A Saint in Graceland

a novel

DEBORAH HINING

Light Messages

Deborah Hining
dhining@lightmessages.com
dhining.lightmessages.com

Published 2016, by Light Messages
www.lightmessages.com
Durham, NC 27713
United States of America

Paperback ISBN: 978-1-61153-157-2
Ebook ISBN: 978-1-61153-156-5

This book is a work of fiction. References to real people, events, establishments, organizations, or locales are intended only to provide a sense of authenticity, and are used to advance the fictional narrative. All other characters, and all incidents and dialogue, are drawn from the author's imagination and are not to be construed as real.

To those intrepid adventurers, the missionaries who have faced danger and hardship in order to share God's Grace.

Foreword

When I wrote *A Sinner in Paradise*, I did not know that a sequel would follow. It wasn't until many of my readers demanded one that I decided to tell the story of what happened to Geneva's crazy cousins and her bevy of disappointed suitors.

Of course, it had to be about Sally Beth—everyone insisted on that—but in order for her to grow beyond the guileless country girl who readers found so endearing in *Sinner*, I had to get her out of Tucker, West Virginia and onto the larger stage of 1978 world affairs. The events that test Sally Beth and her simple faith are so extraordinary you may find them difficult to believe, but they are, in fact, true. I invite you to read the notes at the end of the book for more information about the trials Sally Beth faced in her journey from artless innocent to mature woman.

I have to thank a number of people who have been a godsend to me during this process of birthing another book. Thanks to all of you who read *A Sinner in Paradise*, made such kind comments, and insisted on a sequel, and especially to Jean Lesesne, Delores Crotts, and Phil Hollingsworth. Your frequent friendly reminders that you were still waiting were a great incentive to keep going.

My sisters of LOL3, your constant encouragement and inspiration have been more treasured than you realize. Laura Brown, thank you for doing the tedious task of finding and correcting my many mistakes. Many thanks to my musician friend Jim McConnell for the beautiful music he wrote for both *A Sinner in Paradise* and this sequel, my pilot friend Mike Bensen for educating me about flying small amphibious planes, and to Dr. Eldred Wiser for serving as my medical consultant.

I am very thankful to my husband, Michael, who endured my moanings and groanings, read very bad early drafts, always offered encouragement and sound advice, and for that marvelous road trip when you cheerfully drove hundreds of miles with me across the American Southwest so I could envision that rollicking road trip for Lilly and Sally Beth.

A big, squeezy hug to my publisher and friend, Lady Betty Turnbull, for your constant enthusiasm and for the opportunity to claim friendship with a real Baroness. And finally, to my editor, Elizabeth Turnbull, who made everything possible, then made it better, thank you.

Part One

In Search of Graceland

One

June 24, 1978, Tucker, West Virginia

Annilee slapped her leg and threw her head back, her mouth wide open with delight. "I declare, you two are the worst young'un's I ever saw!"

She had a laugh that would limber up the neck of a sour Presbyterian cleric, and today its wholehearted abandon made Sally Beth's heart dance. Her mother had been through some hard, unhappy years, what with Daddy dying and her heart problems, and then all the mess with the house falling down around her ears and not enough money to fix it. She wanted this moment to last a little longer, to give Annilee a little more time to steep in happiness.

"Don't blame us, Mama," she giggled. "You were the one egging us on to sing Mr. Hawkins' new song! Now, hold on til you hear the second verse," and she and her cousin Jackson launched again into the song they had already begun.

Annilee leaned back, clutching her stomach and laughing until water gathered in her eyes. Sally Beth was enjoying the brightness of her face, when suddenly she saw her mother wince and sit up straighter. Before Sally Beth and Jackson could begin the refrain, Annilee stood, lurched forward, and tumbled down the ten steps of the front porch. As she lay sprawled at the bottom, her head cocked at an absurd angle, Sally Beth's heart leaped again, this time with fear. She gasped, dropped her guitar, and flew down to her.

She knew Annilee was dead even before she had come to a complete stop on the patch of gravel and dirt at the bottom of the steps. There was something about the way she fell, clutching at her chest with her face gone gray that made Sally Beth know that her mother's frail heart had finally given out. Grief and shock exploded through her gut, but still, she couldn't stop a part of herself from taking in the scene with a critical eye and wondering what she could do to make Annilee's passing a little more dignified.

Annilee would not want to be caught dead upside down, with her dress bunched up around her waist so that her drawers were exposed. Not only that, but she had those awful knee-high hose on, and they looked even tackier than the panties. Sally Beth had told her mama not to wear those knee-highs, that bare legs were better, but Annilee had been concerned about her varicose veins showing, not to mention the fact that she hadn't shaved her legs since Easter. Now, here she was, dead at the bottom of the steps, with those ratty panties and those hose exposed—one of them even had a *run* in it—and Jackson seeing all of it, after Annilee had taken such pains to make herself look good for his visit. Sally Beth sobbed aloud while she straightened her mother's dress, and then her head.

She wondered if she ought to try to fix her hair a little. She just looked so pitiful with it all wild and covered with dust, the faded blonde turning ashy against the gray of the gravel. One shoe still teetered on the edge of a step, and her eyes were wide open, empty of the joy that had been there just a moment before. Sally Beth hoped she wasn't still hovering nearby, looking at herself the way they say people do before they rush upward into the arms of Jesus. If she could somehow spare her mother the humiliation, she would do whatever it took. But Sally Beth wasn't capable of much more than what she already had done. Knowing she would have to go on without her mama was more than she could handle right now. She put Annilee's shoe back on, smoothed her hair, and gathered her mother in her arms, hugging her close and weeping inconsolably.

Jackson made his way gingerly down the steps. "Is she gone, Sally Beth?" he asked gently. She nodded, sobbing, rocking her mother.

Her cousin patted her on the shoulder before going inside to call the ambulance. It seemed like no time at all before they got there with their sirens blaring and their equipment clanging. She was still cradling Annilee in her arms when they gathered around her, big men who, by their very presence, made the scene more clumsy and painful. Sally Beth wanted to tell them to be more respectful of her mother's sleep, but she let them pull her away so they could examine the body. She stood hugging herself in the shade of the sugar maple tree and wondered how on earth she was going to tell her sister that their sweet mama was gone.

June 27, 1978

Doc Alvers pulled Sally Beth aside, motioning for her to follow him into the bedroom, away from the crowd that milled softly in the living room. He closed the door behind them before turning to face her with a slight grimace.

"Sally Beth, I heard you telling some of the folks out there that Annilee grabbed at her chest and went gray before she fell off the porch."

"Yeah, Doctor Alvers. I think her heart just went, and maybe she died before she even hit those steps. I hope she did. I hate to think how much it hurt to fall like that."

"Now, honey, I want you to listen to me real good." He looked at her intently but with compassion. "The fall killed your mother. She broke her neck. I have written 'accidental fall' on the death certificate, and I don't want you giving anybody the idea that she might have died of a heart attack, or any natural causes. So you need not say another word to anybody that might shed some doubt on her dying accidentally. You got that?"

"Well, why on earth not? It seems to me that dying of a heart attack is a little more dignified than just falling off your own front porch. Mama wouldn't like anybody thinking she would do anything that foolish."

Doc Alvers sat heavily on the edge of the bed, his hands between his knees, the posture of a tired, old man. After a moment of looking at the floor, he returned his gaze to Sally Beth's face. "After your mother's first heart attack, after your daddy died, she knew she didn't have much longer to live, so she tried to buy some life insurance. She couldn't get any regular insurance because of her heart, so she got the only kind she could get—accidental. A bunch of policies with small death benefits and no underwriting." Dr. Alvers held eye contact, dipping his head meaningfully.

An ugly conclusion wormed its way into Sally Beth's head. "You mean my mama fell down those steps on purpose so she could *cheat* the insurance company?" She was shaking her head before the sentence was completed. "No, Mama wouldn't do that, never! She never cheated anybody in her whole life. And besides, she wouldn't kill herself, either. That's a sin."

"No, I'm not saying that. I'm just saying that she had *accident* insurance. It was the only kind she could get, and she wanted to make sure you and Lilly were taken care of just *in case* she died of an accident, which, in my opinion, she did. She acted above-board. The insurance companies were willing to sell it to her without requiring any medical exam—to collect all those premiums—and now I don't want them latching on to any excuse not to pay the claims. They find out there's even a possibility of her dying of natural causes, they'll give you a world of grief, and you and Lilly need that money."

Horrified and ashamed, Sally Beth blinked back angry tears. He hurried on. "It was the only thing she could think of she could do for you. Just—just think of it as an act of Providence that she happened to die accidentally, even if she might have been having a heart attack at the same time. Sometimes people panic when they feel pain in their chest, and they'll jump up like that." The doctor took Sally Beth's hand. "Your mama was a good, honest woman. She wouldn't ever do anything to hurt or cheat anybody. I believe she happened to die of a broken neck falling down the stairs, and that's what I put on the death certificate. There wasn't any need to do an autopsy, so I never checked her heart. Now don't you go putting me in jeopardy by giving anybody the impression that I told a lie or that I didn't do my job proper. And don't give anybody the impression that your mama was nothing less than the righteous woman we all know her to be. Do her the honor of enjoying this money. Lord knows, she had a hard enough time making ends meet and still make those payments."

Sally Beth bit her quivering lip. "How did you know about the life insurance?"

He sighed, a long, painful sigh full of resignation, his eyes sad and burdened with forty years of the closeted confessions of dying patients. "She told me." He held up his hand. "Not that she had anything in mind. She just mentioned in passing that she had been getting these offers in the mail for accident insurance with no medical questions asked, and she wondered if it would be all right to get some. She never implied that she had something fishy in mind." He put his arm around Sally Beth. "You hear me, now? She didn't know how she was going to go. She was just hoping the Good Lord would arrange something. And it looks like maybe He did. You hear me? I just don't want you casting any doubts on the nature of her death."

Her head began to swim.

"Sally Beth," he said gently, "you need to breathe, honey."

Sometimes, when she felt overwhelmed and there was absolutely nothing she could do to make the situation better, Sally Beth forgot to breathe. This was one of those times, for such news was more than she could comprehend, and although something in the back of her mind was insisting she should do something to fix this, she did not know how to begin. She forced the air into her lungs, put her head on Doc Alvers' shoulder, and cried afresh.

June 28, 1978

Sally Beth woke to a beautiful blue and green morning, fresh and glorious after last night's rain. There was a moment of appreciation for light and warmth before the weight of her loss hunkered down on the edge of her bed and crept over to press down on her. Grief did that, hiding behind the sunshine, skulking in the corners to come and spoil every moment of hope and life. She remembered how ugly it was from the weeks and months after her daddy's death, how it lurked and leered.

Breathing in the morning air, she decided she would not wallow in the foulness of grief, but would give it over to the Lord. She sat up in bed and began, trying not to complain, but nevertheless taking her grievances before Him in a rush of words.

Lord, this is hard. My sweet mama is gone. Only forty-two-years-old and still pretty, still full of fun—gone. Lilly and me, well, we're officially orphans, even though we're technically grown, but just barely. Lilly is turning twenty-one tomorrow. Bless her heart—having an important birthday just two days after we buried Mama. That's sad, just as sad as me living here in this tumble-down house, all alone, because Lilly has up and moved off to Las Vegas and is acting up something awful, rubbing elbows with gamblers and Mafia people and goodness knows who else. It just plain grieves me. It grieves me, and it makes me glad Mama is dead so that she can't see how awful Lilly has become, back for the funeral in a tight dress nearly up to her fanny, looking about as trashy as that poor Mrs. Parker down the road whose no-good husband has left her with three little children and she having to turn to whoring just to feed them. I'll have to have a talk with Lilly. Maybe get her to straighten up and come on back home.

It was a while before she realized that she wasn't really praying any more but simply fuming about the mess her sister had become and how unhappy she was. She took a breath and began again. *Lord, I just don't know what to do! What about these insurance policies? I want to do the right thing, and I want to honor my mother. How on earth am I supposed to handle this?*

She sat back against the pillows to prepare herself for that moment of quiet, where she emptied her mind and waited for the Lord to answer her. But before she fully settled in, her eyes fell on a puddle in the corner of her room, and she remembered that the roof was leaking. She had already placed a pot in the middle of the bathroom floor, but this was a new breach. "Darn," she muttered, followed by, "Sorry, Lord." The Lord did not like swearing, even if it wasn't the real swear word. He knew she was thinking the real word.

Well, that was no good, and there's no use whining. Sunshine was already making its way across the floor and lighting up the colors in Granny's old quilt, and her heart felt it warming the air around her. The age-spotted, wavy mirror in the ancient dresser reflected her sleep-tangled image back to her. *Lord, my hair looks like a stump full of granddaddies.* She resolutely picked up her brush. Things would improve when she got this mess brushed into some sort of shape.

Her mama could see her, she was sure. Mama was happy now, and she would want her to be happy for her, up there with Daddy and Granny and Pappy, and probably sitting in Jesus' lap. Yes, she should be happy for Mama's sake, and besides, for Lilly's sake, she needed to be strong. Goodness knows Lilly needed to borrow some strength from somebody. She was a pure mess over all of this.

"Lilly, I need to talk to you about something," she said as she chopped orange peels and dropped them in the boiling water along with mint and some loose black tea. "I'm thinking maybe we should sell the house."

Lilly looked aghast. "No!" she exclaimed. "This is home!"

Something in her tone made Sally Beth feel infinitely weary.

Lilly had no idea what it took to keep the place up, and she didn't have to deal with it, living a thousand miles away. She felt her patience grow thin over Lilly's self-indulgent weakness. Still, she tempered her words with a soft tone.

"Mama didn't hardly have a dime to her name, nothing except this house, and it has a mortgage on it, and it's falling apart. I'm not making enough to cover the expenses, and Daddy's pension check quit the day Mama died. Even if we do decide to sell it—or maybe we can rent it out—but we need to fix it up first either way. The roof is leaking and the windowsills have rotted out, and I think the pipes in the bathroom are leaking, too." She stopped, regretting her complaints when she saw Lilly's tears spilling down her pale cheeks. Lilly couldn't help it because she was the youngest and never really had to deal with the hard stuff. She changed her tone. "Do you want some tea? I ran out of lemons, so I'm using the oranges Rachel brought over yesterday."

Lilly sniffled, laid her arms on the table, and put her forehead down. She didn't attempt to speak. Sally Beth felt so sorry for her, looking so little and hurt, so plumb deflated, that she thought she might go ahead and mention the insurance. She picked up Caboodle and sat down beside her sister.

"Here, I put some honey in it. It's real good," she coaxed. "I think the orange peel is better than lemon." Lilly rolled her head on her arm, ignoring the cup Sally Beth set on the table.

There was a long silence before Sally Beth could bring herself to say it. "She had some insurance," she ventured cautiously as she stroked the soft spot behind the dog's ear. "But I'm not sure we should file for it." Lilly's head came up.

"She had insurance? How much?" She had perked up considerably. Color came rushing back into her face.

"Yeah." The words came out slowly, guardedly. "But it was accident insurance. I'm not so sure she died of an accident."

"Doc said she broke her neck falling off the porch. He was telling everybody. If that's not an accident, I don't know what is."

"Well, he did that on purpose because he knew Mama had that

accident insurance, and he didn't want anybody to question how she died because he wants us to get the money. But, Lilly, I'm not sure that would be right. Before she fell, she went all pale, and she grabbed at her chest. Then she jumped up, and honey, I'm telling you, she practically *dove* down those steps. I'm thinking maybe she felt that heart attack coming on and just made that accident happen. To tell you the honest truth, I'm thinking maybe she had thought about it, and had decided to find a way to make sure we would collect on the insurance." It pained her to say the words indicting her mother that way, but it had to come out.

"Sally Beth Lenoir! Don't you dare say that my mama killed herself! That's just plumb blasphemy! And besides, Jackson was there. He saw the whole thing, and he never said anything about any suicide."

"He wasn't looking at her. I was. And I think she knew she was dying and did it because she wanted us to get the money."

"Well, for Pete's sake, if she wanted us to get the money, then you should have the sense to let her have her way! What good does it do for us to lose our family home and starve just because you thought you saw something you probably didn't see? I declare, Sally Beth, you are the orneriest girl that ever lived!" Lilly sat back in a huff, then grew quiet.

After a long silence, she spoke again in a small, soft voice. "Sally Beth, I could quit my job in Vegas, and maybe move back here, if I had some money. There aren't any decent jobs around here, and you know it. I could live here with you. We can fix up the house some, and. . . " she bit her lip and glanced away, "maybe I can go to college."

Sally Beth's jaw dropped. "Go to *college?* Lilly, you never said you wanted to go to college! Where on earth did that idea come from?" She kept herself from speaking what was truly on her mind. Lilly had never done well in school, not because she wasn't bright— Sally Beth had always known that Lilly was the smarter one—but Lilly did not like challenge. She always just quit if she was faced with anything resembling hard work. Could she even get into a college? And if by some miracle she did, how long would she last?

A sudden rush of pity for her little sister and her limited prospects washed over her. What could she look forward to, as ill-equipped as she was to make her way in the world? Sally Beth had her cosmetology license, and she had a bigger capacity for work than Lilly did, and she knew she had the ability to make things happen. Lilly, though, was unfocused and, she hated to admit, lazy. Her sister's next words confounded Sally Beth.

"Oh, I've been thinking about it since before I graduated. But I didn't have the money, and I couldn't very well ask Mama for it, could I? And, let's face it, I didn't have the grades to get any kind of a scholarship. I just went to Las Vegas to work and save up so I could go." She made a wry face. "But I don't like it out there. It's too hot, and the men are just out for a good time. And it costs so much to live, I wasn't able to save up much." She sighed a long, woeful sigh before adding, "It's not like what they show on TV."

Sally Beth could not believe her ears. This was the first time Lilly had ever mentioned doing anything productive with her life. For her, it had always been about men and money. "What do you want to study?"

"Oh, that doesn't matter." She fluttered her hand with a dismissive little wave, then her eyes brightened as she leaned toward Sally Beth. "I just know I want to go to Tech. They have four men to every woman there!" she said, splaying four fingers in Sally Beth's face for good measure. "Imagine that! *Four!* To every girl! I figure I just need to go for a year or two, and I'll find a good man there. One that majors in law or medicine, or maybe engineering. I looked it up. All those jobs make good money."

Sally Beth's hopes sank. "You mean you want to go just to get a man? *Lilly!*"

"Well, sure! Why else would any girl want to go to college? And there's nobody around here that's going to be any good to me. This little town? There's nothing here, that's for dern sure. And I'd rather die than marry some dirt farmer!" She ran a hand over her gleaming pale hair as she gazed into the distance. "When I catch me a college man, I won't ever have to worry about being poor again!"

Sally Beth felt so sorry for her sister that she wanted to cry. Lilly could make something of herself if she would just put some starch in her spine. She was bright enough, but she had always depended on others ever since she figured out that people would do things for her just because she was so pretty. Sally Beth suddenly realized that poor Lilly never would amount to much, and the best thing she could do for herself was to marry well. She lifted herself from her chair to feed Kit and Caboodle and fill their water bowl, thinking about what she should do.

Bills were piling up. Her paycheck would not stretch enough to cover them and the mortgage, and what about all these repairs the house so desperately needed? Maybe she could get a second job— they had said something to her down at the nursing home about that, but even a second full time job wouldn't bring in enough to stop this house from falling down. She was beginning to feel the weight of poverty pressing down on her and choking her, as if a sack full of dirty coal had landed on her head. Shutting her eyes, she forced a breath and, out of habit, asked for the Lord's help. She did not really seek an answer, but used the minute to push aside all her sorrows for a little space where she could think without all this pressure.

Prepare yourself to go, came an unexpected—and baffling— thought, right out of the blue, with no frame of reference, nothing to provoke it. Just a single, nearly audible, *Prepare yourself to go*. She knew it came from God, because that was the way He always spoke to her, not making any sense, never saying anything she might have thought of herself. But she knew from experience the sense would come later, and she felt a moment of clarity and trust. God knew what He was doing, and she had better heed Him, even if she didn't know how. Opening her eyes, she looked out the window, and that's when she saw the gutter hanging off the eaves. She didn't know what the thought had meant, but it was a sure-fire thing that something had to be done about this house, and she might as well get busy about it while she waited for God to reveal His plan.

She drained her teacup. "All right, Lilly. Let's look and see what we can find. Maybe she had enough insurance to fix the roof and enough left over for you to go to college for a year or two."

It took them the better part of an hour, but they found the papers under the bed in the box where Mama kept all the family pictures. They were under the one of Daddy looking dapper in a white suit and fedora, leaning against the fender of his 1942 Special Deluxe Fleetline Chevrolet that he was so proud of. He was between two women, neither one of which was Mama, and his arms were draped over their shoulders with his hands on their titties, and he was grinning that crazy grin of his, looking like the cat that had got into the cream.

Mama had showed that picture to them once, and they had a good laugh over it. It was funny to them because it showed a side of their daddy that they had never seen, and Mama hid it back after that because she said Daddy would likely destroy it if he knew it was still in the house. He had gotten saved after he married Mama and became their daddy, and he surely wouldn't want his girls to know what a ladies' man he had once been. It secretly delighted Sally Beth that Daddy had been such a rakish sort in his youth, as it delighted her that Mama had fallen in love with him when he was still something of a bad boy. She liked to remember the passion that smoldered beneath the surface of their quiet, respectful lives, back before Daddy had gotten so sick.

They giggled again when they saw the picture and had a good time remembering how much fun he had been before things got hard, and then, just under that picture, they found a big envelope with eight accidental death policies in it. The benefits ranged from $500 to $4,000, and the total of all of them combined was $22,000.

Sally Beth felt the blood rushing from her head, and she had to lean over and put it between her knees until the dizzy spell passed. Clutching the stack of papers tightly in her hand, Lilly sank down on the bed and grew quiet, too, before she drew a long breath and said, "Oh, thank you Mama! It would take me twenty years to save up that much money!" They looked at each other, and Sally Beth wondered again what on earth their mother had been thinking when she ran to the edge of the porch and fell head first down those steps. She squeezed her eyes tight, pondering what her mama would say if she could speak to her now.

Give it to her now, came a voice that sounded just like Mama's. She sat up and looked around, but all she saw was Lilly looking at the insurance policies and pressing a hand to her mouth.

"Okay," she said, and slid off the bed.

"What?" asked Lilly.

"I have something for you. From Mama and me. I know your birthday isn't until tomorrow, but we won't have time to celebrate since you have to leave so early. So I'm going to give it to you now." She went to her room and returned carrying a guitar case with a red bow on the handle.

"Here. We figured you were tired of that old beat-up thing you were playing." She handed it to Lilly who took it with a look of astonished delight.

"Oh! It's a Gibson!" breathed Lilly. "It's beautiful! How could you? I mean, it's a good one!"

"I found it at the pawn shop, and yeah, it really is a good one. I've been playing it. It's got a real good tone. You like it?"

"Oh, Sally Beth! Thank you!" She burst into sobs. "I wish I could play it for Mama!"

"I know, baby." She took her sister in her arms, and they both wept enough tears to fill up the holes in their hearts.

Two

July 7, 1978, Swallowtail Gap, West Virginia

Geneva awoke to Howard's caress. The smile came before she even opened her eyes.

"Mornin', beautiful. Big day today."

"Yeah." She stretched and blinked at him. "Oh, it's good to be home! I could just lie here all day, but I guess we should leave early. Rachel probably needs some help." She paused mid-stretch. "What are you looking at?"

"Your happiness," he responded seriously.

"Do you see it?" she teased.

"Yes. Right here." He touched her forehead, then kissed it. "And here," he added, kissing her left breast, over her heart.

She giggled. "You missed a spot."

"Really? Where?"

Pushing her foot from under the sheet, she wiggled her toes. "Here. I am happy from my head to my toes."

"Ah, yes. I need to kiss those toes," he said as he moved to the bottom of the bed. After he kissed all five toes, he made his way upward, kissing her foot. "How about your foot? Is that happy?"

"Oh, yes, my foot is happy. It feels like dancing."

"Uh huh. And your ankle. Is it happy?" He nibbled at her inner anklebone.

"Mmm. Yes, my ankle is definitely happy."

He kissed her leg. "How about your calf? Is that happy, too?" She paused to think about it before nodding. "Yes, it's happy. I think it's even happier than my ankle. Maybe even happier than my foot."

He was just beginning to nibble at the inside of her knee when a baby's cry invaded her bliss. A sudden stinging rush pricked her nipples, then a warm wetness trickled down into her armpits. Quickly, she sat up, pressing her breasts with the heels of her hands.

"I got him," Howard said, reaching into the bassinette where the baby lay, gathered him up, and placed him in Geneva's arms as she snuggled back into the pillows. Pulling her close, Howard rested his chin on her head, humming a lullaby as he watched her with quiet eyes. Presently, he spoke.

"Listen, love, I've been thinking," he said seriously. "I know you want some fancy touches to the house, but I'm worried that if we make it look too good, folks will start getting suspicious. It's good you've still got your place in DC, but that can only account for so much income. If folks get wind of that gold up on the mountain, there'll be no more peace for us."

"Yeah, I've been thinking the same thing," admitted Geneva. "But really, Chap, we don't have to spend a lot. Just a log cabin will be fine, really."

He shook his head. "No, I've got this figured out. You know that piece of land my grandfather left me in Oklahoma? Well, there's oil somewhere out there." He laughed. "A hundred or so miles away, but nobody has to know that. Since Jimmy Lee's out West right now, why don't we let it out that he's there to check it out. Maybe if folks think we have an oil well, we can get by with spending more money. We don't have to live so tight and nobody will be suspicious about where it's coming from."

"Chap, that's brilliant! Does that mean I can get the fancy bathtub? And the washer and dryer?"

He laughed again. "Honey, I got all kinds of things I can't wait to give you."

"Really, Mr. Oil Baron? I'm still waiting for you to buy me a wedding ring."

Snorting, he rolled away from her. "Woman, if you don't beat all. I took you to all over Europe! I'm building you a house! I gave you a baby! Now you think I'm supposed to buy you a ring? What do you need one of those for?"

"Hey, just because you got by without one when you married me doesn't mean you can get by with it forever. It's embarrassing, taking little Blue to the grocery store and people seeing me without a wedding ring. You know what they're thinking."

He grinned, leaning in close. "They're probably thinking you caught me back when you chased me around that barn. Don't fret. I'll get you that ring when I'm good and ready," he said, then jumped up and hastened out the door as she threw a pillow at him.

Raven Creek, West Virginia

The party had already become noisy by the time Sally Beth arrived at Rachel's house. The little ones were running around in what appeared to be a frenzied game of who could shriek the loudest, while the older children, most of them cousins two or three times removed, played kick-the-can out in the pasture. As she parked the car, John Smith pulled in behind her.

"Hey John!" she called.

He was glad to see her. It was going to be hard, seeing Geneva for the first time since that awful day when she had married Howard, and walking in with Sally Beth would ease the rough edges. He reached for her, squeezing her shoulders as they made their way up the steps. "Hey, Sally Beth. You doing okay?"

She smiled warmly at him. "Yeah, we're fine. Thanks for coming to the funeral and all. And the roast you brought was really good."

They made their way into the kitchen where Geneva and her sister, Rachel, were putting the last swirls of frosting on the pink and white birthday cake. It was evident to Sally Beth that neither John nor Geneva was quite prepared to see one another. She saw how the agony had flared in his eyes, and Geneva's face had fallen with sadness and shame. Hoping to give the painful thoughts floating through the empty air a chance to scatter and hide, she rushed in with a bright "*Hello!*"

"Rachel! So good to see you!" she said, laying two small packages wrapped in pink paper on the counter. "I can't believe these babies are a year old already. I can't wait to see them!" She glanced at John again. His face was pale with grief. He would not want Geneva to see him suffering like this, and it wouldn't do her any good, either, knowing how much she had hurt him. Quickly, she stepped into her cousin's line of vision. "Geneva! Welcome home! When did you get back?"

Geneva hugged her. "Oh, honey! I'm so sorry about your mama, and I wish we had made it to the funeral. We didn't call home but once, and it was already over by the time we did. I really hate that I wasn't here to be with you." She gazed over Sally Beth's head toward John. "Hi John, good to see you again," and her eyes met his briefly, sending a look that said, *I'm sorry. I know I hurt you.*

He returned her smile as he willed the awkward moment to pass. If he had wondered if he should have told her how much he loved her, he realized now that it would not have mattered; she had moved far beyond his reach, so far that his longing could bear no weight upon her consciousness. The very fact of her radiance, large and luminous, made him understand that she was no longer simply herself, a spinning, dancing, free-floating planet, but that she had been pulled into a larger, completely contained galaxy that had no need for heat or light or life beyond itself. He looked across the vast expanse of cold space to her contented, connected heart and felt himself shrink into the loneliness of his own bruised one. After the briefest of glances at him, Geneva turned back to Sally

Beth.

"How are you? Really?"

"We're just *fine*," Sally Beth said. "Did you know Lilly's moving back home? Now, where's little Clayton? I've been waiting *all day* to see him!"

John saw the look of sympathy in Sally Beth's eyes, which reminded him that she, too, was suffering with grief. Even so, she was mindful of the pain of others, going out of her way to extend comfort, even a kind of gladness to them, and he couldn't help but feel his troubles ease in the light of her smile. She was like a Labrador who had just grown out of puppyhood, learning to be well behaved, not jumping all over people with kisses and goodwill, but wanting to, and restraining herself with sheer force of will. It saddened him to think of her boundless heart suffering with loss, and he felt small and petty as he realized that his own heartache was trifling compared to hers.

"Really? That's great," replied Geneva. "It'll be good to have her back. Blue is outside with everybody."

Sally Beth looked at her, puzzled. "You're calling him 'Blue'? I thought his name was Clayton. After Uncle Clayton?"

"Oh, yes. Clayton Bluefeather Knight. Bluefeather because his hair is blue-black and looks exactly like little feathers. That got shortened to 'Blue', and it stuck. When's Lilly getting back?"

"In a month. Mama left us some money, so we're fixing up the house. It needs a new roof, and some of the pipes are leaking, and, well, there's lots to do. So I'm going to fly out to Las Vegas while they're working on it, and then I'll help Lilly drive back." Her face split into a wide grin. "I'll get to see some of the country!"

"What a great idea. Do you want us to go by and pick up your mail while you're gone? Feed the dogs? Our house won't be finished for another few months, and I know Jesse's getting sick of us all piled up at his place, so I'm always looking for excuses to get out of the house."

"Would you? Oh, you are so *sweet!* The folks at the nursing home say I can leave Kit and Caboodle with them, so you don't have to worry about the dogs. I can take two weeks off, and it would be nice not to have to hurry back."

Geneva wondered what Sally Beth and Lilly hoped to accomplish putting that tumbled-down old house back together. Annilee could not have left her daughters much, certainly not enough to fully repair it, and while she wished she could do something to mitigate their hardship, pride ran so high in the Lenoir family, it would be insulting to even suggest she help out with expenses. She smiled inwardly while she contrived a plan. Although she could not spend money on Sally Beth and Lilly with their knowledge, she could make things happen without them knowing. If she had the keys to the place for two weeks, she and Howard could make Annilee's money go farther than they might expect. She continued casually, "Maybe we can even stay there some, get out from under Jesse's feet. Would you be okay with that?"

Sally Beth lit up as she clasped her hands together with glee. "Thank you, Geneva! That would relieve my mind, knowing you'd keep an eye on things. I want to see the Grand Canyon! And the Painted Desert, and Carlsbad Caverns, and we'd love to stop at Graceland, and oh, *my goodness!* There's *lots* to see between here and Las Vegas!"

John spoke up, "Well, let me do something. Can I at least drive you to the airport?"

"Would you? Oh, John, that would be *just great.*"

"Of course I'm happy to take you. I'm out at the airport all the time these days anyway taking flying lessons, so that will work out just fine."

"John! You're taking flying lessons? Wow, that's something I've always wanted to do," broke in Rachel.

"Me, too!" exclaimed Sally Beth. "Ever since I was little."

"Yeah, it's great, and I don't know if you've heard, but I'm going back to Kenya. There'll be a plane available to me, and it's really the only way to get around—the place is so remote, and Africa is so big."

Rachel was surprised. "You're going back to Kenya?"

"Yes, I am. Things are happening over there right now with the program, so I wouldn't be surprised if I stay six months this time." He didn't say that he needed at least six months or more to be away from Geneva before he felt he could resist the urge to take her in his arms and beg her to run away with him. He forced himself to keep his eyes on Rachel's.

"When are you leaving?"

"Six weeks. Not long after Sally Beth takes off for out West. I guess it will be a quiet summer around here without all of us."

Just then, Howard walked in with Blue in his arms. "Somebody says he's hungry," he began, but seeing Sally Beth, he stopped to put his free arm around her shoulders. "Sally Beth, I'm so sorry about your mother. We didn't find out about it until too late, and—"

She cut him off, "Howard, don't you think a thing about it. I would have just *died* if you cut your honeymoon short to come back for the funeral, and we're doing just fine. Lilly's coming home! I'm going out to Las Vegas to help her drive back."

Howard grinned at her. "Did you know Jimmy Lee's out in Texas right now? He's got some cousins there, and—I guess Geneva told you about my oil well?" he said as he handed the baby to his wife.

John did not miss the look that passed between them as Geneva took the baby from Howard before leaving the room. It was a look filled with secrets, secrets of pleasure, of longing fulfilled, the kind of look that passes between people who have shared hearts and minds and flesh and have discovered the magic of it. The implications of it lodged themselves deep in the crevices of his ruined heart, but he managed to nod at Howard. "Welcome back, buddy," he said. "What's this about an oil well?"

"She didn't tell you? Well… My grandfather left me some land out in Oklahoma a few years back. My mama's family. It wasn't anything but a truck farm, but they're finding oil around there. I sent Jimmy Lee out to take a look, and, well, I'll just say Geneva's already made a list of all the things she's going to buy." He paused before chuckling. "She's got an eye for pretty things."

From the living room, Geneva stifled a laugh. Without actually lying, Howard had managed to let everyone know they could expect them to start throwing a little money around, so there would be no suspicions of his enormous wealth, even after everyone saw the new house. Maybe she could even buy a new car. Maybe she could get that fancy dryer after all. She moved Blue to her right breast and settled into the indulgence of a heart drowned in happiness.

Three

August 6, 1978, Tucker, West Virginia

It felt good to be able to do something kind for Sally Beth. Today she seemed to have shaken off the grief that had enveloped her since her mother's death and was back to her sunny ebullience. John couldn't help but inwardly chuckle at the rush of her monologue as he drove toward the airport through the bright mountain air.

"I'm so nervous! I've never been on a plane before, and the farthest away I've been from Tucker is DC when we went there on our senior trip, and now I can't *believe* I am going to *Las Vegas!* I'm real nervous about being there. You know they call it Sin City, don't you? And I could tell Lilly had changed after living there. I've never gambled before. It even scares me to think about it. I've heard of people losing their *shirts!* But I want to see the Elvis impersonators, although I don't think there are any Elvis shows going on. But we are going to see *Frank Sinatra.* And then, we're going to go to the *Grand Canyon.* I can't wait to see it!" She balled her fists, giving an excited little grimace and shiver, her eyes wide with the thrill of the thought.

"I bet we will see some Elvis impersonators when we go to Graceland, and do you know he died a year ago? And that he and Mama are *exactly* the same age? They were both born on January 8, 1935! We're going to put a flower on his grave from her, because she just *loved* Elvis, and we know she'd want us to. We might even get there on the anniversary of his death. Wouldn't that be something?" She paused to take a breath. "That's kind of silly when you think about it, putting a flower on his grave from her, because they're both up in heaven and probably just having a good old time together."

She grinned at the thought before moving on. "There's so *much* to see. I wish we had more time, because I've never seen the desert, and I want to see the place where you can see *all* the stars because there's no light way out in the desert. Have you seen the Milky Way on a clear night when you're away from town? I have. It's like that up at Holy Miracle's place up on Jacob's Mountain, but I bet it's different in the desert because you're in a different place. Come to think of it, I bet you have seen a whole set of different stars out there in Africa.

"Well, yes," answered John. "The stars are beautiful there, and there's no light pollution out on the plains so far from the cities. The Milky Way looks just like that—a milky wash spread out over the sky."

"I *know!* It's that way up on Jacob's Mountain. But I bet it's even *better* out in the desert, and probably in Africa, too, because the air is dryer—is the air dry in Africa? Oh yeah, there's desert there and all, isn't there?"

He smiled, wondering if he would be able to answer before she broke in again. "In some places. In others, it's a rain forest. There's lots of different climates and terrain in Africa. I haven't seen nearly—"

Sure enough, she cut him off. "*Oh!* I would *love* to go to Africa and see giraffes! I love giraffes. And elephants! Did you know they mourn when one of them dies?"

"So how do you know so much about the American West, Sally

Beth? And Africa? Have you ever thought about traveling?"

"Oh my goodness. Daddy subscribed to *National Geographic* for *years*. And we've got stacks and *stacks* of them. I think we've been through them all about a *million times*! Mama and Lilly and me? And Daddy, too, before he died, and we would pretend we were going to all these places, and Daddy would make up stories about them, about tigers and walruses and flying pigs all living together, although I know they don't live in the same place, and there's no such things as flying pigs, but they were *so funny*.

She then launched into one about a toad who fell in love with a mockingbird who taught the toad to sing, and they started up a traveling show, going all around the world singing at palaces and such, until the toad developed laryngitis and could only croak again. The story went on for some time, and John suspected that Sally Beth had gotten parts of it mixed up with another story, but he finally decided to just enjoy the telling of it because she seemed to get such a kick out of it. The tale was still going on when they pulled up to the airport curb.

"Oh, my! You didn't get to hear all of it, so I'll just tell you how it ends so you won't be worrying about it. Anyway, the toad recovered, although he never could sing as beautifully as before, so they learned another act, where he learned a hundred different croaking sounds and the mockingbird copied them exactly, and they turned the act into a comedy, and they lived happily ever after. It's a *great* story. Oh my goodness—I've got to *hurry!*"

Nearly in a panic, she bounded out of the car, yanking a suitcase out of the back seat before John had a chance to open his door. He rushed out to help her, and as he pulled the second bag out to place it on a waiting cart, she swung around, bumping her voluminous purse into him.

"Ouch, Sally Beth! What do you have in there?"

"Oh, just the usual stuff, and two canteens of water," she said, hoisting the strap higher on her shoulder. "In case the plane crashes in the desert. Bye, John, and thank you. Have a good time in Kenya!" She hurried into the terminal building, leaving him standing at the curb, then turned and waved at him before the doors closed behind her.

John felt a little dazed, as if a storm had just blown through and he had been hunkering down, knocking back tree limbs and bits of houses that flew in his direction. Sally Beth was different from anybody he had ever met. On the surface, she seemed like just a blonde airhead, always chattering near-nonsense, but he knew there were depths of her hidden below her milky skin. Ever since he had seen how coolly she worked to stop the blood streaming from Geneva's leg while he stood aside, feeling sick, helpless, and weak with despair, he had learned not to judge people too quickly. And Holy Miracle Jones, the wisest person he had ever met, had loved and honored her above everyone.

Yes, Sally Beth was *unique*. That was the only way to describe her. He smiled as he drove to the hangar where his instructor waited for his flying session. After today he would be a fully licensed pilot, and Kenya, the new home he hoped would burn the ache out of his heart, would become smaller and more welcoming.

August 6, 1978, Las Vegas, Nevada

The first thing Sally Beth saw as she walked through the gate was Lilly's smooth, pale hair, as sleek as a river otter and the color of winter sun. Her sister was the prettiest girl there, and she looked so much like Mama it was all she could do to keep from running to her with her arms outstretched. But Mama had taught her not to act like an ignorant hillbilly, but to hold her head up and be dignified. *Las Vegas. Oh my! What would Mama think now? Both her girls loose in Sin City.* She almost laughed aloud just thinking about it. But she glided over to Lilly with as much dignity as she could muster and squeezed her baby sister until Lilly protested, "Sally Beth—you're choking me!"

The airport wasn't far from town, and Sally Beth was tickled that they got to drive right down the main drag so she could get a good look at the place she had heard such awful things about. It made a little shiver run up her spine. Even in the daylight, the Las Vegas Strip was wonderfully glittery, but in a tasteful way: not at all tacky and garish as she had anticipated. There were big signs of cowboys and stars and funny little glasses that looked like they were clinking together because they were made of lights that ran around and around, and Sally Beth thought they were the cutest things she had ever seen. It was all just so exciting! She squealed when they drove past a row of palm trees.

"Lilly, look—*palm trees!*" She craned her neck around as they drove past them. "Do you think they have coconuts in them? Can we get fresh coconuts here? *"Oh , look!* There's a big picture of Elvis and he's swerving his hips around. *Lilly!* This place is *amazing.*"

Half of her was in love with the glitter and excitement, the other half full of disappointed trepidation. Las Vegas was cleaner and classier than she had imagined. Truthfully, this disappointed her a little because she had anticipated being shocked by its tawdriness. No gunslingers sauntered down the streets, and there didn't seem to be any prostitutes hanging out on the corners. She wondered if they only came out at night, like vampires, and if the place magically transformed into some apparition from hell once the sun went down and the lights shone brighter. She tingled all over at the thought.

They drove slowly through town, and then, suddenly, they were out in the desert, and Sally Beth's spirit sank at the brown ugliness. She had expected the desert to be an ocean of undulating, pale sand piled up in mountains with little riffles sculpted by the wind, like the pictures she had seen of that desert in China, but this lifeless, bleached soil boasted no such elegance. There was nothing but scattered rocks and scrawny, woebegone little bushes, some without roots that roamed hungrily in the wind. Not far ahead mountains shimmered behind the rising heat, but her glimpse of them seemed like only a dream dissipating into hopelessness. A strange, unsettled aura skulked about the place, and she had a momentary sensation of falling off the edge of something, as if the ground was too malevolent to keep the promises of the solid earth. Perhaps Las Vegas was built upon sin after all, and this is where the dregs of it resided. Hell was surely close by. She pulled out a canteen out of her purse and just about sucked it dry.

"What are you doing? You brought a canteen?"

"It's dry here. And *hot*. I'm parched to death. My *eyeballs* are even drying out. Lilly, how on earth can you stand this?"

Lilly laughed. "You get used to it. But I know what you mean. Why do you think I want to come home? Here's a Carl Jr. We can stop and get you a Coke. It'll be another fifteen minutes before we get to my place, and as soon as we get you unloaded and changed, we'll head back here for a night out. Sally Beth, you're going to *love* Vegas!"

Sally Beth suddenly wasn't so sure. She squinted through the haze and the heat wavering on the highway and looked toward the inhospitable, colorless mountains that did not beckon, but sat brooding in the heat like the unhealthy, sad parents of an unhealthy, sad landscape.

Oh, Lord! Do You ever come to this place? It looks like something the devil would love. She would have given a year of her life for a glimpse of a green tree just then.

Lilly lived in a shabby apartment building, but there was a pool, and Sally Beth hoped they would have time for a quick dip in it before they headed for the marquees and the spinning lights.

"Can we swim?" she asked.

"Sure. We have about an hour and a half before we have to leave."

The pool felt like bath water, not as refreshing as the river where Sally Beth was used to swimming, but it was so hot here that even tepid water felt good. As she paddled around, careful not to get her hair wet and full of chlorine, she heard laughter, and she glanced up to see a beautiful, dark-haired man standing above her. He was wearing a bathing suit so tiny and tight that she could see all his man-bulges, which, from that angle, were significant. Face scarlet, she averted her eyes, pretending to look at something over by the building.

A moment later, he jumped in right beside her, so close that he splashed chlorine-laden water all over her hair. Making her way quickly to the other end of the pool, she eyed him discreetly from a safe corner.

There was something about him—well, a lot, actually—that she found discomfiting. He was too slick, flawless, really, with curly black hair and blue eyes fringed with the thickest, blackest lashes she had ever seen, white teeth, and a body that was beyond perfect. There were no laughing crinkles around his eyes, no scars or calluses, no sign that he lived in the real world of hard work and joyful living. He wore a smug expression that didn't look friendly. And that bathing suit! Sally Beth kept her distance, trying not to look in his direction.

Seconds later, a sweet-looking woman with a wild halo of dark auburn hair strolled into view. Sally Beth was struck by the sheer size of her: she was huge, both tall and broad, and typical of girls who are self-conscious about their weight, she wore a shapeless muumuu that billowed out like a stiff tent, covering her from neck to ankles. She carefully sat down on the edge of the pool, tucking her legs underneath her.

The man in the tiny bathing suit swam over to her, laying his hand on her knee, and all of a sudden, Sally Beth's perspective changed. If this was his girlfriend or his wife, then there was more to him than she had thought, for anybody that good looking who would prefer a lovely, angelic face to a beautiful body must have some goodness in him.

"You coming in, Tiffany?" he asked.

The woman glanced at Sally Beth. "No, I'll just sit out here awhile." She leaned forward to dabble her hand in the water.

"Oh, come on," he insisted, splashing water at her. "It's hot out there." He splashed her again, laughing as she jumped up and backed away.

"No," she said again, but she laughed. The man pulled himself out of the pool and walked around behind her. He nudged her with his knee.

"Oh, come on! You won't melt! I dare you!"

She stood, then turned to face him. "No, I just don't feel like it right—" but he shoved her hard, nearly pushing her into the water. Recovering quickly, she stepped backward for a moment before she reversed her stance to lean solidly into him, then she put her hands on his shoulders and shoved him back.

It was quite a shove. The woman was as tall as he was, at least six feet or more, and her arms looked powerful. Laughing, she leaned into him again, and when he wrapped his arms around her to try to throw her into the pool, she spun quickly. A second later, so fast that Sally Beth wondered if she had missed something, the woman stood at the pool's edge, relaxed and serene, and he was in the water.

"Hey! No fair!" he sputtered, his eyes dark and hard, despite his laughter. The woman casually reached into her bag and pulled out a cigarette.

"I'm going back into the apartment," she said as she stuck a match. "Take your time." She strolled nonchalantly into the building behind them, leaving pale blue smoke in her wake.

He turned his attention to Sally Beth, pushing off the side of the pool toward her and giving her a coy smile. It was time to get out, she decided, but as she glanced toward the shallow end, she felt her face go hot with embarrassment. Lilly had stepped into the glare of the white sunshine, wearing a tiny bikini almost as revealing as the man's.

"Hi, Lawrence," came Lilly's voice. She strolled to the water's edge. "Haven't seen you in a while. How've you been?" She flashed him a smile that was, in Sally Beth's opinion, a hair too friendly. Surely, she knew he had a girlfriend.

"*Lil*-ly!" he hollered, rolling over into a lazy backstroke. "Hey, beautiful! Missed you, too. What's up?"

"Lots. I see you've met my sister. She's come out to help me pack up 'cause I'm moving back to West Virginia. We're headed out day after tomorrow." She sat by the pool and splashed at him with her foot seductively.

"Awww. Too bad!" He made a silly-looking pouty face, pursing his lips at Lilly and eyeing her legs. Sally Beth decided she had had enough. She heaved herself out of the water, picked up her flip-flops, and said, "We'd better go, Lilly." She wanted to get her sister out of there before she made a complete fool of herself.

Oh, Lord! What a day I've had. I hate the desert. Which I'm sorry to say because I know You made it, but it's so hot here. And dry. But even though I can see why they call Las Vegas "Sin City," I did have a lot of fun. That magic show was the most incredible thing I have ever seen.

Sally Beth stopped praying then because she realized the Lord would not have approved of everything that went on that night—certainly not the way Sally Beth had handled things with her sister, who had dragged her to the casino right after the show. Sally Beth had tried to object, but Lilly grumbled about her being an old stick-in-the-mud, and she decided it would be wrong to fuss at Lilly after she had taken her to that wonderful magic act.

Lilly had marched straight up to the Blackjack table, sat down and won three hands in a row. "See?" she said. "There is nothing wrong with this. It's just a game of skill, and you can win at it if you know what you're doing."

Sally Beth didn't say anything. Something didn't sit right in her gut, but she didn't know how to argue. It was late, and she was tired and not thinking entirely straight, so she simply watched while Lilly racked up a considerable pile of poker chips.

"Wanna try, Sally Beth? I'll show you." Sally Beth shook her head. "Come on, you sit here, and I'll tell you exactly what to do. It's okay. We're way ahead, and nobody's going to lose the farm tonight." She stood, pushing Sally Beth into her seat.

The other players smiled at Sally Beth. Most of them didn't look like outlaws, but the one right beside her did kind of look like he might belong to the Mafia with his slicked-back hair and gold chains showing underneath his mostly unbuttoned shirt. The girl beside him looked like a part of a matched set. She had big bosoms and lots of chains, too, and her blouse was halfway unbuttoned.

Another glance at the woman told Sally Beth that she ought to spend less time in the sun and that she should take better care of her hair. She wished she could give her some of the leave-in conditioner she had in her purse. That hair would look a lot better if it weren't so dry and had a little shine.

Lilly was talking. "Pay attention, Sally Beth. You have a jack and a nine. That's nineteen. The dealer has a five. That means you don't take a card, because it's likely he won't do better than you've got without busting. Wave your hand like this." She leaned over Sally Beth's shoulder and passed her hand over the cards, and Sally Beth was surprised when a moment later the dealer pushed two chips over to her.

"Hey, good for you!" said the woman with the bleached out, dry hair.

Sally Beth smiled at her over the head of the man with the gold chains. "Thanks. My first time at this. I'm a little nervous."

The woman smiled back, and it was a nice smile. Sally Beth decided her tan was kind of pretty. It made her look exotic. "Where are you from?"

"West Virginia. And you?"

"Orange County."

"Look, Sally Beth," said Lilly. "You got a five and a three. You want to take a hit. And another."

The woman next to Mafia Man had a big pile of chips in front of her, but her boyfriend was losing, and he was looking sullen.

"Twenty! Ha!" said Lilly.

Sally Beth spoke to the blonde over the head of Mafia Man. "Where is Orange County?"

"California. It's where Hollywood is."

"Oh," said Sally Beth. That explained a lot.

"He busted!" shouted Lilly, and Sally Beth was astonished to see her little pile of chips grow. "Sally Beth, isn't this *fun?*"

Well, yes, it was kind of fun, she guessed, even though it was late and she had been up since six o'clock this morning, Tucker time, and she found the game baffling. Lilly played Sally Beth's hand while Sally Beth talked to the blonde woman over the head of Mafia Man next to her. Sally Beth felt bad for him because he was losing, but she figured since his girlfriend was winning, they would turn out okay, and she hoped he wasn't worrying about the rent or anything. She gave him a smile. "Don't worry, I think she's making up for you," and was surprised when he glared at her and got up from the table as he downed his drink.

"Hillbilly bitch," he sneered and walked off.

Sally Beth was taken aback at first, then she remembered that men didn't like to lose to women, and he probably had felt that she had been making fun of him. She was about to apologize to him, but before she could open her mouth again, Lilly jumped into his seat, mumbling, "Screw you! Take a hit, Sally Beth," and the opportunity was gone.

The woman from Orange County rolled her eyes. "Don't pay him any attention. He's just mad because he's losing. He usually calls me worse than that when he loses," she laughed. "We girls are stomping them, aren't we?" Lilly laughed, too, and so did the dealer, and Sally Beth thought, *Oh, if Mama could see us now, she would just spin in her grave.* But she didn't want to hurt the feelings of the girl from Orange County, so she laughed, too, before turning to Lilly to say, "I'm getting tired, Lilly. Why don't we get on home now?"

"Oh, no! We got this winning streak going on. Oh, look, two aces. Thank you, Jesus! I'll split these."

"Lilly, don't take the Lord's name in vain!"

"That wasn't in vain. I really was thanking Him."

Sally Beth wanted to argue that it wasn't right to thank Jesus for helping you gamble, but she didn't feel up to it. She suddenly felt lonely and homesick, and she knew for certain that Lilly wouldn't let herself be dragged from this place even if it was on fire.

The woman from Orange County leaned toward her. "So what do you do in West Virginia? I'm Carla, by the way."

Sally Beth perked up. "I'm Sally Beth, and I'm a hair stylist." She thought for a second and added, "and a cosmetologist. But mostly I just do hair. This is my sister, Lilly."

"Oh yeah? I need to do something with this mess," said Carla. "I got it colored last week and the woman did an awful job on it. See how dried out it is?" she said, running her hands through it and lifting the ends with a grimace. "Yours is so pretty. Is it naturally that color?"

Sally Beth saw her opportunity. "Oh yeah, but it takes some work, it's so fine and delicate. Hey, I have some leave-in conditioner that'll put some shine right back in your hair. I use it." She rummaged around in her purse to find a small tube. "If you don't mind, I'd like to try it out on you."

Lilly glared at her. "Sally Beth! Don't you dare. You can't be rubbing stuff in people's hair right here in the middle of the casino! People will think you are nuts. Don't take a hit. You've got sixteen and the dealer is showing a six."

"Don't be silly, Lilly. There's people acting crazy all over the place here and nobody pays one bit of attention. See that woman hollering over there?"

"It's okay," spoke up Carla. "I wish you would do something with this. You hair is so shiny. And your sister's too. Does she use it?"

"Yes, and it's real easy. Here, I'll just work some of it through your hair. You'll be amazed." She opened the tube and put a small dollop in the palm of her hand as she got up to move behind her. "Lilly you can play my hand," she said, plunging her hands into the woman's tresses and massaging vigorously.

"Sally Beth, you are embarrassing the heck out of me. Hit her," Lilly said to the dealer. "Hit her again. It looks plain trashy to be rubbing stuff in people's hair you don't even know right here in a public place. Hot dog! Dealer busted again! I'm going to up my bet. You want me to up yours, too?"

"Sure, okay. Oh, gosh, this is making a big difference already. Here, I'll brush it through to get it distributed better." She pulled a brush out of her purse and went to work. "Oh, that looks *so much better*! I've got a mirror in here so you can see. Isn't that nice?"

"Shoot, I shouldn't have taken that card. Oh my, yes! I can really tell a difference." She smiled tentatively at Sally Beth. "I hope you don't take this the wrong way, but you sort of remind me of Elly Clampett on the *Beverly Hillbillies*. I mean, that's a compliment."

Sally Beth nearly grimaced, particularly after what the boyfriend had just called her, but she could tell the woman was being sincere, and she did not want to offend her by acting put-out.

"Well, I will take it as a compliment, then. Elly May's real pretty."

"Yes, you do look like her, but you're really sweet, too, like she is. Sort of innocent. Not spoiled. I really appreciate you fixing my hair."

"Oh, you're welcome. It's so dry out here, no wonder your hair is dried out. Mine would be, too."

"Darn it!" exclaimed Lilly. "That was lucky. He took five cards and managed to pull out a twenty-one."

"Are you starting to lose, Lilly?" Sally Beth was tired and feeling anxious. The blonde with the now-shiny hair had lost three hands in a row. "Shouldn't we go now? I'm real tired."

Lilly sighed, "Okay, Sally Beth," she said, then seeing the tiredness in her sister's face, she added, "It's time we got you home."

Lord, I can see why You don't like gambling. But I did like meeting Carla. You never know how nice people can be. Just goes to show I shouldn't be quick to judge. She yawned. *Give my love to Mama and Daddy, okay? And Holy Miracle. I sure do miss them all.* Sally Beth rolled over and fell into a dead sleep.

August 7, 1978

They spent the day packing up Lilly's belongings and then had an early dinner before going to the Sinatra concert, which, Sally Beth decided, was the highlight of her life. She didn't know which was harder: not singing along with Mr. Sinatra or enduring the dirty looks of all the people around her when she did. It also was hard not to dance out of the auditorium when it was over. "Strangers in the Night" was buzzing around in her head so beautifully, it was all she could do to walk steadily, one foot in front of the other. She thanked Lilly for bringing her a dozen times, as they strolled back through the casino.

"I'm thirsty. Let's get a drink before we go home," Lilly suggested, nudging her through the crowds toward a plush lounge. To Sally Beth's surprise, she soon found herself sitting at a bar across from a grinning Lawrence.

"Hey, ladies. What can I do you for?" he wiggled his eyebrows at Lilly. She pretended to roll her eyes, but Sally Beth caught the smile she flashed at him. "Surprise us," said Lilly.

"Nothing strong," broke in Sally Beth.

"Hey, let the man do his job. Bring us something special. Something Sally Beth will like. She's about to die from the heat here."

"I got just the thing." Lawrence kept up a lively chatter as he dished ice and a variety of liquids into glasses. "You ladies having a good time? I'm getting off in about an hour, and I'm happy to show you around town, some of the—ahem—*special* places I know about."

Lilly laughed. "Don't, Lawrence! Sally Beth already thinks you are awful. And besides, your girlfriend might not like it if she finds out you've been out with a couple of natural blondes." She flung her hair back with a toss of her head.

Lawrence looked at Lilly as if she was some kind of dessert he couldn't wait to devour. "She isn't my girlfriend as of last night, so consider me a free man, up for grabs." He winked. "In every sense of the word. Come on. Let's show Sally Beth how to do Vegas right. Hot time in the old town tonight?" He placed two frosty glasses in front of them and dropped cherries on top with a flourish.

"Thanks, but I've had enough of hot," countered Sally Beth as she picked up her drink and sipped. "I'm just ready for a good night's sleep so we can hit the road tomorrow." She frowned at the glass. "Is there liquor in this?"

He chuckled. "Not much. Just enough to help you relax. Go ahead. I won't let you get drunk."

Doubtfully, she sipped again. It was very good and fruity, and even though she could taste alcohol, it didn't seem too strong. Not wanting to appear prudish or ungrateful, she took another swallow and felt the cool sweetness slip down her throat, then turn warm when it hit her stomach.

It seemed odd, drinking at a bar with Lilly, but it didn't feel as unholy as she might have imagined it would be. The place was pretty, with soft lights and classy décor. The thrill of the concert was still buzzing in her blood, and the pianist was playing the most beautiful version of "Moon River" she had ever heard. When she glanced up at Lawrence, he smiled at her. It seemed like a nice smile, and she thought maybe he wasn't so bad, after all. He was much too pretty and soft-looking, but his teeth were big and white, and she liked the way they lined up so straight, so she smiled back, and then they had a pleasant conversation about how hot it was and what the mountains east of there were like. Before she knew it, her drink had disappeared and Lawrence was placing another one in front of her.

"So you're leaving tomorrow," he said.

"Yes, thank the Lord," said Sally Beth. I don't think I can take another day of this heat."

"You're going back to West Virginia?"

"Yes, but we're going to see lots of sights along the way. The Grand Canyon, and I've heard the high desert is real pretty, and maybe Carlsbad Caverns."

Lilly spoke up. "And Graceland. We're going to see Graceland."

"Uh-huh. Our mama was born on the very same day as Elvis, January 8, 1935, and she always loved him. We're going to put a flower on his grave for her," added Sally Beth.

"Oh yeah? I'd like to see Graceland, too." He paused for a moment, looking thoughtful. "Say, why don't I come along with you? At least to Memphis. I'm from St. Louis, and I've been wanting to get back for a visit. I could just catch a bus from Memphis. I'll help pay for gas," he added.

Lilly lit up like a Christmas tree. "You want to?"

Sally Beth thought that might not be a great idea, but somehow it didn't seem important enough to say anything. She was feeling cozy, as if she was nestled down in a bed of cotton balls, and the room around her was full of shimmering, fuzzy lights, and the music was soft, and it seemed to shimmer, too. Come to think of it, it might be nice to have a man along, if they had a flat in the desert or something. She knew there were long, dry stretches of desert in their near future. Yes, a man could be a big help, and besides, she hated to turn down anybody who wanted to go home. It was the right thing to do, letting him come with them. She nodded, smiled, and listened to the dreamy music, floating along its currents as if she was riding on a cloud.

Lord, I sure wish Mama could have seen Mr. Sinatra tonight. Daddy, too. He was every bit as smooth and glamorous as I thought he would be, and he was so much bigger than he seemed when he was on Ed Sullivan, *and much more alive. It was all really good..."* Sally Beth was asleep before she could finish the sentence.

Four

August 8, 1978

*O*h Lord, I think I need to confess. I got sucked right into this place, and I've been drinking and gambling for real, and I was a terrible example to Lilly. Tell Mama and Daddy I'm sorry I let them down, but thank You that we are leaving today. Bless this trip, Lord. Let Lilly and me get along, help me to be nice to Lawrence who is coming along, and help Lilly not to flirt with him too much. Give my love to Mama and Daddy. Tell them I miss them, and I wish they could have seen Mr. Sinatra last night.

It was hot, with a dry wind blowing from the west. Sally Beth had a little bit of a headache, but she was feeling a lot better in her heart because she knew they were on their way out of this godforsaken place. She and Lilly loaded the car, careful to make room in the trunk for another suitcase. Just as they nudged Sally Beth's cosmetic case into a corner, Lawrence and Tiffany strolled into sight. They both carried a suitcase. He also had a smaller bag slung over his shoulder.

"Hey!" said Lawrence. "Look who's coming with us!"

"Oh!" said Lilly, looking as if she had just eaten a green persimmon. She glared at Tiffany, who was smiling at Lawrence, so Lilly's dirty look went completely wasted.

"Isn't it funny?" Tiffany turned her smile toward Sally Beth and Lilly. "We just had a big fight two days ago, and then last night, he came over and asked me to come with him and meet his family!" Sally Beth thought she had never seen a prettier face, or hair, either, for that matter. She wondered if those highlights were natural. It looked like a million lights of copper and gold woven among the dark brown curls. It was just too bad that she dressed so unattractively: cowboy boots and an awful muumuu that covered her up from her collarbone to her calves and made her look like she weighed at least three hundred pounds. Such a pretty girl, otherwise, and an air of kindness, and so in love with this guy who didn't treat her right.

"Lawrence said it was time I met his parents. And to think I thought he wasn't serious about me!" Tiffany slipped her arm around Lawrence's back and leaned toward him, eyes rich with love.

Lilly made a funny noise, then, after a pause, said, "I don't think there'll be room for all of us and our luggage, too. And there's two guitars in the back seat."

"Oh, don't worry, I'm good at packing, and all we have is just one suitcase each. If we have to, we'll just put them under our feet." Lawrence threw his suitcase into the trunk, and then shoved in Tiffany's soft-sided bag, massaging and prodding it into a shapeless mass.

While he shoved, Tiffany smiled at Lilly. "Lilly, thank you so much for offering to take us! I've been wanting to get out of this place for the longest time. We promise we won't be a bother." She laughed, a rich, musical sound, and added, "At least we'll try." Sally Beth found herself really liking her new travel companion.

It was obvious by the set of Lilly's shoulders that she was mad as all get-out. It was going to be a long trip to Memphis with her in this mood, but Sally Beth hoped it was going to be enough of an adventure to get her over her pique. After all, today alone, they were going to see the Hoover Dam and the Grand Canyon. What more could they ask for?

Sally Beth found the desert no less inhospitable as they drove across Nevada. It was very hot, and the air was so dry her mouth went cottony, and she wondered how Lilly had managed to live here for six months—indeed, how anyone could live here at all. But they were headed toward the mountains, and she thought she would feel better when they began to climb. She would find a tree to sit under and get out from under this relentless sun. Restless, she turned on the radio, but no sound came out.

"Radio's busted," Lilly said.

"Oh, yeah. Tiffany, will you hand me one of those guitars? We need to have some music."

"Sure. Here. And I have a harmonica." Tiffany handed Sally Beth the Gibson, then, before Sally Beth could even get tuned up, she put the harmonica to her lips, launching into a wailing version of "Me and Bobby McGee". The air seemed to cool with the whine of the harmonica, and Sally Beth warmed it up again by picking fast to keep up. Lilly opened her throat to let the music slide out while Lawrence pulled a camera out of the case and began snapping pictures. He took advantage of the wavering light bouncing through the car, taking pictures of Tiffany and sometimes leaning over the back of the seat to focus on Lilly and Sally Beth. Sally Beth got tired of him asking her to turn around and smile, but she was feeling so happy she didn't care. They were on their way to the Grand Canyon, the place her daddy had always wanted to see, and he would be pleased to know that his baby girls were going to see it for him. It felt as if they were on an important mission.

As they neared Boulder City, the terrain became more unfriendly. Sally Beth searched the landscape for trees, but the only things in view were the same scrabbly soil, big rocks, and little bushes scattered here and there. Past the town, the scant vegetation gave way to towering piles of red, fist-sized rocks heaped on both sides of the road, and then, to her dismay, the landscape was further violated by hundreds of high voltage power lines and towers. To her, it was awful: the worst unnatural industrial scenery imaginable. Gaps in the hills of boulders afforded glimpses of blue water between the power lines, but it did not soothe Sally Beth's parched soul. It didn't even look like real, thirst-quenching water, but simply a swathe of blue paper stuck upon the miserable landscape.

Hoover Dam, enormous and impressive, loomed before them. It might have been considered beautiful in a man-made sort of way, but Sally Beth found it bleak, even suffocating. The earth all around the startlingly blue water was not earth at all, but just rock, glaring, hot, and desolate.

"Whoa, look at this!" exclaimed Lawrence, impressed. "Let's get out and go swimming down at the lake. And we can take a tour of the dam. This is incredible!"

"Huh-uh." Lilly shook her head. "I don't even want to get out to look." Staring straight ahead, she gripped the steering wheel with white fingers as she slowly drove across the slim, silver thread of the dam.

"Hey!" protested Lawrence. "You're not even going to stop?"

"Nope," replied Lilly. "It's time to head for the hills and find some green grass."

They stopped for lunch shortly after they crossed the dam and into Arizona. Over dry hamburgers and Cokes, Sally Beth tried to keep the conversation light "Are you two taking a vacation? Will you be going back? Or are you staying in St. Louis for good?"

"Oh, I guess we'll be going back," laughed Lawrence. "We've both got pretty good jobs in Vegas. At least we did. They probably won't like the fact that I didn't show up for work today, and that I won't be back for a few weeks, but everybody needs bartenders, and they're used to us taking off now and then. I'm not worried."

"What do you do, Tiffany?"

"I work for a Mercedes dealership."

"Oh really? Do you sell cars?"

"Sort of," Lawrence snorted. "I mean she *sells cars*. She makes rich old farts think she comes with the deal if they buy one." Tiffany scowled at him.

"Lawrence, you make me sound like a hooker." She turned to Sally Beth. "I help customers decide on accessories and interiors when they custom order a car. I'm sort of a Mercedes interior designer." Sally Beth had never heard of such a thing.

"Is that a common thing?" asked Lilly, bewildered.

"Not really. Just in high-end areas, like Vegas or Los Angeles. People get real picky about how their cars are accessorized. You'd be surprised."

"Yeah. They're pretending to pick out the color of their leather upholstery, and old Tiffany makes them think she'll be all over the back seat with them if they choose alligator hide or ostrich. She gets them to spend an extra grand or two." He winked at Tiffany. "Tell them about your showgirl days."

"I was not a showgirl. I was in a band."

"That's not what I heard," sniggered Lawrence. "I heard you had a real stunner of an act going until they shut you down." He grinned at the others. "Seems Tiffany here had herself a little run-in with the law."

"I did not. I quit as soon as I found out minors aren't supposed to perform in the clubs."

"Not what *I* heard," countered Lawrence.

"Well, you heard wrong. It's getting late. If we're going to get to the Grand Canyon before dark, we'd better move on," Tiffany said, standing abruptly and tugging at the neck of her muumuu to cover the cleavage that had begun to show.

"We need to get gas," Lilly said as they left the restaurant.

Sally Beth shook her head. "I checked before we got out. It

looks like we have more than half a tank."

"It always says that," countered Lilly. "It's stuck there. You just have to get gas every couple hundred miles so you'll be sure not to run out."

After they had stopped for gas, they drove fast until the mountains finally yielded up cooler air, and, *Oh, thank You, God! Trees.* Although they were not the lush, rolling, uninterrupted green of the stands of the forests at home, Sally Beth was glad to see them. At first, these trees reminded her of someone who had had a bad hair transplant, with each one standing singly, isolated from one another, with bare scalp showing between them. But when she rolled down the window, she breathed in the essence of pine, and her parched soul settled and soothed, and then, to her delight, the scent of rain came billowing upon the wind. As they reached the outskirts of Flagstaff, a deluge began. Gusts of wind and rain rocked and buffeted the car. Lilly turned on the windshield wipers, but because they worked only on the driver's side, all Sally Beth could see was water streaming down the windshield in front of her.

"We're getting close to Flagstaff, Lilly. You're supposed to turn here someplace, on 64, and I can't see a thing in this rain. What's wrong with your windshield wipers?"

"Oh, it's busted on that side. But that never bothered me because my side works fine. I'll just drive real slowly, and I'll keep a lookout. Oh, look—here it is. Hot dog! The Grand Canyon in sixty miles!"

Sally Beth's heart lifted as she looked at the rain and saw the dark forms of trees gliding by. Las Vegas, the sin, the heat, the dry, dry desert was behind her, and the Grand Canyon was before her. She took a deep breath of the moist, cool air.

And then they were there. Just as they entered the park, the rain rolled back as suddenly as it had come. The sparse, pinyon forest fell away to reveal miles and miles of rain and cloud and sun, spires of rock and empty space, light and shadow of every possible and impossible hue. When Sally Beth jumped out to look into the great chasm and felt the cold wind rushing upward, she nearly fell to her knees, suddenly feeling insignificant, overwhelmed with awe at the glory. It was not brown, as she had come to believe it would be, but all colors, red and purple and golden, and the air was pungent with the scent of juniper and pine. She nearly wept with gratitude when a rainbow appeared, flooding down from above the tallest peak into the abyss. It was everything she could have hoped for, and more. Her eyes roved and worshipped.

The rain did not stand abated for long. After a short glimpse, they were forced back into the car by an icy downpour, so they drove back to the small community outside the park where accommodations would be cheaper. After an awkward moment when it became evident that Lawrence and Tiffany were planning on sharing a room, Sally Beth decided not to be a prude about it. She registered for a double for herself and Lilly, then stepped away from the desk so Lawrence and Tiffany could have some privacy as they arranged for their room. After that, they ate a quick dinner, then put on their jackets and went back to the rim to watch the sunset.

Slowly, dusk rose up from the great rift, spreading enchantment and mystery over the spires within the canyon, until at last it was full dark below while the last glow settled upon the rock facing them. The sky turned from blue to turquoise to indigo, and the stone cathedral around them deepened into purples and mauves.

The stars came out, pricking their way one by one into the deep blue dusk, and then, suddenly, the light from the sun completely disappeared, and the wash of the pale Milky Way stretched across the sky, a glowing iridescence, a mother of pearl milkiness that did not so much spangle the sky, but draped across it like the finest of silk illusion.

Dear Lord, thank You, thank You THANK YOU for letting me see this place! I am just overwhelmed by Your goodness, Your beauty, Your grandeur, Your glory. Sally Beth wondered if her parents could see all this from heaven. *Yes, of course. Maybe that's why we came here. They wanted us to see it, and they arranged it. It's like a gift from them.*

August 9, 1978, The Grand Canyon

The early morning was bright with stars. Sally Beth woke Lilly, whispering through the darkness. "Come on, let's go back and see the sunrise. Lilly groaned before she threw back the covers and sat up, but she did not need coaxing. They were out the door within five minutes, traveling back to the rim where they sat on a bench to wait.

The sun came up slowly into the frigid morning from behind a promontory to their right, turning the sky from inky dark to a dusky wash of pearly gray, then pink, to sudden daylight above them. Below, the darkness still gaped at them, but slowly lost its battle against the pearlescent light that probed even the darkest corners. Then the sky blazed, and so did the canyon, brilliantly red, gold, pink, green, purple, and mauve. Birds swept across their line of vision, squawking, winging their way westward, chased by the light. And then true daylight began to pierce the depths, pushing the darkness down and spreading color at their feet. When the breeze came up sharp and cold, the beauty seemed to freeze in a brief moment of chilly stillness, and then gave way to awakening woodland sounds and smells. In a way, it reminded Sally Beth of home, although it looked and sounded and smelled very different from the mountains of West Virginia. But it held the same rightness, the same honesty that made her soul settle into a peaceful place that she had not seen for days. She stood at the very edge, her toes bridging out into the vastness, and felt the texture of the cold, searching wind winging its way over her skin.

Something new and bright began to stir in Sally Beth as she gazed into the airy abyss. She felt exposed, but instead of feeling vulnerable, she found herself emboldened. This place marked a beginning, an awakening, as she become aware that all the other wonders of the world that she had dreamed about were more than just dreams. They were real, and they were there, waiting for her.

If she wanted to, she could see them all. The thought startled her. Until now, her mountains had been not just the center of her universe, but her only reality. This place, yes, even the hot, dry desert, had stretched her imagination, shattering the illusion that home was all there was, all there ever could be. She breathed as deeply as her lungs could expand, inviting the great Grand Canyon to become a part of her.

Not until the sun was fully up and the clear sunlight spangled the air both above and below them did they drive back out of the Park to the motel. They went straight to the café where Tiffany and Lawrence sat eating breakfast as they thumbed through the guidebook.

"Did you go back to the rim?" Tiffany asked.

"Yes," said Lilly. "The sunrise was beautiful."

"I wish I had gone with you. Tomorrow, be sure to come get me, okay? Now, what do you want to do today? We're thinking we want to hike the South Kaibab trail, at least to Skeleton Point. We probably shouldn't go much farther since we're getting a late start. What do you think?"

"I don't have any preference, since I've never been here before." Sally Beth figured any trail they chose would be good.

"I'm not going," Lilly said mildly.

"Not going?" asked Tiffany. "Why in the world not?"

Sally Beth explained. "Lilly has a problem with heights." She stopped, feeling that was enough, but Lawrence wanted to know more.

"Why are you afraid of heights, Lilly?"

"I just am. I don't like it."

"But the trails aren't that steep or anything. Come on," he wheedled. "You'll enjoy it."

"No, I won't. It's already hot, and any time there's a 'spectacular view,' it means looking down, probably from a narrow trail, and I'm just not going to do it. You can go without me."

"But we're here, and it's silly..." Lawrence began, but Tiffany interrupted.

"Lawrence, she said she didn't want to go. So just drop it. Now, it's getting late, so let's go. Lilly, what will you do while we are gone?"

"Oh, I'll find plenty to do. Just hang out here, maybe go shopping. I'll have the car, so you're on your own. Try not to throw Lawrence off a cliff, or if you do, make sure nobody sees you."

To Sally Beth's dismay, they had not made it more than half a mile into the Canyon before thunderclouds rolling in from the west brought lightening, hail, and rain swarming up so fiercely they were forced to turn back.

They caught a shuttle back to the village and made their way through the driving rain to the warmth of the café where they ate lunch, dried out, and strolled through the museums, then went back for coffee and pie. They were just dawdling over the last bites when Lawrence spotted Lilly through the window and waved her in.

She was dressed in new clothes: jeans, cowboy boots, a Western shirt, and a cowboy hat. She looked adorable.

"Lilly!" That is the cutest outfit I ever saw!" exclaimed Sally Beth. You look like you belong out here."

Lilly giggled. "I know! Isn't it great?" She twirled around, showing off her new clothes and turquoise cowboy boots. "And I know your birthday isn't for two days, but I got you an outfit, too. We'll be on the road after today, so there's no reason not to celebrate now," she said, placing two large shopping bags in front of Sally Beth.

"It's your birthday?" asked Lawrence.

"Yeah, day after tomorrow."

"The ripe old age of twenty-three! Back home, that's considered 'old maid' territory," laughed Lilly.

"Shoot, where I come from, you're an old maid at eighteen," added Tiffany. She smiled at Lawrence. "It's a good thing you came along. My family was starting to feel right sorry for me."

Lawrence's tight smile and darting eyes were not wasted on Sally Beth. She wished she could tell Tiffany that she could do a whole lot better than this man, but she bit her lip and reminded herself that it wasn't her business as she picked up Lilly's packages.

Within seconds, she had forgotten Lawrence. Lilly had outfitted her with a hot pink miniskirt and a white peasant blouse, as well as hot pink cowboy boots, stamped to look like ostrich, with gleaming silver tips at the toes. A matching pink cowboy belt with a shiny pink stone at the buckle completed the ensemble. Sally Beth squealed as she hugged her sister. "I'm going to *love* strutting around in these, Lilly! Won't we be a sight in Tucker!"

"You know it, girl!" cried Lilly. Sally Beth thought her heart would burst with happiness.

Tiffany threw on an enormous, orange University of Texas sweatshirt over her voluminous muumuu, and the others fetched warm jackets from the car before walking back to the rocky perimeter to watch the sunset. They settled themselves on a bench, huddling into their jackets against the searching wind as the light seared its way across the tops of the Canyon spires.

After snapping a few pictures, Lawrence sat down beside Tiffany. "Out of film," he mumbled, then threw his arm around her, stroking her hair and neck. His hand strayed below her collarbone.

"Stop that." She pulled away.

"What, I can't touch my girl's hair?"

"I just don't like being pawed in public."

"Good grief. This is hardly pawing. I bet Lilly doesn't mind it if her boyfriend touches her hair, do you Lilly?" He pulled his arm from Tiffany's shoulder, extending it to give Lilly's hair a soft tug. Lilly glared at him, rose, and ventured closer to the edge of the rim. After the briefest of glances into the rising dusk, she danced quickly away.

Lawrence guffawed at her timidity.

"Leave her alone, Lawrence," Tiffany snapped. "You can be such a jerk sometimes."

Lawrence fell quiet, then after a few sullen moments, he shot Tiffany a hostile glance, jumped up, grabbed Lilly around the waist, and, with a booming laugh, swung her close to the edge of the abyss. Lilly did not scream, but went pale and clung to Lawrence's arm, pushing herself hard against him.

"See? It's not that bad," he insisted, nudging her forward, closer to the brink.

"Lawrence!" warned Sally Beth. "Let her go. She's scared!"

"But she shouldn't be, that's the point," he insisted. "See, Lilly? I've got you. You can get close to the edge, and you won't fall. I'm holding on to you."

Lilly began to tremble, her breath coming in short gasps. She didn't say anything, just pushed with her feet, trying to force herself and Lawrence away from the edge. Suddenly, as if a signal had passed between them, Sally Beth moved into the two-foot space between Lilly and the edge of the void to put her arms around her sister while Tiffany slipped up close to Lawrence's back. Encircling her arm around his neck, she jerked him backward, forcing him to let go of Lilly.

"I thought you said you had her, Lawrence," said Tiffany softly into his ear. "Seems to me you let go awfully easy."

"Well, yeah. You've got a choke hold on me," he gasped.

"Oh, so you think it's okay to let her go if you are uncomfortable? What if something scared you while you were dangling her over the edge of the rim? Would you think it's okay to drop her?" She spoke mildly, almost sweetly, but kept her forearm pressed against his neck.

"Let go of me, Tiffany!"

"Oh," she said, with a note of surprise and dropped her arm, stepping back nonchalantly, as if she had merely been giving Lawrence a friendly hug. Lilly was trembling and glaring at Lawrence as if she wanted to compete the job Tiffany had started.

"You okay, honey?" Sally Beth asked. She was shaking nearly as hard as Lilly was.

"Yeah." Lilly took a deep breath as she tossed her head to cover her embarrassment and fear. Lawrence looked embarrassed as well, and sullen. They sat silently, watching the sunset, and although it was glorious, they all felt a certain regret that tainted the experience. This was their last evening at the Grand Canyon, and they spent it probing their wounds.

August 10, 1978

Sally Beth and Lilly were awakened in the darkness of the small hours by a banging on their door. Sitting up, Lilly called out, "Who is it?"

"It's me, Tiffany. Let me in!" Sally Beth jumped up, opening the door to find Tiffany standing at the threshold, dressed in a frumpy housecoat that fell to her knees. Below that swirled a shimmering blue nightgown, and below that, Sally Beth could see her cowboy boots peeking from under the gossamer fabric. Her suitcase and a few parcels were in her hands.

"What is it, honey?" Sally Beth asked, stepping back so Tiffany could enter.

"That no-good louse. I am so done with him." She brushed her way past Sally Beth, threw down her load, and flopped on the bed, crossing her arms and blowing a pent-up breath through pursed lips. Her eyes flashed so angrily Sally Beth could see them even in the dim light that shined from the lamp outside.

"What happened?"

"I caught him calling another woman! Can you believe it? He gets up out of *my bed,* sneaks the phone into the bathroom and calls another woman, and I can hear every word he says! He's telling her he'll be there in a week or two and they can go to Mexico together." She clenched her fists, then ran her fingers through her crinkly hair, grabbing it in the process and pulling it distractedly.

"Oh no! What did you do?"

"I threw everything I could into my bag and got out of there.

What do you think I did?"

"You didn't confront him?" asked Lilly.

"Ha. If I did, I'd kill him!" Her lower lip began to tremble and she ran her hand over her face. "No good, sorry—"

"Well, you did the right thing," interrupted Sally Beth. "You can just stay here tonight, and we can sort things out in the morning."

"I already have sorted things out. We are leaving. Now. He might still be talking to that poor, stupid girl, but if I know him, once he's figured out I'm gone he'll be over here trying to sweet talk his way back in, and none of us will get a lick of sleep anyway. We have to get out of here before he comes sniffing around, all whiny and apologetic. *Come on!*" She jumped up and threw her bag on the bed, rummaging through it.

"Oh, no. My good underwear was in the bathroom. All I have is this slutty stuff he bought me, and I can't stand it. I have to wash my decent things out every night, and it was in there drying." She flung thongs and delicate, silky bras the size of tires onto the bed, then stood, unbuttoned her housecoat, and yanked it off.

Both Sally Beth and Lilly blinked and gasped.

Tiffany wore a diaphanous silk negligee that clung to the most stunning body either of them had ever seen. Her breasts were enormous, high, and firm, and her hips were huge but perfect, sitting proudly on long, strong, and shapely thighs. Her broad shoulders and arms gleamed, muscular and smooth, and her waist and belly were slim and tight. Then she yanked off her gown, and she became even more astonishing. She looked like an over-endowed Barbie doll, with every ounce of muscle and fat placed perfectly. Sally Beth wondered how a body like that was possible. She did her best not to stare, but failed.

"I thought you were fat," said Lilly in a small voice.

"Yeah, well, parts of me are," muttered Tiffany as she stepped into a tiny thong. "I hate these things. How anybody can even walk with this crammed up your crack is beyond me. I've got to go to Penny's and get some decent underwear just as soon as we can." She grabbed a bra and strapped it on. It was so flimsy it looked like it wouldn't do any good at all, but then, she also looked like she didn't need it. Every inch of her body was so firm she could have been sculpted from stone. "Look at this stupid thing. Any bra that hooks in the front isn't worth a plug nickel. The thing probably will break if I sneeze. I hate Lawrence and what he's done to me. Don't ever let a man shop for you or pack for you," she grumbled. "Come on!" she added, as she put her housecoat back on and buttoned it up. "He won't wait long—just until he thinks I'm not mad enough to bash his head in."

Lilly jumped out of bed, picked her underwear off the floor, and started flinging her clothes on. Sally Beth, who had put her clothes away neatly, ran to the bureau and put on the first things she came to. They all were completely dressed in a moment, then they rushed around hurling clothing and makeup into their bags and slipped on their shoes. Lilly struggled for a moment longer to pull her new cowboy boots on, but still, they were out the door within five minutes.

"Oh Lord, here he comes!" whispered Tiffany while they were slinging their suitcases into the trunk. Lawrence spotted them, and realizing that he was about to be left behind, he sprinted toward the car. "*Hurry*," Tiffany hissed. Lilly let out a shriek, starting the engine and throwing it into gear as Tiffany jumped into the back. She slammed the door in Lawrence's face, and they careened out of the parking lot, squealed around the corner and disappeared into the night, leaving Lawrence churning after them in the fumes of the exhaust. Sally Beth, her heart thrumming adrenaline through her arteries, began to laugh uncontrollably. Lilly joined her, her mouth wide open, shrieking with excitement, and Tiffany added her musical laughter to the cacophony.

"Go, girl, go!" she shouted, leaning over the back of the seat, fueling Lilly's screams, urging her to press her foot down hard on the accelerator, to run stop signs and take the curves like a madwoman. Lilly laid rubber on the deserted road as she careened away into the night, leaving the Grand Canyon and the small, white moon shining over the hapless head of Lawrence.

"Where are we going?" Lilly finally asked after they had gotten their giggles under control. "Back to Flagstaff?"

"No!" exclaimed Tiffany. "Not yet. I didn't get to see the sunrise over the Canyon yesterday. Let's go back and watch it come up." She checked her watch. "It's nearly four o'clock. We've got less than two hours before sunrise."

"Yeah, let's," added Sally Beth. "We may never get back here, Lilly."

Lilly slowed to make a U-turn in the middle of the road. "Might as well," she said. "This has turned into the best adventure I've ever been on, and I don't want to miss any of it."

Stopping at the overlook at Grandeur Point, they leaned back into the seats, dozing as the wind howled and danced with the pine trees until Tiffany's voice broke into the pre-dawn.

"Come on, girls. I see some light," she said, rummaging in her bag to pull out her sweatshirt. Sally Beth and Lilly put on their jackets, and they stepped out into the morning chill.

They were not disappointed. Silver-gray light pricked the outline of trees and rocks close by, and then a delicate pink kissed a pinnacle just below them. The pink deepened as the sky lightened, and then, suddenly, a small sliver of gold graced the eastern horizon, and glorious light spilled out over the spires, gilding the air and the rock until they gleamed in the milky dawn. Light rained down upon Lilly's face and sleep-tangled hair. Tiffany's hair lit up with copper beside the gold and silver of Lilly's.

"Sally Beth, you are so pretty," said Lilly. This light makes you look like the Virgin Mary. You've got a halo."

"I was just thinking that about the two of you," she countered as she stepped forward to insert herself between Lilly and Tiffany. Putting her arms around both their waists, she raised her face into the glorious light, a perfect hymn to the morning. They watched it for several minutes as the Canyon below them faded from black to gray to purple and red and colors indescribable. She felt herself floating into the abyss of light, and somewhere in the corner of her mind, she felt a stirring that told her something she could not quite grasp, something important. She searched her soul for the meaning, but all she could discern was that she was certain her life was changing.

Five

They could not bring themselves to depart. Instead of leaving, they continued eastward along the Canyon drive, stopping at each overlook for yet another burst of splendor until they finally came to the end of the Canyon. Continuing east, they stopped for breakfast at the first settlement they came to.

Tiffany squirmed in the seat, adjusted her thong, then leaned back into the booth and sighed. "I can't believe I gave that man nearly eleven months of my life. Just being here, away from him, sitting around with girls, makes me realize how stupid I was."

"What you ever saw in him is what I want to know," declared Lilly. Sally Beth did not think it would be helpful to mention that Lilly herself had seen plenty in him, at least until he tried to throw her into the Grand Canyon, so she sipped her lemon tea in silence.

"I don't know," sighed Tiffany. "Seems like I can't see the bad in a man until he rubs my face in it. I hate to date, and the only guys I get involved with are the ones who chase me until I stop saying no. I'm just lazy, I guess. I can't seem to go to the trouble to find myself the right kind of man. You think I'd learn." She looked so forlorn in her frumpy housecoat buttoned from neck to calf, without makeup, making every attempt to hide her beauty that Sally Beth wondered if she had been badly hurt by some man, or perhaps several. Her looks seemed to be a millstone that weighted her down rather than giving her the freedom beauty should.

"So where are you going now? Back to Las Vegas?" It was sad thinking about Tiffany being alone in Las Vegas. The more she thought about it, the more she was convinced that it was a bad place. Girls like Tiffany were paraded around like prize heifers. Even though they were taken care of well enough, fed, watered, and bedded comfortably, there was always the uncertain future when the milk dried up.

"No. I hated it there. My boss was one of those sleazy characters who thinks he can pimp you out just because he writes your paycheck. You wouldn't believe all the things he tried to get me to do so he could make extra money on a car. It was bad enough that I had to wear their stupid 'uniform'." She made air quotes with her fingers. "I wasn't about to intentionally lead men on. Some of those old guys were pitiful; they were so lonesome, even with all their money, and they would have spent any amount if they thought it might make somebody love them. And then others thought I was supposed to come along for the ride with them if they bought the car. I never want to put up with any of that again."

"What did your uniform look like?" Lilly was curious.

"Oh, not too bad, for normal-looking girls, but I have to be careful. You have tits and a caboose like this, and if you show any of it, even hint at showing it, everybody thinks you're a slut, and they treat you like one. No-good men decide they're going to own you, and good men don't know how to act so they try to pretend you don't exist—that, or it brings out the no-good side of them, too. The only reason I took that job is so that I could save enough to get it all whacked off." She made a slicing motion at her breast, and after thinking a moment, added, "Well, that and get my sister through college."

"You mean you were going to have surgery?"

"You bet. Do you have any idea what it's like carrying these globs of fat around?" She hefted her breasts with her hands. "I just wish I could *take them off!* You can't sleep on your back, or your stomach, you have to wear bras the size of peach baskets, and any boyfriend you get keeps trying to cram you into the world's most uncomfortable, stupidest clothes he can find just so he can strut around and show you off to other men." She turned down the corners of her mouth. "What I wouldn't give to just look *normal.*"

"So you have a younger sister?" Sally Beth asked, hoping she wasn't going through the same kind of agony.

"Yeah, Sarah Jane. She's twenty and starting her junior year at UT, and she's the brightest little thing! She got a scholarship, so all she needs is enough money to pay for room and board, and I've been helping her do that. She has a job, too, so I don't have to do too much."

"Any others?"

"Nope. Just Sarah Jane and me, Edna Mae."

"Huh?" Lilly asked.

"Edna Mae. That's my real name. Tiffany is just a made-up name that my boss wanted me to use because he thought Edna Mae was too country for the likes of his fancy dealership. Back home nobody would know Tiffany. I kind of liked it at first, but now I can't stand it. You can call me Edna Mae. It feels good to hear it. It feels like home."

"So... Edna Mae," said Lilly, trying it out. "What do you want to do next? Do you want to ride east with us?"

"If you don't mind. I'd like to go as far as Texarkana, where my granny lives."

"Your granny? Is that where the rest of your family is?"

Edna Mae's face tightened as she glanced away. "My granny is my family. Her and my sister." She shifted her gaze back to her coffee cup. Edna Mae was holding something back tightly, something that she hated so badly that she wanted to thrust it from her rather than hold it in, and she was fighting herself to keep it close. She fairly quivered with the strain of it.

"That's okay," said Lilly gently. "We can take you right to Texarkana. We'll be going through there, and it's fun having you along. I like to hear you play the harmonica."

"Let me get the gas, and I'll drive awhile," said Edna Mae as they stopped at a gas station.

Lilly opened the back door. "Okay. I'll sit back here," she said, shoving bags and guitar cases across the seat. "Hey, here's Lawrence's camera. He left it in the car."

"Oh yeah," laughed Edna Mae. "He actually didn't. I just happened to grab it on my way out the door. Consider it yours. It's the least I can do for you driving me all the way home."

"Edna Mae!" scolded Sally Beth. "You can't be giving his camera to Lilly. We have to send it back to him."

"No we don't. I bought that camera for him, and now I'm taking it back. He took it under false pretenses, and I'll be dadgummed if I let him have it. I'll throw it in the river first."

"Here are four rolls of exposed film," said Lilly. "All those pictures he took of us? Hey! Let's find a one-hour photo shop and have them developed when we get to Flagstaff."

The rain began again. Since she couldn't see out of her side of the flooded windshield, Sally Beth leaned back into the passenger seat to gaze at the streaming desert through the side window. *Funny. I'm watching the desert and there's standing water all over it.*

It was true; the desert streamed with flowing water. Each wash and gully was filled with raging torrents, frothing at the banks and spilling over ravine walls. Grass seemed to grow and flower as she watched, as if it had been released from a fisted hand. Slowly, she realized that the desert was not dead at all, but full of life and sound and color. Even when the rain abated and the water stopped streaming, she saw and appreciated the lean, rough beauty of the place.

"This place is very... muscular. Like a really hard-working man," she mused. "Home is like a woman. It's soft and sweet, and curvy. This place is all bristly and calloused. Hard edges."

"But you like it?" asked Edna Mae.

"Yeah," admitted Sally Beth. "I think I do." She looked again, letting her eyes wander over the solid, endless plateaus. They were rough, but if you looked hard enough, you saw a sweetness, too, even in the craggy hills. The stone walls hinted at secret, honeyed places where color slept and life surged beneath the rocky soil. She sighed as she leaned her forehead against the window, sleepily watching the play of light and shadows of rain upon the land.

As they drew near Flagstaff, they agreed that with visibility so poor, they might as well push on toward Winslow to get a jump on the long haul to Albuquerque. Edna Mae turned eastward on the highway, but they had not gone very far before she suddenly yawned. "I just got really sleepy. I didn't sleep much last night, thanks to Lawrence, and after getting up at, what? Three o'clock this morning? I'm ready to call it quits. Let's stop here for the night. Unless somebody else wants to drive."

"Yeah, let's stop," agreed Lilly. "I want to get these pictures developed."

They found a cheap motel before tracking down a pharmacy with a one-hour photo service where Edna Mae bought a toothbrush. After an early dinner, they went straight to bed, each falling into her own private dreams.

Friday, August 11, 1978, Moqui, Arizona

"Happy Birthday, Sally Beth!"

She woke to see Lilly and Edna Mae standing over her with gifts in their hands. Lilly dangled earrings that looked like a string of glittering stars. Edna Mae presented her with a bubble-gum pink cowboy hat with a rhinestone princess crown set into the front. Squealing with delight, Sally Beth put on the earrings and the hat. She felt like a princess indeed: pampered, loved, and oh, so cute, all dolled up. "Where did you find these?" she asked. "And how?"

"There's a great truck stop just down the road. We sneaked out while you were still asleep. Now, come on Birthday Girl! We got some celebrating to do!"

The first stop was at the drugstore to pick up their developed film, then they went to breakfast where they took their time looking at the photographs. Lawrence proved to be quite the photographer. Although his pictures of the Grand Canyon were remarkable, the images he had shot of the women were astonishingly beautiful. He had used the close-up lens on Edna Mae, capturing the delicate nuances of her extraordinary face and hair.

Lilly was fascinated. "How did he get this effect, where the light seems to shine right through you?" she asked. "And what did he do here, to make the background so crisp, when here it is all fuzzy and soft? Oh, look at this one of you, Sally Beth. You look like an angel! The light is giving you a halo. And look at your *eyes*— Sally Beth, you are just *beautiful*." She kept thumbing through the photographs, marveling and studying them. "These look like real art, not just pictures."

"Yeah, he went to school to study photography," said Edna Mae, and he's this good even with his old camera. I just bought this one for him." She gave a snort of laughter. "I bet he's mad now that he'll have to use that old camera on his other girlfriend." She pondered this for a moment, eyes flashing. "Wonder if she will let him take pictures of her naked? That's all he ever talked about to me—just *had* to take pictures of me naked. Man, I'm glad I never let him. Who knows where those would have shown up? Seriously, girls," she added, "don't ever let a man take a picture of you naked. That's one bit of decent advice my mama gave me, and she was right."

Sally Beth laughed. "I don't think you ever have to worry about me, Edna Mae. Lilly, now, that's a different story." She punched her sister in the arm. Lilly punched her back, but not as hard as she might have. Clearly, Lilly was in a better mood than Sally Beth had seen her in a long time. "Let's go," she said, her voice light and happy. "I want to take our pictures standing on the corner in Winslow, Arizona. Somebody else drive. I need to read these instructions and figure out how to work this thing."

Behind the wheel, Sally Beth drove fast across the miles of mesas and hills. They stopped in Winslow before driving on to see the Petrified Forest, and then as the Painted Desert opened up before them, she couldn't help but pray her thanks. *Thank You, Lord! You are magnificent! Beyond magnificent! I can never be grateful enough, but I am as grateful as any human can be.*

The desert bloomed now; it was not dry, but wet, colorful, almost lush. The lean and rocky land spoke in a whispered voice, telling Sally Beth that she was too soft to understand the secrets here, no matter how much she might yearn to know them. She was satisfied just to look and not intrude upon the mysteries. It wasn't her place to know all places intimately just as it was not her place to know all people intimately. Her mama had taught her that the secret to enjoying life was to open herself to it as much as was proper without intruding; to appreciate and love, but to accept whatever constraints a place or a person—or she—needed to impose. Like a dance, there are rules, a form within a certain space.

"You are free to move all you want within that space, as long as you make the steps," she had once said. "You can improvise on the dance, but the reason to dance in the first place is to show your love. Hold people carefully. Don't step on anybody's toes or trip anybody up. If everybody remembers that, we all get to dance and nobody gets hurt." Sally Beth was grateful to her mama for teaching her that. It made it easier to navigate, knowing these simple rules.

Edna Mae pulled out her harmonica, Lilly took up the Gibson, and before long, the three of them had settled into a nice harmony. Lilly sang with a robust, full voice. Sally Beth's was higher, pure and sweet, not strong, but she blended well with Lilly. Edna Mae's voice was raspy and breathy, but she could carry a tune, and she could belt them out.

Edna Mae pulled out the beat-up old guitar. "Here's a little something I'm working on in honor of our favorite pretty boy," she said, giving the guitar strings four long strums in a minor key, then bellowed out:

You're better off with the fury of hell than with a scornful wo-man.

The devil will let you ride his tail while he heats up the frying pan.

But a lady full of scorn won't give you that spin.

She'll scorch you to cinders for all of your sin.

I'm a scornful woman, you are the scorned

I disdain your sweet-talking ways

You can cry all you want, look sad and forlorn

But I'm done with you for all of my days

Lilly picked up the backup quickly. Sally Beth found a counter melody as Edna Mae tinkered with a second verse.

A loving woman won't be tight with wages that you're due

If the sweet words that you spoke to her came from a heart that's true

You'd feel like a king if you'd treated her nice

But a rotten man's pay is fire and ice

The refrain rolled out of their mouths lustily. They rolled down the windows and sang it loud. Lilly leaned out of the window, shouting it to the dusty road, and Edna Mae joined her. Sally Beth stomped on the accelerator as she hollered at the windshield, skewering poor Lawrence as they stormed their way across the lovely, silent desert.

At Edna Mae's insistence on stopping early enough to celebrate Sally Beth's birthday, they found a motel on the outskirts of Albuquerque. As soon as they threw their suitcases on the bed, Edna Mae slapped the pink cowboy hat on Sally Beth's head and announced, "Let's go honky-tonking!"

Lilly shook her head. "Sally Beth won't want to go to a bar,

Edna Mae. Let's just go to a nice restaurant." Edna Mae shrugged off her disappointment. "Okay, she's the princess today." Sally Beth breathed a sigh of thanks.

Lilly and Sally Beth both dressed in their new cowgirl outfits and took pains with their hair and makeup, but Edna Mae scrubbed her face and pulled her hair back into a tight ponytail. She put her dowdy housecoat on, buttoning it all the way up, and shoved her feet into her plain, scuffed brown cowboy boots. Sally Beth looked her over. "Don't you want to at least put on a little lipstick? Really, Edna Mae, it looks like you're trying to make yourself look unattractive."

Edna Mae laughed. "You're right about that, girlfriend. I've spent my whole life trying not to attract attention. Thanks, but I'd just as soon be as ugly as a one-eyed, one-eared mutt tonight. Now, come on. The man at the desk told me about a nice restaurant right down the road." She picked up her purse and strode out the door.

Sally Beth grew suspicious about how "nice" the restaurant was when they pulled into a parking lot full of pickup trucks and Harley Davidson bikes and heard the thumping of country music. "This looks like the place," observed Edna Mae. "Hope you girls are set for a good time." She and Lilly both bounced out of the car, leaving Sally Beth to trail behind as they wriggled through the crowd and into a corner booth. A waitress appeared right away. "I'll take a Jim Beam, neat, and a glass of water," said Edna Mae.

Lilly glanced at Sally Beth before she said, a little timidly, "I'll have a mojito and a glass of water." Sally Beth didn't know what a mojito was, but by the way Lilly was acting, she suspected it had liquor in it. She gave her sister an apprehensive glance. "Lilly, does that have alcohol in it?"

Lilly rolled her eyes.

"Why shouldn't she have alcohol, Sally Beth?" demanded Edna Mae. "It's your birthday and you need to cut loose a little." She turned to the waitress. "She'll have one, too. It's her birthday, and it's time she learned the ways of the Wild West." Sally Beth's eyes grew wide, but she didn't say anything. This was a side of Edna

Mae she had not seen before.

The drinks came. Sally Beth sipped hers carefully, watching with alarm as Edna Mae tossed her shot of whiskey back in one gulp, then signaled for another. Sally Beth gnawed at her lip. Lilly had already finished half of her drink.

"Lilly, don't you drink it fast. You need to be careful."

Lilly glared back at her. "Oh, chill out, Sally Beth. You aren't my mama, and I can do anything I want. I'm twenty-one years old. Now just shut up and leave me alone."

"But Lilly…"

"She's right, Sally Beth. She's twenty-one years old and you aren't her mama. Now, it's your birthday, and I'm not going to let you get out of here until you've loosened up a little and had a good time. Drinks are on me." She lifted the second whiskey in Sally Beth's direction. "To Sally Beth. Happy birthday to the sweetest girl in—where are we?" she said loudly to the crowd in general. "New Mexico? To the sweetest girl in New Mexico." She tossed it down in a single gulp, then slammed her glass down with a big, breathy, "Ahhhh!"

Lilly lifted her glass, too, proclaiming, "To the sweetest, busy-body sister in the world, but the one I wouldn't trade for anything. I love ya, sis!" She guzzled her drink and slammed the glass on the table as well.

Despite her alarm at Lilly's recklessness, Sally Beth felt a knot in her stomach begin to loosen the tiniest bit. It had been a long time since she had sat at a table with girlfriends and just had a good time, and it felt good to hear Lilly's and Edna Mae's praise, as it felt good to think about her sister as her friend, not someone she needed to mother and protect. She gave a timid smile and said, as primly as she could while her heart swelled with friendship, "Thank you," and she took another sip.

Before long, the music, the smoke in the room, and the alcohol made her feel giddy, but she was having such a good time, she didn't care that she was laughing too loud or that they might be making fools of themselves, singing along with the band while bouncing in their seats to the rhythm of the music.

A man dressed in tight jeans and boots, with slicked-back hair approached the table. "Hey, Birthday Girl," he said. "Care to dance?" Sally Beth was taken aback. Usually men asked Lilly to dance first. She hesitated, looking at Lilly and Edna Mae.

"Go ahead, girl!" urged Edna Mae. "Show these cowboys a step or two!"

Lilly gave her a shove toward the dance floor. As Sally Beth let herself be led into the dance, Lilly and another man joined them. She glanced back at Edna Mae, wondering if she ought to go back and sit with her, but she didn't look like she was lonesome; she was just sitting back, smoking a cigarette, smiling at the band, the dancers, and the waitress, who was bringing her another whiskey.

The evening flew by faster than she could have imagined. She and Lilly danced with several partners, then they ordered dinner and ate, and afterwards, the waitress brought a whole cake, and complete strangers sang "Happy Birthday" to her as they passed out cake to everyone who wanted some. Then someone sent over a round of drinks, and although Sally Beth wasn't sure it was right to accept them from a stranger, Edna Mae and Lilly laughed at her and lifted theirs to the guy at the bar who was waving at them. Sally Beth smiled and waved back, just a little, before she sipped at it.

Right after that, he appeared at their table. He was good looking in a rough sort of way, but Sally Beth didn't mind that. She preferred real men to sissy ones, unlike Lilly, who seemed to like pretty boys like Lawrence and her cousin Geneva's old boyfriend, who drove a fancy car and wore a suit even during the week. No, this man who was asking her to dance was the kind she liked. Big and burly and not a dandy, and she was feeling so good and happy with the music thrumming in her veins, she jumped right up.

The band was playing a fast tune, but as soon as they stepped onto the floor, that song melded seamlessly into a slow dance number. Sally Beth began to regret her lack of caution when her partner moved in close, tightening his grip. As politely as she could, she put her hand on his chest, pushing lightly and shaking her head. He didn't get the message, but pulled her even closer, then, to her horror, he pressed his groin into hers as he leered and breathed into her face.

Up close, his teeth looked ragged and dirty, his breath was beery, and when she saw his red eyes focused on her with a hard and ugly stare, she felt a sudden fear creeping up her backbone. Struggling in earnest, she clawed at his shoulders, but the more she resisted, the more it fueled his cruelty. He moved his hands down to cup her buttocks, roughly jerking her toward him to grind his crotch against hers. When he began to steer her toward a dark corner, she panicked, forgetting to breathe until the room started to spin.

Suddenly, Edna Mae appeared behind the man. "Hey, darlin'," she drawled. "I think you've got a little too tight a grip on my friend here. I'm cuttin' in."

The man mumbled an obscenity at Edna Mae without unlocking his drunken gaze from Sally Beth's face.

Edna Mae said nothing, but smiled brightly, as if she was having the most delightful conversation, then, as gently as if she were giving him a loving hug, she wrapped her forearm around his neck and slowly pulled him backward.

He brought his arm up sharply behind him, hitting Edna Mae with his elbow, then he spun around and glared at her. "Get the hell away from me, you fat dyke, before I bash your teeth out."

Edna Mae's smile grew tight and her eyes hardened, and one second later, he was lying flat on the floor with one of Edna Mae's scuffed boot heels delicately balanced on his throat. The sole of the other boot stood in his open palm on the floor.

The dancers stopped, then the music stopped, and Sally Beth wished she were anywhere but there. A thought flashed through her head. *This is what happens when you go to bars and drink and dance with strangers.* The bouncer materialized by her side.

"What's the problem here?" he asked.

Edna Mae smiled at him, all soft sweetness. "Sorry, sweetheart. This bozo decided to molest my friend right here on the dance floor, and she isn't big enough to discourage him by herself. I just gave her a hand." She stepped away from the man on the floor. "We'll just go back and sit down now, if that's okay. I think he's learned his lesson." The bouncer nodded as Edna Mae grabbed Sally Beth's shaking hand and led her back to their booth.

Sally Beth was mortified, but after a moment, she felt kind of good, too, that Edna Mae had come to her rescue like that. But then again, no one had ever done anything like that man had done to her.

The man jumped up and yelled at Sally Beth's and Edna Mae's backs, "You ugly, fat bitch!" he yelled, lunging at them, but when the bouncer made a threatening step forward, he turned back to his friends at the bar, muttering something that made them look in the girls' direction and hoot with laughter.

Furious, Lilly jumped out of her seat, but Edna Mae grabbed her arm. "Huh-uh, honey. I know how to deal with their kind. They'll be whimpering before we're done with them." Slipping back into the darkness of the booth, she rummaged in her purse. "Sally Beth? Do you have any red lipstick?"

"What?" She had not yet recovered from the shock.

"Red lipstick. I don't think I brought any with me. And eyeliner. You got any?"

"Uh, yeah. In here somewhere." She opened her purse to pull out a handful of lipsticks and eyeliner pencils.

"Oh, good. Let me have that," she said, grabbing the assortment and a compact mirror.

"Don't you want to do that in the bathroom?" asked Lilly.

"Nope. It's better if we do it right here," said Edna Mae as she peered into the mirror. "It terrifies them when we just bust out of the corner like this." After she put on a thick ring of black around her eyes and slathered on lipstick, she untied her ponytail, shaking out her hair until it bloomed around her face in a fan of copper and honey curls. Sally Beth gasped at the transformation.

"Got any earrings in there? Big ones?

"Uh—"

"I do. I bought them for Sally Beth, but then I found the starry ones and decided to give her those instead." Lilly produced a pair of large gold hoops.

"What are you doing?" asked Sally Beth.

Edna Mae grinned as she put the earrings into her ears. "You two had better spiffy up, too. Here, put some on," she said, handing the lipstick to Sally Beth. She unbuttoned the top five buttons of her housecoat and tugged it off her shoulders. Reaching under the table, she unbuttoned her housecoat nearly up to her crotch. "Sally Beth, give me your belt."

Sally Beth hesitated only for a moment before stripping it off and handing it over to her. She was only slightly surprised that Edna Mae had no trouble buckling it just two notches away from where she had worn it. It cinched in the voluminous garment, making Edna Mae's waist look tiny between her breasts and the huge swell of her hips.

"Lilly, undo a few of those buttons, honey," Edna Mae said, as she tugged at the elastic top of Sally Beth's peasant blouse, bringing the shoulders down to the middle of her upper arms. "Here, that isn't enough." Taking the lipstick from Sally Beth, she applied it thickly on her lips, then did the same for Lilly. Eyeliner came next, and then she pulled the pins out of Sally Beth's chignon, ruffled up her hair, fluffing curls around her shoulders. Finally, she carefully replaced Sally Beth's bubble-gum pink cowboy hat with the rhinestone crown atop her blonde head, leaned back with a sultry look and said, "How do I look?"

Sally Beth grimaced slightly. "A little trashy," she said, then immediately regretted saying it, so she added, "but real pretty!"

"Perfect," came the reply. "Before we're done, these guys will be crawling. Here, drink this down," she said, handing Sally Beth a fresh mojito. "You're going to need it." Sally Beth wasn't sure she should, but Edna Mae was so authoritative and so intimidating that she felt she really had no choice. "Good girl. Now heat it up."

She pushed them both from the booth and she slid out, revealing a long, chiseled thigh. Head held high, she strode to the stage, stepped up beside the lead singer, and stood perfectly still in the spotlight.

The room fell silent while all eyes turned to her. Every inch of her, from her wild hair and painted eyes and lips to her scuffed cowboy boots looked like an Amazonian goddess. No one there had ever seen anything like her outside of the mud flaps of an eighteen wheeler. Her breasts billowed out of the top of her dress; her slender waist accentuated the round, perfect, massive hips. A long thigh pushed forward through the open dress as she stood, quietly smiling. Then she simply lifted the mic from the stunned singer's hand and spoke into it with a low, throaty voice. Her eyes were half closed; her lips were pursed slightly, as if she wanted to kiss the mic.

"I just love hearing you boys play, and me and my girlfriends just *had* to get up here and join you. You don't mind, do you?" The band members broke into grins, and the audience fell to clapping. Edna Mae glanced slyly to the bar where Sally Beth's dance partner sat with an open mouth. His friends all wore the same expression.

Lilly was the first to recover. Standing below the stage, she nudged Sally Beth. "Here's your chance, honey. Make that jerk suffer." Tossing her head and running her fingers through her satin blonde hair, she stepped up on the stage and leaned into Edna Mae.

"Anyway," Edna Mae was saying, "I'm Tiffany, and these here are my girlfriends, Silver Gilded Lilly, and Sweet Sally—come on up here, Sweet Sally. She's shy. Boys and girls, why don't we help her out?" Lilly reached out to pull Sally Beth up to her while the audience cheered and applauded, and suddenly Sally Beth felt the alcohol send courage and strength pulsing through her veins. She realized that this was her moment. That man had humiliated her in public, and now Edna Mae was up to something to pay him back, and she was going to do her best to help her. She threw her head back and stuck out her chest as she heard the applause and felt a warm buzz go through her.

"That's right, boys and girls. Give Sweet Sally a hand. She's real shy at first, but once she warms up, she can be *hot.*" She turned back to the lead singer, draped an arm over his shoulder, and looking dead level into his eyes from about four inches away purred, "Would you boys mind if we sang a little song? In honor of Sweet Sally's birthday?" He shook his head no, dazed, but grinning as he gazed down at her breasts pressed against his chest. Slipping his guitar strap smoothly over his neck, Edna Mae handed it to Sally Beth, then took her harmonica out of her pocket, sat on the stool, and crossed her legs. The crowd erupted in cheers. Lilly approached the bass player and just as neatly took his instrument from him.

"Now, we want to sing this song for that little creepy man over at the bar there, the one who thought he could put his nasty old hands all over Sweet Sally and call me a fat, ugly bitch." She pointed directly to him, holding the pointed finger out long enough for his friends to edge away from him. After she was sure everybody knew who she was going to honor with the song, she stuck out her chest and put both hands up to fluff up her hair, then gave a mighty stretch, lifting her leg and pointing her foot forward. When she had finished stretching, her hands slid downward across her body, stroking her curves. "Do you think I'm fat and ugly?" she crooned into the mic.

A chorus of "NOOOOOs" rang out.

"He needs more than just glasses. He needs a shrink!" shouted someone from the back.

"My thoughts exactly. Crazy little man thought he could get by with pawing his nasty old hands all over Sweet Sally right on the dance floor, and on her *birthday.*"

Another round of enthusiastic "NOOOOOs" echoed around the room. Sally Beth was past caring about maintaining a ladylike demeanor. She preened and blew them a kiss.

"Now, the way I hear it, the only men who do that kind of thing are the ones who have a little..." Edna Mae held up her thumb and forefinger two inches apart, "problem," and she winked. "It makes them feel like a *maaaan* when they can intimidate and molest nice

girls. Isn't that right, creepy little man at the bar with the little…"
Again, she held out her finger and thumb, but shrank the distance
between them while drawing them in front of her right eye. She
closed her left eye and squinted, "…problem."

Then she blew into her harmonica for a few bars before
launching into the song about a scornful woman. Sally Beth and
Lilly moved into the second mic to back her up, stomping their
cowboy boots, swinging their hips and hair, and playing for all
they were worth.

"We need a drink up here, boys!" shouted Edna Mae while Lilly
played a riff, and within seconds, both bartenders brought them
drinks—whiskey for Edna Mae and mojitos for Sally Beth and
Lilly.

They sang both verses twice, then Edna Mae spent some time
making the harmonica as insulting as she could, and then, to Sally
Beth's surprise, Lilly leaned into the mic and on the spot, came up
with another verse.

*He's way too dumb to understand what he can't and
what he can*
*He struts around all day and all night thinking we're all
his fans.*
He ain't no kind of man to a real wo-man
*But he's a REAL BIG FELLA TO HIS OWN RIGHT
HAND!*

Lilly shouted the last line, her fist pumping the air. "Let's all
sing it!" She yelled to the crowd. *"He ain't no kind of man to a
REAL WO-MAN,"* and they sang back with one loud voice:
*"BUT HE'S A REAL BIG FELLA TO HIS OWN
RIGHT HAND!"*

Sally Beth was so embarrassed to hear those words coming out
of her sister's mouth that she had to distance herself from the whole
scene, falling into the laughter of the music and pretending she was
someone else while Lilly sang. The crowd went wild. Hats flew in
the air. Women jumped up and down, laughing hysterically, and
men gawked, whistled and stomped while Lilly and Edna Mae

breezed through the chorus again. Sally Beth's face flamed, but she tried to laugh through the rest of the song. The man who had humiliated her stormed out the door as the crowd jeered at him, then turned back and cheered the trio.

When the song ended, Sally Beth was breathless, and her feelings were so mixed up she didn't know what to think. She felt such an outrush of love for her baby sister and this unreal super woman who this afternoon was too shy to put on lipstick, all painted up and strutting, slinging her hips and shaking her boobs around in front of a crowd just to vindicate her, little Sally Beth. On the other hand, she was embarrassed to death. She chugged her drink and hoped for courage. It didn't occur to her to pray.

Edna Mae made a deep bow, exposing enough flesh to make the crowd cheer and whistle louder. "Thanks y'all. That was real nice of y'all. We enjoyed it a lot, and you just *made* Sweet Sally's birthday. Come on, Sweet Sally, take a bow. She's twenty-three years old today, and isn't she the prettiest thing you ever saw? Our little princess. Our honky tonk princess." There were more shrieks and whistles. Sally Beth blushed and made a tiny curtsey. She was feeling warm and really good. Sometimes liquor was just what you needed to get you through an embarrassing time, she decided.

"Now, we're just leaving," continued Edna Mae, "and we have a little suspicion that some *little somebody* just might be waiting in the parking lot for us, so we would greatly appreciate it if maybe one or two of you nice gentlemen would escort us to our car. Sweet Sally's had enough excitement for one night. And, oh! By the way, who's got our dinner tab this evening?"

"I got it, darlin'!" came a voice from the back.

"It's on the house!" came another voice.

Edna Mae smiled again. "Thank you all so very much. And that pretty little lady over there is Charlotte, our waitress, and she needs a big tip, okay? A twenty ought to do it."

"She's got it," came the first voice from the back, and Charlotte whooped. Lilly and Sally Beth gave their guitars back to the musicians in the band.

"Thank you," Sally Beth whispered gratefully. The guitarist laughed as he stuck out his hand. "My pleasure, ma'am. You can come back any time."

Everyone in the bar ushered them out. The obnoxious dance partner was nowhere to be seen, but Edna Mae kept looking around warily, even as she smiled and shook hands with people who were congratulating her. She slipped into the back seat of the car, Lilly got behind the wheel, and they drove slowly out of the parking lot. The crowd ran after them until they hit the street and accelerated.

"Don't go straight back, honey," came Edna Mae's voice from the dark back seat. Wind around a little. Let's make sure they aren't following us. Something prickled Sally Beth's scalp. It suddenly occurred to her that they might be in danger. "Let's go to the downtown area and see if we can find the police station."

Lilly objected. "I've been drinking, Edna Mae. We can't go waltzing into a police station."

There was a silence. "Okay. I don't see anything, but we don't want this guy following us. Drive into that A & W, and let's just get something to drink." They pulled in and sat for some time until the place grew quiet. "I guess it's okay. I haven't seen anything, and I don't think that guy was too sober. Let's go."

Deep into the night, Sally Beth awoke to find Edna Mae standing tense and solitary at the window. The curtains were closed, but she gripped the edges as she peered out into the parking lot, like a sentinel standing guard over her troops. Sally Beth slipped out of bed.

"What's wrong?" she whispered. "Is there somebody out there?"

"No," answered Edna Mae. "Just checking." She kept her face turned to the window, and in the filtered light, Sally Beth could see she looked sad and drained, as if a light that had blazed blindingly bright for a brief time had been extinguished.

"What is it, Edna Mae. What's wrong?"

"Nothing, honey. Go back to bed. I just want to stand here for a minute, just to make sure." After a long silence, Sally Beth turned and got back into bed with Lilly, but she did not sleep until much later, after Edna Mae finally stopped her vigil and stumbled back into the other bed.

Lord, shine Your love down on Edna Mae and heal the hurts she is living with. Bring her a good man, Lord, one who will love her for who she is, treat her right, and make her feel special and safe. And Lilly, too, Lord. And maybe me, if You've a mind to, if that's what You want for me. We all want to be cherished.

Six

August 12, 1978, Albuquerque, New Mexico

Sally Beth woke early, feeling a little hung over and saddened by what she had seen during the night. Lilly still slept, but Edna Mae was up and dressed in cutoff jeans and a tank top. Her hair was pulled back into a tight ponytail, and her face shone with scrubbing. She sat on a chair tying her tennis shoes, and even in the awkward, bent-over position, she looked stunning.

"Hey," said Sally Beth, rubbing her eyes.

"Hey. There's a gym next door, so I'm going to go work out. Why don't you come with me?" She paused to study Lilly briefly. "Lilly ought to come, too."

Sally Beth had not been in a gym since high school, and she was not anxious to go back to smelly locker rooms and shouting boys. "What do you do there?"

Edna Mae laughed. "Gotta stay in shape, and you should, too. Come on, I need to teach you how to take care of yourself. Lilly! Get up. I'm going to show you how to handle men who think they can bully you."

Lilly moaned from under the covers. Sally Beth felt a tremor of apprehension. "You mean, beat them up? No Edna Mae, we're Quakers. We don't fight. It's against our beliefs."

"Oh, don't worry about that! You don't have to hurt anybody. You just learn how to repel somebody who wants to hurt you. Like that guy last night. I didn't hurt him. I just showed him I won't be pushed around. It's not fighting. It's self-defense. It's perfect for you."

Sally Beth wasn't convinced. She looked askance until Edna Mae spoke again. "Do you know this kind of self-defense was invented by priests who were absolute pacifists? Bandits and murderers used to come and raid their temples, and they got tired of being robbed and raped and murdered, so they developed this style of defense to protect themselves without hurting their attackers."

Sally Beth thought about that. Edna Mae had thrown the man to the floor last night, but he had not appeared to be hurt, and she had thrown Lawrence into the pool when he had tried to push her in. She also had dragged him away from Lilly when he threatened to push her off the Canyon rim.

"You sure they don't get hurt?"

"Did he look hurt?"

"No," broke in Lilly. "He just looked mad. You could have hurt him, though. Standing on his windpipe like that."

"Yeah, but I didn't. Most of the moves are evasive and non-confrontational. You just learn to side step and make an attacker go off balance. Come here, Sally Beth, I'll show you." She jumped up on the bed. "Come on! You'll see. It won't hurt a bit. Come up here on the bed."

Sally Beth reluctantly climbed up beside Edna Mae. "Okay, now come at me like you're going to choke me." She bounced a little on the bed, moving her shoulders like a boxer.

Sally Beth tentatively put her hands forward, and before she even touched Edna Mae, she found herself flat on the bed with Edna Mae's tennis shoe resting lightly on her throat. "See? You didn't feel a thing, did you?" She bounced back and pulled Sally

Beth up on her feet. "Do it again. This time try to hurt me."

Sally Beth knew hurting Edna Mae was not likely to happen. She halfheartedly lunged for her, but again, she ended up on her back, looking up at Edna Mae's perfect leg.

"Come on, Lilly. You get in on this. I know. Both of you get dressed and let's go outside, and I'll show you how easy you can throw somebody, and you won't even hurt them."

Lilly jumped up enthusiastically and began throwing on her clothes. Sally Beth wasn't so sure. She pulled on shorts and a T-shirt, but she wasn't certain that she should be taking part in this. Fighting was fighting, and this sure looked like fighting to her.

They moved to the dew-laden grass outside. "Okay, now both of you rush at me like you're going to grab me or stab me or something. Lilly and Sally Beth looked at each other, and Lilly started to giggle. This wasn't much different from what they had done as girls when they wrestled with each other and their cousins. Maybe it wouldn't be so wrong after all. They rushed in toward Edna Mae, who sidestepped them easily. She swept her foot under Lilly, who stumbled and fell, and then she grabbed Sally Beth around the waist and flipped her so gently that she found herself lying on the grass, unhurt and unruffled.

"Did that hurt?" asked Edna Mae.

"No…" mused Sally Beth from the ground.

Lilly jumped up. "Not a bit! How do you do that?"

"Come on, let's go down to the gym and I'll show you." She pulled Sally Beth up and returned to the room briefly to get her University of Texas sweatshirt, pulling it over her head as she trotted into the parking lot. Twenty minutes later, she was showing the sisters how to use the weight of an opponent against him.

It was surprisingly fun and fairly easy to catch on to the basics. Within an hour, both Sally Beth and Lilly were able to throw not only each other, but Edna Mae as well. Laughing, they agreed that the time might come again when they needed to know how to be as tough as Edna Mae. Sally Beth hoped it never came to that, but it did feel kind of good to know she was stronger than she realized.

By the time they had showered and changed and had sat down to breakfast, she felt that she was standing just a little taller.

Swallowtail Gap, West Virginia

"Hey, Chap! Slow down!" Geneva called to her husband. "Blue says he doesn't like being jostled so much."

Howard halted his horse and drew up the packhorse he was leading beside him. "Sorry, darlin'," he said, looking back. "Why don't you let me take him the rest of the way up?"

"No, I don't trust Lightening. He may try to throw you just for spite, and you have your hands full. I can manage okay."

"Maybe I'll go on up ahead? I can get some firewood in and pick some dinner from the garden, and you can take your time."

She shifted in the saddle, nodding. "Yes, go on. I'll take it easy the rest of the way."

Howard nudged his stallion into a fast trot, leaving Geneva alone with her baby and her thoughts. It had been a year since she had been to this cabin. She remembered the night she and Howard had first loved each other, with the sound of the waterfall thundering in their ears, the smell of mint and the wild, summer night. Her heart pounded just remembering, and she felt the familiar, sweet, melting sensation when she thought about how Blue was the result of that night. What kind of divine intercession had occurred, sending that thunderstorm and her illness? Had that storm not come, she would have turned her back on Howard and taken a different path, and the thought made her shudder with dread. She closed her eyes, smiling. God had used her foolishness and wantonness and turned it to good. She breathed a prayer of thanks and nudged April forward.

When she arrived at the cabin, Howard had already nearly unpacked their supplies. He stopped to help her down from her horse before lifting Blue from her back. "I see he made it okay," he said, smiling into his son's face. "That's about the most even-tempered young'un I ever did see."

Geneva smirked at him. "Blue got my sweet temper."

Howard's eyes laughed at her, but he said nothing as she unbundled the baby and carried him inside while he finished the unpacking. He took the horses to the stable, then pulled vegetables from the garden, and went out to shoot some game for supper while Geneva washed and cut up potatoes and made a little relish out of onions, cucumbers, and the two ripe tomatoes they had found. Blue stared at her with his bright blue eyes as she hummed while she worked, contented. The honeymoon in Europe had been nice, but this was home.

After supper, they built up the fire outside, and like they had just a year ago, they filled the zinc washtub with water and placed it over the coals. First they bathed Blue, then Howard said, "The last time you took a bath here, I didn't get to watch. But you watched me…" He settled himself on the porch step and leaned back on his elbows. "Now it's my turn."

Geneva blushed, remembering how beautiful he had been, standing on the cliff above the creek, holding himself still and calm, then plunging into the water, how she had been unable to move, how he had risen from the water and they had discovered each other. The memory made her want to strip for him, but although she attempted a little seductive dance, she soon began to giggle from embarrassment, and ended up just tearing her clothes off quickly and lowering herself into the tub.

He shook his head with mock disgust, sighing. "I think you could've done a little better than that. I might as well go on over to the creek. Not much of a show tonight." He pretended indifference, but his eyes lingered on her as he made his way down the path.

Somewhere near the Texas Border

To Sally Beth's dismay, both Lilly and Edna Mae had refused to stop for Carlsbad Caverns on the grounds that "bats bite and get tangled up in your hair," and closed spaces gave Edna Mae the heebie jeebies. They did agree to take the back road from Albuquerque so she could at least see White Sands, which finally quenched her desire to see a "real" desert, with towering, undulating dunes of pure white sand. Other than that, the road between Albuquerque and Pecos was a long, dry, hot stretch. Yet, the uninspired scenery soon took an unnoticed position behind the comfortable space made up of music, feminine talk, and laughter. Lilly proved to be even more obtrusive than Lawrence had been with the camera, sticking the lens right up into Sally Beth's and Edna Mae's faces and constantly telling them to look that way or smile or make a face until Sally Beth started mugging and positioning Edna Mae into sidesplitting poses.

At one stop, Edna Mae talked them into mooning for a shot. "Come on!" she laughed. "Nobody will ever know it's us if we don't show our faces." She instructed Lilly to place the camera on the front seat of the car and set the timer, then laughing uncontrollably, they pulled down their panties and sat on the hood of the car, mashing their bare bottoms against the windshield. By the time the camera clicked, they were howling, and then they rolled off the car and onto the sand, hysterical. A car drove by slowly, its occupants staring at them, which made them laugh even harder. Sally Beth had forgotten how much fun pure silliness could be.

By dinnertime, they had nearly made it to the Texas border, but there was little to offer in the way of food or respite. They drove a long time on a deserted road before they finally found a decent-looking place offering Mexican food.

"It's a half-hour wait for a table," Edna Mae informed them after she had talked to the hostess. "Let's sit at the bar." She led them through the throng waiting at the doorway and moved a couple of barstools around so they could sit together.

Lilly perched on her seat as she picked up a menu. "Oh look! They've got a special on pitchers of margaritas. Let's get one."

"Lilly, we were drinking last night," warned Sally Beth. "We shouldn't get in the habit of doing this."

"Come on, Sally Beth. Once we get home, we can't kick up our heels like this."

Sally Beth was about to declare that she'd had enough heel-kicking, but then she looked at her sister's face and saw it more relaxed and happy than she had seen it in a very long time. The old, pinched look she had worn for years, ever since Daddy had gotten so sick, was gone. A pitcher of margaritas was not worth arguing about, not when she, Lilly, and Edna Mae were on the adventure of a lifetime. "Okay," she conceded, "but just one."

"They're not that strong when it's the special," soothed Edna Mae. "You'll hardly feel it. And I bet they know how to make them here." She settled happily on the bar stool and hiked up the neck of her muumuu.

Somehow, a full pitcher of margaritas managed to disappear before they even ordered food, although Sally Beth limited herself to one glass. Lilly, too, seemed to be a little more careful. Edna Mae was not. She drank with abandon, and ate with equal gusto. It was remarkable how much she was able to put away.

"So how did you learn judo, Edna Mae?" asked Lilly as she put a dollop of sour cream on her third taco.

"And *why*?" added Sally Beth.

Edna Mae grew thoughtful. "It comes with the territory. I started having to fight guys off when I was in the fifth grade." She splayed both hands across her chest, making a wry face.

"Oh. That's tough. I didn't get boobs until I was fourteen, and they were pretty little for a long time. Both of us were still climbing trees and playing in the creek when we were eleven."

"I envy you two. I had to give up running when I was ten; they were so sore from growing so fast. It was too bad, because I had been athletic as a kid. My dad taught me to play baseball, and I was real good at it. But these monsters got in the way."

"Daddy taught us to play baseball, too. Lilly was really good at it."

"I bet you two had a good daddy," Edna Mae said wistfully. "I had a good daddy, too. He didn't get a boy, so he taught me all those boy things like fishing and baseball and fixing stuff around the house, and he was *funny!* He could make me laugh without even saying anything." She looked into her margarita with melancholy eyes that suddenly misted with tears. "But he died when I was ten. Worst thing that ever happened to me."

Sally Beth and Lilly fell silent while she continued, "My stupid mama took up with the biggest pervert you ever met just a few months later, and he hadn't been in the house any time before he started trying to feel me up." Her face tightened.

"Oh, Lord," said Lilly. "What did you do?"

"I got my friend Sammy Johnson to teach me how to fight. Sammy was this real cool black dude who carried a knife and would cut anybody who tried anything on his little sister. I told him about Clyde, and he took me under his wing. His sister was the same age as me, and we hung out together, and I guess he just felt sorry for me.

"I try to fight clean now, but back then I learned to fight dirty, and I do mean dirty. Sammy always said, 'Anybody who picks on a little girl is about as worthless as they come, and you can forget all those notions of honorable fighting. You need to be as low-down as he is, and believe me, little white girl'—that's what he called me, 'little white girl,' but he had to look up at me while he was saying it 'cause I was already a head taller than him—'that's more low-down than you can imagine.' He taught me how to gouge out eyes, how not to be afraid to bite and hang on even if you get slung around, and how to break a man's neck."

"One night, Clyde came home while Mama was working, and he got right in my bed while I was asleep. He grabbed me and pinned me down before I could even wake up, and he was slobbering all over me, but I had a knife under my pillow—thank you Sammy—and I stabbed him in the arm, left a five-inch gouge right here." She made a slicing motion on her forearm and gave a bitter smile at the memory. "He never laid a hand on me again, but then, about a year later, he started in on Sarah Jane. She was just eight."

Sally Beth could not believe her ears. Somebody's *daddy* would do that? Well, technically, he wasn't her daddy, but any man had a responsibility to protect children. "Did you tell your mama?" She could only imagine what her own mama would do, and it wouldn't be pretty.

"Oh, I tried. But he had already been talking trash about me to her, and well, I think she was suspicious of me because I looked so mature." She sighed sadly. "To tell you the truth, I think she was jealous of me. My boobs were bigger than hers by then, and Clyde would make snide comments to her about her being a skinny sack of bones. I think she wanted me out of the picture because it was important to her to have a man around."

"What did you do then?"

Edna Mae laughed again, but this time the sound was cheerful. "I beat the living tar out of him. I came in one day and he had little Sarah Jane backed into a corner, and she was sitting there whimpering while he pawed at her, and I got an iron skillet and sneaked up on him, and—*Wham!* I busted his head good, then grabbed up Sarah Jane. I took his wallet and his car keys, then cleaned out the mayonnaise jar Mama kept her cash in, shoved Sarah Jane in his car and we took off for Texarkana to my granny's."

"How old were you?"

"Twelve."

Lilly gaped. "Lord have mercy! What happened then? You didn't get caught driving that little?"

"I wasn't little. I was already taller than any grown woman I knew, except for Granny—I take after her, you'll see—and I looked a lot older. Nobody batted an eye." She laughed. "Old Clyde was too afraid to report us 'cause he knew we would tell what he had done to us, and I could point to that scar on his arm as evidence. Sarah Jane had some bruises where he had tried to hold her down, too, and I was ready to do whatever it took." Sally Beth looked at the set line of her jaw, and she figured Clyde probably had an inkling of what he was in for if he made trouble.

"Good for you, honey. He deserved worse than you gave him,"

she said, patting her arm.

Edna Mae flinched at the touch, then laughed. "We kept the car, and I managed to steal almost a hundred dollars off him, and another twenty off Mama. Me and Sarah Jane lived it up all the way to Granny's. We probably had ten milkshakes on the way down."

"Then what happened?"

"When we got there and told Granny about it, she called up Mama and cussed her out and told her if she didn't throw that creep out, she'd never speak to her again. Last I heard, he was still there, and Granny nor any of us haven't seen or talked to her since." She dusted tortilla flour off her hands with a gesture of finality. "Hey bartender! We need another pitcher here."

The bar began to fill up, the band arrived, and Lilly found a dance partner. When someone asked Sally Beth to dance, she forgot her troubles of the night before and leaped into the music and the energy bounding through the room. Even Edna Mae was persuaded to get out on the dance floor, dancing and singing along with the band until everyone in the bar joined in. The later it grew, the more celebratory they felt. Sally Beth learned the Texas two-step and was breathless and dizzy from spinning around, and, she admitted, from margaritas, even though she sipped at them slowly, drinking a glass of water between each one as Edna Mae had instructed her.

The music grew louder as more people arrived, including several odd-looking characters and three very small men. She thought at first they were children, but on closer look, she realized they were just very petite, like jockeys.

"Look!" exclaimed Lilly. "Munchkins!" The men stared at her.

"Lilly. Don't make fun of them."

"Sorry." She looked over at the little men. "Sorry guys! I thought you were munchkins."

"Lilly!" Sally Beth gave the men an embarrassed smile. "Don't mind her," she apologized. "She's from the hills and doesn't get out much."

"Yep! That's me, Silver Gilded Lilly straight from the hills of

West Virginia. I've never danced with a munchkin before." She stood up and made her way to the small men. "Who wants to be the first?"

One of them jumped up and grabbed Lilly's hand. Another approached Sally Beth, and the next moment, she was kicking up her cowboy boots in the Electric Slide. The three little men got down on the floor and went through an amazing break-dancing routine while Sally Beth whirled around with a man who didn't talk, but danced a funny, disjointed dance like a puppet on strings. Someone else pulled out juggling balls, and soon after, people were juggling, tumbling, and break-dancing all around them. Someone behind her said, "They're from the circus. They've been in Midland all week. Wonder what they're doing way out here?"

After another fast dance, a slow waltz started up, and Sally Beth let herself be pulled out to the middle of the floor to dance with her little partner. She was a bit tipsy, but when he mashed his face into her breasts and wrapped his arms around her waist, her mind sharpened, remembering the night before.

"Excuse me, but you're dancing a little close," she said quietly.

"Sorry," he said, and backed off. But a moment later, he pulled her close again, breathing hot air into her blouse. At first, she was merely embarrassed, and she wondered how she could get out of the situation gracefully, but when he moved his head and his mouth zeroed in on a nipple, her embarrassment turned to mortification. A second later, something she had never felt before came washing over her.

She thought about eleven-year-old Edna Mae, missing the love and protection of her daddy, being awakened from a sound sleep by rough hands and foul breath. The image of the little girl exposed and afraid, fighting for her childhood, sent her into a hot rage against perversity and meanness. Before she knew what was happening, the little guy lay on the floor, and Sally Beth's boot heel pressed heavily on his throat.

Edna Mae appeared at her elbow, pulling her away, "Good job, sweetie," she said loudly enough to cover the sound of his coughing and choking. "That'll teach him to mind his manners." Reaching down to grab the man's hand, she pulled him upright with one swift move and gave him a vigorous brushing off, as if he were covered with clinging sawdust. The scene was absurd: Edna Mae's enormous bulk bending over the tiny man, her muumuu billowing out like the Big Top, whacking at him with far more force than necessary. It wasn't clear if she were helping him or beating him up, but Sally Beth wasn't about to stick around and find out. Flooded with shame and panic, she fled to the parking lot.

Lilly followed her out. "Hold on, honey!" she called, catching up with her and steering her toward the car, then she unlocked it, jumped in, and started the engine. Sally Beth flung herself into the front seat, and as Lilly backed out of the parking space, Edna Mae hurried out. She yanked open the back door, jumping in as the car lurched forward, and Lilly roared away, laughing hysterically. Edna Mae whooped and screamed.

"It's not funny!" wailed Sally Beth. "I don't know what came over me."

"Oh, yes it is, darlin'! You should have seen that little guy trying to get at your tits. It looked like he thought you were his mama. And you had him on the floor before he knew what hit him."

"Good for you, Sally Beth!" exclaimed Lilly. "You took down a man and just about broke his windpipe; I didn't know you had it in you. *Wahoo!* My sister, the Destroyer. Look out perverts—Sally Beth will take you *down!*"

"He was a *midget!*" sobbed Sally Beth. "Half my size—I could have hurt him!"

"But you didn't," soothed Edna Mae. "He was fine, just surprised, that's all. Besides, he's a clown in the circus; he's used to tumbling around. You saw him earlier. He was just taking advantage of you, just like that guy last night. I am so glad I taught you that move. Now I don't have to worry about you." And she and Lilly laughed and laughed as Lilly stomped her cowboy boot down on the accelerator and blazed her way southward.

The adrenaline did not began to ebb from their blood until after they crossed the border into Texas, when the memory of the night could no longer fuel them and the dusty miles sucked away their energy. Lilly and Edna Mae continued to giggle between yawns, but Sally Beth felt a small, hard knot forming in her chest, and she realized it had been a while since she had had a good talk with the Lord. She felt small and sad and disconnected when she realized that she hadn't been a very good influence on her sister.

Lord, I feel myself changing, as if this country is making me coarse and rough. Make me gentle again, Lord. Forgive me for my anger, my violence. Forgive me for being a bad example to Lilly. Take off this hardness that I feel creeping up on me, and shape me to be like You want me to be.

August 13, 1978
On the mountain where Singing Eyes wept

Deep into the night, he woke her, shaking her gently and kissing her forehead. "Wake up, darlin'. Time for the show." Geneva blinked, not comprehending, but when he pulled her from the herb-scented bed, she suddenly realized what was afoot. Quickly, she slipped on her shoes, gathered up the sleeping baby, and wrapped them both in blankets. Then she slipped her arm around Howard's back, and together they went out the door and up the mountain.

The stars were already falling in a sky so clear and black it looked like quicksilver streaming across black satin. She swaddled Blue tighter, and then lay down, placing the baby beside her, knowing what delights were to come.

For a while, Howard lay quietly beside her, before he seemed to make up his mind. He flung his blanket aside and rose to stand still under the falling stars, and then he began his dance. It was just as she remembered, his naked, smooth body twirling and leaping, his voice rising and dropping into a sustained note. She stood so that he could enclose her in his warm embrace, lifting her high into the cascade of stars. Flinging her neck back and her arms wide to embrace the night, she wept with gladness as she enfolded him to her, and even as the spinning stopped and the night stilled, she could not let him go. Arms and legs wrapped around him, she held him, feeling his warmth seeping into her, filling her with dreams and desire and laughter and more tears than she could hold, with the bittersweetness of knowing how beautiful, how fragile, how lovely, how temporary this life was. She wanted to make him understand just how much she loved him and how much more she wanted to love him in this short time they would have each other on this earth. But she could not speak.

At last, he broke from her and said, "I owe you something."

"What else could you possibly give me?"

He slipped a ring onto her finger. "This is a year late."

She blinked back the salt water, trying to make light of her deep emotion. "No, only a few months late."

"No, Geneva. I married you one year ago tonight. You didn't know it then, but I did. I told you then this was a marriage dance."

The tears ran freely now, as she felt the ridges along the band and knew what they meant: a stream of comets stretching around the circumference. A mark of this night, a mark of her, *Strikes fire in the soul.* He had let her go after that, because he believed he could not live up to her vain notions of what her life should look like. But he had released her only to bring her back again when she had finally grown enough to realize what he meant to her. Now she knew how much he loved her, how much he had loved her then, and that they truly had been wed that night twelve months ago. She marveled at the knowledge that nothing in this creation could ever pull them apart.

The soft breath of the Milky Way whispered, "You are home now, and safe," and she heard her heart singing a hymn.

Seven

Pecos, Texas

L et's go to the gym again," said Edna Mae the minute Sally Beth
opened her eyes. "You need to get these self-defense moves
down good so you won't forget them." Before Sally Beth could
object, Lilly was already out of the bed and pulling her hair into a
ponytail. "Today, you're going to learn how to break a man's neck
before breakfast. How many people can say that?"

Sally Beth's eyes flew open with alarm, but Lilly whooped, "Hot
dog! I've always wanted to know how to do that." Sally Beth was
so taken aback by the image of her delicate sister forcefully twisting
a man's head that she wondered what other strange thoughts
she might be harboring underneath that platinum hair. She said
nothing as they trooped to the gym, pondering how to discourage
Edna Mae and Lilly from becoming too violent, but once she saw
Edna Mae stepping as lightly as if she were dancing, she found the
moves so interesting, so graceful, and so beautiful that she forgot to
feel guilty about learning them. Before the morning was gone, she
had learned how to dance away from an opponent before leaping

in to surprise him, grabbing his head in a gentle, almost loving embrace before giving his neck a quick snap. It was almost fun, if she didn't think about it too much.

After they left the gym, they showered quickly and put on their coolest dresses before loading the car and heading eastward. It was proving to be a hot Texas day, hotter than they had seen so far in the high deserts of Arizona and New Mexico, so they were glad to be on their way in the coolness of the air-conditioned car.

"If we push it, we can make Dallas tonight," said Lilly. "I want to go shopping at the Galleria, and we'll have enough time to stay a couple of days and still make it to Memphis in time for the Elvis anniversary."

"Sounds good," said Edna Mae from the back seat. "Let's not go out for breakfast, but just get some stuff to go."

When they stopped at the gas station, Sally Beth pumped gas while Lilly went inside to get snacks. As she lifted the nozzle, the distinctive odor of fuel wafted to her nose. "Somebody has spilled some gas here," she commented to Edna Mae. Better not be lighting up right now."

Lilly returned with doughnuts and Cokes. "Wow, this took a lot of gas," said Sally Beth. "We just filled up last night."

"Not really. I was tired and the pump was slow. I probably didn't put more than a couple of gallons in. Besides, it's been getting really bad gas mileage lately. I think something is wrong with the fuel pump," she said as she put the key into the ignition. The car sputtered and died twice before it finally started. "Darn it. I'm going to get a new car just as soon as I can get another job. It's gotten to where it costs more to keep this one repaired than car payments on a new one would be."

The car finally started and Lilly rolled back onto the highway. Edna Mae picked up Lilly's old guitar, strummed a few chords, popped the top of a Coke and munched on a donut, then stretched out across the back seat, picking out a tune. Sally Beth leaned against the window while Edna Mae tried out some new lyrics, and before long, Lilly joined in. The air conditioning, turned up high, felt good; the sun shimmered in the morning sky, and all of Texas lay before them. Sally Beth smiled a sleepy smile as she listened to her sister's sweet voice and let her thoughts slide up the long rays of sparkling sunbeams. Time had ceased to be a taskmaster. The day was long, they had no particular plans, and they were flying across miles and miles and miles of sand and road while music floated around her. She felt, not just free, but free-floating, disconnected from the reality of the world, free from her nagging fear that Lilly was making bad choices that she could not stem. She felt free in a way that she had never felt before, and she wondered if maybe it was because Lilly was acting happier and less artificial than she had seen her in a long time. It was wonderful to see how her baby sister was opening her mouth wide and letting the music flow unbridled and joyful.

The day grew hotter. Edna Mae leaned forward. "Turn up that AC, will you? It's getting really hot back here." Sally Beth punched the buttons, but when she put her hand to the blowing vent, she felt a blast of hot air.

"This is just warm air coming out. Lilly, I don't think this air conditioner is working."

"Oh no," said Lilly. "I had it fixed before we left, but the guy said the compressor probably wouldn't hold out all the way home. I had hoped it would last until we got closer."

"You reckon there's any place around here that might sell some dry ice?" said Sally Beth. "We can put it around in the car and let the air blow over it."

Lilly shook her head. "We aren't far from Midland, but it's Sunday, so it's likely we'll just have to make do with regular ice."

They rolled all the windows down. In the back seat, Edna Mae rummaged through her bag, complaining. "I can't wear this muumuu in this heat." Hope you girls don't mind, but I'm changing into something cooler," she said as she tore the dress off, exposing her transparent bra and tiny thong panties. Intimidated by Edna Mae's beautiful bulk, Sally Beth averted her eyes. It was easier to talk to Edna Mae when she was covered up.

"I hate these panties, and this bra, and look at these stupid shorts! Lawrence, you jerk. I haven't been comfortable since I left my good things in the bathroom back at the Grand Canyon." She lay on the back seat, struggling into a pair of shockingly short cut-off jeans and yanked a tank top out of her bag.

Sally Beth was sweating, but the heat was kind of nice, she thought. The sun before them was bright and friendly, just high enough to be shaded by the lowered visors, and it seemed to be leading them, pulling them gently across the vast Texas horizon. She idly gazed out at the sagebrush and the hypnotic, shimmering sand until something oddly familiar caught her eye.

An old truck, blue with a rusty red door, was parked on the shoulder. Just beyond the truck was a slim man, waving a cowboy hat over a dog that was having some sort of a fit, spinning in a tight circle, snapping at his tail.

"Stop!" she yelled, sitting upright. Lilly tapped the brakes, then tapped them again until she had slowed dramatically.

"What?" she yelled back. "What's wrong?"

"Stop the car! That's Jimmy Lee."

Lilly careened to a stop, pulled over to the shoulder, then backed up to within feet of the man and the spiraling dog. Jimmy Lee, still waving his hat, did not see them until the sisters jumped out of the car and ran to him. He startled when they both yelled, "*Heyyyy, Jimmy Lee!*" Sally Beth was so happy to see him it was all she could do to keep from hugging him. "You are a sight for sore eyes!"

His face lit up with a luminous grin as he shaded his eyes against the morning sun. "Why, Sally Beth! Lilly! What on earth are you doing here?" He grinned wider, until his face just about cracked apart, and he grabbed Sally Beth in the hug she had been too shy to give. She could feel his joy as he caught her up and spun her around as the traffic whizzed by and the dust and sand blew up around them.

"What's happened here?"

"Radiator hose sprung a leak, and poor old Lamentations nearly got run over, and, well…" He trailed off, giving his dog a sad glance. Recovered from his fit, Lamentations slunk over to him, whining, and tucked his head up under his master's hand, his tail low, but wagging. Jimmy Lee gave him an affectionate caress before turning back to beam at Sally Beth and Lilly. "Boy, am I glad to see you here, not just because it's you, but because the truck won't go nowhere. Can you give me a ride up to Midland?"

"Why, sure, Jimmy Lee. Just get on in. Hey, Lamentations," Sally Beth added, holding her hand out to him.

The dog cringed as he licked Sally Beth with timid little thrusts of his tongue. He always was embarrassed after one of his episodes, and she had learned to be gentle with him until he got over it. Carefully, she squatted down to put an arm around him.

"Hey, Lamentations. Did all the traffic scare you? Huh?" She ruffled the fur at his neck. "Did you just get all bent out of shape? Well, that's okay, you just come on with us. We'll keep you safe." He licked at her face, this time a little more enthusiastically, and trotted after them to Lilly's car.

Edna Mae had remained in the back seat. She had put her extra-extra large orange University of Texas sweatshirt on and had tucked her knees up inside it, her bare feet on the seat. A line of sweat trickled down the side of her face. She sat quietly, looking like a big, sweaty pumpkin.

Sally Beth believed that pity was an ugly thing and that Edna Mae would be mortified if she thought she was the object of her pity, but she couldn't help but feel sorry for her in her silence and stillness, knowing how uncomfortable she must be. She jumped in the back seat next to her, moving the guitar cases around.

"Jimmy Lee, you sit in the front with Lilly. This is Edna Mae, our friend who's traveling with us to Texarkana. Edna Mae, this here is our real good friend Jimmy Lee from back home." She paused, then added gently, "He's real nice, Edna Mae, one of the nicest boys I know." Edna Mae smiled tightly, averting her eyes until Jimmy Lee ducked his head and grinned at her. His face was honest and friendly.

"Hidy ma'am," he said, touching the brim of his hat with his fingertips. Edna Mae's smile grew a little more relaxed and she wiped the sweat off her forehead. Her red face clashed something awful with her burnt orange sweatshirt.

"Sorry it's so hot, Jimmy Lee," offered Lilly, "but the AC is busted. We're hoping we can pick up some dry ice in Midland."

They arranged themselves as comfortably as they could. Jimmy Lee and Lamentations sat in the front seat with Lilly; Sally Beth and Edna Mae shared the back seat with the two guitars, the camera case, and various bags the short distance to a service station outside Midland, where Jimmy Lee picked up a hose for the radiator and a can full of water. The three old friends chatted, but Edna Mae endured quietly, smothering and steaming silently in her sweatshirt as she perspired and fanned herself with a magazine, even when the others took refuge in the air-conditioned service station. Sally Beth brought her an icy drink, which she guzzled gratefully, but by the time they got back to Jimmy Lee's truck, she looked like she was roasted and ready for the barbeque sauce.

"Why don't you get out for a minute and cool off some," urged Sally Beth as Jimmy Lee tinkered under the hood of his truck. Edna Mae shook her head.

"I'm fine," she said lightly, but she didn't look fine. She looked like she was about to die from heat stroke.

"Here," said Sally Beth, putting some ice in a bandana and handing it to her. "This should cool you off some." Edna Mae took it gratefully, pressing it to her neck. She pulled up the sleeves of the sweatshirt and rubbed ice along her arms.

Jimmy Lee withdrew his head from the depths of his engine briefly. "Did you see that place up on the right? Go on up there and cool off. I'll get this radiator fixed and catch up to you. Let me buy y'all lunch! And I'll find you some dry ice."

Lilly's car failed to start even though she ground the starter several times, pumping the gas pedal. Jimmy Lee looked up. "What's wrong?" he asked.

"I don't know. Car won't start," said Lilly, then paused and added, "I smell gas."

Sally Beth sniffed. "Me too." She got out of the car to take a look, and to her dismay, saw a puddle directly below the gas tank. "Oh, no!" she cried.

"Oh no!" echoed Lilly, kneeling beside her. "I'm afraid this car isn't going to make it all the way home."

Jimmy Lee came over to see. From underneath the car, he called out to them, "Yep. Hole in the gas line. Won't be hard to replace, though. My truck is nearly fixed, so we'll just go back to that station and get you a new hose and some gas. I can take care of it. You all want to ride back with me? You'll stay cool. Just let me fill this radiator up, and we can go."

Sally Beth and Lilly looked at each other and then cast a glance at the suffering Edna Mae. "Come on, Edna Mae," Sally Beth coaxed. "Jimmy Lee's a good friend. We can all cool off in his truck." Edna Mae shook her head, looking miserable despite her smile.

"No, that's okay. Somebody ought to stay with the car, and we won't all fit, anyway. It's not far down there, and I'll be fine. You go on."

Sally Beth hesitated. She was really starting to worry about Edna Mae, but it was clear she wasn't going to budge as long as Jimmy Lee was around. "Okay, we can leave Lamentations with you, and we'll hurry back. Here, let me wrap up some more ice and you can put it on your neck, and maybe you can step outside and cool off some, okay? Lamentations? You want to stay with Edna Mae while we go get some gas and a new line?"

To her surprise, Lamentations glanced back at Jimmy Lee once, then scrambled into the back seat to lick Edna Mae's face. "Yeah, boy, you keep the lady company. We'll be right back." Jimmy Lee smiled broadly at Edna Mae. "I never seen Lamentations take to anybody right off like this. You must be real quality, ma'am."

They returned shortly. After Jimmy Lee slid back under the car to replace the hose, he poured most of the gas into the tank while Sally Beth and Lilly hovered, fanning themselves. After checking his work one more time, he fumbled in his pocket for a package of cigarettes, lighting up before he opened the door for Lilly. "Start her up," he told her. Lilly inserted the key and cranked the engine. Nothing. She tried again, pumping the pedal a few times. Again nothing. Jimmy Lee took a few thoughtful puffs, nodding.

"I figured this. You were so plumb out we'll have to prime the carburetor. Pop the hood."

Lilly released the hood, then turned to Edna Mae. "Hand me that camera, would you? And my purse. Might as well record the bad moments as well as the good ones. Here, Sally Beth," she said, rummaging through her purse to find a comb. "Comb your hair and stand there beside Jimmy Lee. You've got it all blown out sticking your head out the window. Edna Mae, you don't have to get out. Just poke your head out the window and smile."

Sally Beth gave her hair a quick comb, then replaced her pink cowboy hat before leaning toward Edna Mae for one still, smiling moment. Jimmy Lee barely looked up. Cigarette pinched between his teeth, he picked up the gas can and carefully poured what was left of the gas into the carburetor.

The sun was high in the sky by this time, and Edna Mae had begun to squirm in the back seat. In this heat, her stamina was breaking apart, especially since the ice had completely melted, and she was steaming in the warm, soggy, sweatshirt. Her hair was wet from sweat, and more poured down her face. She was breathing a little funny, too, in short, shallow gasps that did not seem to draw much air into her lungs. Suddenly, her face scarlet, she ran a hand through her hair, gave a couple more gasping breaths, and said in a panicky voice, "I can't stand this heat another second!" Flinging open the back door, she jumped out and ripped off the sweatshirt.

The timing could not have been worse. Jimmy Lee glanced up just in time to see her struggling to pull it over her head. In her haste, she had grabbed the edge of the tank top with the sweatshirt, and it came off, too, revealing her lacy bra and the whole expanse of her tight, muscular torso. Her breasts, the size of basketballs, strained against the transparent bra. The waistband of her skimpy shorts sat low, several inches below her belly button, while the elastic of her thong panties rode well above, lying just at the place where her hips began to swell out from her waist. As the shirts popped off and her arms stretched high above her head, the front clasp on the bra snapped, releasing her breasts, which bounced, flinging themselves upward with happy abandon.

Jimmy Lee looked like he had been hit upside the head with a tire iron. Stunned, he sloshed gasoline all over the engine block, and then, almost in slow motion, Sally Beth saw his mouth fall into a wide-open gape. The cigarette practically leaped out of his mouth, falling onto the engine, which caught fire with a loud *Swoosh!* Staring and frozen, Jimmy Lee did not notice the flames leaping up at his face, even after Lilly screamed at him. Sally Beth rushed forward to push him aside and slam the hood of the car down, but her attempt to quell the blaze was too late. Flames roared out of the front grille.

Edna Mae, seeing the conflagration, yanked open the back door to pull Lamentations out by the scruff of his neck, just before the flames followed a trail of gasoline toward the puddle under the car, then up into the gas tank, which exploded into a fireball that blew it apart and flung them all to the ground. They rolled, then jumped up and fled onto the grassy roadside just as the rest of the car burst into flames. Lamentations, terrified out of his wits, leaped backwards and started cartwheeling. Nobody except Jimmy Lee noticed that Edna Mae was topless. On the other hand, Jimmy Lee still seemed not to notice the fire, although his face and clothes were blackened and his eyebrows were scorched off.

Passing cars swerved. One clipped the fender of another and careened toward them. Sally Beth screamed at Jimmy Lee as Lamentations tumbled around his leg, and, confusing his master's knee with his own rear-end, bit him on the kneecap. Jimmy Lee jerked into action, grabbing the dog mid-whirl and fleeing away from the car skidding toward them. In the melee, Lamentations bit Jimmy Lee again on the hand and the chin.

By the time Sally Beth, Lilly, and Edna Mae thought it was safe enough to disentangle the pair, several cars had wrecked. One had run into Lilly's car, now totally engulfed in flames, but somehow the driver had managed to pull away and had escaped becoming a part of the inferno. Jimmy Lee bled from his chin, hand, and knee, Lamentations lay limp and quivering, and although Jimmy Lee was trying his best to comfort his helpless dog, he could not quite keep his eyes from straying to Edna Mae.

Sally Beth glanced at her. She blinked and tried to say something, but all she could manage was, "Oh, honey! You're— you're…" and she feebly pointed at her until Edna Mae glanced down and noticed her state of dishabille. She ran back toward the car, and, braving the flames, rescued her partially-burned sweatshirt from the road, whacking it against the ground just enough to put out the glowing cinders before she jerked it back on. The back was nearly burned off and the front was full of holes, but at least it gave her a modicum of decency. She reached under the sweatshirt and tried to fasten the flapping bra, but it was hopeless. The catch was broken.

Long seconds dragged by as the cars piled up all around them, until everything but the fire in Lilly's car grew still. In the long, unbearable silence afterwards, the wrecked, still vehicles made little ticking noises in the heat.

No one said anything for a long time, until Jimmy Lee breathed softly, "Lord God Almighty. I have ruined you."

There was another long pause. A motorist opened the door of his bashed-up truck and stood in a daze, staring at Edna Mae, at Lilly's car, and at his own smashed fender. Slowly, other people began to emerge from their cars and trucks.

"It was my fault," came Edna Mae's voice, full of grief and fury. "I am so, so sorry!" She choked back a sob as she turned away. "It was just so dadgummed *hot!*"

A small crowd had gathered. People spoke in soft murmurs, as quietly as if they were attending a funeral. No one attempted to put out Lilly's flaming car; it was clearly too late to salvage it. Miraculously, no one other than Jimmy Lee was injured, and the damage to the other cars was minor to moderate.

When the police arrived, it took quite a bit of explaining to sort out what had happened. Lilly took a deep breath and slowly related the bare bones of the story, leaving out the parts about Jimmy Lee's cigarette and Edna Mae ripping her clothes off. Sally Beth, afraid of saying the wrong thing, busied herself tending to Jimmy Lee's injuries with supplies from the policeman's first aid kit.

"It's okay, Sally Beth," he said, waving her away. "He's had his shots, and I've been cut up worse than this." The misery in his eyes belied his cheerful tone. Edna Mae stood despondently on the far side of his truck, trying unsuccessfully to make herself look small. Lilly sat on the gate of the truck, mumbling something about the heat and the gas container to the state patrolman, darting her eyes to Sally Beth, pleading for her to come rescue her, but Sally Beth wasn't about to. Lilly was doing just fine all by herself, she reckoned.

It took a long time, but finally everything was sorted out to the satisfaction of the trooper. No one wanted to press charges against Lilly; no one wanted to admit they had lost control of their vehicles because they had caught sight of a near-naked giantess standing beside a flaming car, so they did not mention Edna Mae's strip show. At last, after an hour of filling out reports, exchanging insurance information and soothing Lamentations, they found themselves alone and staring at the blackened hulk of Lilly's car.

"Oh, *noooo!*" wailed Lilly. "Both my guitars. And my new boots."

"Mine, too," Sally Beth commiserated. "But look, Lilly, you at least have your pocketbook, and your camera. And Edna Mae saved Lamentations." She touched the top of her head. "Oh—I still have my princess hat!" This made her feel infinitely better.

Edna Mae picked at one of the holes in her sweatshirt and fought back tears.

"This is all my fault," said Jimmy Lee miserably from his blackened face as he brushed away some ash that used to be his eyebrow. He took a deep breath before adding, "And ma'am, I am eternally beholden to you for saving my dog." He was looking somewhere in the vicinity of Edna Mae's feet, but, with effort, managed to drag his eyes up to her face. "I don't know what I'd do if I'da gone and killed poor Laminations. He's the best dog I ever had."

He brightened a little as he knelt to stroke the dog's back. "But don't you worry none. I'll buy every one of you all new things. I'll buy you a new car, too, Lilly." He paused again, thinking. "It's Sunday, so everything's closed, but we can head on to Dallas today. I've got a cousin has a dealership there, and he'll give us a good deal on a new car. Tomorrow, I'll make all this right."

Lilly looked dumfounded. She stared at Jimmy Lee, who, frankly, was about the sorriest looking thing imaginable. His bandaged hand stood out starkly white against his sooty clothes. His face was unrecognizable: blackened, bleeding, and bald. Standing beside his rusty, beat-up old pickup truck, cradling a pitiful excuse for a dog in his arms, promising to buy them all new clothes and a new car was just too much for Lilly to handle. She snorted with disgust and looked away.

Sally Beth put her arm around her sister and said gently, "Come on, honey, let's not make him feel worse."

Lilly crossed her arms. "Sally Beth, Jimmy Lee doesn't have two nickels to rub together. How's he going to replace any of this? And a car? Come on! He's crazy."

Sally Beth was about to agree that Jimmy Lee had probably taken leave of his senses when she suddenly remembered the last time she saw his cousin Howard, and what he had told her about the reason Jimmy Lee had come out West. She turned to Lilly thoughtfully. "He might not be as poor as we think he is."

"What do you mean? Just look at that old truck! Just look at *him!*"

Sally Beth looked. Jimmy Lee—and his truck—did look poor, but the tires were new Michelins, and earlier she had noticed that the interior of the truck had been nicely repaired since the last time she had seen it. There was a new floorboard and a newly-upholstered seat. Upon a closer look, she noticed that his cowboy boots looked new. A silver and turquoise belt buckle gleamed through the soot.

"Let me talk to him for a minute." Approaching him cautiously, she laid a hand on his arm and spoke softly. "Jimmy Lee, I know you feel responsible for this, and I know you want to make it right, but you don't need to go buying anything, at least until you talk to Howard."

"What do you mean, Sally Beth?"

"I mean, I know he has come into money, and he probably would tell you to go ahead and get us home, but I think you should check with him first."

Jimmy Lee narrowed his eyes. "What are you talking about?"

She was taken aback by the suspicion in his face. "Well, I don't think this is a secret or anything. I mean, he told us how he sent you out here to check on his oil well, and I know he'd loan you the money and all, but..."

"Oil well?" He looked genuinely puzzled.

"Yeah. He told a bunch of us how they found oil on the land his granddaddy gave him in Oklahoma. How you were out here checking on it? And how he's probably going to be rich?"

Jimmy Lee thought a moment, then slowly looked back at her, his eyes glimmering with caution and something else she could not understand. "Oh. He told you about that?" There was another long silence before he spoke again. "Well, yeah," he said, his voice halting and careful. "And there is a lot of money coming out of that dirt. But... Howard has made me a... partner, and I do my share of the work. I got a bit of cash, too."

She glanced at the truck thoughtfully. Despite the new interior, it was the same, beat-up old wreck he had always driven. When he saw her looking at it, he moved a little closer to her, speaking softly but earnestly. "We decided not to go showing off none. You know, get above our raisin'. But believe me, Sally Beth, I could afford to buy a new one. I can afford to buy Lilly a new car, and I'm derned sure I can afford to buy you all some new clothes. Let me do this, please." He looked at her, pleading.

She nodded. She was certain Jimmy Lee was exaggerating about how much he could afford, but she would die before she poked any holes in his pride. "Okay, Jimmy Lee. But we have to tell Lilly and Edna Mae about the oil well and all, okay? They have to know this won't hurt you."

She turned to tell Edna Mae and Lilly about the sudden windfall that had befallen the Knight family, explaining that Jimmy Lee felt that he could easily afford to replace their belongings. Lilly perked right up, and a bright gleam came into her eye, but Edna Mae shook her head defiantly. "Huh-uh. This was mostly my fault. I was stupid and crazy from the heat, and if I'd kept my clothes on, this never would have happened." She blushed violently. So did Jimmy Lee, and there was a long, awkward silence while Sally Beth and Lilly tried to ignore their flaming faces. Jimmy Lee finally spoke, and there was a kind of dignity in the way he stood, his hat in his hands, his head up, and his eyes direct.

"Ma'am, I got eyes, but that don't mean I got the right to go crazy just 'cause I see something beautiful enough to knock them out. It ain't your fault I acted a fool. It would ease my conscience greatly if you would let me make this right. My mama and daddy, they would be disappointed with me if I was to let you suffer for what I done." He blushed again.

A surprised look bloomed on Edna Mae's face. She looked at him, then took a breath and suddenly smiled, not exactly at him, but beyond him, as if she were thinking a very pleasant thought. Sally Beth realized that Edna Mae had probably not met many real gentlemen before.

She amended her thoughts. Jimmy Lee would never be classified as a gentleman, exactly, but he was, indeed, a gentle man, and she was proud of him, proud of the people of her home, proud of the way they raised their children with dignity. Jimmy Lee may look like a raggedy old hillbilly, but she knew he had a chivalrous heart.

He cleared his throat, and looking at the ground around Edna Mae's dirty, bare feet, manfully offered, "I reckon you might want to put some different clothes on. I got some pants and a shirt..."

he trailed off, his face scarlet.

Edna Mae looked at his feet in return. "I would appreciate it, Jimmy Lee." Neither of them moved.

Sally Beth figured she'd better step in before one of them burst into flames. "That's real sweet of you, Jimmy Lee. Edna Mae, you can change in the truck. I'll help you find something."

Sadly, and much to the embarrassment of both Edna Mae and Jimmy Lee, nothing fit, except Jimmy Lee's socks and shoes. His pants wouldn't go over her hips, his shirt wouldn't button. Edna Mae fought back humiliated tears while Sally Beth did her best to sooth her. "Your shorts are fine, and the front of your sweatshirt isn't burned too much, and it's so long you don't see the shorts anyway. Look, I've got some scissors in my pocketbook..." She trailed off. Her purse was a smoldering lump in the back seat of Lilly's car.

"Jimmy Lee, you got a knife?" He handed Sally Beth a pocketknife. "Thanks. Let's just cut off the sleeves, so you won't be too hot, and you can put a shirt on over it. That'll cover the back. Tomorrow we'll get you something real quick." Edna Mae took a deep breath and nodded, then looked down while she brushed at her sweatshirt and tugged at her shorts.

"Come on, Edna Mae. You look just fine. You've got such pretty legs, and you've got a beautiful face and hair. Why, you look downright cute in that shirt and those shoes! Here, I'll fix your hair a little, and you'll look just like the prettiest thing in Texas."

She fussed at Edna Mae's hair for a minute before stepping back to eye her critically. "Oh, honey, you look just *fine!*" Leaning in, she giggled, "A sight better than Jimmy Lee," she whispered.

It took some doing, but all four managed to squeeze into Jimmy Lee's truck: Sally Beth sat on Edna Mae's lap while Lamentations was relegated to the back. They made it the mile or so down the highway to the diner, but it was awkward: if Jimmy Lee shifted gears, he had his hands between Lilly's knees, so he just chugged along in first gear the whole way. They parked in the shade so Lamentations wouldn't get too hot, then managed to clean themselves up a bit in the restrooms before Jimmy Lee took water to his dog while the girls found a booth.

"How are all of us going to get to Dallas in Jimmy Lee's truck?" asked Lilly after they had ordered. "There's no way you can sit on Edna Mae's lap that whole way. It's even crowded with just three in the front seat."

Edna Mae spoke up. "Just take me to the bus station. I can get on home from here." This was followed by an uncomfortable silence. It did make sense for Edna Mae to leave them, but Sally Beth did not want to part company so soon, and Jimmy Lee looked stricken. It was clear he did not want to part company, either.

"Oh, don't do that!" she chided. "You can't go riding in a bus in those clothes and we'd just hate for you to leave us, and we want to meet your granny and all." She considered their dilemma. It would be difficult for them all to ride very far in Jimmy Lee's truck. "I know! I'll ride in the back. I just *love* riding in the back of a truck! I used to do it all the time when I was little."

Edna Mae shook her head. "No, I'll ride in the back. I'd like to be back there with Lamentations. He needs the company."

"Well, we can ride back there together," countered Sally Beth. She did not want Edna Mae to be lonesome or feel awkward, and to tell the truth, it would be terribly awkward if even three of them rode in the front seat all the way to Dallas.

"No lady is going to ride in the back," announced Jimmy Lee. "I'll ride back there with Lamentations, and you three can ride in the front. And that's the end of it."

There was some more arguing. Lilly kept her mouth shut. It was clear she wasn't about to ride in the back of a pickup truck with a crazy dog all the way to Dallas. Sally Beth knew what was on Jimmy Lee's mind: he wanted to be with Edna Mae, but he was too shy to say it.

"I tell you what," she said. "We'll take turns. Lilly and I will ride in the back first, and then after an hour or so, Jimmy Lee and Edna Mae can take a turn."

Lilly glared at her. "Sally Beth," she hissed in her ear, "I am not about to ride down the highway in the back of a pickup truck. In Texas. When it's a hundred degrees and the sun is just *beating* down. I'll get sunburned in about five minutes, and you know what that wind will do to my hair, not to mention yours. Besides, I went all the way to Las Vegas and worked my tail off just so I could get up in the world and could stop being a raggedy old hillbilly, and here you are wanting me to ride in the back of *a decrepit old pickup truck* with an old *hound dog*, getting beat to death by the wind! I'm just not going to..."

She stopped suddenly, staring at the double door of the diner, her eyes wide, and her mouth open. Sally Beth glanced up, and she, too, felt her own eyes and mouth fly open.

In the doorway, in a shaft of bright sunshine, his arms flung wide to hold the twin doors open, his jeweled, white jumpsuit glowing, stood Elvis. She blinked. He looked like an angel. An Elvis angel all jeweled and in white. She expected him to break into song, and wondered for a moment if he had exchanged his guitar for a harp. She blinked again as Elvis stepped inside, followed by another Elvis, and another, and another. Before Sally Beth even noticed that she had forgotten to breathe, the room was filled with at least twenty Elvises, all dressed alike in jeweled, white bellbottom suits. They took seats at the tables all around them.

"Lordamercy!" she breathed, staring. She thought her heart was going to just melt in a puddle. It already felt like Jell-O, and it was warming up fast.

Edna Mae turned to look, then scooted farther down into the booth, muttering, "Looks like an Elvis convention. This is all we need."

Slowly, meaning dawned on Sally Beth. She had been all the way to Las Vegas and had not seen an Elvis impersonator the whole time, and now, here in the rough lands of West Texas, were a whole slew of them, all dandied up in their finest clothes. She couldn't believe their good luck. Smiling broadly, she gave them a little wave. "Hi, you all. Nice to see you."

Lilly was just as happy to see them. She waved as well, and then, after a tiny hesitation, jumped up and went right to them. "Gee, you all look *great!* Where are you from? Where are you going? My sister and I are headed to Graceland, and we're just thrilled to see you all here. We just love Elvis!"

As much as Sally Beth wanted to join her, she was a little too bashful, so she just sat in the booth and grinned at them. She surely hoped they would come over and talk to her. They were the cutest things she had ever seen, and it was hard to hold herself back from busting out of the booth and running over to stand by Lilly.

Lilly's efforts were far from wasted. At least half of the Elvises warmed right up to her, introducing themselves and inviting her to join them, and then some of them moved over to the booth where Sally Beth, Edna Mae, and Jimmy Lee sat. Edna Mae made herself as small as she possibly could. Jimmy Lee looked confused and dazed, but he shook hands as Lilly urged each Elvis toward them.

"This here is my sister, Sally Beth, and this is Jimmy Lee, a friend from back home, and this is Edna Mae; she's a little shy, so don't spook her. This is Elvis Tommy and Elvis Cliff and Elvis John, and Elvis Harry, and..." Sally Beth's head began to spin with all the Elvises in their dazzling costumes. She smiled and smiled and vowed that *this* moment was the highlight of her life. Twenty Elvises! It even beat the Sinatra concert.

"What are you all doing here?" asked Lilly.

One of them pointed at the window. Outside in the parking lot was a bus with letters written in fancy script, *Love Me Tender Gospel Choir.*

"We're on tour. We just left a church service at the Baptist Church around the corner, and we stopped here to get something to go for lunch. Tonight we've got another concert at a church in Fort Worth, so we're in a hurry. We don't have much time."

Another Elvis spoke up. "Did I hear you say you were on your way to Graceland? We'll end up there for the service on Wednesday. It's the anniversary of his death."

"I *know!*" exclaimed Sally Beth, her eyes glowing. "We're planning on being there for it. *Imagine that.*"

Lilly clapped her hand over her mouth to stifle a laugh, her eyes happy and bright above it. "You're headed for Fort Worth *today*?" She looked at Sally Beth, who, reading her mind, grinned back at her and gave a perky little shrug, hoping that Lilly was about to open up a world of delights.

"Say," said Lilly carefully. "We're in a little fix here. My car caught fire just down the road and burned up. Did you see it?"

"Yes, we did," spoke up one of the Elvises. Sally Beth thought it was Elvis Tommy, but she wasn't certain.

"Anyway, our friend, Jimmy Lee happened to be here, and he has a truck, but we don't all fit in, and I was wondering if maybe, if you don't mind, and if you have room, maybe we could ride as far as Fort Worth with you?" She gave Elvis Tommy her most beguiling smile. Sally Beth added hers.

A few of the Elvises looked at each other, and one shrugged. "Hey, Elvis Sam!" One called to an Elvis standing at the cash register. "We got room for three more as far as Fort Worth?"

"Oh, not me!" exclaimed Edna Mae. "You two go on. I'll ride with Jimmy Lee." She glanced at Jimmy Lee, smiled and blushed. Jimmy Lee looked like he had just won the lottery. He glowed through the soot he hadn't been able to completely remove from his face

"Just two more," corrected Elvis. "That was their car burned up back there."

Elvis Sam did not look happy. He didn't really look like Elvis, either, being short and skinny and a little old. He scowled at Lilly and Sally Beth and started to shake his head, when another Elvis spoke up. "Oh, come on, Sammy boy! These ladies are in need here. We got room to take them as far as Forth Worth. All the way to Graceland, even. They won't cause trouble." He winked at Lilly and said under his breath, "You look like a lot of trouble sweetheart, but I think we can handle it." Lilly giggled and twinkled back at him.

Another Elvis cajoled, "Yeah, Sammy, they're damsels in distress. Elvis would never leave distressed damsels stranded. This was followed by a general chorus of, "Yeah, Sammy. Come on!"

A few minutes later, Sally Beth and Lilly climbed aboard the Love Me Tender Gospel Choir bus, bag lunches grasped in their hands, and waved goodbye to Edna Mae and Jimmy Lee. All four of them thought they had died and gone to heaven.

Eight

Sally Beth was too excited to eat her lunch. The Elvises argued over who got to sit next to the girls, and her heart was all aflutter because they were all so handsome, and most of them looked so much like the real thing that she had to remind herself that the real Elvis was dead, and these were just pretend. She so wished her mother could have been there to see it, and she sent a little prayer heavenward to ask that if she could take the time, would she just take a glimpse down here and see what her girls had landed in.

She settled by the handsomest one in her opinion. He was a little rough looking, with a bit of burr on his face, and he had a nice smile with even, white teeth. He was the biggest of all the Elvises, too. His name was Elvis Chuck. Lilly took longer to decide which one to sit beside, and spent a good forty-five minutes taking pictures and talking to each of them before she finally settled on sitting in the back with Elvis Tommy. As thrilled as Sally Beth was, she was even more thrilled when Elvis Sam stood in the front of the bus and blessed the meal before anyone took out their sandwiches and cups of Coke. Not only was she on a bus full of Elvises, but a bus full of Christian Elvises. Christian Elvises who could *sing*! Her heart sang its own little number over that.

She turned to the one beside her. "Do you do this all the time? Be Elvis, I mean."

"Pretty much. We travel a lot, and we're especially busy right now, it being the anniversary of his death." He laughed shortly and leaned in toward her. "Although some people who should know say he isn't really dead."

Sally Beth drew up in surprise. "I had heard that, but I thought it was just a rumor. You mean he really might not have died?"

"That's what they say. He faked his own death because he was sick of the way his life was turning out, and he just wanted to retire. Supposedly he lives over in Hot Springs now."

"Do you think it could be true?" Sally Beth tingled at the possibility.

Elvis Chuck shrugged. "Could be. I'm not going to dispute it."

Elvis Sam stood up at the front of the bus again. "Okay, boys, we need to practice before we get to Fort Worth. This show's going to be a little longer than the others, so I want you to leave the ladies alone while we add four more numbers." He pulled out a pitch pipe. "It's been a while since we ran through "I'll Fly Away" so let's try that one first." He blew into the pipe, and suddenly, heavenly voices rose up all around Sally Beth, and they all sounded just like Elvis!

> *Some bright morning, when this day is o'er, I'll fly away*
> *To that home on heav'n's celestial shore, I'll fly away*
> *I'll fly away, Oh, Glory, I'll fly away*
> *When I die, hallelujah, by and by, I'll fly away!*

She and Lilly couldn't help themselves. Within the first two lines, they were singing along with the choir. After that, they ran through "Are You Washed in the Blood?", "In My Heart There Rings a Melody", "The Old Rugged Cross", and many more. They sang until their voices were tired, they sang to the glory of heaven. They sang with their hearts making more music than their voices.

It was heavenly, this trip down the dusty Texas highway in the plush, air conditioned bus, sitting beside a handsome Elvis, and Sally Beth thought her heart would fly away, right out of her chest and up into the sky where her mama and daddy and her good friend Holy Miracle Jones, not to forget Jesus, watched and smiled.

All too soon, Elvis Sam made them stop so they could rest their voices, and the bus grew quiet. She and Elvis Chuck talked. Rather, Sally Beth talked while he mostly just looked at her, smiled, and nodded. Sometimes he asked her a question. She talked until she was hoarse, and then she laughed about how much she had talked, and Elvis Chuck looked at her and smiled and told her about his home and about how she reminded him of his mother, in a way, who was from Denmark and whose hair had been the same color when she was younger, and how her face was the same shape. He stopped talking after a while and started looking at her funny, and before she knew it, she wanted to lean in toward him and smell his skin, and maybe ruffle his hair a little and smooth out that cowlick right in the front. She got to wondering what it might feel like to place her palm on his cheek and feel the whiskers there. But he was a professional Elvis impersonator, and she was just a country girl from a hick town, and she knew she was being silly, and she hoped she hadn't acted foolish. When he leaned toward her, as if to kiss her, she shrank back a fraction, smiled and looked away. It made her sad to think about how many girls he probably had kissed, and she didn't want to be just one in a long string of them.

Sally Beth was saving herself for the right man. Oh, she had kissed plenty of boys before, at least five to her recollection. There had been Darryl Millsap whom she had loved in the ninth grade. She was sure he was The One, but then he moved away when his daddy got transferred to Charleston, and although they swore they would write and stay true to each other forever, the long distance relationship had lasted only about six months. She had not been good at writing—every word had been a struggle, and then she had gotten so busy with the horses, she didn't really notice when his last letter came. Then, when she was in the eleventh grade, there was Lonnie Odem. She had gone out with him for a few months before she realized she liked his twin brother, Johnnie, better, after she had been caught in a rainstorm and he picked her up and drove her home, and then, when she was just about to get out of the car, he leaned over and kissed her, surprising her both with the suddenness of it and the fact that her insides disintegrated into effervescent fire, and she realized she was with the wrong brother. She had kissed him back like she had just discovered kissing, but afterwards, she felt bad about cheating on Lonnie.

It wasn't fair to break up with Lonnie and then start dating Johnnie, so she just quit going out with boys altogether until after high school, when she started keeping company with Sam Abel, a nice Quaker boy her parents really liked, but it didn't take long before she realized he was as dull as dirt. It was hard to break up with him because he really loved her, but she thought she would go out of her mind if she had to sit through one more evening of him talking about his prize heifers. Besides, he didn't care for music and couldn't sing a lick. He tried for her sake, but she found it painful to listen to him.

And finally, there was Jay Hambly, who she thought was going to be The One as well, but they broke up last year after she got her cosmetology license. He got to acting funny and implied that she was going to start putting on airs now that she would be traveling in high-fashion circles. He wanted her to get a job down at the mill with him until they got married and started having children. She didn't pay much attention to that until he started talking about some of the things dutiful wives were supposed to do, and being an independent woman with her cosmetology license was not one of them. She woke up one morning realizing she could do a sight better than Jay Hambly.

Now that she was free, she could have kissed anybody she liked, and although she certainly found Elvis Chuck very attractive with lips that looked kissable, she cautioned herself that he was a stranger, someone who didn't know her, and neither one of them could possibly know the true value of one another. Her mama, and her daddy, too, had talked to her about how important it was for her to guard her heart, and how she should keep her love safe and pure for The One that God had picked out for her, who would be with her all of his days, and she well knew the veracity of their counsel. She remembered how her old friend Holy Miracle Jones had teased her about when she would find that man.

"He is both near and far, Sally Beth," he said to her once, "and he will flee you before he comes running to you. And he will love you truly for all of his days." Holy Miracle always spoke in riddles that way, but he knew what he was talking about, and she did not doubt the truth of any of his words. Elvis Chuck was near now, and his traveling would take him far, but in her heart she knew she probably would never see him again after today. Besides, he wasn't fleeing her now. It wouldn't do to think of him as anything other than a happy afternoon on the Texas highway, and it certainly wouldn't do to be leading him on by letting him kiss her when she knew there was no future for them.

She smiled at him, drew a breath, and launched into a new topic, and the moment passed. Elvis Chuck was funny and kind, and she was having such a grand time that she wondered if Lilly was having fun, too. When she turned around to look for her, she was shocked and pained at what she saw.

Lilly was in the back seat of the bus with Elvis Tommy, her arms were wrapped around him, and she was kissing him for all she was worth. She was practically lying down on the back seat and Elvis Tommy was just *all over* her! At least she thought it was Elvis Tommy, it was hard to tell with them all in a tangle like that. He had taken off his pearly, jeweled jacket, and he was kissing her as if he had earned the right to. If her daddy had been here, he would have given him a good talking to about how he was being disrespectful to Lilly and that he certainly had not earned any rights at all regarding his baby girl.

Sally Beth wished a hole would open up in the floor of the bus and swallow up both Lilly and herself, but she steeled herself and did what she felt she ought to do: she marched to the back of the bus and stood over Lilly until she came up for air, then she said, keeping her face and voice as pleasant as possible to keep from embarrassing everybody too much, "Lilly, I thought maybe you'd want to come up to the front of the bus and spend some time with Elvis Chuck and me, and some of the others. You won't have this chance again, and they are real interesting. Elvis Chuck is from Utah." She couldn't think of anything else to say, so she just stood there and smiled at Lilly until she was sure her face would crack, then she sat down beside her and nudged her with her elbow.

"Sally Beth," I am doing just fine here, thank you," said Lilly, her face a mask of smiling ice. You can go on back to the front of the bus and enjoy yourself there."

She leaned in and spoke more softly, "Lilly, as your older sister, I think you need to behave a little better in public." Sally Beth's eyes narrowed, but she kept the smile in both her face and voice. Lilly kept no such pretentions.

"Sally Beth, you leave me alone!" she hissed into her ear, searing the air around it with fiery disdain. "I am not doing anything wrong, and you just need to stop being such a prude if I want to kiss somebody. I happen to *like* Elvis Tommy, and I might not ever see him again, and so you shouldn't begrudge me a few little kisses, thank you very much!"

"Well, does Elvis Tommy like *you*?" She kept her voice barely above a whisper so no one other than Lilly could hear her. "If he does, then maybe he'll go to the trouble to see you again, and so this *wouldn't* be the last time you see him. Otherwise this is just a you-know-what!" She mouthed the last three words rather than saying them. It wouldn't do for anybody to hear what she was thinking about Lilly at that moment.

Elvis Tommy, looking decidedly uncomfortable, began to edge away from Lilly, casting nervous glances at Sally Beth. She smiled at him over Lilly's head. "I am sorry if I am embarrassing you, Elvis Tommy, but my sister doesn't have good sense sometimes when it comes to men. I don't mean to blame you or anything."

"Why, Sally Beth Lenoir! You're making me out to be a regular slut—and I am not. I just happen to really, really like Elvis Tommy, and so what if I want to kiss him? You aren't my mama, and you just need to *back off.*"

Sally Beth felt like knocking some sense into Lilly. It just about broke her heart that her baby sister was wantonly giving away her precious kisses to a virtual stranger, and to know that she had not listened to Mama about how important it is to guard your heart and save it for the one man who would treasure you above all others. She wanted to make Lilly understand that she was making a mistake here that might follow her all the rest of her days, that throwing her love around to just any good-looking guy who paid attention to her would hollow out her soul and change her in ways that she could not fathom, but she was acutely aware of a few pairs of eyes on her, and she suddenly felt very small and vulnerable and in the most uncomfortable position she had ever been. She wanted to drag Lilly out of the back seat and make her behave herself, but it was obvious Lilly wasn't going anywhere. She was very grateful when she looked up to see Elvis Chuck standing before her, guitar in hand.

"Sally Beth? Do you play guitar? I've been working on a ballad, and I'd like for you to hear it and maybe sing it. It's perfect for your voice, I think."

Sally Beth felt a rush of thankfulness for his rescue. Although all the Elvises were politely looking in other directions, she knew she was on the brink of making a fool of both herself and Lilly, and maybe she had already stepped over the line. She wanted to get away, but then, again, she didn't want to walk all the way back down the aisle of the bus past all these men, not when she was already embarrassed to death by Lilly and their argument. She turned back to Elvis Chuck with grateful appreciation. "Why, I'd love to, Elvis Chuck. But Lilly here has the best voice for ballads. Would you like for her to join us? She smiled demurely at Lilly and scooted closer to her, making room for Elvis Chuck.

Lilly sighed heavily, rolling her eyes. Elvis Chuck sat down beside Sally Beth and began strumming and singing.

My darling has hair like summer wheat, and skin as pale as pearl

Her heart's as big as the harvest moon, as big as the wind when it starts to unfurl

But she doesn't know how lovely she is, how kind or gentle her ways

Nor does she know how she lights the path of all she holds in her sway

My darling has hair like summer wheat, and lips that beckon like wine

Her voice rings out and touches me, and how I long to make her mine!

But the burden she carries she carries alone, too high, too far to address

She dances away as lightly as wind, not knowing I yearn for her caress.

My darling has hair like summer wheat, and a smile that glows from her heart.

She cannot know how my own heart thirsts, how it dreads the moment we part.

My darling has hair like summer wheat; her eyes are blue, as blue as a song.

I cannot but wonder what else they hold. Do they cry sometimes when she is alone?

My darling has hair like summer wheat, like summer wheat, like summer wheat.

My darling has hair like summer wheat, and I long to make her my own.

Although Lilly was still miffed at Sally Beth, she couldn't help but smile after just a few lines. "Why, Elvis Chuck, that doesn't sound like a song for a woman!" she teased. "At least for a woman to *sing*. Are you sure you wanted Sally Beth to sing it—or to *hear* it?" He didn't answer, but continued to strum, while Sally Beth blinked and wondered if he had just made up the song or if he had been working on it before they met. She felt a little flattered, but also a little uncomfortable. She knew she was just a simple girl from the mountains and that some men might try to play on her unsophistication and use flattery for the wrong purposes, but she surely hoped Elvis Chuck was not capable of it. He remained silent, trying out a few new chords before he suddenly stood.

"Sally Beth, let's go back up front and you can help me work out a harmony for this, okay?"

She didn't know how to answer, she was so confused by the way Elvis Chuck was acting. But she was glad for the opportunity to get away from Lilly, now that they had publically argued and Lilly had acted so awful, so she made her way back down the aisle and spent the rest of the afternoon making sure Elvis Chuck knew that she was not going to be seduced by a song, although when she really thought about it, it was a song worthy of seduction. If she had been that sort of girl.

They didn't feel dressed enough for church in their slightly sooty summer dresses and sandals, but Jimmy Lee and Edna Mae were not due to pick them up until after the concert, and besides, all the Elvises cajoled them until they finally agreed to sit in the sanctuary with all the well-dressed people who had come to see the performance. As soon as the concert began, they were glad they had been persuaded. Sally Beth closed her eyes, trying hard not to sing along while the Elvis voices filled the church with the sacred gospel songs. It was the most beautiful thing she had ever heard.

Halfway through the concert, Elvis Sam stepped forward and announced, "Ladies and gentlemen, we have a very special guest with us tonight. Elvis Jesse has driven over from Hot Springs and is going to perform with us." To Sally Beth's complete astonishment, someone who looked *exactly* like the real Elvis strode out onto the stage and took his place with the other singers. She studied him closely. He looked better than the real Elvis did; at least he looked better than he did in the months before he died. He looked like Elvis did back when he was healthy and happy, before he got so fat and strung out on pills, back when he looked like he liked living, and when he stepped forward to sing a solo of *"Amazing Grace"*, she began to believe that Elvis was not dead, but stood before her in the sanctuary of the Sugar Creek Baptist Church of Fort Worth, singing like an angel. She wept softly and took Lilly's hand. Lilly squeezed it and joined her in the weeping.

Oh Lord, if You're listening to this, and I hope You are, would You please get Mama and Daddy to come listen too? I know You probably have angels that sing as good as this, but I think this is about the closest thing we have to angels down here on earth, and I want Mama and Daddy to know what a good time we are having, and although we miss them very much, we are grateful for the life we still have in us.

When it was over, it was hard to say goodbye, but the Elvises packed up quickly, and before she had a chance to seek out Elvis Jesse to tell him how much she appreciated his singing, he had disappeared through the back door and the Elvises of the Love Me Tender Gospel Choir were filing onto the bus, waving at them. Lilly ran up to give Elvis Tommy one last kiss, and Sally Beth was wistfully hoping she would be able to say goodbye to Elvis Chuck, when he suddenly materialized beside her.

"Sally Beth, here is my address, and my phone number. Can I have yours?" He pressed a piece of paper into her hand. She managed to stammer out, "Okay, but I'm not good at writing. I'm not sure how often you'll hear from me." She suddenly felt like crying again. Elvis Chuck had been so nice to her, and they had had such a good time together. She began to regret her suspicion that he had been playing games with her. She didn't want him to leave. She wanted to throw her arms around him and kiss him the way Lilly had kissed Elvis Tommy, but she didn't want to give Elvis Chuck the wrong idea, and she certainly didn't want to compromise her heart. On top of that, she was afraid she would embarrass them both if she did. So she stuck out her hand and mumbled something about how nice it was to have met him, and sadly watched as he took the steps into the bus. He hung out in the doorway for a moment, waved at her, looking very sweet and sad, and disappeared.

Jimmy Lee and Edna Mae were waiting in the parking lot. Edna Mae wore a new dress. It was about the ugliest thing Sally Beth had ever seen, but it did cover her up well, with yards and yards of brown splotchy fabric billowing around her from her neck to the tops of Jimmy Lee's white socks and scuffed brown shoes. "Where did you get it on a Sunday?" Sally Beth wanted to know.

Edna Mae beamed. "Jimmy Lee and me, we drove around the shopping areas, and we found a place. It wasn't open, but the owner had just come in to do some work, and Jimmy Lee talked him into letting us in! I was feeling so dirty and ragged, and Jimmy Lee was determined to find me something to wear. He knocked on the door for a long time, and the man kept waving him away, and finally, Jimmy Lee slapped a fifty dollar bill up against the window, and the man came over and let us in! I found this dress on the sale rack, and isn't it just perfect?"

"Perfect" was not how Sally Beth would have described it, but she was glad to see Edna Mae happy. "Yes, it's perfect, Edna Mae. I bet you feel real relieved to have it on."

"Oh, I am!" breathed Edna Mae, looking at Jimmy Lee as if he was just perfect, too.

Jimmy Lee stepped up and almost put his arm around Edna Mae but stopped himself just before he touched her, then waved his arm around a little as if he didn't know what do to with it, finally bringing his hand up and scratching his head. "We've found a motel just around the corner, and we've already checked in, so let's get on over there and get some rest. Tomorrow we can replace all your things and head to Dallas to find a car for Lilly. We took the liberty of getting you a few things for the night." He blushed and looked away, making Sally Beth feel somehow worldly in the face of his bashful gallantry.

Sally Beth insisted on riding with Lamentations in the back of the truck the two miles to the motel Jimmy Lee and Edna Mae had found, and she enjoyed the breeze and the warm Texas night, even though the mosquitoes were pretty bad until they got up some speed. She couldn't see the stars very well because there was so much light all around, but just looking heavenward and dwelling on the music of the day made her think of her mountains and how happy she was to have a home under the glorious heavens, so close to the sky and these stars, and how happy she was to be on this adventure. Even though Lilly had upset her earlier in the day, the bad feeling between them had dissolved, and once again, she felt glad just to be alive in this beautiful world, and she stopped worrying about Lilly or what pain her recklessness may cause.

Lord, this is changing me. I don't know how, and I don't know if it's all for the good, but I ask You make it work together for good. Use me, changed or not. Whatever happens, show me a way to serve You better.

Jimmy Lee and Edna Mae had food for all of them back at the hotel, and they had managed to find new toothbrushes and some big T-shirts to sleep in, as well as clean clothes for tomorrow, which were especially welcome. Sally Beth noticed that while Edna Mae had chosen an ugly and shapeless dress for herself, she had picked out bright and beautiful ones for Lilly and her. Her heart swelled for Edna Mae and her kindness as she and Lilly held the dresses up against themselves and twirled around in front of the mirror.

Jimmy Lee stood awkwardly in the doorway while they exclaimed over their new things, then mumbled something about how late it was as he opened the door to slip out. Edna Mae jumped up to walk outside with him, returning half an hour later, smiling. Sally Beth had to smile, too, but when Lilly opened her mouth to tease, she shot her a warning glance to silence her. It was easy to change the subject; they all had plenty to say about their day's adventures.

It was pure luxury to wash their faces and brush their teeth, shower, and climb into the clean T-shirts. When they finally snuggled down into the soft beds, tired and happy, sleep came slowly, dragging its feet and lingering at the foot of the beds for a long time. They all had a lot to contemplate, and all of their contemplations were about men. Sally Beth thought about three: Elvis Chuck, her daddy, and Jesus.

Nine

August 14, 1978, Fort Worth, Texas

Lilly had only a few hours to buy an entire wardrobe, so she didn't want to waste a minute. They went to the shopping mall around the corner, where she ran straight into The Gap and launched into a buying frenzy. Within two hours she had visited four stores, bought six new outfits, three pairs of shoes, and a set of matching luggage, and it looked like she was just getting warmed up. Sally Beth set aside the minimum she would need to get home, and then enjoyed helping Lilly. She tried to mostly steer her toward the sales rack.

Edna Mae quietly headed to JC Penney's alone, mumbling something about finding things that fit, and Jimmy Lee managed to do some shopping of his own, saying that if he was going to hang out with three beautiful women, he might as well start looking like a man about town. Lilly laughed, "Be sure you buy yourself an ascot, Jimmy Lee!" He grinned at her, but Sally Beth could tell he didn't have a clue as to what she was talking about.

They all joined up for lunch at the Woolworth's. Edna Mae was sporting a new pair of sandals and a surprisingly soft, light green muumuu that looked more like a casual, comfortable dress than a camouflage tent. The color brought out the honey in her hair and eyes. She also was sporting a smile as wide as Texas every time she looked at Jimmy Lee. He looked at her like—well, Sally Beth tried not to think about it. She felt like she was getting a little too close to their personal feelings.

"How much more shopping do you all need to do?" Jimmy Lee spoke to the three of them in general.

"I'm done," answered Edna Mae.

"Me, too," said Sally Beth.

"I just have a little more to do," said Lilly, "but I'm anxious to look for a car this afternoon, so I can finish up later. I still want to get some cowboy boots, and I'm dying to buy *something* at the Galleria in Dallas."

Jimmy Lee nodded. "My cousin's dealership ain't far, just this side of Dallas, so we can head over there any time you're ready."

Edna Mae looked thoughtful. "Well, then, you all go on. I'll stay here and hang out a while, maybe catch a movie."

Sally Beth knew Edna Mae was just being considerate about how little room there was in Jimmy Lee's truck, and she thought she would bow out gracefully, too. "I'll stay here, too, and keep you company." But her apprehensions about Lilly's extravagance forced her to pull her sister aside. "Now listen, Lilly," she said firmly. "You can spend *exactly* the blue book value of your old car, and not a penny more, you hear? Jimmy Lee's already spending a fortune on us, and I don't want you taking advantage of him just because he's nice enough to let you."

Lilly sighed, rolling her eyes. "Sally Beth, I wish you would just trust me!" This irritated Sally Beth a little. Lilly had a way of making people feel guilty while she got away with murder, and she couldn't come back with any more admonishments without making herself out to be a suspicious old curmudgeon.

"We'll be back in a couple of hours," said Jimmy Lee. He said this to Edna Mae, as if he were wishing the time already gone. He almost forgot to look at Sally Beth.

When Sally Beth and Edna Mae emerged from the movie theatre, they found Jimmy Lee just outside, lounging beside a nearly new, bright green Chevy truck. "Lilly's still shopping," he grinned. "We got her a real nice car, probably the best deal on the lot, and, well…" He suddenly went red in the face. "I figured I needed a new truck, too. That old one could only be patched up so many times." His eyes slid over to Edna Mae, seeking her approval. "My cousin gave us a real good deal."

"It's nice, Jimmy Lee." She dropped her eyes, smiling, but she could not let them remain away from his face for long. They kept flickering back and forth between the man and his new truck. He couldn't stop grinning. Sally Beth reckoned she had better intervene before they embarrassed themselves any more with their surreptitious yearning for one another.

"What kind did she get, Jimmy Lee?"

His smile broadened to include Sally Beth. "You just have to see for yourself."

Sally Beth felt a tingle of foreboding. She suspected Lilly had pulled a fast one over him, cajoling him into not only buying her something beyond the blue book value of her old car, but also into buying himself a new truck. That Lilly! Poor Jimmy Lee probably had shelled out far more than he could afford just because he felt guilty and because Lilly had led him to believe that with a new truck, Edna Mae would like him better. She bit her lip in worry over her friend and his wallet. That was proving to be one expensive cigarette. One expensive glimpse at Edna Mae's bosoms. But Jimmy Lee was probably thinking it was worth it.

"We need to get you some new boots," Jimmy Lee reminded them. "There's a Western wear store just up the road. Lilly's there now."

The new truck was roomy, with a large space behind the seat where Lamentations lounged in luxury. The ride to the Western wear store was a pleasure, but Sally Beth sort of wished she were sitting in the bed of Jimmy Lee's old truck, feeling the Texas wind on her face and looking forward to the four of them going out and maybe getting into a little mischief. Their glorious adventure with their new friend was coming to an end, for it was clear that Jimmy Lee would have the honor of delivering Edna Mae to her granny in Texarkana.

Lilly was wearing a new pair of tooled blue-green boots that looked very expensive, and she had stacked up several piles of boxes for them to see. "Sally Beth, try these on. I found you some pink ones, but here are some brown ones that I think are adorable, and I love these blue ones. They're the exact color of your eyes. Edna Mae, I don't know your size, but over there are some gorgeous ostrich ones. I put them right there."

She preened and pranced in the new boots, "These are a whole lot better than the ones I got us," she said, twirling in front of the mirror. Sally Beth tried on the pink ones and the blue ones, and ended up being talked into getting real ostrich boots dyed a rich cherry red. They were very expensive, but Jimmy Lee grinned and grinned when he saw her trying not to dance in the aisles in them, and he said, "You have to get those boots, Sally Beth, and I'll do anything to make you get them. Why, if you don't, I'm going to tell everybody back home that I caught you brawling in a bar." He said it with complete innocence, thinking it was the most absurd thing imaginable.

Lilly burst out laughing. "Oh, Jimmy Lee, who on earth would believe such a thing about *Sally Beth?*" Edna Mae turned her head and sniggered while Sally Beth bit her lip and blushed. *If only he knew.* She nodded, acquiescing, hoping that Edna Mae or Lilly would never speak about her encounter with the little man in the Pecos bar.

Jimmy Lee also talked Edna Mae into trying on new boots, and although she kept saying she didn't need any new ones, he noticed when she paused and smiled in the mirror at the plain dark brown pair she had tried on. When she wasn't looking, he took them to the counter and paid for them before she noticed.

As they were leaving, Edna Mae whispered to Sally Beth, "Jimmy Lee's the nicest man I ever met. Lawrence would have made me get high-heeled slave sandals or something covered with rhinestones, and he would expect me to pay for them ten times over."

"Jimmy Lee, you are the *best!*" exclaimed Lilly, prancing through the doors. "Sally Beth, you are not going to believe the deal Jimmy Lee's cousin gave us on my car. Did you see his truck? Isn't that just the sweetest thing you ever saw? It almost made me want to get a truck, but look what I did get!" She swept her hand toward the parking lot.

Sally Beth couldn't see anything out in the direction Lilly was pointing except for a fancy red two-seater sports convertible, but when Edna Mae hollered, "Lilly, you are one bad mama!" it began to dawn on Sally Beth what Lilly had done. Various thoughts ran through her head, all along the lines of, *How on earth are we going to be able to fit all three of us in that? How much did it cost? Lilly, you are acting the fool if I ever saw one!*

"I know!" shrieked Lilly. "It's a 1974 Corvette Stingray, and Dylan gave it to us for his cost, only $2,500, which he said he practically stole. He said it was the best deal on the lot."

Sally Beth was stunned. She felt as if Lilly had just slugged her in the gut; her knees went weak, and she could not catch her breath. "You spent $2,500 on a *car?* Oh, *Lilly!*" she said weakly.

A voice in the back of her head said, *Turn around and take those boots back right now.*

From a distance, she could hear Lilly's voice. "Sally Beth—don't be mean!"

Take back Lilly's boots, too. Maybe we can take back all the clothes…

"Sally Beth? Sally Beth? Breathe, honey. Here, come on over and you can sit down." Lilly took her arm. "It's not that bad, Sally

Beth. Really." Lilly opened the door of the convertible and gently shoved Sally Beth down onto the plush upholstery.

"Really," she repeated in a rush. "I had insurance on it, so that will cover about five hundred, and Jimmy Lee said that he owed us so much more than that. I argued with him, but he swore he wanted to buy it. Oh, Sally Beth, don't be mad!" Lilly's eyes filled with tears that threatened to spill down her pale cheeks. "I promise, Sally Beth, I'll get a job, and I'll pay him back! You don't have to worry."

Jimmy Lee chimed in, "Sally Beth, it's fine. I reckon I put you all through at least that much trouble, and I owe Lilly something for all that. Shoot, I owe you more than you'll let me pay for. I plumb ruined your trip." He stood anxiously, waiting for Sally Beth to answer.

Edna Mae chimed in, "Sally Beth, for Pete's sake. You're acting like you're about to pass out over a car! Shoot, I'll pitch in another $500 myself. I owe you a pile for rescuing me out of Las Vegas. Don't make Jimmy Lee feel bad."

Sally Beth looked at Lilly, suddenly pale and trembling, and her heart went out to her baby sister, who had always wanted nice things but had never had them, not in her whole life, looking so distressed and sad, and Sally Beth wanted to cry for her. She felt terrible that she was acting so upset about it, but then, there were lots of repairs to make on the house—*the roof alone was going to cost $1500, and it's for sure there's a problem with the foundation, not to mention the fact they had wanted to get it painted and the windows fixed. And the plumbing.* The numbers swam through her head. *College was going to cost close to $2000 a year, that was just tuition and room and board, and Lilly would have other expenses for four whole years. They weren't going to have enough left from Mama's insurance to pay off the mortgage, and she couldn't afford the payments on what she was making. And now they owed Jimmy Lee at least $1000, and Edna Mae another $500, and she didn't know how she was going to make the dollars stretch.* But Lilly looked so disappointed, whereas just a moment before she had been excited and happy, and Sally Beth couldn't bear to be the cause of such grief, so she took a deep breath and smiled, "Lilly, it just surprised me, that's all. We can't let Jimmy Lee pay for all of it, but we'll manage. It's a beautiful car."

Lilly threw her arms around Sally Beth. Her smile came back as she hugged Jimmy Lee and Edna Mae, then Sally Beth again. Sally Beth swallowed her feeling of doom and hugged her back.

Despite the brief crisis over Lilly's extravagance, the rest of the day was a celebration. Lilly spent an hour trying on her new clothes and deciding what to wear for dinner. "I've never had all new clothes before! Shoot, even most of my 'new' clothes were secondhand." She held a blouse to her nose and sniffed it. "The whole suitcase smells like new. I love Jimmy Lee!"

Sally Beth felt her joy, as she, too, reveled in the new outfits she had bought that day. She had ended up getting more than she intended, although fewer than she had lost in the fire. The only thing she regretted losing was the necklace her mother had given her last Christmas and the Bible she had had since elementary school. The Bible had been tattered and marked up, and the necklace had not been expensive, but she had treasured them. She wondered if Lilly regretted the loss of her own similar necklace and Bible. She guessed maybe not. The Bible was still pristine, even after all these years, and the necklace hadn't been to her taste.

"Wear this one," said Edna Mae, holding up a lacy blue sundress. "It's the perfect color for you. And these sandals. Sally Beth, what are you wearing?" Edna Mae rummaged through the bags piled on the floor.

"I like the pink, and I *love* these shoes!" Sally Beth couldn't suppress her enthusiasm as she pulled out a pair of tiny thong sandals studded with pink jewels and held them next to the new dress. It had a few sparkly sequins around the neckline that matched perfectly. She knew exactly how Lilly was feeling. All this new was making her dizzy.

Edna Mae looked at them wistfully for a moment before taking a white, sleeveless A-line dress off a hanger. It was surprisingly immodest, by Edna Mae standards. When she put it on, she did not look fat and frumpy, but statuesque and elegant. Lilly whistled. "Whoa! Edna Mae, you look fabulous in that. Throw those muumuus away, girl."

"Yes, you look really nice," agreed Sally Beth. "You look like you are stepping out to have a good time. And you don't look like you are afraid somebody will look at you."

Edna Mae laughed. "Yeah," she admitted. "I feel safe around Jimmy Lee." She paused, fingering the linen. "He's nice, isn't he?"

"Nice?" laughed Lilly. "If I thought I had a chance, I'd try to take him away from you."

Sally Beth smiled. It was not true—no matter how much money Jimmy Lee spent on Lilly, she would never see him as anything other than a country boy, not worthy of her, but she was happy that Lilly had said it because it made Edna Mae feel good.

"Wait, let me take your picture," said Lilly, grabbing the camera on the way out the door. "You too, Sally Beth. Stand here. Hey, Jimmy Lee!" she called to him as he emerged from his room. Come over here and let me take y'all's picture. Lamentations, too." She set the camera on the railing, set the timer, and jumped into the frame. As they all stood smiling into the lens, Lamentations wedged between Edna Mae and Jimmy Lee, Sally Beth couldn't help but feel a sense of newness and anticipation in everyone, like it was Easter Sunday and the scent of spring made the air sweet and hopeful. Her heart was filled with the celebration of promise.

Almighty God, what a day! Yesterday started out so awful, and it got so good, and today was even better. Thank You for sending Jimmy Lee to us and thank You that Edna Mae is feeling safe around him. Thank You for the Elvises, especially for Elvis Chuck and the concert, and for the chance to see more in one week than I have seen in all my life. Thank You for Lilly's new car, but I will be sure to pay Jimmy Lee

back, please just show me a way to do it. Bless us, Lord, especially Edna Mae. My love to Mama and Daddy, and to Holy Miracle, too. You are good, Lord.

August 15, 1978

The night had erased any possible feeling of guilt Lilly may have felt over conning Jimmy Lee into buying a Corvette Stingray, for at breakfast she began talking about what else she planned to buy as they rolled through Dallas. Sally Beth put a stop to that with a sudden glare and a violent shaking of the head. "Huh-uh, Lilly. You aren't getting *another penny* out of poor Jimmy Lee." Lilly stopped talking, looking contrite and sad. Sally Beth knew what she was feeling: it had been a good ride, and it was hard to give it up. She felt a little sorry for her sister, but she refused to soften. Lilly was getting too good at playing on people's emotions, and she wasn't about to let her play hers or Jimmy Lee's for one more minute.

They took their time going to Texarkana. Jimmy Lee, Lamentations, and Edna Mae rode in the truck, while Sally Beth and Lilly happily settled into the Stingray. They stopped in Dallas long enough to see the place where John F. Kennedy had been shot, and then, at Lilly's insistence, having lunch at the Galleria. After that, Jimmy Lee and Edna Mae left them while Lilly and Sally Beth did a little window shopping; once they saw the price tag on things, even Lilly decided that she had had enough, so they sat by the ice skating rink and waited until Jimmy Lee and Edna Mae came striding toward them. He carried a shiny turquoise guitar case with a big red bow tied on the neck. Beside him, Edna Mae looked as happy as a bluebird bursting with springtime. Her face glowed as Jimmy Lee presented the case to Lilly, who jumped up with a squeal.

It was another Gibson. A brand new one, in turquoise and tortoise shell, and it had a sound like angels humming. Lilly cried, hugged him, then took it out and played and sang until shoppers gathered to listen. Sally Beth and Edna Mae were both too bashful to join her, in this swanky place where every woman wore very big hair and big diamonds to match, so Lilly's impromptu concert did not last long. She said she didn't feel like singing if her best friends in the whole world didn't join her, which made both Edna Mae and Sally Beth feel warm and happy.

They finally left the mall and climbed back into their vehicles, heading eastward. The three-hour drive to Texarkana seemed like a celebration parade.

When they arrived at Edna Mae's grandmother's apartment complex just on the border with Arkansas, they found her wearing a muumuu exactly like one of Edna Mae's. It was apparent which side of the family the body—and the taste in clothing—came from. Granny looked fat above her hemline, but below it, her sixty-five-year-old legs were fabulous. There was plenty of beauty above the neckline as well. Sally Beth couldn't help but feel happy for Jimmy Lee: if he played his cards right, he could well be in for a life of bliss.

After hugs, tears, and introductions, a puzzled Granny said to Edna Mae, "I thought you said your fellow was Lawrence, honey."

There was a short, uncomfortable silence until Sally Beth stepped in, not minding in the least telling a near-lie in order to save Edna Mae's pride. "Oh, Lawrence was Lilly's neighbor; he just came along with us as far as the Grand Canyon." She paused to smile at Jimmy Lee and Edna Mae. "Jimmy Lee is an old friend from back home, and it's a good thing we ran into him back in Midland. He rescued us when Lilly's car caught on fire."

"Well, I'm so happy you brought my baby home to me. I can't thank you enough. Now, you all sit down. I've got a pitcher of margaritas in the freezer with your name on them, and we're all going to just sit right here by the pool and enjoy our time together."

"Thanks just the same, but we have to get back on the road," said Lilly. "We're just passing through on our way to Memphis.

The Elvis tribute is tomorrow. You know, it's the anniversary of his death, and we have friends who are performing."

Edna Mae's granny snorted. "Oh, honey, be there if you have friends to meet, but you don't need to be mourning for Elvis. He's not dead."

Sally Beth sat up. "What makes you say so?"

"Why, 'cause I just saw him down at the Piggly Wiggly this afternoon. He was pulling out of the parking lot as I was getting there." She adjusted the neckline of her muumuu, pulling it up well above the exposed cleavage. "He's out here visiting all the time—his great-aunt is here, and one of his musician buddies lives in town. Why, I thought everybody knew he faked his death last year!

Sally Beth nearly jumped out of her skin, she was so excited. She and Lilly looked at each other with astonished delight. "Well, I'll be," said Sally Beth. *"Imagine that. Elvis alive.* I thought that really was him at the concert on Sunday..." Her head churned with possibilities. "But we still want to go see Graceland, don't we Lilly? They've opened the gardens to the public, and it would be nice to get a glimpse of the house."

"Yeah," agreed Lilly. "I think Mama would like us to see it. We should head on over there."

"Naw, stay the night with us," insisted Granny. "Have some margaritas. I got all of us steaks at the Piggly Wiggly, and I've made a big salad, and there's potatoes baking right now." She pressed. "Tell me your stories. Help me celebrate me getting my Edna Mae back home. You can run over there in the morning to see your friends. But you won't see his grave!" She slapped her knee, accompanied by a hearty laugh. "Oh, you'll see a tombstone, but there's nothing under there except a wax dummy, and besides, it doesn't even pretend to be *his* tombstone. They misspelled his middle name on purpose because his daddy thought it would be bad luck to have the right name on it."

Sally Beth gave her a quizzical look. "I'm serious, honey. You think his daddy would go and spell the name wrong on his own son's tombstone without a good reason? Why, he threw a fit when they got it wrong on his birth certificate and made them redo it. Oh, yes. He is Elvis Aron Presley with just one A in Aron, and if you go look at it, you'll see plain as day, Aaron, with two As." She shook her head and put her fist on her hip in a gesture of finality. "No, siree. Elvis is as alive as you and me, just down the road, visiting his great-aunt Fanny Jane over on the Arkansas side of town."

They did not need much coaxing. They stayed, cooking the steaks over a grill poolside and eating as much as they thought they possibly could, and then eating more when they discovered Granny had made fresh peach ice cream and chocolate pound cake. The margaritas went down easy, too, and before the evening haze settled in and the waxing moon rose over their heads, they felt as comfortable with Edna Mae's granny as they did their own.

Edna Mae picked up Lilly's new guitar. Jimmy Lee borrowed her harmonica, and as the two of them played, Sally Beth, Lilly, and Granny slipped into the kitchen to wash the dishes.

"Tell me what's going on between those two," Granny demanded the minute they were out of earshot. "I know good and well Lawrence has been Edna Mae's boyfriend for close to a year now. Your little story about Lawrence just being Lilly's neighbor doesn't hold any more water than my spaghetti strainer."

"No, it's true. He was my neighbor. And it is true we left him at the Grand Canyon—" Lilly giggled, "after Edna Mae caught him cheating on her." Sally Beth had to laugh, too, remembering the drama of their exit with Lawrence chasing them through the parking lot of the Day's Inn. "And he was Edna Mae's boyfriend, but I don't think she wants Jimmy Lee to know that right now. Sally Beth was just saving her the embarrassment."

"Oh," mused Granny. "Well, I sure hope this Jimmy Lee's a good man. Edna Mae doesn't know how to pick them out, and I tell you the truth, I worry about her. She's dragged in some real sorry ones, and I hate to think of her getting mixed up with another bad man."

Sally Beth patted her shoulder. "I can vouch for Jimmy Lee. I know he's kind, and he will be good to Edna Mae. He comes from real proud folk. They don't go running over their women." She did not see the need to discuss Jimmy Lee's infatuation with Geneva or his tumultuous relationship with Myrtle. She was certain that once Jimmy Lee found the right woman, he would be as true to her as he was to Lamentations. If nothing else, his grandmother Lenora would see to that.

Granny nodded. "I think losing her daddy so young messed her up. Bad as it was on me losing my only boy, it was a whole lot worse on Edna Mae and Sarah Jane. I don't know what would have happened if they hadn't gotten away from that sorry louse their mama took up with." Blinking back tears, she picked up a platter to wipe dry. "John Harold was a good boy, sweet as an angel, and he turned into a fine man, a real good husband and daddy. But he lacked discernment when it came to women." She paused, shaking her head. "Maybe little Edna Mae got that from him. No discernment. That's a gift not everybody has."

It was late when they finally went to bed. Jimmy Lee ended up sleeping in his truck with Lamentations. Sally Beth and Lilly shared the only guest bedroom, and Edna Mae slept with Granny.

Holy God, thank You for people like Granny. And Edna Mae, and Jimmy Lee, and thank You for giving me a loving family and for the gift of discernment. I like that, she mused, letting her thoughts drift to the boys she had loved… *no, not loved, not really. I guess I nearly loved them, or maybe thought I loved them, but… anyway, thank You for sparing me the pain of wrong love, and for giving me the goodness of right love, especially Your love.*

August 16, 1978, Texarkana, Texas

Their leave-taking the next morning was bittersweet. Edna Mae hugged them tightly, and so did Granny, and Jimmy Lee did as well, explaining that he intended to stay on another day or so, just until Edna Mae "got sorted out," whatever that meant. They finally left around midmorning, after eliciting a promise from Edna Mae that she would soon visit them in Tucker. Jimmy Lee stood aside, grinning and nodding like the little bobble head dog that sat on the dashboard of his truck. He looked very, very happy. So did Edna Mae.

The traffic into Memphis was awful. As they got closer to the exit on Elvis Presley Boulevard, the traffic crawled to a near stop. After noticing an ELVIS LIVES bumper sticker on the car in front of them, Lilly and Sally Beth realized that the traffic jam was due to the number of people who, like themselves, were on the way to the ceremonies at Graceland.

Sally Beth began to feel a little claustrophobic. "Do you think we will even get near the Elvises? The choir, I mean."

"I don't know," answered Lilly uneasily. "And even if we do, I'm not sure we'll get the chance to talk to them. I'm beginning to think this is a bad idea."

"Me, too," offered Sally Beth thoughtfully. Without Edna Mae or Jimmy Lee, the trip had lost its flavor. She suddenly felt a wave of homesickness, made even worse as she looked out over the miles and miles of creeping cars ahead and the blue haze of exhaust fumes swimming along the road. This was not the way to honor Elvis, alive or dead, and she felt sure her mother would forgive her if she missed the events of the day. "I'm ready to be home," she said.

Lilly fell quiet for a moment before she sighed and said, "I can get off here and head east. Just say the word."

"Don't you want to see Elvis Tommy?"

She shrugged. "He knows where I live. It's going to be a madhouse down there, anyway. Do you want to see Elvis Chuck?"

Sally Beth thought about it. Elvis Chuck had been nice, but when she probed the depths of her heart, she knew that it was unruffled and unstained with any hope for Elvis Chuck. He was nice, and the song he had written for her had made her feel pleasantly achy inside, but music alone could do that, she knew. It didn't necessarily mean she had developed an ache for him. Lifting her arms high into the empty air above her, she laughed as she opened her hands to release the last, lingering desire for the handsome man from Utah. "Let's go home!" she said, as she snugged the string tie of her pink princess cowboy hat up tight under her chin.

Ten

August 17, 1978, Tucker, West Virginia

When Lilly and Sally Beth rolled into their driveway, they were met with the sight of their pretty little house, looking extraordinarily neat and new. It took them a minute to realize that not only was there a new roof, but the repairs to the windows were so well done they looked like brand new windows. Also, the house had been painted, the flowerbeds had been weeded, and the flowers had multiplied during their absence. Lilly was happy to see it all looking so good, but Sally Beth grew alarmed as she noticed more things that had been done.

Inside, the place looked even better. The hardwood floors gleamed. The cabinets had been repaired and painted. The Knights weren't there, but Lilly found a note on the kitchen table. She read it aloud as Sally Beth looked around the house in wonder.

Dear Sally Beth and Lilly,

Welcome home! Sorry we weren't here when you arrived. Lenora is canning this week, and she needs me up there to help. I guess you can tell the house is painted! Some people came by, they wouldn't say who they were, but I think maybe they were from some church? They said that they take on one big "surprise!" project a year and you had been picked this year because of the work you do at the nursing home and the hospital, Sally Beth. Nice of them, huh? That just goes to show how much you are loved and appreciated!

Howard fixed your cabinets and did a little painting on the inside. He just felt like puttering around, and before we knew it, we decided to paint. Hope you don't mind! I wanted to see how the colors I have picked out for my house looked in a real room, so we tried them out here. If you don't like it, we'll come back and repaint for you.

I found this new floor wax that I tried out on your floors, too. I wanted to see how it worked before I put it on mine (we sure have been experimenting on your house), and I think it made the floors look good. It's the least we could do after missing your mother's funeral.

It was great to be so close to town and have the place to ourselves. We got a babysitter and went to a movie twice, and I got a level place to stroll Blue around every day. It felt like we were on vacation! As a thank you, I have a little housewarming gift for you on the beds—some sheets I got at my favorite outlet in DC—they are seconds, but I don't think you can even tell.

Geneva had loved writing the little lies in the letter. The sheets were 1000-count Egyptian cotton from the best store in Paris, and the painting and extra repairs had been done by the craftsmen who were building her own house up at the Jumpoff. She hoped that Sally Beth and Lilly would not notice the fact that they also had shored up the foundation, installed new windows, fixed the termite damage in the attic, replumbed and rewired the whole house, refinished the floors, deepened the well, and pumped the septic tank. She was a little nervous that they might notice that the roofing had been upgraded substantially, or that everything that could not be seen easily in Sally Beth's car, from the windshield wiper blades to the brakes had been rebuilt or replaced. Howard wouldn't let her put new tires on it, even though they were looking worn, because that would be too obvious. Geneva felt a delicious little thrill as she thought about all the things they would not notice, but that would improve the lives of her two cousins. She had laughed as she signed her name. "I could get used to this!" she exclaimed. "It's better than hiding Easter eggs."

Howard shook his head. "It's a good thing they were gone only two weeks. It would be hard for them not to notice the whole house had been rebuilt. You'd better watch it, sweetheart. Until that mine is all played out, we can't let nobody know how much we got. I don't know how much we can pretend to get from our 'oil well,' but we don't want to have to put a fence around that whole mountain."

"I know," replied Geneva sadly. "I almost wish you hadn't found that new vein. We have so much more money than we need, and until we can really start giving it away, it isn't much fun. But you know, oil wells can pump out a lot of money, so maybe we can get by with a little more, especially if we can spread it out so nobody gets enough to be suspicious. And there's always 'Mr. Anonymous,' and 'church groups.' "

"Yeah, but if word gets out about that gold, you can kiss that pretty creek—and that mint patch—goodbye."

She smiled and put her arms around him, kissing him soundly. She would do anything to preserve that mint patch.

Oh, God, I am so happy to be home! Thank You for the best trip, thank You for getting Lilly back home, and for Geneva and Howard, who did a lot of work, too, and oh, these sheets!. I feel like a queen. They are the prettiest shade of pink, and they exactly match the paint that Geneva has put on the walls of my bedroom. And the living room is the nicest, softest green I've ever seen.

And thank You for those complete strangers who painted the house. I wish I could thank them. You know, it would be fun to go and do something nice for somebody and not let them know who it was. Maybe Lilly and I can find some project like that. Just go and surprise somebody who really needs help. That seems like the most fun thing in the world to do....

She let her gaze slide over the pink walls in the moonlight and forgot she was praying, letting her mind dwell on the highlights of the trip. She was just thinking about Elvis Chuck when the Voice came to her so plainly and so different from her train of thought that she couldn't mistake it for her own meditation:

Prepare yourself to go.

Her drowsiness left her. *Lord, I already went! And now I'm back. What on earth do You mean?* But silence echoed in her ears, and presently, sleep crept over her, and the next thing she knew it was morning with glorious, golden light streaming in through the window. She was so happy to be home as she fluffed up her pillows in their new pillowcases that she felt like singing.

Some bright morning when this day is o'er, I'll fly away
To that home on heav'n's celestial shore, I'll fly away!

August 18, 1978

She made breakfast for herself and the sleeping Lilly before tiptoeing out the door, leaving a plate of pancakes for her sister. She didn't have to be back at work until Tuesday, but Fridays were always busy with walk-ins, so she figured they could use her today. Besides, she wanted to tell everyone about her adventures. *Just wait until Fanny Sue finds out about Elvis being alive.*

The engine cranked up just as smooth as could be on the very first try, which surprised Sally Beth. It had been sitting for two weeks, and usually she needed to give it a jump if it had been a while since she had driven it. *Thank You, Lord,* she breathed, and backed out of the drive. Everything about her life was good.

The Corvette was parked in the same place when she returned, and Sally Beth guessed Lilly had not been out all day. She found her sitting in Daddy's big armchair by the window, a pile of photographs in her lap.

"*Heeey Sally Beth!* Guess what I found out today?"

"What's that, Lilly?"

"The community college over in Mt. Jackson offers an Associate's Degree in Photography! I didn't know you could study something like that. I mean, there's a *whole lot* you can learn about photography, enough to take years to learn. And some colleges have a major called photojournalism. That means you can become a newspaper photographer, or—*get this*—a photographer for a magazine like *National Geographic!*" Her eyes were wide with delight. "Imagine that. You can get a job where all you do is take pictures all day long."

"Really? That sounds like fun."

"I know. I thought you had to study something boring when you went to college, like history or math or something. I didn't know you could learn *fun* stuff. I've been on the phone all day. I talked to this guy in the photography department, and he said that graduates go on and do all kinds of things, like become fashion photographers, or travel photographers, or take pictures of famous people. Sally Beth, this is *perfect!*" She glowed with excitement. "I could do just a two-year program at the community college and I don't have to go on to the University. I could get a real job taking pictures right away. Classes start next week, and this guy said his classes aren't full and I could get in right away. And if I decide to, I can get a full degree, 'cause they have a photojournalism program at State."

Sally Beth was astonished. Lilly had wanted to go to Tech, not State, because Tech had more male students. Now she was not even mentioning her desire to get a man. She was talking about getting a real job, doing something she really wanted to do. She was so proud of her baby sister she could have popped.

"Now, come look at these," said Lilly, picking up a stack of photographs. "Here are the pictures I took with Lawrence's camera. I've been going through them and trying to figure out what I did that worked and what didn't. See, look at this picture Lawrence took of you, and here's a similar one that I took. You see how in this one you stand out real sharp against a fuzzy background and the light seems to pour out all over you? And in mine, you just look flat against the background, and the light isn't great. I've been reading the instruction booklet, and a lot of it has to do with this F-stop thingy. You can change it to make the background come in or out of focus. And you have to pay attention to the angle of the light. And sometimes you use a flash even in the daytime to get rid of sharp shadows."

She went on, talking so fast and excitedly that Sally Beth could hardly keep up with her, but then, Sally Beth was more interested in seeing the change in Lilly than she was in photographic techniques. It was nice to see her learning, and so happy about it, she thought, watching her glowing face as she talked and gestured, and she wondered and hoped that Lilly was finally growing up.

Thank You, Lord, for Lawrence. Even though we sort of stole his camera, it has opened up a whole new life for Lilly. Thank You, Lord, for Edna Mae. Oh, speaking of Lawrence, would You please make sure he is okay? And help him to be a better man. I don't think he was too happy with himself, but You can change that. Just open up his heart.

August 21, 1978

It was nice that her day off came on Mondays. Sally Beth could run down to the nursing home, get the dogs, and see everybody. She dropped by Mr. Hawkins' room, where she was saddened to see that he seemed lethargic and uninterested in her trip.

"You got a new song for me, Mr. Hawkins?" She hoped that would brighten him.

"Naw, honey. I don't feel like much today. My Tilly, she told me to cut all that out. All the cussing, too. She's left me until I can behave better." His sad, old eyes grew red.

Sally Beth couldn't help but smile. Mr. Hawkins' wife had been dead for eight years, and still, she was constantly fussing at him for his bad language and his lusty songs.

"Aww, Mr. Hawkins, she hasn't left you! She's just gone to see Jesus, to get that new place ready. And she's expecting you to have some songs for her when you get there, but I bet she'd like a nice one. Do you know "I'll Fly Away"? I heard Elvis sing it last week, and it sounded real good."

He perked up. "Oh yeah? Tilly likes Elvis." His face clouded again. "I used to know how it went, but I can't remember."

"It goes like this," she said gently, as she settled on the bed and sang about some bright morning when he would see his Tilly and remember everything important again.

Dr. Sams stopped her in the hall as she was leaving Mr. Hawkins' room.

"Sally Beth, I'm so glad I ran into you. Come here into the conference room; I want to talk to you about something." He guided her into a small room furnished like a cozy living room. Once she was settled, he began without preamble.

"I belong to a medical mission group, and we all take turns going to Africa every few months. I went three years ago, and I'm due to go again in a week. It's a great group, and we do an amazing amount of work in just the few months we are there. We had our group together, but one of the women who was to serve in a support capacity had to back out at the last minute. I was wondering if you'd like to go in her place?" He hesitated, watching her closely. "I thought you might be at loose ends since you lost your mother this summer, and, well, it would be something different for you to do." He added quickly, "Your way would be paid, and we might be able to put together a little salary for you, if you think that's something you'd like to do."

Sally Beth blinked. "Dr. Sams, I don't know what I could do to be of help. Why would you even think of me?"

"You're one of the best I've ever seen when it comes to relating to people, especially people who are sick. You have such empathy, and there's something about you that makes people feel at ease. You're a great organizer, and you aren't squeamish around sickness or injury. We need someone like you to check people into the clinic, to, well, just help out. We can teach you to give shots and administer pills, and you already know how to bandage wounds. Believe me, you'd be a great asset to us."

She didn't know what to say. Sally Beth had always thought it would be nice to see Africa, ever since she had sat with her daddy looking at all those *National Geographics*, but the reality of Dr. Sams' offer was bigger than she wanted to consider at the moment. She had just gotten back from her trip out West, and she was just getting Lilly squared away with her school. She would surely need her for a while, at least.

"I'll think about it," she began, but before the words were out of her mouth, a thought flashed into her head: *Prepare yourself to go.*

Sally Beth sat quietly, stunned, and then heard other thoughts welling up inside her mind. *It would be fun to go and do something nice for somebody. Just go and surprise somebody who really needs help. That seems like the most fun thing in the world to do...*

Mama was gone. The house was in good shape. Lilly was going to start classes, and she really didn't need Sally Beth to mother her anymore, as much as she might want to. There were some things she would have to iron out—but they had a new person just starting at the salon, and... She took a breath and began again, "Well, Dr. Sams, if I go, I'm not so sure I would have a job when I got back, but I'll talk to my boss and see if I could take a leave of absence."

"I have a feeling you're going to learn so much on this trip to Tanzania that you may not want to be a hairstylist when you get back. There's more to you than meets the eye, Sally Beth, and maybe it's time you found that out for yourself. I need to find somebody to fill this role right now, tonight, even. I can give you until tomorrow morning to think it over, I guess, but it's already almost too late to get you a passport and visa. Fortunately, I know some people at the Tanzanian consulate, and we can drive over to DC and get it all done in a couple of days. I know it's sudden, but something tells me this is what you need to do. And we need you."

Prepare yourself to go. Just go and surprise somebody who really needs help. That seems like the most fun thing in the world to do.

She sat up straighter, filled with a power that welled up to push the words out of her mouth. "No, I don't need to think it over, Dr. Sams. I'll go."

Part Two

The Hymns of Graceland

Eleven

September 4, 1978, Kyaka, Tanzania

Sally Beth woke to the sound of a rooster crowing. As she rose from the depths of unconsciousness, she thought she was talking to her mother. *I thought you got rid of Doolittle. Oh, I did, but he keeps popping back up. We'll have to put him in the freezer, I guess.*

That didn't make sense. She rolled over, fighting her way through wispy shreds of visions. The bed creaked, and new smells wafted into her dreams, dissipating them like water vapor under a scorching sun. Doolittle crowed again, a raw, raucous screech that jerked her, floundering, into a bright, scented, noisy morning. A cracked concrete ceiling swam above her in the shimmering light; an unfriendly, narrow expanse of canvas embraced her from below. This was not her own bed with the glorious pink sheets from the outlet mall in DC, but a slender cot, made up with scratchy sheets in a small, concrete room that smelled faintly of disinfectant. A stunningly bright shaft of sunlight streamed through the window, reminding her that she was halfway around the world from her pink room, her pink sheets.

The rooster crowed a third time, prompting her to fling back the covers. Dirty and sweaty, she was wearing panties and the limp shirt she had traveled in. Her pink princess cowboy hat lay on top of jeans, a bra, and her jeweled sandals resting on the floor. When they had arrived in the middle of the night after a day and a half of flying and waiting in airports, she had been so exhausted she had crawled gratefully into the narrow cot without even brushing her teeth or washing her face for the first time she could remember.

A makeshift screen stood in the corner of the room, concealing a toilet and a sink with a small mirror above it. Making her way across the cool, cracked floor, she gazed into the mirror, but she could not see much in the murky reflection. Just as well. She could imagine how bad she must look. A quick search through the luggage piled on the floor yielded toothpaste and personal grooming items, and pulling a chair over to the sink, she placed her toiletries there and went to work.

After she felt a little cleaner, she pinned her hair up into a modest bun, put on a fresh dress, and stepped out into the most glorious sunshine she had ever seen. She imagined she was walking inside a diamond.

The light amplified and enriched the color of everything she saw, from the vibrant red dirt at her feet to the towering celadon trees over her head. The sky above was a pale azure, while the colors of the land were deeply saturated, steeped in light and life. She was standing at the edge of a garden that sang to both her eyes and her ears: green, gold, red, and countless other hues lay carelessly flung on bushes, on trees, on the ground, on slender stalks and fat ones. Monkeys and frenzied birds laughed and frolicked in the huge trees. She had never seen such an extravagance of color, light, noise, and life. The place sang of innocent sensuality, as if the Serpent had never entered Eden and shamed it into modesty.

Beyond the garden lay a large, flat lawn that surrounded a stone church more than two hundred feet away; the bell tower rose like a sentinel into the soft blue air. To her left and right stood a cluster of buildings linked together in a continuous arc, and where the buildings ended, a stone wall with an iron gate beyond the church completed an irregular circle.

The buildings beside and behind her were utilitarian, concrete structures that looked as if they had been hastily thrown up decades ago and had aged poorly, the blocks chipped and roughed-up, the windows cracked and leaning. The plain, hard surfaces were softened, though, by all manner of vegetation: bushes and spires of flowers, blooming vines surging upward in pulsating tints, growing over the roofs and even into the cracks in the windows. Next to one of the buildings stood a young man with red hair and skin the color and texture of badly-tanned leather. When he saw her, he waved as he called out to her.

"Hello! You're Sally Beth, right?" His voice carried a relaxed, friendly American accent that sounded like home. "We met last night, but you were so tired I think you were past caring. I'm Red." He laughed. "For obvious reasons. Red Thompson.

"They're still serving breakfast, so I'll walk you over to the dining hall. Your group is still there—at least, they were just a minute ago when I left them. Come on." He led her through a maze of more old, tired concrete structures to a large building that exuded breakfast smells and noises.

Suddenly ravenous, Sally Beth hurried forward, but between herself and the door of the building stood a knot of women, the most colorful people she had ever seen. Some were very black, blacker than she could imagine people could be, like the purple-black tail feathers of Doolittle, the Marans rooster of her dream. Others were lighter, the color of milk chocolate, but all of them were beautiful in their own way, dressed in wildly colorful clothing, glowing with health, with dazzling white teeth and shiny skin. Some of them were slim and tall, sporting completely bald, perfectly shaped heads, balanced on long, graceful necks. Others wore bright headscarves and lengths of cloths wrapped around lush bodies. Sally Beth blinked, taken aback by their openness, then suddenly she found herself surrounded by at least a dozen of these stunning, shining women, smelling of warm woman-flesh and spice.

Red halted, touching Sally Beth's arm. The women were staring at her. Some were laughing openly, others hid their smiles behind their hands, but all had friendly, bright, inquisitive eyes, and some seemed to want to reach out to her. They all murmured in musical voices. "They are fascinated with you, Sally Beth. They rarely see fair-skinned people. When I first got here, I could tell they were dying to touch me, but they didn't because I'm a man. But they want to feel your hair. Would you mind? They mean you no harm. They think you're beautiful."

Sally Beth hesitated, but only for a moment. These women looked so beautiful, of body and of spirit, she was not wary of them. She smiled, nodding, and reached up to pull the pins from her bun, then, as the hair was freed, shook her head and let it flow out toward the women.

They rushed to her, hands outstretched, stroking and petting her, exclaiming over the texture and color of her pale hair. They rubbed it between their fingers and then brought it to their faces to stroke along their cheeks. "Beautiful!" they cried. "So soft, so fine! So pale, like silk, like the moon! Like the moonflower!" Some brought it to their noses and sniffed the floral scent of Sally Beth's shampoo, and then they exclaimed more. Sally Beth reached out likewise, running her fingers along the smooth, supple skin on their arms and faces. Suddenly, they all began to laugh, and Sally Beth felt the happiness welling up in her chest like a flower blooming. There was nothing here that she had ever seen before. It was nothing like home, but somehow, she felt as welcomed as if it were.

It took her a week to get used to the light, and even then, she was astonished by it every day the minute she stepped out of her room. It came quickly into the mornings, splitting open the cold, indigo nights, blooming upon the land with a suddenness that never ceased to surprise her. At home, in her mountains, the light came creeping in softly, at first barely perceptible, and then gradually turning the air into a soft, watercolor dawn before it stretched up, tiptoeing over the tops of the trees and the mountaintops until the day sparkled through prisms of dew or ice. At home, the light flirted demurely, playing with shadow and wind; here it rained down uninhibited joy, unfettered and free.

Thank You, Lord, for bringing me to this. I have been living in a watercolor world, not even imagining that this kind of color existed.

In the beginning, her job was undemanding. All she had to do was check in patients as they came to the medical clinic, taking their names and performing basic triage. Most of the people spoke a musical, highly formal-sounding English; those who did not were sent to Falla, a small, black-skinned woman, delicate as a bird, who wore floating, colorful dresses and bright scarves on her head. It seemed that Falla's primary task was to lend serenity and grace to the aura of the waiting area, although she also made tea and translated, for she spoke several languages. Sally Beth fell under her calming spell the moment she came into the room each morning, sensing that everyone who received one of her smiles immediately felt better, no matter how bad their condition. Falla's face was the first of the healing anyone received at the clinic.

Before a few days had passed, Sally Beth began to soak up knowledge that floated among the medical personnel: how to give injections, how to irrigate eyes and wounds, to palpate for broken bones and sprains, when to merely clean and bandage a wound by herself and when to bring it to the attention of one of the doctors or nurses.

She became used to the privations and general poverty of the area, the scarcity of clean—and especially hot—water, the intermittent hours of electricity, and the lack of anything soft or luxurious, but she never grew used to the unbridled joy of these African people she had come to serve. They brought their wounds and their illnesses like offerings, cheerfully submitting their pains and their bodies to the hands of the medical workers who touched and prodded them. Smiling, laughing easily, speaking in soft, musical murmurings, they made Sally Beth's heart expand with what seemed like a never-ending flow of joy.

Oh, Lord, I came here hoping to share Your love, and now I find it is heaped upon me. This must be what heaven looks like.

September 9, 1978

On her first day off, Sally Beth spent time getting to know the people who worked at the mission. The pastor of the church was Mr. Umbatu, a tall, slim young man who informed her that he was of the Haya people who had lived on this land for thousands of years. By his side was Lyla, a beautiful young woman, a little lighter skinned, dressed in a purple, blue, and yellow dress. Around Lyla's head was an elaborately tied scarf, and she wore large gold earrings that hung halfway to her shoulders. Sally Beth found her elegant and glamorous.

"I am happy to meet you, Sally Beth," Lyla purred in a soft tenor. "My fiancé Pastor Umbatu is proud of his people, but I, too, am of a proud people. I am of the Sukuma." She laughed as she looked up at Pastor Umbatu. "We are rivals from generations back, but our hearts are bound together, so we are like Romeo and Juliet!"

September 16, 1978

The second Saturday, Dr. Sams took her through the gates set in the stone wall surrounding the mission to the village and adjacent countryside. They walked down a road as red as poppies in the shimmering sunlight to the banks of a wide, muddy river.

"This is the headwaters of the Nile, Sally Beth. Here it's called the Kagera, but it flows into Lake Victoria, and it becomes the Nile when it leaves there. If you've seen the movie, *The African Queen*, some of it takes place on this river."

"I've seen the movie. I never dreamed I would see this. It's wide to be a headwater."

"Yes, but it's much wider at Cairo. And below there, it can be vast during the flood season. I'd love for you to see it."

They turned to walk back up the hill toward the village. "You look happy, Sally Beth. I knew you would thrive in this."

"It does beat doing hair all day long. I mean, I love making people beautiful, but it's even better making them well. Being here is more than I ever thought it could be. Thank you for bringing me here."

He laughed. "Thank you for coming! It was very brave of you, actually. I understand this is only the second or third time you've been out of the mountains."

"Yes. I went to Washington, DC, on my senior trip in high school, and, well, you know I just went out West last month. Gosh, it seems like a year ago. I've done more traveling in the last month than my whole family has in generations."

"Well, I have a feeling that now you've stretched your wings, you'll be flying off to all manner of new places." He glanced ahead to the ramshackle village they had passed on their way to the river. "Here we are. This is Kyaka. It isn't much, but soon I'll take you down to Bukoba, which is much more impressive, and you can see Victoria Lake, although you won't be seeing where the Nile comes out. That's in Uganda, not a place we want to be going right now. It is a country in crisis, run by a despot, backed by an army of thugs. I'm sure you'll be hearing more about that. Since we're only about twenty miles from the border, we often get refugees from there coming to the clinic. They're lucky to find a way out." His face grew sad for a long moment before he brightened again.

"But the lake is really beautiful. And in a month or so, we'll shut down the clinic for four days so we can all go on safari. You'll get to the see the Serengeti, and Kilimanjaro. You'll get to do the whole

African experience." He laughed. "Well, not the whole thing. That would take years. Just a part of it." He fell quiet again before adding almost shyly, "An extended stay after our three months stint here might be possible. I could show you more."

They spent an hour wandering around the village, where some of the people recognized Dr. Sams. Most were friendly and very curious about Sally Beth's pale skin and hair underneath her cowboy hat, but they did not give her the same enthusiastic reception the women had given her at the mission on that first morning. A very few looked openly hostile.

"Don't mind them, Sally Beth. Some people here hate whites, for various reasons, some of them legitimate, some not. His voice dropped to a low, almost warning register. "They are not like us. They have their own way of doing things, their own line of thinking, and some are still resentful of the colonial government that was here until the early part of this century." In a lighter tone, he added, "Well, the Christians are welcoming, especially the ones who have been living or working at the mission. As followers of Christ, we have something in common, and they are slow to take offense when we come off as arrogant or condescending.

"But you'll find that kind of thing anywhere—people who are suspicious of anything that is alien to them. Just keep to yourself when you're off the compound and don't be too friendly. They will come to you if they want to be social, and eventually they'll come to accept you. Most of those who have been to the clinic appreciate what we do, although surprisingly few of them have been there because they can treat their own illnesses very well. The Sukuma especially have a very good knowledge of herbal medicine." He nodded to a tall, thin, somber man wearing a burnt orange-red, tunic-like garb and carrying a spear. "*Habari ya asubuhi*, Mubabe?"

"*Nzuri*," came the reply. The man gave a dignified nod before slipping away as silently as a shadow.

He turned back to Sally Beth. "He is a Maasai warrior. There aren't very many in this region. Most of them live over on the other side of the lake, but they are cattlemen, and there is good grazing here, so a few have migrated."

He continued to stroll along the dirt road, glancing at people as he passed them. "There are several distinct tribes here. They each have their own dialect, but most of them speak English." Pausing to watch villagers set up shop in the dusty street, he added, "Remarkable people, and very self-sufficient. The ones who don't know us or what we can do for them don't really appreciate our ways, and some resist coming to us, unless they need us for something acute, like broken bones or infections that get away from them. And of course, we try to immunize the children. That's been going on for several generations now, and we've pretty much wiped out the most serious illnesses that we can immunize against. Really serious things requiring surgery or long-term treatment, we take down to Bukoba or Ndolage. The hospitals there can handle most things. Do you want to look at anything in particular?"

Sally Beth stopped at a stall to look at jewelry, but since she didn't know if she was supposed to haggle or not, she merely smiled at the woman and turned to another stall displaying bolts of bright fabrics. "Dr. Sams, do they have sewing machines at the mission?" she asked him.

"Yes, and please call me Jim when we're off campus. There's a pretty strict protocol here, and everyone likes more formal forms of address, but when we're away from everyone, I'd like it if we could be friends." He smiled at her, and she wondered what he meant by that. He was nice, but if she was going to be working for him, she thought she'd better keep things more formal. She nodded, but said nothing.

When the sun rose directly overhead, they returned to the mission where Sally Beth went to her small room to wash the red dust off her hands and face before lunch. Walking back toward the dining hall, she heard the sound of an airplane engine above her, dipping lower, then circling back and dropping behind the church. She ran to it as it rolled around into her line of vision.

A small amphibious plane was taxiing toward her through the grassy meadow that lay behind the church. Sunshine glinted off the pristine, white body and wings and crisp, red letters on the side stood out as if they had been newly painted: MORE MOOJUICE. She laughed aloud, thinking that the owner of the plane would be surprised to know what that would mean to an American.

When he touched down on the grass inside the mission compound, John scanned the field ahead of him carefully, hoping to avoid potholes and bumps. He wouldn't have been so careful in the old plane, but he didn't want to bang up this new one. Glancing ahead, he saw a woman running toward him, and his heart skipped a beat before the sun coming in through the windshield blinded him temporarily. He blinked and looked harder. Was he going insane? Geneva, the woman he had loved and lost was standing in a watching pose, holding her hat on her head, the wind whipping a light pink dress tight against her legs. He rubbed his eyes. Surely, he thought, the sun was playing tricks on him, but still, his heart beat out a syncopation of hope cavorting with alarm. Pushing the brakes until the plane jolted to a stop, he leaped out, ready to race to the woman in the pink dress.

"John!" she shrieked, running to him, and his breath stopped, but then he recognized her and he felt a momentary surge of disappointment, followed by a surprising flush of relief. It was not Geneva, but her cousin, Sally Beth. *Sally Beth, of all people.*

He broke into a wide grin, whooped, and ran to meet her, his arms opened wide, laughing as he hugged her. She was so light, he almost felt he could toss her in the air like a child, but settled for spinning her around and squeezing her tightly.

"What are you doing here?" she asked, amazed at the sight of him. He was bronzed and beautiful, and she was so happy to see a familiar face, she almost kissed him.

"What am *I* doing here? I *live* in Africa. For now, anyway. The question is what are *you* doing here?"

"Oh, it's a long story. I thought you were in Kenya. Isn't that a long way from here?"

"Not really, just over the lake. Nairobi is only a little over 350 miles from here, and I come here all the time to deliver supplies and mail. It takes about two and a half hours in this baby," he said, gesturing toward the plane. "And as of last week, we're going to set up a station at Kigemba Lake, only about ten miles from here."

"Oh my goodness, I'm just beside myself! *Imagine.* You being just a couple of hours away. And coming here. And what a *beautiful* plane."

John's face shown with pleasure. "Yes, I just got it three days ago. I didn't think our program was very well known outside of Nairobi, but apparently, someone who was at the conference where I delivered a paper last year got interested in my project and has made a big donation. He gave us two planes. Along with about $500,000 to set up another station here in the Kagera Region.

"It was the oddest thing," John continued. "About two weeks ago, we got this call from a bank saying a group interested in world hunger—I had never heard of the group—but they wanted to wire money to our foundation, and it was to be used specifically to buy land in Kagera for another experimental station, and they gave us two planes. We're supposed to get involved with local missions, too, but mostly we're to expand this new milk enhancement program. No reason, no other stipulations, just that, so I've been over here looking at places. I found the perfect land for sale at Kigemba Lake just yesterday, and our offer has been accepted." He closed his eyes in a long, slow blink, baffled by his new circumstances. "It's unbelievable. First, we get all this money and these planes, we're buying land, and now here you are. All these impossible things happening all at once." He looked at her closely. "So what are you doing here, 8,000 miles from Tucker? The last time I saw you, you were on your way to Las Vegas. Did you take a wrong turn?"

Sally Beth laughed. *Oh my. It's so good to see him!* "Sort of. Rather, we had some car trouble—that is, Lilly's car caught fire and burned up in Texas, and we just happened to run into Jimmy Lee who saved our hides, and when we got home, the doctor down at the nursing home—he comes here to do mission work, and he had this team all ready to come here, but somebody backed out at the last minute, so he asked me to come, and I had exactly *five minutes* to make up my mind, because we left about a week later. I had to drive over to DC to get my passport and visa and had to go to the Tanzanian consulate, and to Senator Byrd's office to get it all done, and I've only been here since last Monday." She took a breath. "I think that was the fourth. What is the date today, anyway?"

He laughed. "I know what you mean. The time passes differently here. It's Saturday, September 16. Gosh, I can't believe it's you." He hugged her again, knocking the hat off her head, and they both chased after it as it spiraled through the grass, laughing like schoolchildren running through the fields on a summer day.

John ended up staying the night at the mission, with plans to stay off and on indefinitely, for he would be in the region for several weeks while he finalized the purchase on the land, looked at cattle, and talked to contractors about building the barns to house them. That suited Sally Beth just fine. John's familiar face and the cadence of his Appalachian accent, reminders of home in this beautiful but strange land, were a balm to her soul.

September 17, 1978

John joined the staff for Sunday service at the mission church, then for lunch at the dining hall. Sitting at the table with John and Sally Beth were Dr. Sams, Dr. Price, the other American doctor at the mission, the two nurses Janie and Francine, Pastor Umbatu and Lyla, and three people she had not met before: two quiet African men and a very young woman with watchful eyes.

Sally Beth turned to the minister. "Pastor Umbatu, I'd never been to a Lutheran service before I got here. It is very interesting." This was true, at least for about half of the sermon, and then it had ceased to be interesting and instead had become very long. She wondered if all Lutherans went on like that. But the music had been good. They had sung a few traditional hymns, probably for the benefit of the American congregants, but for the most part, the music was very strange to her: loud, joyful, and colorful, with people clapping and dancing, lifting their hands high. Some people jumped about and flailed their hands and arms. It was far different from the quiet Quaker services she was used to.

"Thank you, Sally Beth," he said in his deep, melodic voice. "But I am guessing that you found it too long, and perhaps too noisy? That is what I am told Americans tend to think when they first come to this country. We go on too much with our worship."

Lyla interjected, "Pastor Umbatu! You must not tease our friends. Sally Beth will think you are being serious and she will feel compelled to insist that she liked the sermon very much, and you will force her into telling an untruth." She turned to Sally Beth. "He is only teasing you, my friend," she said. "Although I think maybe he will be fishing for compliments. You must not encourage his vanity."

At that, Pastor Umbatu threw back his head and laughed a deep, long, booming laugh. "Ah, Lyla, you chastise me too much. Our friends will come to the wrong conclusion, that my sweetheart is a shrewish woman—and we know that she is not!"

The elegant, constrained flirtation between the pastor and his lady became more generalized to include everyone at the table. Before long, they all, except for the three newcomers, were teasing and laughing. Not wanting them to feel left out, Sally Beth turned to them.

"We haven't met yet. I'm Sally Beth from West Virginia, in America."

The men remained silent, but the young woman looked at her curiously, lifted her head, and smiled. "Good afternoon," she said in a low, gentle voice. "We are happy to meet you, and hope that you will be our friend in Jesus. I am Alice Auma, and these are my companions, Francis and Joseph. We are soldiers for the Holy Spirits."

Pastor Umbatu stepped into the conversation. "These are our friends visiting from Uganda, Sally Beth," he said, laying a hand on the younger man's shoulder. "They are fleeing the persecutions of Mr. Amin, and we are sheltering them until they feel they must move again." Alice's head came up sharply. She shot him a disapproving look.

"Mr. Amin?" asked Sally Beth.

"Idi Amin," explained the pastor. "The ruler of Uganda, just north of here. Some say he is the president, but some say he is the scourge of Uganda. He has not been known to treat his people well."

Alice spoke up. "We do not fear Mr. Amin. He has no power over us," she said, her eyes steely, and her voice grew stronger. "We move on the orders of Lakwena, the emissary of the Holy Father, and he has sent us here merely for a respite. We will be returning to Uganda soon to continue the battle against evil, and when we win it, we will have a new Uganda, purged of sin and injustice."

The table fell silent for a small moment, and then Dr. Davis spoke. "We are happy to offer you shelter, and we hope you win your battle against evil. None of us is fond of Mr. Amin, either." He brightened as he turned to John. "So, John, that's a beautiful plane. When did you get it?"

"Just three days ago. An American organization. Nice, huh?" He wiggled his eyebrows.

"I'll say. And when do I get to take a ride in it? This afternoon?"

"Hold on! I can understand why you want to ride in it, but I think I need to take the ladies up first." He turned to the nurses and to Sally Beth and Lyla. "Any takers, ladies?"

Janie, a tall, sleek African-American spoke up. "Silly question. We all do! Is it a four-seater? I guess we'll have to fight it out, since there are five of us."

John laughed at the teasing. "We'll draw straws to see who goes first. I'll take you up two or three at a time."

Alice shook her head, "Lakwena forbids me and my soldiers to move up into the sky. We have not purchased that right."

Again, there was a puzzled silence until John spoke again, "Well, okay, then let's see who's going first," he said, reaching into his pocket for a book of matches. Sally Beth was dying to go, but she knew the others were, too, so she said, "That's okay. I have a few things to do. You can all go first. I don't mind waiting."

Lyla looked at her compassionately. "You are a kind girl, Sally Beth. I will wait with you, and we can go up together on the second trip."

Lord God, what a beautiful, beautiful, wonderful day! Just wonderful. What a creation You have made. I have never seen anything like the plains and the forests and the lakes like I saw them today in John's plane, skimming right above them, and the monkeys running everywhere, and when I saw the giraffes—oh! It was just the most wonderful thing ever. They float. They just stretch their necks out and float across the plains as if they are flying.

And Lord, I just love Lyla. She is so kind and funny. I think she will be my best friend here. And thank You for John being here. He looks so much happier now. If it weren't for Howard being so perfect for Geneva, I almost wish she had married John so she could be here, too, and I bet they would have been happy. But Lord, I know I shouldn't make such speculations. I'm just excited and wish everybody could be this glad. I love You, Lord! Thank You. Hi to Mama and Daddy, and to Holy Miracle, and don't forget Edna Mae and Jimmy Lee and Lilly, and poor Lawrence, too—make things work out for good for them. Oh, and please take care of those people I met today who are taking shelter here, and all the good people at the nursing home, and... Sally Beth fell asleep listing all the people she cared about.

Twelve

The days, and the work, became routine and comfortable. Although John spent most nights at the mission, he was seldom seen, for he usually left before sunrise every morning to oversee construction of the new facility at Kigemba Lake, and he returned quite late. Every day as he looked over the day's accomplishments, he felt his heart swell and flutter. Each of the new calves born into the program meant that another child might survive the awful drought that had crippled Kenya, Ethiopia, and Somalia for years. He would breed cattle here in the lush grasslands around Kigemba to give them a good start before moving them to the drier and harsher climate near Nairobi. It was a good plan, he thought, as he murmured a silent thanks to the anonymous donor who had suggested it and made it possible.

The only part of Sally Beth's work that she didn't like was the paperwork, but after Falla stepped in to help with that, she found working in the clinic quite enjoyable, especially since she had learned how to do minor medical procedures. Giving immunizations, taking temperatures, bandaging wounds, and offering comfort to the suffering was satisfying, even fun. Every day new wonders opened up to her.

Friendships grew. She became close to the nurses and to Falla, but she became especially close to Lyla, who taught Bible classes to the children from the village. They managed to take their lunch and tea together almost every day, except on those days Sally Beth was too busy to take a break.

"You must come to visit me at my home this Saturday," Lyla announced one day as she peeled a banana. "My mother and my father, they say I talk so much about you that they are tired of not knowing what your face looks like. It is hard to explain that you are as beautiful and as pale as the rain, so they must see for themselves."

"Pale as the rain? Lyla, the rain is not blonde. It's gray. Or it is colorless! You don't think I am colorless, do you?"

Lyla looked at her closely. "You have not seen the rain come during the day here yet, have you, Sally Beth? When it rains while the sun is shining, it is not colorless at all, but both transparent and all colors. You have pink in your face, and your eyes are very blue. And your spirit sparkles like a prism. Yes, it has no color, and yet it is full of color. I say you are the color of rain, or maybe of gentle music. Will you come for lunch on Saturday?"

September 23, 1978

Lyla met Sally Beth in the foyer of the church and led her out to a large, black car, dusted in just barely enough red dirt to cover the glint of a flawless paint job. Beside the car stood a liveried chauffer who crisply opened the door for them. Lyla obviously was farther up the social ladder than anyone she had ever met before, and Sally Beth felt a fleeting apprehension as she remembered how much she had teased her, elbowing her in the ribs over silly jokes and making fun of her formal style of speech. She should have minded her p's and q's a little better, she thought, as she leaned into the leather seat and felt the cool air conditioning blowing on her skin.

But once they were on the road, her surprise at the car and the chauffer soon turned to alarm as they drove the twenty miles to Lyla's home. She had never seen such awful drivers or such horrible road conditions. It seemed there were no rules here: people herded goats, geese, and cows down the middle of the road amid a cacophony of cars that rushed up behind them, blaring their horns, then swerved around, running up the sides of hills, bumping over debris piled up on the sides of the road. Cars passed donkey carts and each other, even though there were double yellow lines, curves and hills, with cars and trucks coming, with monkeys, cows and herders, and donkeys meandering along the road. They passed on one-lane roads with three or four cars abreast, blaring their horns and jockeying for position as they sped over the potholes.

Dala-Dalas, buses about the size of mini vans meant to carry six or seven people, were crammed with twenty or more. The seats had been removed, and the people all stood packed inside or clung to the sides and back, or swayed on the roof as the driver careened along, seemingly oblivious to the mayhem around or the fact that people almost went flying off every time he hit a bump. The only car that was not badly dented or damaged was the one they were in. Sally Beth had seen some crazy drivers in the mountains at home, but this was far beyond the worst she had ever seen.

If she was feeling dazed by the time they arrived at Lyla's home, she was downright dazzled by where her friend lived. They turned off the main road, through an ornate gate flanked by guards, and drove down a long, shaded drive that ended at formal gardens surrounding a mansion. As far as her eye could see stood hundreds of acres of a banana plantation. When she stepped out of the car, she was immediately greeted by a large, uniformed household staff, just like in one of those English movies.

"This is where you *live?* Oh, Lyla!"

Her friend laughed. "Do not be overly impressed, Sally Beth. We are simple people. My father just has had good fortune and a head for business."

Sally Beth fell silent. There was nothing in her experience to prepare her for this, and she spent the rest of the afternoon feeling like a country bumpkin dining with the Queen.

Oh my Lord! Another stunning day. I was so surprised by Lyla's family; they are rich—but they were so nice. And good-looking, and elegant. It's hard to describe them, except to say they were classy. But that sounds cheap, when I don't mean it to be. They are really, really nice people. But I'm kind of sorry I went. It was nice to think that Lyla is a girl like me. Now I really don't know how to act around her. I nearly passed out when she showed me her wedding dress. It has a six foot train and is covered in pearls. I've never seen anything so fine. I'm sorry we will be leaving here before the wedding in December. She's going to be a beautiful bride.

Anyway, I'm having such a good time here, and it's so full of surprises. One minute I'm ducking because a Dala-Dala *is about to run over us to keep from hitting a goat in the road, and the next, I'm having this elegant lunch with real china and silver, and talking to the richest, but nicest, people I have ever met.*

Thank You for sending me here. Thank You for Lyla and Falla and for Dr. Sams who goes out of his way to be nice to me. He says I am the fastest and neatest bandager he has ever seen, although I really doubt that's true. Everyone here is so good to me, and I'm glad I came.

My love to everybody up there. Give John safe travels as he returns from Kenya, and the people who are running from Mr. Amin. I'll be glad to see John. I hope he will take me flying again.

After that, the days flew by so fast Sally Beth hardly noticed their passage. She got over her awe of Lyla, falling back into the comfortable joking and teasing relationship they had begun, and their friendship deepened over the children. They dallied under the sun; they gamboled across the courtyard and sang songs. It was the highlight of Sally Beth's day when she got to hold a baby or play horsey-ride with a one-year-old bouncing on her knee. Lyla had a playful streak, and together, she and Sally Beth kept the children laughing. In the evenings, Sally Beth talked the staff into playing games with them. She got pretty good at soccer out of necessity; she could not really get them interested in either basketball or softball. When John found out about these after-dinner games, he started returning earlier so he could join the fun. Before they knew it, September had evaporated, and they were facing the month of October, wondering how it could have gone by so fast.

October 1, 1978

Sally Beth was just putting on her hat to go to church when someone knocked at her door. Opening it, she saw John's large form framed in the doorway, looking rugged, yet fresh, like he was well-rested and happy in his element. She was so glad to see him she let out a little gasp of pleasure.

He was wearing a cowboy hat that he had bought the last time he had been to Nairobi. The moment it caught his eye, he had found himself chuckling over the image of Sally Beth and her cowboy hat with a rhinestone crown and bejeweled sandals, bandaging up bloody wounds in the heart of Africa, chattering to patients in her West Virginian drawl, totally unaware of the image she made. He had bought it just because of that happy reminder of her. Today, when she greeted him with her bright face, so full of joy, whether at the sight of him or just the fact of the day, he could not say, he felt a little bubble of happiness rise to his chest and pop like a balloon full of confetti. He took off his hat and swept it into a low bow.

"Milady," he said. "Do you care to go a-flying with me today?"

"You mean now? It's Sunday. I was just going to church."

"Never mind. Most of the Americans skip out whenever they can, and you've been a very good girl up 'til now, so you get to take a day off. Pastor Umbatu understands, and I think he pretty much expects it. These services can be a bit much for us Westerners. And

I've got lots to show you today."

Sally Beth bit her lip. She hated to insult Pastor Umbatu, but to be honest, his sermons were a little tiresome, at least after the first hour, and those seats could get mighty hard. The idea of spending a day with a relaxing, undemanding old friend who shared her roots seemed an easier choice. She grinned at him. "Let me get my canteen. And my purse."

It was a glorious day. They headed straight east into the morning sun, out over the vast, blue waters of Lake Victoria. After about half an hour, John turned slightly and lowered the nose of the plane, bearing toward the southern shore. Flying low over a cluster of huge, white stones jutting out of the water, they disturbed a flock of white and silver birds that spiraled up in noisy song under the shadow of the plane.

"Mwanza Rock," he said, pointing. "And this is the city of Mwanza. It's the second largest city in Tanzania." He pushed the plane's nose upward again, skimming along the eastern edge of the lake. Presently, he circled back and dropped altitude, settling into the water and skating into a sandy beach.

"We'll stop here for a break," he said. "I'm hungry, and besides, I want the sun to get a little higher before I show you some things. I would say it's time for brunch, milady."

He pulled a cooler out of the backseat while Sally Beth spread a blanket on the sand under the cool shade of the baobab trees that grew along the shoreline. He laid out a basket of fruit and bread and handed her a cup filled with mango juice. Leaning back against one of the huge trees, Sally Beth looked out over the blue lake and into the western morning sky, blue and white and as clear as a gemstone, and found that she couldn't stop smiling. Just a few months ago, she had never even been on a plane before. How impossible it was that she should be here, sitting on the sand beside a vast African lake, drinking fresh mango juice and eating oranges. It took her breath away.

"The weather has been perfect the whole time I have been here," she remarked. "Of course, it's always perfect at home in September, but I expected it to be hot here."

"I know, it's remarkable; it's nice all year round, even in the rainy season. We're so close to the equator and so high up, especially in Kyaka, that the temperature is really very consistent and mild."

"Is it high? I see mountains that are higher from there."

"Yes, believe it or not, the elevation is a lot higher than it is in Tucker, but there are much higher mountains all over Africa, Kilimanjaro being one of them, of course. It's the highest freestanding mountain in the world—over 19,000 feet, and where you are at the mission is close to 4,000. Tucker is at more than 1,000 feet below that. One day I'll take you over the Rift, and you'll see just how high it is. The land falls away for thousands of feet."

Sally Beth looked northward across the water. "Is Uganda that way across the lake?"

"Yes. Uganda is in trouble, and the mission is in an uncomfortable place, being only a few miles from the border. There have been some border skirmishes, but thank goodness they always leave the church alone. Uganda and Tanzania have not been friends for some time now, since '71, I believe, when Idi Amin overthrew Obote, the President of Uganda then. Obote came to Tanzania, and he is still here. The rumors say that he is planning to take back the country someday."

"Who do you think those people were who came to dinner last month? They seemed—well, odd, I guess. That girl was so young, yet she acted like she was in charge, and who was that Lakwena she said is giving orders?"

He shrugged. "I don't know. Pastor Umbatu seemed to imply they were hiding from Idi Amin. He's a brutal man—some say the worst since Hitler and Stalin. He's responsible for the deaths of thousands of Ugandans. He even murdered the archbishop of the Ugandan Anglican Church, among others. Rumor has it that he eats the livers of his enemies, and he keeps the heads of some of his victims in his freezer." He shook his head. "The people of Uganda have had it tough for a very long time. Obote was pretty bad, too, I hear."

She breathed a grateful prayer for her own safe home back in Tucker, then sat back to let the peace of the lake and the bush land around them seep into her soul. She tried not to think about Mr. Amin or the terror clawing its way through his country. It was hard to believe that this peaceful place bordered such horrors.

After a few comfortably silent moments, John stood up. "Come on," he said. "There's lots more to see."

Back in the plane, they traveled southwestward, over the great Serengeti, where herds of wildebeests, elephants, giraffes, and countless other creatures ran beneath the shadow of their wings. Sally Beth watched the sun arc over the bulge of the earth: gold, blue and green sailing below her. She delighted to chase filmy clouds, darting in and out of them like a dragonfly through a spring mist. Everywhere she looked, there was beauty and wonder and more splendors. She prayed aloud as much as she talked to John, and always the theme of her prayer and her conversation was *Thank you! Thank you! Thank You!*

Again, he pulled the nose of the plane upward, and as they rose into the morning sun, lifting high above the land, John pointed straight ahead.

"Look, Sally Beth," he said.

She squinted into the glare. John changed angles slightly until she could see, and she breathed a long, *"Ohhhhh."* In front of her, distant but dazzling in the sunshine and cool, bright air, stood Mt. Kilimanjaro, its snowcapped peak rising above a golden cloud.

She could not speak. She had seen pictures of this sight dozens of times, sitting by her daddy's side, thumbing through the worn pages of his *National Geographics,* but nothing could have prepared her for the grandeur, the awesomeness of this natural wonder. "Oh, John," she sighed, her eyes brimming with tears. *"Thank you."*

He could not help but be moved by her simple gratitude, her childlike wonder. "I take it you know what that is."

"Oh, yes. Daddy always said he would love to see it. I imagined it standing over the Serengeti, with elephants in front of it, but never from the air like this. It's... it's... *magnificent!* She believed it might have been the first time she had ever used the word, and she was glad she had saved it for this moment, for it held all the weight that it should as it formed in her mouth. Then she burst out laughing, and John, caught up in her joy, was so delighted with her delight he wanted to show her everything at once. He hoped the time was right, for he knew about a secret place that bloomed with flamingos at some point during the spring months. Murmuring his own hopeful prayer, he headed farther east.

Before long, they came to a bowl in the plains, and to his delight, and to Sally Beth's, the bowl was filled with crimson-winged flamingos sailing through the air, thousands perhaps hundreds of thousands of them, darting in and out, flying in formation, breaking, and reforming again in great waves of scarlet and pink. Below them lay a crucible filled with fire—a deep red lake, and in this lake floated hundreds of what looked like pink icebergs. On these floating islands were thousands more flamingos, dancing and strutting across the water in their elaborate mating dances.

"*Oh*—what is it?" shouted Sally Beth.

"This is about the only breeding ground for scarlet-winged flamingos. The water is red because of an algae that blooms here. The flamingos eat it, and that's why they are so pink. They'll stay that color until the rains come again and dilute the water.

"They build their nests on those floating islands. They're made of salt, basically, or rather sodium carbonate, and it's so alkaline that nothing can live here except for a very few species, the flamingos and the red algae being two of them. That makes for a safe place to raise their young. I don't want to get too close and disrupt them, but if you were to be down on one of those islands, you'd be amazed at how hot it is. It can get up to over 140 degrees. The flamingos build up the nests out of that sodium carbonate that are more than a foot or two high in order to get up out of the heat. It's brutal, and it's an amazing feat of nature that they can even live here, let alone breed and thrive."

He turned the plane south. "Up ahead, that's *Ol Doinyo Lengai*, 'Mountain of God' to the Maasai. It's an active volcano, but with a different kind of lava than other volcanoes. It doesn't erupt, but is always seeping lava made of sodium carbonate, called natron. It's what causes the chemical makeup of the lake, what makes it so caustic. This is Natron Lake."

Sally Beth looked out at the moonscape of the volcano below her. The ground was completely barren, rugged with jagged peaks, burned black, but crusted over with white sodium carbonate. It was miserably, horribly lifeless, but behind her, she could still see the cherry-colored cloud of flamingos, wheeling and dancing their seductive, sensual dance, making ready to mate and start their families.

"Amazing. Out of this dead-looking mountain comes all that glory."

"Yes," he said. "You have it exactly. This is where the legend of the Phoenix comes from. The scarlet-winged flamingo is the inspiration for the myth of the Phoenix."

They flew all the way to see Kilimanjaro up close, then stopped to refuel and returned to the shores of Lake Victoria where John once again landed in the water and skied up to a resort where they had a late lunch on the veranda before heading back to Kyaka.

The mission came into view under the afternoon sun, which sat at the perfect angle to fix a glow upon the church spire, turning it snowy white against a field of green and gold. As they left the plane to head back to Sally Beth's room, her soul felt deeply satisfied and peaceful, and John, too, felt that the day had lifted a burden from him. Flying was, indeed, liberating, and the beauty of Africa and Sally Beth's simple appreciation of it was just the thing he needed to put things in perspective.

Loving Geneva had been complicated. He had never quite known how to relate to her—she had been changeable and unsettling, and he had always felt slightly off balance around her. Of course, that had been one of the things he had found so attractive about her: her restlessness as well as her recklessness and her desire to take hold of everything within her reach. She had seemed to constantly be grabbing and embracing things, including himself. While it was exciting to feel her reaching into him to take possession of everything he was, it was also scary to know that she was capable of it. Being around Sally Beth was the perfect, healing antidote. She was the reverse of Geneva: undemanding, always giving. It wasn't exciting to be around her. She did not have the fire and gusto that Geneva had, but she was a good place to rest when he was weary. He watched as she walked across the meadow, wishing he could be happy with someone like her, but deep in his heart, he was certain he never could. He needed Geneva's intensity, her veneer of sophistication, not Sally Beth's softness and simplicity. His heart would grow fat and lazy in Sally Beth's easy embrace, and that was not something he ever wanted.

As they made their way past the church, Sally Beth's thoughts dwelt on other things: how the beauty of this place existed alongside the pain being borne just across the border twenty miles away. She wondered what Alice Auma had meant when she said the country would be purged from sin and evil, and if there was something she could do to help. *If only people let others exist in peace, if they did not try to grab from others and try to overpower, the world would be better for everyone.*

They both were so absorbed in their own thoughts that they hardly took notice of each other, until she thought of how happy she was that John had revealed such beauty to her this day, and then, suddenly, when he slowed to give her time to catch up to him, she became aware of his physical presence. She had always thought of him as a nice man, someone she felt sorry for because he was so hopelessly in love, and hopeless in his love. But now, as she drew close, she saw the bits of pale stubble on his chin that the razor had missed and the light brown hair curling out from under his hat, and she had a sudden urge to take the hat off and ruffle the curls. She slowed her pace, willing herself to look at the path ahead of them, not the expanse of his shoulders or the way he strode so confidently across the yard.

When they reached her door, she was filled with gratefulness for what he had done for her today, a gratefulness that was mixed with a desire to feel the strength of his arms around her. But she reminded herself that no matter how kind he was to her, John's heart was closed to anyone but Geneva. Looking into his beautiful green eyes and wanting him to know how grateful she was for all the beauty he had given her today, she settled for squeezing his arm and saying softly, "I don't know how to thank you. It was the best day of my life."

He smiled down at her. Sally Beth was a beautiful girl, sweet, and honest, and for a moment, he had a wild urge to lean to her and kiss her pink lips, but a vision of Geneva laughing into the sun and leaping into his arms swam before his eyes, and he felt a great, cold hand clutch at his heart. He tipped his hat and bowed before he walked away.

Lord, I am still stunned from today. You made all this! Your imagination knows no bounds; Your Glory is greater than even this. Oh, Lord, I love You. Please protect this land and the people in it. I hold them up to You, Lord. Please keep them in Your hands.

Thirteen

October 2, 1978

The clinic was short-staffed because Francine was suffering from a stomach bug. As soon as Sally Beth sat at her station at the admitting desk, two young men were brought in with severe burns. One had fallen into a charcoal fire pit, and his friend also had been burned while trying to get him out. The two physicians, Dr. Sams and Dr. Davis, were tending to them, and Janie, the only nurse on duty, was busy with another young man with scalp lacerations and a possible concussion. As Sally Beth sorted through a throng of people with less severe ailments, a young black woman with an American accent came into the clinic with a moaning child in her arms. Sally Beth motioned her to the front of the line when she saw the state of the little girl.

"Your names?" she asked, pen poised over the lines of the admitting register.

"Alethia Bagatui. This is Mara Anihla. We need to see the doctor right now."

"Can you spell that? And what's wrong with her?" Sally Beth

asked the woman as she labored over the names.

The young woman looked grim. "B-a-g-a-t-u-i. They know me here. Never mind the baby's name. You can get that later. She has infection." Her eyes glared, her lips were pressed into a thin line. "Excisement and infibulation." She seemed to fairly quiver with rage.

Sally Beth had no idea what that was. She struggled to write it all down. "How do you spell that?" she asked.

"E-x-c-c—." The woman's impatience got the best of her. "Just put down FGM."

"Triage is right around the corner here, there is a long line, but she looks pretty bad…" Sally Beth stopped. The woman had hurried around the corner, carrying the child and yelling, "I need someone here, please! I've got a baby with a really bad infection from FGM!"

There was a flurry of activity. Dr. Sams rushed from one of the examining rooms with Janie following close behind. He turned to her. "You need to stay with him. I think concussion is evident, and you need to stop the bleeding. Go ahead and stitch him up." He turned to Sally Beth.

"Sally Beth, I need you in here. Alethia, did you just find her?"

"Yes. Her sister brought her in an oxcart. They've been traveling for four days from over near Natron. I asked her why she didn't go to the hospital there, and she said somebody had told her I was the one to care for these children. She's Somali, but this looks like the worst hatchet job I have ever seen. They've used acacia thorns." She blinked her eyes hard a few times, battling the tears that leaked from the corners before she squared her shoulders and turned her attention back to the little girl. The child was nearly gray, chalky looking, and although she was unconscious, she moaned constantly.

"All right. Let's get her clothes off her. Sally Beth, I'm sorry you have to see this, but it may not be the last one you have to see, so you might as well get used to it. Alethia, you just hold her and talk to her. Sally Beth, help me take her clothes off." Gently, Dr. Sams began to tug at her traditional Somali dress. When he had stripped her, he gingerly pulled her legs apart.

Nothing could have prepared Sally Beth for the horror of the wounds between the child's legs. What she saw looked nothing like the genitals of a little girl, but like a swollen, misshapen plum, pierced with inch-long Acacia thorns. Sally Beth gasped, trying hard to choke back the bile rising in her throat, and she had to grab hold of the gurney to keep from collapsing. She blinked, not believing her eyes. The child was almost completely sewn up with thorns.

Dr. Sams gasped. "Oh my ever-living God. This is awful; I've never seen a circumcision this bad. They're usually good with preventing infections, but this looks like they didn't even try."

Though Sally Beth could feel as well as hear the pain and horror in his voice, she could not comprehend what she was seeing, the meaning of what had happened to this child. Her brain fought against the image, disorienting her and causing the room to tilt and the light to swarm. A slow dawning came to her: this was no accident. Someone had inflicted an incomprehensible cruelty to an innocent little girl on purpose. *But why?* Such brutality didn't make sense, did not correspond to her conviction that children should always be protected and sheltered, to be innocent of pain. An amorphous darkness crept across her vision in denial to the sight before her. She simply did not want to see this.

Sally Beth, you are here for a purpose. Do you not know that I suffered more than this?

The darkness fled and the light stilled. She took a breath, standing straighter, and the details of the room clicked into sharp relief.

"Did the sister say anything?" Dr. Sams looked at Alethia while Sally Beth forced herself to listen to his voice. He glanced at her. "You okay?" Sally Beth nodded and took another breath, trying to think about what needed to be done. She could think of nothing, for she was fighting an overwhelming need to cradle the child in her arms.

Alethia shook her head, averting her eyes from the grotesque scene. "She looked sick and poor, and she was very frightened, not only for her sister, but she was afraid someone would be coming after her. I think she may have tried to stop the cutting, or she may not be circumcised and she's an outcast. But whoever she is, she hasn't been well cared for, whereas this child seems fairly healthy other than this."

"I'm starting an IV," he said, reaching for an IV packet and some tubing. "Get me some penicillin, and an irrigation syringe," he barked. Sally Beth jumped to find the supplies.

"How old is she?" he asked.

"Five," answered Althea.

"That would have been my guess. Sally Beth, find Janie and see if she has finished sewing that boy up. If she has, you trade places with her and watch him. Let me know if he tries to go to sleep on you," he added as he turned to find a vein in the tiny arm.

Sally Beth left the room to find the nurse, then, her head still swimming with the image of the suffering child, she sat down to cuddle the boy with the head lacerations. Holding his hand, she focused on his face, smiling as she told him about the antics of her funny little Kit and Caboodle. From a distance, she could hear her own laughter ringing out clear and unforced while the heart within her screamed into subterranean darkness, *Lord God Almighty! Why? Why?*

Later that afternoon, Sally Beth waited until the lines disappeared and Dr. Sams sat down at her desk for tea. She was still reeling from the horror of the morning.

"I know, Sally Beth," he said before she could ask. "You've never seen anything like that child this morning, have you?"

"No, I haven't. Nothing near as awful as that. What happened to her?"

He spoke slowly, with great sadness. "It is a practice among the people here—in all of Africa—to circumcise their boys, as we do in America. Of course, we do it when they are babies, and they are anesthetized. Here, it's considered an important rite of passage, done in a coming-of-age ritual at around puberty. It's very painful, but people regard the ability to withstand pain an important part of being an adult. Unfortunately, it also sometimes leaves them scarred for life, with a lot of problems.

"In some families—some tribes—many, actually, girls are not exempt from circumcision. Some do it at puberty as a symbol of entering adulthood, and some do it early, for a different purpose. I've seen it done as early as three, or as late as fifteen or sixteen. They will cut off part or all of a girl's clitoris, and sometimes the inner labia."

Sally Beth gasped, "Why?"

"It's considered an important step for girls, tradition, a matter of family honor, an entry into womanhood—various reasons— and it's important for some because it ensures chastity. A woman is less likely to be promiscuous if she doesn't enjoy sex." His eyes clouded and he gazed out the window for a long moment before he heaved a great sigh and looked more directly at her. "And then, sometimes, for good measure they infibulate—they sew the outer labia together so that it scars over and seals up. Traditionally, they used Acacia thorns, although not many do now."

Sally Beth stared at him, horrified, as he continued, "As you can imagine, it can cause all sorts of problems. Once the danger of infection is over, you still have to deal with damaged urethras, and although they leave small openings for urine and menstrual blood to pass through, it can be inadequate and urine backs up into the vagina as well as the urethra. Then there's terrifyingly painful sex once the girl is married."

"But why? Why do they do it? And to little girls like Mara?"

He shrugged slightly, his head down. "It's their way."

"Why don't you do something to stop it? Aren't you supposed to be educating people so that they are healthier?" She had never felt such anger. "You have to make them understand how bad it is!"

Looking pained, he brought his hand up sharply to stop her. "I know how you feel. It's more complicated than that, and to tell you the truth, Sally Beth, I can't talk about it right now. I'm just too… tired." He rose, slowly, as if a great weight pressed against him. "We can speak about it again another time, but please, for now, try not to think about it." He walked out the door. She watched him go, her mouth open with rage and horror.

October 5, 1978

Francine was back on duty and the lines had dwindled to nothing. No one sat in the waiting room. It was a cool afternoon, but to Sally Beth it seemed the air inside the clinic lacked oxygen. She looked up to see Falla watching her, eyes eloquent with sympathy, although she said nothing.

"Falla, I think I need to leave early today. Could you handle things the rest of the afternoon?"

"Of course, Sally Beth." Falla's voice was as soft as the warm spot behind Caboodle's ear.

She jumped up, leaving her desk just as it sat, without straightening it up or putting anything away. She could not stand to be in the room another minute. Walking past the shower building to where the bicycles were parked, she took one from the rack and made her way along the Ugandan Road for a short way before she turned east onto a lesser road. She had never been out into the community alone before, but she was not afraid, despite the fact that Pastor Umbatu and Dr. Sams had warned her to be wary. Many of the people she passed along the way recognized her, smiled, and waved. Only once did she see someone scowl and look in the other direction.

She had traveled perhaps two miles when she came upon another fork in the road, where she turned south onto a very rutted, grassy dirt road. She hoped she was following the instructions Janie had given her. The grasslands had given way to bush and forest. The huts she passed looked more dilapidated. Monkeys swung over her head, and she found herself startling at the forest sounds: loud, invisible things crying into the stillness of the day.

By the time she arrived at the white clapboard house with the big front porch beside the grassy meadow, she was covered in red dust. Her pale pink dress had taken on an orange hue, and she was sure her face was reddened by it as well. She brushed herself off before mounting the steps and knocking at the door.

Alethia Bagatui opened the door. Sally Beth smiled, holding out the bolt of fabric she had brought with her, a geometric matrix in bold blues on a white background. At least it had started out as a white background. She wished she had wrapped it up against the red dust. Not knowing what to say, she spent a moment brushing it off before she handed it to Alethia.

"Alethia? Do you remember me? I'm Sally Beth, from the mission clinic."

"Of course, Sally Beth. Please come in. I never got a chance to thank you for your help the other day."

She stepped inside. The house seemed to be laid out like an American house, with a living room/dining room combination. The area was filled with a haphazard assortment of Western toys, books, backpacks, and lined school papers. A crib sat in a corner, and bright clothing lay all over. A vase of lilies sat on the table. Sally Beth could see a messy kitchen off to the left. Four little girls peeked around the corner of the doorway.

"It's okay, girls, come on out. Come meet my friend from America. She helped me the other day when I took Mara to the clinic."

The girls poked their heads around the doorframe, and then one by one, they shyly eased themselves into the main room. Alethia moved about, picking things off the couch and chairs. "Excuse our mess, Sally Beth. We've been very busy lately and haven't had much time for keeping the house up. These are my children, at least four of them. Priscilla, Juliette, Becky, and Lizzy. The others are upstairs doing their homework. Mara and her sister are napping right now. Did you come to see her? To see how she is doing?"

"Yes," replied Sally Beth, grateful that Alethia seemed relaxed and friendly. She glanced at the children. The oldest looked about thirteen or fourteen, the youngest was missing three of her front teeth.

"I..." She faltered, and bit her lip. The image of thorns pinned into Mara's flesh haunted her. "I brought you some material to make the girls some clothes. There are sewing machines at the mission, and I will help you with them. I thought maybe we could teach them to sew, if they want to."

"Sit down, please," said Alethia, picking up little dresses off the sagging couch and piling them onto a table. "Thank you. We have a sewing machine here, and if you would like to help us make up some things, you are more than welcome." She turned to the children. "Girls, please go make Miss Sally Beth some tea. Do you care for regular tea or herbal? We have orange and chamomile." She sat quietly, her hands folded in her lap, offering Sally Beth tea in the most civilized, quiet Southern accent, as if she were not aware that a child that had been hacked and butchered in the most brutal way was sleeping in the same house.

"I... uh, orange, please. It's my favorite. I make it at home. I put orange zest in mine..." She stopped. She wanted to cry.

The girls disappeared into the kitchen, and within seconds, had begun a happy chatter in a language Sally Beth did not recognize. She smiled timidly at Alethia.

Alethia smiled back. "You are wondering about my story? Mara's story?"

Sally Beth relaxed. Alethia was just a Southern girl, just like herself, and open. She felt her preconceived barriers dissolve.

"Yes. They told me about you at the mission, and I have to say, I admire you very much. Taking in children as you do, taking care of them all alone."

Alethia shook her head. "No, don't admire me. Just look at this house. I love these girls, but I am not much of a mother. It's all I can do just to get them bathed and fed and get their homework done. With Mara being added to the mix, and her sister, too, I've been falling apart. Things haven't been getting done."

Sally Beth laughed. "If I were taking care of six little girls—eight counting Mara and her sister—I wouldn't get anything else done, either! Here, let me help you straighten things up. Have you got supper going? I can help." She stooped to pick toys up off the floor.

Alethia did not hesitate. She laughed, jumping up. "Sally Beth, I have prayed for a friend to come and help me. I think the Lord has sent you, and I am not too proud to pretend I don't need your help. Would you mind helping the girls clean up the kitchen so we can start supper? I have to give Mara her antibiotics now, and I left two girls working on their math, and they really need my help. I'll be right back."

She returned a few minutes later while Sally Beth was in the kitchen breading okra and slicing onions. "Stay for supper," said Alethia. I'll radio the mission and tell them I'll bring you home later so they don't worry about you."

Supper with Alethia and the eight young girls was lively and fun. The girls chattered in English, squirming in their seats while trying to be on their best behavior for Sally Beth's sake. Priscilla, the eldest, kept nudging the younger ones, reminding them to eat with their forks, not their fingers. She looked like a prim mother fussing over her little ones. Mara was very quiet, and she still looked ill, but she smiled shyly at Sally Beth. Her sister also was quiet and sickly looking. Neither joined in the general conversation, but talked to each other in subdued tones. She did not understand any of their words. The two went directly upstairs when they had finished eating.

After the dishes were done, darkness descended over the big white house, and the girls gathered closely around Sally Beth. She could tell they were longing to touch her, but they held back, too shy or too polite to reach.

"I bet you girls have never seen blonde hair before, at least not this long and straight," she said to them. Or maybe you haven't

ever seen skin this white? We call this fish-belly white at home."
The girls giggled. She slipped the elastic band off the end of her
braid and began to unravel it. "Would you like to touch it? It feels
different."

Jayella reached a tentative hand forward. The others looked
to Alethia, who smiled and nodded, and before Sally Beth could
completely shake out the braid, they all six were sitting on her lap
or next to her, reaching up to stroke the pale strands.

"Oh!" they cried. "It's so soft. And fine. It's beautiful."

Lizzy made a face. "But your skin looks sick. I can see your
veins through it." She traced a faint blue line on the inside of Sally
Beth's arm.

"Lizzy!" admonished Alethia.

"Oh, I *know!*" exclaimed Sally Beth. "It's no fun at all to have
skin like this. It bruises easily and I can't get out in the sun without
covering up or using lots of suntan lotion. It *is* kind of sickly. I
wish I had beautiful brown skin like yours, or soft black skin like
Prissy's. I bet you don't get sunburned easily." She stroked her hand
along Prissy's thin forearm.

The girls looked at her pityingly. "We still like you, Sally Beth,"
said Prissy. "Your eyes are very pretty." The others nodded. Jayella,
the youngest, patted her cheek. "And white isn't so bad, even
though it looks like a fish belly."

Neither Alethia nor Sally Beth laughed, although both felt
like it, for neither wanted to offend the other. They were both
remembering the racial tensions that existed in the United States.

"It's a school night, girls, and it's getting late," said Alethia. "You
need to go have your baths. Priscilla, please go get them started.
Miss Sally Beth and I want to have a chat."

The children were surprisingly compliant. Without any
complaint, they let Priscilla herd them up the stairs while Alethia
settled onto the couch, patting the place beside her, inviting Sally
Beth to sit. After a moment of silence, she spoke.

"I know it was hard on you to see Mara the other day. But it's
common practice throughout Africa, although the Somali tend to

do it much earlier than most people. It's not often they get infected. They have their own medicines that work pretty well." She paused before adding softly, "It's rare that they are sewn up with acacia thorns, though. That's what they used to use, but now they tend to use regular needle and thread." Noting the look of horror on Sally Beth's face, she hastened to add, "They do anesthetize, or some do. And the girls bear it pretty well. To them, it's honorable to endure it."

"But why?" burst out Sally Beth. "Why do they do it? *Who* does it? And why do the mothers let them?"

Alethia shrugged. "It's tradition, an important rite, and it's considered a matter of—well—personal hygiene, sort of, and it's considered more aesthetically pleasing—and, to tell the truth— because mothers want their daughters to keep the family honor, just like our mothers back home." She glanced slyly at Sally Beth. "Your mama ever tell you you'd better be a virgin when you get married?"

At Sally Beth's dry smile, Alethia said, "It's just that their methods are more extreme." She touched Sally Beth's shoulder and added gently, "It's a different culture, Sally Beth. It's hard for Westerners to understand."

Alethia took a deep breath and went on, "My grandparents were Maasai; they became followers of Christ right after they got married. My grandfather felt called to preach the gospel, so the priest who ran the mission invited them to America to get an education. After Grandfather graduated, he got a job teaching at Payne University up in Ohio, so they ended up staying in America, but they came back to Tanzania as often as they could. My mother met and married my father here—he was working at the mission she came to every summer when she was in college. Then she started working at a church in Alabama, and they got married the next time she came back. He went back with her, and I was born there. I've lived both here and there for most of my life—my parents came here often. Their church in Montgomery is a sister church to one near here, and we've been the go-between, so to speak."

Sally Beth grew impatient. If Alethia were so comfortable with the people here, why didn't she do something to help raise awareness? Something to stop it. "I don't understand why people don't speak out against such a barbaric practice. I mean, it seems savage, one of those things that make people think Africans are not civilized. I grew up hearing that Africans were cannibals."

Alethia shrugged. "Some of them are, and some of those are kind and gentle people otherwise. But Africa is many nations, many peoples; some are crueler than others, just like anywhere else. My people, the Maasai, are considered savage and warlike, and they circumcise their girls, but they respect the dignity of other humans. They've never kept slaves—have never sold even their enemies into slavery. Then, tribes in Guinea are considered more peaceful, but they enslaved the people they conquered and sold them to slave traders. In the same way, not every tribe circumcises. Different people have different ways of seeing things."

Sally Beth was affronted by Alethia's casual attitude. "But why doesn't the church do something to stop it? Nobody talks about it at the clinic or the mission. It's like they don't care!"

"Oh, they care. We all care very much. But it isn't appropriate for us to interfere." She stopped and looked directly at Sally Beth. "How would you feel if someone from another country came into your home town, set up a church and a medical clinic and began preaching about how awful you and your culture are because you circumcise your baby boys? We have a job to do here, and that's to help people and teach them about Jesus, not to condemn practices that they consider important—and have considered important for a very long time." Seeing Sally Beth's stunned look, Alethia softened her tone. "Many people do give it up on their own once they spend time with us and come to understand that it isn't a universal practice. My grandmother was surprised to find that people don't do it in America. She was circumcised like Mara was and sewn up with thorns. If she had not left here, she may have had my mother circumcised. I have aunts who have been cut, and their children, too.

"But why do they do it in the first place? Hack off parts of little girls that are important?"

Alethia turned to her, hesitating briefly before plunging on. "Okay, which do you think is prettier? This?" She composed her face into a gentle expression, eyes half closed, lips together and smiling slightly. "Or this?" She opened her eyes and mouth wide, baring her teeth and sticking out her tongue grotesquely. "That's the way they look at it. They like a smooth, closed surface. It means chastity and cleanliness, and believe it or not, Sally Beth, it's the women who are the biggest fans of it. Many times, it is the grandmother who performs the procedure, and I've known women who have asked to be reinfibulated after childbirth. That is, they want to be stitched up again."

"Speaking of that, how do they manage? Childbirth, and sex, for that matter." Sally Beth surprised herself at her own frankness with this young woman she had met only two days earlier. But it was important to her to know, to understand. How could these people who seemed so joyful and so kind do this to their children?

Alethia smiled gently. "It's hard to understand. It's a very patriarchal society. It is considered a right of a husband to open an infibulation. It's pleasurable to them. Usually, women have surgery to prepare them for childbirth, but as I said, a lot of women ask to be reinfibulated afterwards."

Sally Beth gasped. "That's awful! And women don't get any pleasure at all, do they? Just the pain!"

Alethia's smile tightened. "People see things differently."

Rage surged through Sally Beth's arteries. She squared her shoulders, resolving then and there that she would change things. "Well, you may think you have no right to interfere, but I don't see anything wrong with it! And I'm going to see what I can do to educate women, to show them that they don't have to put up with that—that—"

Alethia stopped her. "Sally Beth," she said grimly, gripping her hands and looking directly at her. "Do not. Outsiders have tried before, and all it does is insult people and drive them away. It completely reverses the good we can do here. All we have the right to do is to help them and tell them about God's love, not judge them and condemn them." Her eyes grew more intense. "I am serious. You can do a huge amount of damage—to these people, the church, and to yourself." She stopped, started again, and hesitated again.

"Years ago, a Finnish woman went on a campaign to do just that. She went in to educate everybody, especially the women, and told them that FGM was a horrible crime to women—"

"FGM?"

"Female genital mutilation. It's what we arrogant Westerners call it. I shouldn't have called it that in the clinic. It's condescending and belittling, but I was mad and my tongue got away from me. Anyway, this woman from Finland came, preaching against it. She won a few converts, but in the end, the entire village rose up against her, invaded her home one night, tied her to her bed, circumcised her, and then murdered her. This is something you don't go messing with."

Overcome with the knowledge of the horror Mara had suffered, Sally Beth felt like crying, but Alethia would not let her indulge in her anger. "Enough of this," she said. "Let me get you another cup of tea, and then I'll take you back to the mission. I need to get back in time to tuck the children into bed."

"I think I should just go on," Sally Beth said miserably. "It's getting late, and you have a lot to do." She stood.

"Okay," replied Alethia. "I'm sorry I've upset you, Sally Beth. I sort of have gone through the same kind of outrage, although I've had a different perspective because my grandmother has talked about it. Just remember, all cultures do things that other cultures would be horrified about. In America, people get facelifts to keep from looking old. Here, that would be considered an atrocity. I know an American doctor who gets mad at people for piercing their children's ears. It's all a matter of how the culture perceives it. You may not be able to understand it, but you don't have the right to condemn it."

They walked out to the porch. Alethia flipped on the light. "Put your bike in my van. You should never ride into the bush on your own in the dark. You could easily get lost. Most of the people here are kind, and they would help you, but some are not. I don't want to frighten you, but one way some people earn a living here is to kidnap people and hold them for ransom. To tell you the truth, you should not have ridden out here by yourself in the first place. She hurried Sally Beth out to an ancient van that was covered in bright, crudely painted flowers. On one side was written in childish letters:

"For GOD so loved the WORLD, HE gave his ONLY BEGOTTEN SON so that we may have LIFE EVERLASTING. John 3:16."

As she dropped Sally Beth off at the mission, Alethia leaned over to hug her. "God bless you, Sally Beth. I will pray that He will ease your mind about Mara and others like her. Come back any time."

"I'll be back on Saturday," she replied, "and we can start making those dresses."

"I'll pick you up. Stay the night, and you can come to church with us on Sunday. Pastor Kimkutu is no more long-winded than Pastor Umbatu, and afterwards we can picnic on the lake." She grasped Sally Beth's shoulder, giving her a look full of love. "Thank you, God, for Sally Beth. I'll see you Saturday."

Sally Beth felt humbled and beaten, and yet, somehow encouraged. Alethia needed a friend, and so did she, for she was suddenly feeling quite alone and alien in this strange land. She tried to tell herself that she should be less judgmental and more accepting, but the image of Mara's infected wound made her wonder anew what was wrong with people who would allow such a thing.

Lord, I don't know what to do. They tell me my job is not to tell people how to think, even if they think wrong, but just to show them Your love. If You were here, would You allow this? It's hard to know what to do, or even to think, so please show me. And thank You, too.

Despite all this misery, You have given me another friend. Someone from back home. I had forgotten how much I missed it and the people, and just an American accent. And John, too. Thank You for bringing him here. I'm beginning to feel like we all belong to each other.

Fourteen

October 5, 1978

Throughout the next day, Sally Beth nearly made herself sick worrying over the practice of female circumcision. She found herself looking at all the native women differently, wondering if they had suffered through the awful procedure. By teatime, she realized she was obsessing about it. *You should not think about a person in terms of what body parts they have or don't have. That makes you almost as bad as the people who rob these women of them. Think only of their hearts and their spirits.*

She was relieved when, right before supper, John arrived, bringing mail, including a letter for Sally Beth. Glad to have something to take her mind off her conversation with Alethia, she opened it eagerly. "It's from Lilly!" she exclaimed. "John, I'm so excited, I can't read it fast enough," she said, handing it to him. "Will you read it to me? Her handwriting is so sprawly it's too hard for me to decipher." She did not mind if John knew she had difficulty reading. He was as comfortable as an old sweater, and she knew he would never make fun of her.

"Sure," he said. "I'd love to. Now I won't have to wait to hear the news second hand." He took the letter and unfolded it.

September 18.

"Wow, it got here fast! Only two and a half weeks," he said.

Dear Sis, I am having the best—"she's written *best* in all caps and underlined it four times"—*the best time in my photography classes, so much that I don't mind that I am having to take English and math! We have real-life assignments, and for my first one I started going to Tucker High football games and they let me stand right on the sidelines because I told them I was with the newspaper, which of course is a lie, but they are so excited to imagine that a newspaper photographer would come and take their pictures that they let me walk right on the field. I started taking some of the developed prints to the games with me, and their mamas love them—I took close-ups of the boys on the benches, and I am able to capture their excitement—and their misery when they're losing—and they're so cute and little but they think they are grown-up. Anyway, I sold a bunch of prints to their parents, and they went like hotcakes! It's amazing. I haven't even bothered to get a real job because now I am just going out into the streets taking pictures of children playing, and since I'm a girl and I talk to their mamas, nobody minds, and you wouldn't believe it, but I have a real business going.*

In my class we're paired up with a partner for a show for the final—I got the only other "grown-up" in the class (everybody else is only eighteen or nineteen), who is the most fascinating person. He's not my type, in case you're wondering, he's just a little too crazy and rough, (more yours!) but he's very interesting. He has hiked the whole Appalachian Trail and wrote a book about it—he's a real journalist and is taking photography classes so he can include pictures in his books. He also writes real pretty poems. I even understand some of them. Ha ha.

Anyway, he's making me think more (imagine that!), and the professor likes what we are doing so much he is pretty much letting us make up our own projects, which will be worlds above what everybody else in the class is doing. Imagine the difference between Lawrence's photographs and the first ones I took on the road. That's about the difference between our work and the rest of the class.

So, long story short, we are going to finish the project just as quick as we can—there's no need to take the whole rest of the semester to do what we can do in just a few weeks, then we'll keep going and put together a book! Phil, my partner, says he knows a publisher who will publish it! I know these hills almost as well as you do and have a way to get to children, (and to tell the truth, I take better pictures than he does), and he's a writer so we are going to do an "in-depth" (I love that word! Phil uses it all the time) photographic essay with poetry about the mountains, calling it "Flora and Fauna in the Alleghenies," but instead of plants and animals, we're going to call children "flora" and "fauna," because children are as pretty as flowers and as wild as wild creatures. And every picture is going to be either a very beautiful child or one acting wild. Get it?? It's an interesting challenge, making them as beautiful as we can (I'm learning to play with the light, and there are tricks you can do in the darkroom) or catching them acting like a crazy person.

Jimmy Lee is back and guess who came with him??? Ha ha. Tucker has no idea what's about to hit it. So far everybody thinks Edna Mae is fat, and word is out that Myrtle is badmouthing her all over the place. I sure hope I'm there when Edna Mae meets her (tracks her down!) I just hope I have plenty of film in the camera when she does! They're doing it all proper—Edna Mae is staying with Lenora and Ike and everybody is getting along like a house afire. I wouldn't be surprised if you don't come home just in time for a wedding!

I hope you are having fun in Africa, and I wish I was there with you so I could take pictures (and to see you!) Maybe I will come over there someday. Everybody misses you and says to tell you hey.

By the way, Elvis Chuck called you on Sunday, and I just happened to be home for a change. We had a nice, long chat. He said he had called three times before, and he was beginning to wonder if he would ever get the chance to talk to you. Was he ever surprised that you had gone to Africa! Hope you don't mind, but I gave him your address. I don't know what you did on that bus (I was busy myself), but whatever

*it was, it sure made an impression on him. He sounded like he misses
you.*

John stopped here and looked at Sally Beth over the top of the
letter. "Elvis Chuck? On a bus? Have I missed something?"

She blushed and laughed. "Oh, it was nothing. Lilly is just
being silly. Keep reading."

He looked askance at her, but returned to the letter: *The house
is empty without you, but maybe that's because I'm hardly ever there
either. I'm always out taking pictures. Click! Click! Smile! You're on
Candid Camera!*

Love, Lilly.

*P.S. Everybody looooves my car! You wouldn't believe how many
guys have asked me out because of it, but believe it or not, I've been too
busy and working too hard to go out much. I've paid Jimmy Lee $30
already, and I think I can give him $30 every couple of months. He
didn't want to take it, but I told him you would kill me if he didn't,
and he didn't want my blood on his hands. And Edna Mae says she'll
kill me if I mention one more time about paying her anything at all.*

*P.P.S. I'm taking a class called "women's studies" that I signed up
for thinking it would be about how to be a lady—you know, how to
dress, walk, set a table, etc. I thought it would be easy because Mama
already taught all that stuff, and we had it in home ec in high school,
but it turns out it is a philosophy/literature class with stuff written by
or about women. It's not easy, but I sort of am enjoying it. My favorite
author so far is Kate Chopin. Most of those writers have some pretty
wild ideas, but they sure do make you think!*

Love again,

Lilly

Sally Beth made him read it a second time, although she waved
him on when he started reading about Elvis Chuck. She laughed
at the part about Edna Mae and explained to John that Edna Mae
was not fat, except in all the right places and that Jimmy Lee was
acting crazy in love with her. She started to mention that he had
gotten over Geneva awfully fast when she suddenly remembered
that John had been in the same boat, but that John's feelings for

her cousin had run a lot deeper. She fell silent, not knowing what to say without reminding him of his loss.

He made it easy. "It's still early. Why don't we go up for an hour or so after supper, and you can see the sunset from the lake?"

"Oh, John, that would be just *great!*" Her excited little hop made him smile.

By the time they were aloft and skimming over the water, Sally Beth said, "I wish I could fly!" and before he knew what he was promising, John found himself saying, "Why don't I teach you?"

"*Really?*" she squealed. "You'll teach me? When can we start?"

"How about right now?" He started pointing out the instruments to her. "Here, you take over. Keep steady by watching this line here. See? That fixed line is us, and this one that moves is the horizon. Tilt to the right. See how the line is floating? Now, move back to level. That's all there is to it." He sat back in the seat and made a show of stretching and putting his hands behind his head. "Just wake me up when you get back to the mission if you need any help landing."

Sally Beth laughed, and not just at John's little joke. She was *flying*. She held the power of an aircraft in her hands, and she, and she alone, was keeping it aloft. Glancing upward, she pulled the nose of the plane up and sped toward a cloud. She wanted to whoop, she felt so powerful and free. The whole, wide sky belonged to her; she was swimming through air, through clouds, through the golden sunshine and the dust motes alive in the sparkling air.

He broke into her thoughts. "You want to try turning around?"

Yes, she did. She wanted to try loops and spirals and rolls and death plunges, screaming to the earth until the last second, and then pull up sharply into the pale blue sky and then do it all over again. The feeling was marvelous. It was like—like—she couldn't come up with the right word for it, it was so big and freeing and wonderful. She had to make up a word. "It is *tremendglorious!* How *do* you turn around?" She banked to the left over the water without waiting for an answer.

"My word, Sally Beth. You're a natural!"

He let her fly in wide, lazy circles as the sun sank lower, until the huge ball of orange flame just touched the western horizon, and then he asked the unthinkable. "Do you want to learn to land?"

She let out a little shriek. "Oh, *yes!*"

It took her three tries, buzzing the meadow by the mission and setting John's hair on end, but on the third try, she managed a bumpy landing that made him wish he hadn't been so generous with his offer. His brand new Skylane did not need to be jostled by an amateur landing. But he repented of his parsimony when she turned to him, eyes wide and glowing.

"Every time I learn something new, it takes me three tries to get it right, but, by golly, I can *land* this thing. And I can *fly!*"

Walking through the meadow of long, dry grass, gilded by the last sliver of sun, Sally Beth could not let go of the thrilling sensation of taking control of the craft and the air. She took advantage of the growing darkness, falling behind to spread her arms and pretend to swoop and fly. John glanced back once, then forced his eyes forward to give her time to enjoy this moment of sweetness. His own jubilation tickled in his belly.

When they reached the door to her room, he turned to see her gazing up at him, her face luminous with joy, and he felt his heart soften with the pleasure of knowing he had been the instrument of her gladness. She must have heard his thoughts calling to her, for before she could summon the will to govern her actions, she jumped up and threw her arms around his neck, hanging like a sparkling necklace. She was light and warm, vibrating with happiness. There was no choice but to bring his arms up around her.

She felt it first. The strength of his arms, the roughness of his cheek, the breadth and hardness of his chest sent a lightning bolt through her. She caught his scent, like summer grass and wind and sun, and she felt her heart hammering. A soft cry escaped her lips.

It pierced him, too, that lightning bolt, and then he was

overwhelmed by an intense physical response that he never anticipated and did not welcome. Unprepared, he was frightened and angered by how it caught him unawares; he had no business flirting with Sally Beth or feeling this way about her. He tensed.

She felt the sudden apprehension gripping him, making him cold and rigid. Sally Beth let go of his neck; he released her, and she dropped to the ground, face flaming.

"Thank you *so much*, John," she breathed. "Sorry, I got a little carried away there. I've never done anything so *exhilarating* in my whole life!" She gave a little gasp. "Thank you," she said again.

He nodded, ashamed of his reactions to her and of his own fears. "I am real proud of you, Sally Beth. I've never seen anybody take to flying like that. You seem like you were born to it."

"I know!" she agreed. "It felt like it was *me* flying, not just the plane. Like I didn't even need the plane..." She trailed off, then looked up at him hopefully. "Do you think maybe we could do it again? I'd really love to learn and all, and maybe get my license?"

He relaxed. "Of course. I'll teach you. It should take another— oh—couple of minutes for you to learn to take off. Maybe three. I still have my old plane back in Kenya. Maybe I can bring it up here and leave it with the mission so you can fly it when you've learned how."

John swept his hat into an elaborate bow before he made his way back to his room, the shadow of his desire following him like a lost puppy.

Sally Beth was so happy she fell onto her bed with her arms outstretched and reimagined what it felt like to hold the plane in her hands and soar into the heavens. Tanzania was beautiful! People were kind and good. *John* was kind and good. She tried to stop thinking about that, but it was very, very hard.

October 7, 1978

On Saturday morning, Sally Beth packed an overnight bag and

a portable sewing machine and ran to breakfast an hour before Alethia was due to pick her up. Pastor Umbatu stood before the others as he usually did to pray. His face was grave, lined with worry and tiredness.

"My friends," he said. "I have some bad news. Last night I got word that an attempt was made on Idi Amin's life two nights ago. Some dissidents in the Ugandan army who are weary of the way things are staged a raid on his home, but he and his family escaped by helicopter."

There was an alarmed murmur. Pastor Umbatu held up his hand. "Then, yesterday, General Adrisi, the Vice President, was injured in a car accident that he suspects was contrived as a reprisal. As you know, there are many in the government and the military who are unhappy with Mr. Amin. General Adrisi is one of them, and now he and part of the army have declared a mutiny. My friends, it saddens me to tell you that the country is on the brink of civil war, but perhaps some good will come of this. We must pray that this is the beginning of the end of Idi Amin's reign of terror over Uganda, and that God will cause a good and just leader to rise up in his place."

There was a shocked silence before a cheer rose up from the Africans in the room. Pastor Umbatu went on, "Now, let us pray."

The silence descended again. Sally Beth thought about the young Ugandans she had met the month before. Perhaps they had something to do with the attempt on the president's life. They were so young, and they talked of peace; yet, somehow, they seemed to be capable of violence beyond her ken. The thought of death, vengeance, and brutality gnawed at *her* peace, clawing through her mind, until the floor began to spin beneath her and she was forced to her knees. For now, there was nothing else to do but pray for peace and good leadership for the Ugandan people. She took a deep breath, willing herself not to think about Idi Amin or his wrath today, but to concentrate only on what she could do. She would pray for deliverance and she would make dresses for little girls.

Sally Beth and Alethia had a constructive morning cutting out patterns and sewing sundresses, starting with one for Priscilla. "We need to make Prissy's first because all the others get hand-me-downs, and by the time they make it to Jayella, she has way more than she needs," commented Alethia. "Poor Prissy has only four dresses, while Jayella has over twenty." She ran the scissors down a length of fabric while Sally Beth set up the portable sewing machine on the dining table.

"Is this a treadle machine?" she asked as Alethia rolled an ancient contraption over to the window.

"Yeah. We generally go without electricity during the day. I just am running the generator today so you can plug yours in. This treadle machine works fine, and it doesn't use an ounce of power." She wound the bobbin and threaded the machine.

"How did you end up being the mother of six girls?" asked Sally Beth. "Did you get all of them right here?"

"No, I started over in Dodoma. I was studying at the college there my junior year—that was five years ago—and I ended up dropping out so I could work at a mission right there in town. Lizzy was my first. Her mother had died of some sort of wasting disease—nobody could ever figure out what it was, but both she and her husband had it. When her mother died, her father was too sick to look after the children—there were five of them—so her sisters both took two of the younger ones, but Lizzy was left to take care of her dad. She was just seven at the time. When he died, the sisters were overloaded with children of their own, and neither one of them felt like they could handle another child, and they brought her to the mission. I just fell in love with her. I knew she was mine the minute I saw her."

"So you really adopt them officially—you don't just take them in to take care of them?" Sally Beth was growing more impressed with Alethia by the minute.

"Oh, yes. They need the assurance that somebody is going to

claim them no matter what. They've been through so much in their short lives. It wouldn't do for them to think I could just get rid of them whenever I got tired of them. Some of these girls have witnessed unspeakable horrors. What Mara has gone through is the least of it." She bit a thread and held up the partially constructed garment.

"This is going to be cute!" She went on, "There's a law that says a single woman can't adopt, but there are a lot of orphaned children, especially in Uganda. Idi Amin has done his best to make orphans of the entire nation. If kids can make it across the border, they end up in orphanages here, and they're overwhelmed with all the homeless children coming in. The Tanzanian government makes exceptions for Ugandan children with no known relatives, or even Tanzanian children if the orphanages get too crowded. It's not been hard for me to adopt girls. They're more careful about boys, but that's okay by me. I think I am better at mothering girls."

"Are you going to stay here? Will you ever take them to America to live?" Sally Beth wondered if she missed her home in Alabama.

"I go back all the time, but by myself and just to raise money, and I guess my life is here now. I had intended to go back permanently after school—I had a boyfriend back home then, and we were planning on getting married. He was at Auburn, and he'd come over for vacations if I didn't go home, but after I adopted Lizzy, things fell apart for us. I don't think he liked the idea of being a father so soon.

"After that, it seemed like the girls came at just the right time. I got Charlene and Charlotte right after I broke up with David. I was heartbroken over it, and one night I was sitting around feeling sorry for myself, and these two darling little girls, sisters, came to my door and told me they wanted me to adopt them. They were the cutest little things, standing at my door, looking up at me and telling me I had to adopt them because they were afraid the orphanage might separate them. Word had gotten out about me taking Lizzy, and so they figured I could handle two more. It was crazy, but they got me out of my funk in a hurry! I can't imagine my life without them. The rest I got after I moved here. Ugandan." She stopped talking, but her eyes told Sally Beth volumes. Priscilla, Becky, and Jayella did not need to be reminded of their past traumas. Alethia smiled at her girls and gave Jayella a cuddle. "We're a real family now."

Sally Beth was full of questions. She had never met anyone like Alethia before, someone who would sacrifice a comfortable life in America and take on being a single mother to six little girls. And who knew how many there would be before it all ended? "When did you come to Kagera?" she asked.

"Two years ago. I met the pastor at a Baptist church in Kakindu while I was in Dodoma, and he invited me to teach at his mission. I did for a year, then I got Priscilla, Becky, and Jayella, and I got too busy with them to teach anymore. Now I raise funds from America and Canada and that keeps us going. I go over there once or twice a year, do a tour, see my family and old friends. That's how I built this house, with Western donations." She finished a seam and removed a little dress from the sewing machine.

"Oh, gosh, I didn't match up this square up in the front of the bodice," she mumbled through the pins in her mouth. "It's not far off, though. Hand me that seam ripper. I think I can adjust it."

They worked all day. The girls giggled when it was time to try their dresses on, standing on a stool while Sally Beth and Alethia pinned up their hems. If Sally Beth had wanted to broach the subject about how many of the girls had been circumcised, she had learned that it should not be of concern to her as far as Alethia was concerned. But she was curious about something she had said the first day they had met. "Why did Mara's sister say she had heard you were the person to bring Mara to?"

Alethia paused before smiling guiltily. "I know I told you not to get involved, and I have good reason to. I was like you in the beginning, determined to change things. Even though I knew my grandmother had been through it, the first excisement I saw made me so mad I wanted to go storming into every village in Africa and 'enlighten' them." She splayed two fingers on both hands to make air quotes. "I'm afraid I said more than I should have to a village elder once. If you want to know the truth, that's why I am here, and not still over by Dodoma. I am considered a *persona non-grata* there." She smiled again.

"So now you know. I pretty much ran for my life—and for my lady parts!" The smile softened, then disappeared. "I have to be careful, still. My reputation has been hard to live down, and it took a while for the people to accept me. But they mostly have, now, because I have kept my mouth shut. Fortunately, not too many people know about Mara's circumstances. They just think she's another child that lost her family. But she does have a family, and I assume her sister will be taking her back as soon as she is healed."

"Will it be okay for her to go back? Will her sister suffer for bringing her here?"

"No, I don't think so. They love their children, and the fact that she brought her here instead of a clinic nearer her home won't make a difference." She paused, picking at a thread. "I won't reverse her infibulation, in case you were wondering. It isn't up to me, and besides, they'd just do it again once she gets home. I have to do what I can to ease some suffering, and in Mara's case, to get the infection cleared up."

She held up a little dress, eyeing it critically. "Not bad. I am so glad you brought us this fabric." She pointed to the curtains and slipcovers on the couch and chairs made from a bright green, yellow, red, and blue cotton broadcloth, a field of flowers on a meadow. "I have about 2,000 yards of that fabric down in the basement, and I was afraid I was going to have to make every outfit from here on out of it. Some company in America gave their entire stock to me because it has a flaw in it. I mean, it's pretty, but I've made us all curtains and bedspreads and some tablecloths, and everybody a dress out of it. I'll never run out, and I'm sick of it."

"Maybe you could donate it to somebody else. I'm sure people from the village would love it if you gave them some."

"Yes, and then have to look at it every time we go to Kyaka. Sorry. I'll just have to take it to Nairobi next time I get over there."

They went to bed late, after completing four dresses; the others needed only the hems by the time they were yawning so much they finally agreed to call it quits. "We'll finish them up after church tomorrow. Do you want to come to church with us? We go to the Baptist mission a few miles from here up in Kakindu."

"Sure," said Sally Beth. "I haven't been up there yet."

October 8, 1978

They didn't make it to church the next day. During the night, Mara's fever spiked, and by morning, her condition had worsened. Alethia put her in the bathtub filled with cool water. Sally Beth stood in the doorway of the bathroom at six o'clock in the morning and watched as the child lay spread-eagle in the water, her suffering wound red and unrecognizable as part of a human being.

"I called the mission. Dr. Sams said I should just get her to the hospital in Bukoba, and he's going to send someone up here to get us." She looked at Sally Beth with pleading eyes. "I hate to ask this, but—"

Sally Beth cut her off. "You go. I'll take care of the children. I'm sure Prissy can tell me what to do. If you leave your van here, I can drive them to school, and church, and do whatever they need. The mission can live without me a few hours a day. I can go there after I get them to school."

Alethia blinked back tears. "Sally Beth, I know God sent you to me. I could be gone a while. A week maybe? Or more. I just don't know. I'll take Sylvie with me."

An hour later, Sally Beth was on her own with six little girls she had barely met, but that did not stop them from climbing into her lap and asking her to tell them stories. She did the only thing she knew to do. She wrapped her arms around them and told them about the frog and the mockingbird who traveled the world singing before sultans and princes.

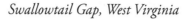

Swallowtail Gap, West Virginia

"Ha!" said Geneva, although it was not so much a snort of laughter as it was an exclamation of disgust. She stomped into the kitchen. "You awful man!"

"Wha'd I do?"

"Lured me up to that rock where you do your thing and got me pregnant. Again. When I am just now starting to get my body back. What on earth has Lenora fed you all—" Geneva didn't get to complete the sentence because Howard was suddenly kissing her so hard she couldn't breathe. Or think. But when he let her go, she could laugh.

An hour later, they lay tangled in the Egyptian cotton sheets they'd bought on their honeymoon, their fingers entwined. He placed his free hand on her belly. "They could have the same birthday. Twins a year apart. I bet this one's a girl."

"No, knowing you, it's another boy! Are you going to get me pregnant every time the stars fall? I'd like to have a year or so off, if you don't mind. I might as well get rid of all my shoes and resign myself to the fact that I'm going to spend my life up on that mountain barefoot and pregnant."

"I'm not so dumb, huh? Making sure you stay that way means I don't have to worry about you running out on me."

She giggled. "Just keep digging up gold. And make sure the mint patch doesn't get torn up. I'll forgive you this time, but you have to promise to take us all to Paris every single year. We keep this up, and you'll have to buy a plane." She fell into the quiet of his arms, pondering the possibility of having a personal plane, then giggled again. "Suppose we could get John to fly us around in his two new planes?"

"Wonder how he's getting along now that he's discovered Sally Beth's in Africa?" Howard mused as Geneva laced her fingers through his and gave a contented sigh.

"I bet Sally Beth would love to learn to fly. You think we should maybe make an anonymous gift to the mission stipulating that one of the American women serving in a non-medical capacity gets a plane and flying lessons?"

He laughed. "You start getting too detailed, and they'll figure something is up, especially if you get specific on every one of them. Telling John he had to set up a station in Kagera wasn't so bad. You can pass that off in a lot of ways. Getting a plane for Sally Beth's personal use, or setting up a scholarship for Lilly is going to be tricky. 'Full scholarship for a twenty-one-year-old female student from Tucker, West Virginia who wants to study photography.' Should we add 'blonde hair'?"

"Snotty personality."

"With a sister serving at a mission in Kagera, Tanzania."

She sobered. "We really should do something for Sally Beth and the mission there. It sounds like they are doing good work."

He stretched his arms over his head and lay back.

"I can't believe I'm saying this, but what do you think about calling up your old boyfriend? Nobody knows money more than he does, and I bet he has to take some sort of oath about client confidentiality. He might be able to find us somebody to help us write these grants to be airtight. And besides, we need to invest in more than land. He might could help."

"Chap! Really? You want to let Howard Graves in on the secret? You trust him?"

He shrugged. "Yeah. I trust him. But we don't have to tell him about the gold. Just the oil." He winked at her before pulling her closer and tucking her head under his chin, then he became thoughtful.

"That morning when he came looking for you up at the cabin, I saw something in him that I liked. He figured out what had happened in a New York minute, and even after I swore up and down you had been too sick to be interested in the likes of me, he knew. We had a stare-down for a minute. He let me win it, and he let me know he was letting me win, like he was telling me your happiness was more important to him than his own. That made me feel like there was something to him. And I guess you trust him. He still manages your money. Do you?"

She thought about it. "Yes," she said slowly. "He is a good man, underneath that slick exterior. And he does know what he's doing with investments. He made me rich enough, and I am happy to let him keep on making good bets for me. It would be nice to keep it in the family, so to speak." She paused. "That's another thing I love about you. You aren't the jealous type."

"Oh, I can be jealous. And mean. As bad as Myrtle. Just try and cross me."

She snorted. "The way I see it, Myrtle has met her match. Have you seen Edna Mae? She's twice Jimmy Lee's size, and at least half again Myrtle's. Sweet girl, though. Pretty face. I think Jimmy Lee's got a keeper there. You think he can keep the secret from her?"

"He'd better." He suddenly shifted, leaning on his elbow and looking at Geneva. "What would you think if I closed the mine?"

"Close it? How?"

"I'd dynamite it closed, seal it up. Clear out all the evidence from the creek and put things back the way it should be. I'm tired of being careful, always watching, always scared somebody is going to come up and find out what's there. We've got all the money we could ever need for generations to come—we can't even spend near all we've got, even if folks think we have an oil well, even if we give millions away. Jimmy Lee can stop working it, and Edna Mae or whoever he marries doesn't even have to know about it. Heck, we can even pass off the money we invest with Howard as income from an oil well. If he finds us a good lawyer to take care of the grants, he'll never know how much we really have." He watched her carefully. "I'm just tired of this uneasy feeling, not trusting anybody."

She laughed out loud. "Howard, I can't even fathom how much money you do have! I just know you told me I can give millions away as long as nobody knows where it came from. If you want to seal up that mine, do it. But keep the cabin. And the garden. And don't mess up the creek, or the mint patch. I'd give up all the gold in the world before I gave up that place."

He kissed her. "That's my girl. Now, I'm hungry. Let's go have breakfast and then we can go check on the house. They're putting on the roof today. Should I tell them to add about eight more bedrooms?"

"Very funny. I look forward to the day you are too fat and lazy to dance down the stars. I'm not safe until then."

Fifteen

October 9, 1878, Kyaka, Tanzania

Sally Beth rushed into the clinic very late. It had taken her longer than she thought it would to get the girls up, dressed, fed, and delivered to school. But nobody minded, for the clinic was quiet. Dr. Sams was sitting at her desk reading a medical journal when she arrived. He glanced up, smiling.

"Hi Sally Beth. Slow day today. Pastor Umbatu came by. You got two letters that were dropped off at his office by mistake." He handed her the envelopes.

"Oh, it's from my sister! And one from..." She stopped, surprised to see the return address. *Elvis Chuck.*

"Well, I'm going to go to the kitchen and get another cup of coffee. You know where to find me if any emergencies come in."

She opened the envelope from Elvis Chuck as she sat down. While it might have been nice if John were there to read it to her so she wouldn't have to puzzle through it all by herself, she really didn't want John to be privy to what might be in it. Flattening the letter on her desk, she picked up two rulers and laid them below and above the first line of script. By hiding lines under the ruler, the words were easier to manage. Still, she read slowly.

September 24, 1978
My Dear Sally Beth,
I have been thinking about you nonstop ever since I got on that bus in Fort Worth.

She stopped, her face suddenly flaming and her heart thumping. Bending over the paper, she continued reading. His handwriting was more legible than Lilly's and easier to read.

I hear you are in Africa! What a surprise to me, and a disappointment, especially since I have the opportunity to spend some time in Nashville next month. Looking at the map, I see that Nashville is not THAT far from Tucker, West Virginia, at least not as far as Las Vegas is. I was hoping that you could either pop down and meet me or I might take a side trip and come to see you. It seems that we might have some things in common that I was hoping to explore more.

But you will be in Africa until December, so I guess that possibility is out. Maybe another time?

Anyway, I hope you will write to me, and if you don't mind, send a picture. I look forward to hearing from you.
Your admirer,
(Elvis)Chuck

She had calmed down by the time she had reached the end of the letter. Elvis Chuck had been nice, and it was sweet of him to offer to see her again, but somehow, that warm night on the road to Fort Worth seemed every bit the half a world away that it was. She knew she was going to have to write him back to tell him she was sorry if she had led him on. She sighed, dreading the task as she picked up Lilly's letter.

Sept 22, 1978
Hey girl!
I am between classes, so I thought I'd write and give you all the

news. Everything is going great at school. These little 18 year olds act like school is hard, but I think that's because all they want to do is party. Phil and I are the only ones who don't cut class. It isn't nearly as bad as I thought it would be.

I am really loving my women's studies class. We're reading The Beauty Myth *by Naomi Woolf, and it got me to thinking about what beauty is, and I realized that all women are beautiful in some way, but most of them don't realize it and try to hide what they think are flaws. You know how Edna Mae covers herself up because she's too beautiful, and some women do it because they think they are ugly, while some try to flaunt what they think looks good, and that kind of makes them look bad because they're trying too hard, and then some don't care what people think and just do what makes them happy, and* that *gives them a certain kind of beauty.*

Sally Beth had to puzzle through that sentence two more times before she finally figured out what Lilly was trying to say.

Anyway, I have to write a term paper and am combining it with a photography project, calling it "Studies in Beauty." You know those skinny Carver girls? I think I can take pictures of them and bring out how pretty they really are even though people call them sacks of bones. And Dawn Hatfield with the scar from the cleft palate? Well, she has a beautiful profile, and she's pretty even with the scar—I think her crooked mouth is actually nice in an odd sort of way. Anyway, I think I'm going to have a lot of fun with it, the pictures illustrating what I mean when I talk about different standards of beauty in the paper.

So, that's keeping me busy, along with the Flora/Fauna project I'm working on with Phil, who is becoming my best friend, and no, not a boyfriend! He actually has a girlfriend. She's a little off-beat, but I like her. She seems real confident and interesting—one of those women who don't care what anybody thinks, and I hope she will let me photograph her for the "Studies in Beauty" project!

Guess who was in town last weekend??? Howard Graves! You know, Geneva's old boyfriend? His mother got real close to Geneva when she was living in DC when she was pregnant, and she wanted to see Blue, so they came down and stayed at Rachel's house, and everybody was just as friendly as could be. Howard and Geneva came over and spent some time with him, although I can't imagine what they talked about for a whole afternoon. Rachel had invited me over for dinner, and when I got there, they all three (Geneva and her two Howards!) were in the study with the door closed. It made me nervous wondering what they were whispering about. I got to wondering if Howard Knight was challenging him to a duel or something!

It was odd being there without you, but I had the funniest conversation with Howard (Graves). I got to thinking how bad I behaved the last time we had dinner over there—I was going through some weird stuff then, and I know I was acting pretty awful, and I just told him I was sorry I had been so terrible, and he was very nice about it! We got to talking about my photography projects, and he said they were real interesting, and then, he said the funniest thing. He said, "Lilly, I think you and I are growing up at about the same pace." I thought that was sweet. He made me feel like a real person, not some backwards hillbilly who doesn't know her a— from a hole in the ground. He says he might come back next month to see the Flora and Fauna exhibit when it goes up at the Student Union. Ours is going to be SOOO much better than everybody else's! The professor is already getting excited about it. He says I have "a real eye for nuance and for photographic commentary within my images," whatever that means!

The insurance money still hasn't come in, but they say these things take a while. Don't worry. I'll pay that mortgage off just as soon as it comes. I had to quit my super-duper photography business for the most part, I'm just so busy, but I'm not spending much and I can make the house payments with the money left in Mama's account for a few more months. I was spending a fortune on film—we have a darkroom so we develop ourselves, but somebody donated a THOUSAND rolls of film, and gallons of developing and fixing solutions to the class, and so now we don't have to buy that either. The professor says we can take whatever we need. Phil and I are going through it like hot you-know-what through a possum! Last night we developed pictures until 3:00 A.M.

I was so tired I couldn't even remember where I had parked my car, so Phil told me I could crash at his and Molly's house (They are living in sin!), and this morning, they said I could stay with them until this project is done so I can spend every spare minute in the darkroom. It's better to use it late at night because we have only three that the whole class uses, and we need it waaay more than our "official" time slot.

Love you. Gotta go. There is a squirrel sitting on the tree outside eating a nut. I'm going to go see if I can get a close-up.

Love and hugs,

Lilly

P. S. You should see the house Howard and Geneva are building up at the Jumpoff. It is going to be really big, and really beautiful! I think that oil well must be doing pretty good. That, or Geneva is making a lot of money renting out her apartment in DC. It might be nice having a rich cousin. Ha ha!

Edna Mae and Jimmy Lee are still getting along just fine, and Myrtle is still badmouthing Edna Mae, but Edna Mae doesn't seem to mind. She just looks sad when anybody talks about Myrtle. She really is the sweetest thing.

Oct 4.

I was just about to mail this, but before I got to the mailbox, Edna Mae called. She wants to rent the house! She loves it—says this is just the kind of house she's always wanted to live in, and she fell in love with Mama's asters that are blooming like crazy now. Beginning next week she's got a job as a receptionist for Bubba Henry right here in town. I guess she's here for good, which means Jimmy Lee is happy. She thought maybe I could use a roommate, but now I'm thinking I can just rent a room from Phil and Molly until I finish my courses at the college, which will save me the hour's drive to and from school every day. If I move to Mt. Jackson, Edna Mae can just take over the house until you get home, and when you get back, you'll have a roommate if you want. I told her she can stay at least until you get home. I hope that's ok with you. It will sure save us a lot of $$.

Sally Beth sat back after reading the letter. "Well, I'll be," she said aloud. "Lilly working past midnight and then just *crashing* at

Phil's house? Edna Mae wants to take over the house?" It was so unbelievable that she read the letter again to make sure she had read it right the first time, but before she could completely finish it, a young woman with a snakebite was rushed into the clinic, and the rest of the morning was gone before she could get back to it.

At lunch, Lyla joined Sally Beth for sandwiches. Afterwards, she pulled out a batch of cookies, which she called "biscuits," and began brewing tea. "I know you like orange zest in your tea, Sally Beth, so I chopped up fresh whole oranges to put in here. I think we're on to something.

"It's going to rain soon," she continued, "so let's go outside for our tea to watch it come in. You can count on it coming every day until the season is over. You'll get to see the color of rain, now, my friend."

Their conversation was interrupted by the urgent clanging of church bells. Pastor Umbatu suddenly came running into the clinic. "I just got a call from the church at Mutukula. Idi Amin's army has attacked the border! I don't know if they are just coming after some who have fled after the assassination attempt or if he really is invading, but there are casualties in the south of the city." He glanced around the room at the few people gathered in the waiting room as he moved to the door. "Come with me. Everyone is going to the church. I will tell you what I know there."

The sanctuary was already half full when they arrived. Pastor Umbatu ran to the pulpit, beginning without preamble. "My friends, there is fighting at the border in Mutukula. Our brothers at the church there tell me that Ugandan forces have pushed their way across, and there is a battle going on right now. They have already had a few casualties. That is all I know."

Soft murmurings rose up from the pews. "Do you think this is a real invasion or just one of Amin's raids into Mutukula?"

"Maybe they have just come after those who attempted to kill Amin? Maybe they found them there?"

"Are we in danger here?"

"Should we go to Mutukula to help?"

The questions started flying faster. Pastor Umbatu raised his hands. "I know nothing more, but I will tell you as soon as I hear anything. The official word is that Idi Amin is just up to his old tricks and nothing will come of it. I think we are safe here for now, and even if they do move south, there is no reason for them to molest us here at the mission. It is, of course, against the rules of battle to harm anyone who is doing God's work. And I don't think any of you should go there. It would be foolish to walk into danger, and if they need us, they can bring patients to us. It is only twenty miles to the border, less to where they are fighting. As a matter of fact, I would not be surprised that if we listen carefully, we will be able to hear it from here."

All fell quiet, then, as if one, they rose to make their way outside, past the courtyard and out to the meadow to the north. The wind was blowing from the southwest, and no matter how hard she strained, Sally Beth could hear only the breath of the wind and the chattering of birds and monkeys. Everyone began milling around, murmuring softly.

"I think we need to get prepared," said Dr. Sams. "Casualties could be coming in at any time, and we need to do all we can to be ready for them. Does anybody know where John is? It would be nice if he could run down to Bukoba and bring some extra supplies."

"He's probably at his place at Kigemba," said Sally Beth.

"Close enough to contact by radio," Dr. Price said. "I'll get over to the office and see if I can raise him. If not, I'll drive to Bukoba myself. I can get there and back in four hours, if you radio ahead and ask them to get the supplies ready."

"Right, but if John can go, you can be here if any casualties come in."

The wind shifted, bringing a low rumbling sound, ominous and malevolent. Everyone froze for a moment as they realized what it meant: that, truly, war was at their door. They suddenly all broke into a run. Dr. Sams shouted orders. Lyla raced for the school, calling for children who had been playing on the playground to come back to the classroom. Sally Beth ran with the others. She didn't know what she could do, but she was anxious to do what she could.

Shortly after that, the rain came, breaking the long dry spell and spreading a shimmering light over the land. The sun was still shining to the west, turning the silver drops into a thousand glistening rainbows. Awed at the sight, Sally Beth understood why Lyla had said the rain is full of beauty, and through her fear and grief, she felt a flutter of pleasure that Lyla had thought that she was the color of rain. She would have to thank her later.

October 10, 1978

No casualties had come in the day before, and after the brief noise of battle they had heard earlier, no sound but the pattering of raindrops hung upon the wind. Still, the tension in the clinic rose as the day wore on, and today, no one had a moment to forget about the death and misery foraging through the land to the north of them. Soldiers from the Tanzanian army were already on the road beside the mission, streaming northward in a steady line of tanks and jeeps bristling with guns and soldiers. Occasionally a truck bearing large-bore guns and bazookas, weapons capable of destroying entire villages and all the lives within them, came roaring by, slinging red mud into the greening grass and disturbing the peaceful rain. Each truck full of soldiers that slogged by deepened the atmosphere of foreboding.

Late in the day, Dr. Sams gathered everyone together in the waiting room. They stood or sat quietly, expectantly, their faces turned toward him. "From what I hear, the Tanzanian army has everything under control. It seems like hundreds have already gone north, if you've been watching the road. But you never know. I know we've had no casualties come here, but if fighting starts up again, we can expect to see some. They won't be able to handle them at Mutukula. Dr. Price has talked to John. He says he can bring in all the supplies we need up to a point, unless of course, he has to fly through artillery fire. My guess is the Tanzanians will set up field hospitals if they need them, so that will keep the pressure off us, unless there are a lot of civilian casualties.

"I hate to ask you all to stay. I don't know if things are going to be more or less dangerous as time goes by. John has offered to take any of you anywhere you want to go. Americans, if you want to go home, we've got clearance to leave any time you want. You're more likely to get flights out of Nairobi." Dr. Sams sounded tired but strong as he looked around the room, searching everyone's faces.

"I'm not leaving," said Francine. "I don't believe we are in any danger at the moment, and it's no good to turn tail and run just because we're nervous."

"She's right," spoke up Janie. "I feel pretty safe here in the compound. The Tanzanians are used to this, and they know how to handle Amin's army. There's no way the Ugandans can make it down here without going through the whole Tanzanian army. I'm staying. At least for now."

Sally Beth wasn't listening. She wasn't thinking about leaving or staying, or the danger they might be in. She was just thinking that she should bring Alethia's girls to the mission until they were assured there would be no war. The Ugandans weren't so much of a problem, she thought, but the Tanzanian soldiers looked like they wouldn't be overly cautious about making sure children were kept safe. Dr. Sams broke into her reverie.

"What about you, Sally Beth. What do you think?"

She blinked. "I need to get the girls here. Alethia and Mara and Sylvie are safe in Bukoba, but I worry about all these soldiers being on the road. And what about the other children in the village? Should we set up some place for them so they will feel safe? Are the rooms in the Bamboo building good enough to house them if we can get some men from the village to come help repair the roof? I'm worried about getting people to the hospitals with the roads so clogged with the soldiers coming up, and I'm wondering if maybe

John could bring his partner here. They have another plane, and we could shuttle the really injured people to Bukoba or Ndolage.

There was a general soft laughter. Falla came over and put her arm around her. "My dear Sally Beth. In you we see the face of God."

Sixteen

October 20, 1978

B attles had been going on intermittently just north of them for eleven days, with neither side seeming to gain control for more than a few minutes or a few hours at a time, and because the fighting was taking place in populated areas, civilian casualties were beyond what the Tanzanians' field hospitals could handle. A river of wounded streamed to the mission, noisy with cries of pain and fear, swelling and surging as the days passed. Everyone was exhausted, not just from the constant work with victims arriving by the hour, but by the emotional strain of trying to remain calm and cheerful around all the children, including Alethia's, who had been moved to the mission for the duration of the fighting.

Yet, life had not become the hell that war could be. The seriously wounded bypassed the mission clinic to go directly to the hospitals at Bukoba or Ndoledge. The injuries Sally Beth saw were relatively minor, but there were so many of them: a wall of bloody humanity that defined her days and towered over her dreams at night. Everyone, from Pastor Umbatu to the maintenance staff, was pressed into helping bandage wounds and begin plasma or saline IVs. They took their meals at their stations, usually just cold leftovers because the cooks did not take the time away from the clinic to prepare much. Sally Beth spent her time soothing crying infants and distraught women, fishing for bullets and shrapnel, and injecting antibiotics, and she even learned how to stitch up superficial gashes. It was not pleasant work, but it was not gut-wrenching either. Mostly it was just exhausting and depressing.

Late in the afternoon, she heard the drone of an airplane she had by now learned was the much-longed-for sound of John's Skylane. Sally Beth shook off her fatigue as she washed the blood off her hands, looking forward to a smile from him, or, when she dared to hope, that he would hold her in his arms for a moment.

"It's John," she said to Falla. "I've finished with this. It wasn't too deep, but it was long, so I stitched it up. One of the docs should check to make sure I did it okay. I'll run out and help him unload." She took off her smock, put on her hat, stepped out into the shimmering rain, and ran toward the meadow beyond the church.

John was tired, so tired he could barely keep his eyes open, and the bad news he had just received had deflated him, but the sight of Sally Beth standing in the rain, her pink princess cowboy hat sitting atop her pale beauty brought a smile to his face. She was simultaneously ridiculous and beautiful, with that ersatz rhinestone crown glinting almost as brilliantly as her genuine radiance. He nearly laughed aloud, and for a moment, he forgot his tiredness.

"Hey, John!" She waved, running to him. "It sure is good to see you! Did you bring penicillin? And some plasma? We've plumb run out." She stopped when she saw his face, gray with fatigue, and her heart lurched with sympathy. "Oh, John! You look so tired! How long has it been since you got any sleep? Do you have time to stop and take a nap? Or at least some coffee?"

He dragged himself out of the cockpit. She took his hand to help him, holding it for a moment longer than was necessary, but he did not mind. Her warmth made him feel steadier. "Coffee sounds great, Sally Beth. I need to get back to Kigemba right now. There's been a raid on the ranch and although my crew was able to keep most of the cattle safe, I need to get there as quick as I can to help round them up and get them secure. I just got the call about a minute ago. And then I need to get back to Bukoba to get the rest of the supplies for here. They didn't have everything you need at Izimbya and I didn't want to take the time to divert because I was afraid you would need the plasma now."

By now, they were joined by Red and Pastor Umbatu, who had already begun to unload supplies from the plane.

"Thanks, John!" Red said, holding out a thermos of coffee to him. "We've got a patient who needs to get to a hospital. He's got a fractured leg and Dr. Price says he's going to need surgery. Do you think you could ferry him down to Izimbya?"

John looked defeated. "I just got back from there, but I have to go to Bukoba to pick up some more things. And I have to get back to my station at some point. Can I take him to Bukoba? It would be quicker for me all around."

"Sure," said Red. "I'll let them know you are coming. Can you eat something before you go?"

John hesitated. He was starving, but he didn't want to take the time to eat. Too many urgent needs demanded he get aloft again quickly.

Sally Beth spoke up. "How about I go with you? You can eat on the way, and then you can drop me off at the hospital in Bukoba with the patient. Red, if you call ahead and have someone at the airport to pick us up, I'll get him checked in and take care of the supplies, and John can go back to the ranch. You can come back to pick me up tonight. And I'll be able to see Alethia for a minute. Let her know her girls are safe."

John felt a tiny lessening of pressure. It would be nice to have Sally Beth along for the company. She had a way of brightening his outlook, and it would be good to sit back and eat and let her fly. He nodded. "That would be fine."

Thirty minutes later, they began the checklist for takeoff. "You need to learn to take off, Sally Beth," he said to her. "You never know when you're going to be called on to fly, so we might as well get a quick lesson in. Now pay attention. I'll show you what to do, and you can try it yourself from a real runway when we leave Bukoba." He took a few extra minutes to walk through the takeoff procedure, then, when they were aloft, he handed the controls to her with the comment, "I'm starving. Take over for me while I enjoy this sandwich. What is it?"

"PB and J. Nobody's cooked in a week."

"Ah, a little taste of home." He peeked at the sandwich. "Blueberry?"

"Blackberry. The church from home sent it over in a care package."

The radio crackled and a voice calling for John broke in. He responded, "Skylane 235 niner Juliet here."

"Some passengers requesting transport from Bukoba to Kyaka. When will you be in the vicinity?"

"Roger that. Will be in Bukoba in twenty, but will be roundabout getting back to Kyaka. Okay to delay delivery? By the way, there's a war on. Passengers know that?"

"Passengers en route to Bukoba now, due to arrive at sixteen hundred. Roger on the war. They are journalists to cover it. Can you accommodate?"

"If they're traveling light. I'll be leaving Bukoba with supplies sometime this evening. Not much room for luggage."

"I'll let them know. Over and out."

Sally Beth shook her head. "What kind of idiots would come to Kyaka with the Ugandans right at the doorstep? It's all I can do to keep from running away!"

John shrugged as he bit into his sandwich. "Journalists are a bunch of daredevils, I reckon. And somebody needs to report what's going on. I, for one, would like to know."

He dropped Sally Beth off at the airport where an ancient van serving as an ambulance of sorts sat waiting. The driver jumped out as soon as they taxied to a stop. John kept the engine running while the driver and Sally Beth unloaded the patient and moved him to the van. They waved to each other as they departed in separate directions.

Oh Lord! Keep him safe!

"Alethia!" she shouted across the parking lot.

"Sally Beth!" They ran to each other and embraced on the wet sidewalk outside the emergency room. "I just got here. One of the nurses called me to tell me you were coming. How are my girls? Are they safe? Are they scared?"

"They're safe and doing fine. There's not been any fighting anywhere near the mission. The Ugandans didn't get past Mutukula, and the Tanzanians are pretty much whooping their tails. I've even heard that the Tanzanians are plowing up into Uganda, although *they* say they haven't invaded. One radio says one thing, one says another. But it's clear the Tanzanians are winning, so nobody's really worried. We've been keeping the girls at the mission, though, and they're doing their lessons with the children there so I don't have to drive them up to their school. I just don't have the time; things are so hectic at the clinic. How's Mara?"

"Oh, thank God! I've been hearing the same sort of thing. She's doing better, but it took a long time to get the infection under control. Sylvie and I have been taking turns sitting with her. I have some friends here in town we've been staying with. They don't have much room, or I would ask you to bring them here. Thank you so much for taking care of my babies, Sally Beth."

The calm oasis of the afternoon where she lounged in Alethia's warm, comfortable friendship was much too small. It seemed as if only a few moments had passed before it was time to walk through the driving rain back to the dilapidated van that stood waiting, loaded with supplies. Parting was painful. Neither of them doubted that they both would remain safe, but in the back of their minds, they both knew that life could be capricious.

"God be with you, Sally Beth."

"And you as well, Alethia," she replied, blinking back tears.

The airport was not busy, but she decided to wait for John out on the tarmac in order to see him as soon as he came in. Leaning against the van, shivering, hunkered under an umbrella as the rain pelted down, she still thought it was better than sitting in the steaming van, breathing the scent of damp cardboard boxes. The air was fresh and full of the greening smells of rain-soaked earth.

After about fifteen minutes, the rain suddenly eased off, then stopped. The sun drifted softly into the misty lake until it sank and drowned, plunging the land into sudden darkness. It was peaceful, and even though death roamed just north of her, the quiet pinpricks of light shone into her soul, comforting it. For a moment, she pretended that she was home again, gazing at the gloaming and the twinkling lights of fireflies at the top of Jacob's Mountain, and she allowed herself the small luxury of pretending she was there with John. Darkness would enfold them, just as his arms enfolded her, and the two of them would become an indistinguishable, single entity underneath the stars.

The breeze that sprang up held the scent of lilies, which made her think of her own pale, beautiful sister, and unspilled tears stung her eyes as she wished she were home and safe, singing and playing with Lilly. The tune of an old ballad found its way into her throat, floating out into the cold night as she leaned back to look deep into the spangled sky and pray for the safety of her loved ones back home. She suddenly understood how acutely painful homesickness could be.

Not much time had passed before a man and a woman loaded with bags and backpacks exited the terminal building, made their way down the steps, and slowly begin walking toward her. She squinted through the darkness, blinked, squinted harder, then, when they were ten feet away, the clouds parted below the gibbous moon and she let out a cry as she sprinted toward them. The woman dropped her bag, running to meet her.

"*Sally Beth!*"

"*Lilly!*"

They collided, laughing, crying, holding on to each other, jumping up and down, and screaming into each other's ear until the man, struggling with all the baggage, caught up to them.

"What happened to your hair?"

Lilly's hair was as short as a boy's.

"I cut it. When I'm out in the field, it gets in the way, and it's impossible to keep it looking decent." She ran her fingers lightly through her shorn locks.

"Well, it looks *awful!* Why didn't you wait and let me cut it?"

"You'll get your chance." Lilly laughed and reached out to brush a stray lock from Sally Beth's forehead. Lilly looked tired and wan, her face scrubbed clean of makeup, the blonde brows and lashes disappearing in the glimmering moonlight. Not even any lipstick. Sally Beth had the sudden uneasy thought that the person standing before seemed insubstantial, like the mere ghost of her sister. Nevertheless, she was beautiful to her.

They were loading supplies onto John's Skylane before Sally Beth finally got the complete story. The man was Phil, Lilly's photography partner, and Sally Beth agreed that he definitely was not Lilly's type. He was big and hairy, with a low forehead and big nose that made him look like a caveman, but intelligence glimmered in his sharp, brown eyes. Lilly introduced him proudly. "Meet my best buddy. The minute he heard the news about the invasion, he talked me into coming.

"He told me this could be the launch of a great career for both of us, that if we covered this story well enough, we would have all kinds of opportunities just falling at our feet. And you're stationed so close to the action, we couldn't be in a better situation. And of course, I was wild to know what was happening to you, so it didn't take long for him to talk me into it. The only thing that kept us from getting here sooner was it took some time to get my passport and visa. I had to do exactly what you did, go to DC and sit on Senator Byrd's doorstep."

"What about your classes? You can't just up and leave school in the middle of the semester!"

Lilly shrugged. "We've already aced our photography class; Dr. Jacobs told us he wasn't going to stand in the way of our fame, and he gave us two hundred rolls of film to bring with us. We're going to send it back to him to develop, and he's going to submit the best pictures to the wire, and he says we'll probably win an award. Phil's going to write about what we see, and who knows—we may get something published."

"What about your other classes?"

"I turned in my English paper yesterday, or I guess the day before yesterday, depending on what day this is. I'll miss the final, but my teacher says she'll accept whatever I write about the war as a substitute, and my women's studies teacher will do the same as long as I write something about how the war is affecting women. I'll just take an incomplete in my math course, and I can finish it when I get back. All the teachers are so excited for me; they are doing everything they can to help." She gave a little laugh. "And I thought teachers were mean! Of course, that was back when I was more interested in boys than in class. I think they like you better when you get serious."

"But how much did it cost for you to get here? There can't be much money left in the account."

"Oh, I sold my car," Lilly answered breezily. "I made $500 profit on it, and I paid Jimmy Lee back." She grinned. "Well, mostly. Partly. He wouldn't take more than $200. Edna Mae told him we both had lost some jewelry in the fire, and I think she may have lied about how much it was worth."

"You sold your car? *Lilly!*"

"Yeah, well, it was a gas hog, and besides, I need something that will take back roads better. I'll get a jeep when I get back. We'll be rich after we sell this war story to the wire service."

Phil laughed. "Rich enough to go chase after another story, anyway."

John shoved the last box into the fuselage. "Right. That's all she'll hold," he said, slamming the door shut. "You're going to have to put your luggage under your feet and on your laps." He turned to Sally Beth. "I'm holding you to that promise. You're taking off this time, and flying the whole way. I can't keep my eyes open another minute. And don't you dare offer me a cup of coffee. I just want to sleep."

Lilly dropped her jaw and she stared at Sally Beth. "You're…" she began, then closed her mouth and shrugged. "If you can fly as good as you can drive, I reckon we'll survive. Take us to the war!"

Sally Beth was nervous, terrified, really, but she remembered almost everything John had told her, and with just a little coaching, she made it off the ground without embarrassing herself or scaring anyone other than herself. Lilly and John were both asleep by the time they had reached optimum altitude, and Phil seemed unconcerned, probably because he didn't know this was only her third time flying and her first takeoff. She wiped her sweating palms on her jeans, said a prayer of thanksgiving, and turned the nose of the plane to 281 degrees northwest.

Fifteen minutes later, she buzzed the meadow by the church when her nerve failed at her first landing attempt. Neither Lilly nor John woke up until her second try, when she landed roughly, bouncing four times before the wheels finally made steady contact with the ground. Phil said nothing, Lilly startled once, then said, "Huh?" John roused himself enough to mutter, "Good job."

October 21, 1978

The next morning, Lilly was still sleeping in Sally Beth's cot as Sally Beth crept around the room, getting dressed in the early morning dark. She was at her post later, irrigating a wound in a young man's arm while Falla worked with a woman with an ugly burn on her back and Jenna, the cook, rolled bandages, when Lilly strolled into the clinic.

"Hey, Sally Beth." Lilly still looked tired and pale without any makeup. Her closely-cropped hair had not been combed, and she was wearing the strangest outfit Sally Beth had ever seen: khaki pants and a vest festooned with at least a dozen pockets in which Lilly had stuffed all manner of items, from film to camera lenses to candy bars. Lawrence's camera was slung around her neck and hung down the front. Another one hung across her body and dangled at her side.

Sally Beth turned back to the young man. "Does that hurt?" she asked him, touching the ragged edges of flesh lightly as she squirted water into it. "There's some porridge on that hot plate there," she said over her shoulder. "And coffee, or tea if you want it, and a pot of yams. And there's plenty of fruit. Help yourself." She turned her attention back to her patient. "I'm just going to put some salve on this and bandage it up. I don't think you need stitches, but you need to keep this clean. Okay?"

The young man nodded. His eyes looked frightened, but he sat up straight as she wrapped the bandage around his thin arm. Finally, he stood, nodded his thanks, and walked out the door.

Lilly ladled out a bowl of porridge, sliced off some bread, and stood against the wall as she ate. "I'm starving," she said, spooning the porridge into her mouth. "Let me eat this, then I'll help. You seen Phil?"

"Yes, he's over by the wall, helping to shore up a few places in case any of the fighting moves down here. We're not too worried, but—" Sally Beth was interrupted by someone shouting, and suddenly more people filed into the small room. One of them was the young woman, Alice, whom she had met over lunch a few Sundays ago. She staggered in with the support of the young man, Francis, who had been by her side on the day they had met. The back of her blouse hung in bloody shreds, and under that, her back was lacerated with stripes. Sally Beth gasped when she realized she had been brutally whipped with a lash.

"Alice!" she exclaimed. "What happened to you?"

Alice moaned, sinking to her knees. Francis knelt beside her. He looked at Sally Beth with great sorrow.

"The Lakwena demanded it. She ordered the men to battle before they were purified."

"The Lakwena? Who is that?" She gingerly cut off the back of Alice's blouse. Lilly had exchanged her bowl of porridge for a camera. From against the wall, she stepped sideways, keeping her distance, and discreetly began snapping. Sally Beth stopped to frown at her, but Lilly shook her head slightly. "I have to do this," she said quietly.

Francis answered her. "He is the spirit who guides us. Alice saw an opportunity, and she ordered our men to battle before they were purified." He looked at his friend with compassion, taking her hand and speaking softly. "You braved it with great courage. The Lakwena will be proud of you."

Alice suddenly looked up, then before Sally Beth could begin sponging off her back, she staggered to her feet, and eyes staring vacantly out the window, spoke in a strangely hard, low, guttural monotone, "God forgives Alice. She has borne her punishment and He knows her regret. Tell the woman to wash her stripes with water and honey, but do not put anything else except the *kitungulu* on them. God will heal His servant Alice in three days."

Sally Beth stepped back, startled. The voice had definitely come from Alice: she had seen her breathe and speak, but it did not sound as if it came from her. It seemed to echo off the walls and come at her from behind, and it definitely was not the voice of the young woman she had met a month before.

Francis looked at her sternly. "You heard the Lakwena. Wash her stripes with water and honey. I will find the *kitungulu* for her healing."

"*Kitungulu*? What is that?"

He paused, struggling to translate. "It is the young wild allium, like an onion. It is one of the cures that has been purchased, and we have been given permission to take it. The salves you use are forbidden."

Alice suddenly slumped again, moaning, her head on her hands, resting on the floor. Lilly inched closer, her camera clicking and whirring as she focused on the young woman's face, her back, her bowed-over posture. No one seemed to notice her as she took frame after frame, moving through the light like a pale shadow, crouching, circling Alice as she focused and clicked, focused and clicked.

Sally Beth glanced at Falla and Jenna. Falla was with another patient, but had stopped to gaze at Alice. The wounded and sick sitting against the wall or standing in the doorway stared silently while Alice moaned, and Lilly danced through the light, all her energies zeroed in on the woman with the hollow face and voice. Sally Beth felt her knees begin to quiver. She wanted to tell Lilly to stop taking pictures, she wanted Alice to look at her, and for all the others to look away, but she felt helpless, rooted in a circle of absurdity as she watched Alice's vacant face and bloody back. Time froze, but after a few breathless seconds, she forced herself to stand straight as she said quietly to no one in particular. "Can someone get me some honey?"

Jenna jumped up. "I'll go," she said, dropping her roll of bandages and passing quickly out of the door. Sally Beth retrieved a small basin, filling it with warm water, while all eyes except Lilly's watched her. A few minutes later, Jenna returned with a small jar of honey.

Sally Beth turned to Alice. "Do I mix the honey in the water?" she asked her, but the young woman looked blank, as if she had vacated her body and there was no one inside to respond. She tried again, turning to Francis. "Do I mix the honey in the water? Or wash her first, and then apply honey?"

He looked at Alice. "Alice? Lakwena?" He asked her gently. "Does she mix the water in the honey?" Alice did not respond, but gazed steadily at the wall in front of her while Lilly eased closer, taking close-up photographs of her empty face. Francis turned to Sally Beth and shrugged. "I don't know. Whatever you think."

She realized that Alice was in shock, and she suddenly felt a piercing terror for this young woman who knelt before her. She was carrying a burden that Sally Beth could not understand, a burden that was far greater than her slight shoulders should be holding, and there was nothing Sally Beth could do to give her ease. She had the nagging feeling that Alice would never be free of it, and that this beating was not the last she would take for the sake of her Holy Spirits.

Sally Beth gave up trying to understand and instead did what she could to alleviate her physical suffering. She simply washed the bloody welts and lacerations with water with a soft sponge, then gently slathered honey on them before applying bandages.

Afterward, she spoke to Francis. "I'll leave it to you to find the onions, but I think she'd better stay here for a while. Seems to me she's in shock. There are some cots out in the courtyard under the trees. Can you take her out there and let her rest? Keep her warm, and I'll get one of the doctors to check on her." She didn't know what else to say. Alice was still staring vacantly at the window. Suddenly the light flickered behind her eyes and she turned to Sally Beth, smiling, her face alight with pleasure and recognition.

"Sally Beth, my friend from America. How nice to see you again. Thank you for helping us. You have been very kind, and we hope to return the favor someday soon." She stood, holding her shredded blouse up to cover her breasts, and slowly, but elegantly, made her way out the door, followed by Francis. Lilly slipped out the door behind her, but she whispered to Sally Beth as she left,

"Sally Beth, *please* go and get Phil, and ask him to find us."

She could not leave, but she turned to Jenna. "Jenna, there's a big, hairy white man out by the west wall. Would you please go ask him to go out to the courtyard and help Lilly and Alice?" Jenna nodded, leaving quickly, as Sally Beth sighed, washed her hands, and turned to the next person waiting in line. She felt like she was a hundred years old.

Sally Beth did not see her sister again until late in the afternoon. She was trying to drink a cup of tea between tending to two young boys who had been in their house when a grenade landed on it, causing part of the roof to collapse. One boy was fine; the other had been hit in the head with the sharp edge of a tin roof and needed to see a doctor. She set him on a cot on the corner by the first examining room before looking up to see Lilly and Phil standing in the doorway.

"I gotta go, Sally Beth. Alice is going back to her soldiers, and Phil and I are going with them. It's amazing, what they are doing. I don't have time to tell you everything, but Alice is a medium for a spirit, who is leading a whole army; they call themselves the Army of the Holy Spirits, and it's a story you won't believe. We've just *got* to cover it."

Sally Beth cried out, "No! Lilly, you can't go. There is a real war out there. The people coming in here aren't even in the fighting; they've just been hurt because they're close. You can't."

Lilly made an impatient gesture. "Don't worry about us. We'll stay well away from any battles. Alice has a whole flock of people with their army—women, children. They are a traveling town, they have church services and school, like a whole community. And they're perfectly safe. They don't get near the fighting, and they can move fast if they need to. We'll try to be back in a couple of days, but don't worry about us. We can't pass this up." Her eyes flashed with excitement, and Sally Beth knew it was useless to try to stop her. She had seen that look before.

Phil spoke up, "I'll make sure she's safe, Sally Beth. But she's right. We can't pass this up. This could be the story of the war, and it looks like nobody is covering it." Sally Beth felt her heart grow heavy, felt it sink like an anchor. She had lost her father and her mother. She had lost Holy Miracle, and now she would lose her sister, for no matter how hard she fought, Lilly would turn and walk out that door and across the threshold into hell.

Lilly hugged Sally Beth tightly. "I love you, Sis. We'll be *fine*."

Sally Beth clung to her even as she pulled away, giving Sally

Beth a bright smile as she skipped out the door. Sally Beth started to follow, but a child sitting nearby let out a wail, pulling her thoughts back toward her duties. When she looked back, Lilly and Phil were nowhere in sight.

Seventeen

October 25, 1978

Sally Beth had seen her mother die, and she had seen her best friend Holy Miracle Jones release his last breath into a vision of an Almighty God, and she had seen an elderly patient at the nursing home slip away into the darkness and the light of death, but she had never seen anyone die in agony. She had never seen anyone who was young, vital, and strong succumb to that seductive pull, the promise of liberation from pain. She had never seen anyone face death in terror, screaming about the claws of Satan, or anyone who whimpered and begged for his mother as the Great Shadow roved hungrily into his being.

Until now, she had been an innocent, believing that death was a great adventure, the threshold across which one must pass as one steps into the Light, like going through a dim cave to get to the brilliant pool of sunshine on the other side. Now she saw the dark, angry, ugly side of death, where people did not simply shrug off their ailing flesh to leap into the arms of God, but where death came and clawed away at them until their bodies and their souls were shredded and bleeding, their humanity ripped away from them. She stopped breathing when the first one gripped her hand and, eyes wide with fear and pain, begged her for a drink of water as blood fountained from his severed legs. She held onto him, despite the blackness swimming before her own eyes, then felt her chest convulse in a burst of self-preservation when it finally realized she was not the one meant to die today.

After that, she forced herself to breathe slowly and regularly through the mask of cool professionalism she put on to shield herself. It was nearly ripped away dozens of times, at first, when she saw the mangled and dismembered, and then again as war presented her with a whole new brand of horrors: raped, tortured, mutilated children.

A little girl, not more than eight or nine was first, followed by so many she could not count them. Many were already dead when they arrived; most were dying, some died in her arms. By the end of the day, she had seen more of hell than she ever could imagine seeing in an eternity.

It had started early in the morning. Ugandan forces, reinforced by thousands of troops from Muammar Gaddafi's Libyan army and Palestinian fighters, had suddenly surged to take the whole Kagera region. They flooded across the border, murdering, burning, plundering, and raping their way southward in a wide swath along the Ugandan Road. Tanzanian forces, overwhelmed, were pushed back well south of the river, but as they withdrew, they laid land mines and booby traps to try to deflect their enemies.

Civilians, fleeing in terror from the monsters who pursued them, ran into these mines, and the bloody, unfathomable aftermath was laid at the doorstep of the mission. What had been a place of grace for people to rest or be treated for minor injuries and illnesses suddenly was overrun by the hell of war.

She could hear the guns and grenades just outside the mission compound; she could smell the smoke from burning houses, and when the wind was right, the smell of blood and the first reek of flesh beginning to rot in the African sun. They had not had time to run; they had only seen the Tanzanian army fleeing, and then the sea of bleeding, dying, savaged civilians who came screaming or mute, alive and dead, terror-stricken, to the gates.

There was nothing to do but rush out amid the ravaging death to try to help one or two at a time, to staunch a river of blood spurting from a woman's armpit, to drag a dead mother off a baby suffocating underneath her, to hold a screaming, terrorized two-year-old who had been raped, then shot in the face. Sally Beth forced her own breath in and out, and with each exhale, she begged God for the life of her sister, for Phil's life, for John's life, for the life of the whimpering child she held in her arms. She had not seen Lilly or Phil for four days; she had not seen John since the night before that, but she knew he might be somewhere nearby, flying through bullets to ferry the seriously wounded to hospitals that might have enough room for them.

Oh, God! Where are You? Surely, You can see this. And surely, it offends You so much You want to make it stop. Please, make it stop. Lilly! John! Oh, God! Where are they? Protect them, Lord. Save this child. Save us all.

They had brought those they thought they could help back into the mission and had laid them on cots or blankets, or even on the grassy lawn. Still holding the child, she made her way back to the clinic, hoping against all reason to find a way to save her. The sun was setting. She had not eaten anything since early this morning, and she felt that she would sink to the floor, into the blood that rose up the soles of her shoes and be swallowed up in its rank redness. She brushed the hair from her face and looked up to see Falla smiling at her and holding out a glass of water. In Falla's face, she saw grace and beauty for the first time that day, but there was no pleasure in it, for it was laid against a backdrop of horror.

"Drink, Sally Beth. And give some to the babe." Falla leaned over to wash the little girl's face with a tattered rag. The child calmed for a moment, but clung to Sally Beth. A bullet had left a hole in her cheekbone: the huge, bloody-black cavity glared at her like a malevolent eye. Sally Beth gave her a sip of water and tried to look at the other side of her face, still flawlessly plump, a baby's face, but she could not manage a smile. All she could do was hold her tighter, close her eyes and cry out in silence.

The little girl died late in the afternoon, still cradled in Sally Beth's aching arms. Sally Beth could not even think clearly enough to lay her down; she merely stood mute and helpless while Dr. Sams gently lifted the cooling corpse from her. As night fell and the small bodies piled up outside the door, she finally crumbled, weeping and begging God to come into their midst, to lift the evil embedded in men's hearts, to rip it out, even if it meant ripping out so much of their hearts they could not survive. But God did not come. He did not speak. He had fled this place. Even He could not face this much evil.

Oh, Lord God. How can You stand us? Why have You not wiped humanity off the earth and started over?

October 29, 1978

The fighting had moved south, and for a few precious moments at a time, there was no one to care for, no dying hand to grasp, no ravaged and tortured woman or child to hold. The air still stank of burning houses, blood, and rotting flesh, but somehow, the mission had not been touched. The enemy soldiers had parted, like a school of sharks swimming around an island as they continued their way toward the heart of Tanzania.

She could not remember when she had last eaten or bathed. She had seen Alethia's girls only once since the carnage began, and then Lyla had taken them and several other children of the village to her home in the mountains west of Kyaka for safety. She had not had the chance to inform Alethia about this, for telephone lines had been down for four days, although they had managed intermittent radio contact. She hoped that Lyla had gotten through to her in Bukoba.

Sally Beth was sick with heartbreak and fatigue; she had

managed to snatch only moments of sleep at a time amid the terror and the violence. Now, even though quiet settled in, she could not bring herself to close her eyes; every time she did, she saw horror and death lunging, and she found herself cowering against the evil gnashing its teeth just outside the boundaries of her sight.

While bandaging a boy's mangled foot, she saw a movement across the room, and her eyes fell on a woman who suddenly smiled at her, then lifted herself from her chair and knelt onto the floor, singing. Her voice rose, rich and joyful, above the stench of the blood on the floor, the pile of bloody bandages on the table, above the basin of bloody water, and other voices joined hers. Sally Beth did not understand the words; they were sung in one of the dialects of the region. Falla leaned toward her and whispered the words to her in English:

> *Oh my Almighty God!*
> *You are the Father who loves us, the Father who gave us*
> *life, who gives us every breath.*
> *You are the Almighty One who conquers death, even as*
> *Death revels in triumph*
> *But Death is only a shadow that flees before the Light*
> *You are the Father, the Father who is the Light, who is*
> *Love, who is Breath*

Sally Beth knelt as well, sitting on her shins as the sounds and her own tears washed over her like a warm balm. For days, she had searched for God without glimpsing Him, without the whisper of His voice to comfort her, but now she felt the strength of the faith of those around her seeping into her soul, even as her own faith faltered. When she rose again, she felt a kind of power in the air, surging like a windless storm, and she grasped at it.

Lord, we have nothing, only You, but surely You, even in the midst of all this, should be enough. Let me see the Enough, Lord. Let me see it through Your eyes. I am too blind to see it through my own.

Late in the day, when Sally Beth felt that she could not stand under the weight of one more blow, she looked up to see Alethia's girls rushing toward her, and then she looked past them to see Lyla, ragged, dirty, and ashen, staring at her out of the face of a ghoul. When she saw Sally Beth, she cried out, running to her, arms outstretched, and buried her face in her hair, weeping as if she had no hope for life.

"What is it, Lyla? Why are you here?"

Lyla lifted her head, and through her tears, managed to stammer out, "They destroyed my home. My mother, my father—they are dead. And the workers who stayed to help. They held them off with rifles until I could escape into the forest with the children, but then the soldiers shelled the house and set it on fire. And then they set the orchard afire. There is nothing there but ruins, and I have been hiding and walking with the children for three days."

She stopped, gave a brief sob, but then, amazingly, smiled at Sally Beth. "But praise be to God. We have made it here, and you are safe! This place is standing." She gave Sally Beth a tight hug. "Is there food? And water? We are so thirsty. We have been living on fruit we found along the way, but there hasn't been much. The army has ravaged the countryside."

Sally Beth was too numb to be astonished, but as the girls gathered around her, hugging her, weeping, but praising God, she began to feel their warmth and their joy. Their clothes were filthy and in tatters; they were scratched and some were bleeding from small wounds, but to Sally Beth, they were beautiful. Lyla was beautiful. She pulled them into her arms, but only for a moment before she ran to find them water.

Later, after she had fed the children and put them to bed, after she had seen Lyla cradled in the arms of Pastor Umbatu, she heard the miraculous sound of John's Cessna engine coming from the east. She was outside and standing at the edge of the meadow when he landed, and he did not have a moment to think about it before she was in his arms, shaking and weeping, covering him with kisses. He kissed her back without thinking about it, for thought had vanished the moment he felt her arms around him.

She was filthy, smeared with blood, her hair hung in pale, limp strands around her ghostly face, and her eyes were hollow and red, but still, there was an aliveness about her in her quivering flesh and in the gasps that accompanied her sobs, and the reality of her pressing herself into him felt perfectly right.

"I thought you were dead. I haven't seen Lilly for days. How did you get here? The Ugandans are everywhere!"

"They aren't around here right now. This is the first time I have been able to get through, and I've been worried sick about you. I've come to get you out of here. Has anybody tried to get out?"

"No. The roads are mined, and soldiers are everywhere south of here. Oh, John, it's been awful! So many people killed; so much horror. I'm so *scared!*"

"I know, darling," he soothed. "Now, let's get out of here. I'll take you to Bukoba, and get out as many of the others as I can, then I'll take you to Kenya."

She shook her head. "Not me. Take the children. Lyla took Alethia's girls home with her, but it's been destroyed, and her parents are dead. They walked three days to get here. You have to take them."

John rested his chin on her head and breathed in the scent of her. Of course Sally Beth would not flee to safety as long as children were in danger. He wondered how many times he would have to fly through treacherous skies full of flying lead before he would be able to take her away from all this.

"Okay, Sally Beth. You go get the girls. I'll fuel up and maybe get some coffee. Is there anything to eat? I couldn't bring any supplies—they're desperate for whole blood at every hospital I've been to, and everything else is running out. If casualties have stopped up here, they've asked if we will send whatever blood and plasma we have where it will do some good. I'll radio ahead and see if I can get Alethia to meet me at the airport to pick up her girls."

Sally Beth ran back inside the mission to wake Lyla and Alethia's girls. "Hurry," she urged. "John is here. He's going to take you to your mama." They woke immediately and trailed after Sally Beth as she made her way back to the landing field. Red and Pastor Umbatu walked out with them.

"You'll have to sit on each other's laps. Prissy, you get in the front and hold Lizzy. Charlotte and Charlene, you sit in the back and hold Jayella and Becky. That's it, scoot over, and maybe Becky can squeeze in between you." She opened the front passenger door. Prissy, in here, sweetheart." But Priscilla stepped back, shaking her head.

"I'm not leaving you, Miss Sally Beth. Or Miss Lyla. You need someone here who loves you, to take care of you. I'll go when you do."

"Prissy! You have to go. I'll be fine here, I promise. And your mama is worried about you. Now, get in here."

But Priscilla refused to budge. "I have seen war, and I am not afraid of it. I can see you are afraid. I will stay here with you." She took another step back. Sally Beth and John looked at each other.

"I can be back in an hour," ventured John.

"Yes, it's crowded anyway," said Lyla. "We'll take care of Priscilla until you get back." She placed her hand on Priscilla's head. "My love, will you go on the next trip?"

"Yes, if you and Miss Sally Beth come, too."

John jumped in the front seat and leaned out toward Sally Beth. He wanted to say goodbye, but he suddenly felt awkward. He had kissed her as if he meant it half an hour earlier, and now he both regretted it and wanted to kiss her again. Geneva still nestled heavily in his heart. Even now, he could see her image, the memory of her laughing in the sunshine, and he knew he was not ready to give his love to anyone else. Yet, Sally Beth looked at him so hopefully, her eyes wide with unfulfilled promise, blood-smeared and filthy, and still beautiful, still innocent after all the horrors she had seen. He hesitated, then reached out and brushed away a lock of hair that had blown across her cheek. She lowered her lids and nodded. She knew what he was thinking, and she did not want him to see the disappointment in her eyes.

He delivered the girls to Alethia without mishap. She met him on the tarmac, clawing at the doors of the plane until she held her children in her arms, weeping with gratitude and thanking John in incoherent gasps. Then she flung her arms around him and kissed him without reservation. When she stepped back to look at him with shining eyes, he couldn't help but think, *War. It hands out kisses as well as bullets.*

"I'll be back with Priscilla as soon as I can," he said, as he grasped her shoulder. Then he got back into the plane and turned the nose northwest.

He was not able to go directly back to the mission. Enroute, he received a call from his station at Kigemba, telling him that soldiers had descended on the ranch and had stolen nearly all the cattle and set the place on fire. All the buildings were burning, half his staff was dead, and the cattle were gone. He groaned as he turned toward the ranch, for even as he lowered altitude to settle on the lake, he could see smoke billowing from the barns. Four men dead. He shut his eyes against the smoke as he landed.

October 30, 1978

John had not returned. Sally Beth, Priscilla, and Lyla sat at her desk in the empty room, waiting for something they could not name. They hoped for peace, but dared not expect it. They could not anticipate what the day held, but their hearts held fear and trepidation.

The Ugandan army was gone, spread out southward across the region in pursuit of the fleeing Tanzanians. The civilians also were gone, fled to the mountains or the cities in fear for their lives. Still, dread echoed throughout the mission.

Dr. Sams and Dr. Price came out of the examining rooms. The nurses Francine and Janie joined them soon afterward.

"Looks like business is slow today," said Dr. Price with a wry smile. "Guess the customers didn't like our service."

No one laughed. Lyla got up to make more tea. "I have oranges. The tree in the courtyard is loaded with them. Sally Beth and I like to chop them up and put the rinds and all in the tea."

"I'll take some," said Janie wearily. "I think we ran out of sugar yesterday."

"Me, too," said the others. Dr. Sams picked up a scalpel and carefully sliced open an orange.

"I guess we'd better think about how we're going to get out of here," he said. "The Embassy knows we are here, and they have made it clear to the Ugandans that the U.S. won't tolerate any harm to us, but I don't think they are willing to send anybody here to get us, at the moment, anyway. If they send in a plane, it could be an excuse to accuse America of interfering in a local conflict. The Ugandans obviously are reluctant to attack this place because they know we are here, but I don't think it's safe to travel on the road. There are enough renegades out there who might try to kidnap us for ransom, and besides, I'm sure there are still mines out there. We're just as good as under siege.

Dr. Price spoke up. "But they seem to be okay with John coming and going. They must know he's American because nobody has shot at him yet. If he makes it back, we can get out with him."

"Yes, but it's going to take some time to clear this place out, and if we're going to abandon it, we need to pack as much as we can in the way of supplies for him to take to the hospitals where they can do some good. We've got a little plasma and IV supplies. But I hear they really need whole blood. Who hasn't given blood this month?"

"I haven't," said Sally Beth. In fact, she had not given blood at all since she had been here. Dr. Sams had insisted she was too small to donate.

"Nor I," said Janie. "Well, I'm just a few days away from it being a month. I feel strong, though, so it'll be okay for me to give some more now."

"I'm good to go," spoke up Dr. Price. "I'm AB positive."

"Sally Beth, you can't. You never were big enough, and you've lost weight this week. Janie, you're A negative, right?" Dr. Sam's voice was abrupt.

Sally Beth suddenly felt slighted, dismissed as worthless. "Look," she said, bristling. "I weigh a hundred and twenty. You've just been too cautious." This might not have been true. When she had arrived nearly two months ago, she had weighed a hundred twenty-one pounds. It was likely she had lost more than a few pounds during the past couple of weeks, but she felt an overwhelming need to give blood. "Maybe only a pound or two under. Go ahead. Somebody could really need this, and I'm as healthy as a mule. I'm O negative. If anybody needs blood, mine will be the most useful." There was a silence as everyone regarded her. To everyone there, she looked pale and thin, but a fierceness in her eyes made Dr. Sams relent.

"Okay, we'll get a unit from each of you, and no doubt it will be needed." He moved to one of the examining rooms to collect the equipment, returning a moment later. Sally Beth jumped up.

"I'll be first," she said, her head up and chin out. Dr. Sams sighed as he wrapped the rubber strap around her arm.

Sally Beth grasped Priscilla's hand, chatting to her as she felt the blood drain out of her body. She downed a cup of tea and held out her cup for another. "Prissy, what is the first thing you are going to say to your mother when you see her again?"

Prissy laughed. "I'll tell her how beautiful she is." Sally Beth forced laughter, drank more tea, and kept her head up. The blood draining from her arm seemed to be taking with it all the strength she had, but she steeled herself against the rising darkness. At last, Dr. Sams smiled at her.

"I'm proud of you, Sally Beth. I knew you were strong, but you've got some real iron in there, haven't you?"

Dr. Price revived the earlier conversation. "How many children are there on campus right now?"

"There are eight young ones, and another three teenagers," replied Sally Beth. "That means John will have to make at least five or six more trips, if adults can carry children on their laps. He can carry only three adults at a time, and it wouldn't be fair to hold you all up. You nurses and one of you docs go as soon as you can. I can't leave until I know Lilly is safe, and I have to get Lyla and Priscilla out with me."

Lyla shook her head. "I'm not leaving without Pastor Umbatu, and I'm sure he'll be the last to leave, so don't worry about me."

"We'll worry about that when and if John comes back," said Dr. Price, "but I agree that Janie and Francine need to get out of here as soon as they can. Francine especially. Being black, you may not be recognized as American. The rest of us have the advantage of being the only whites in the area. They have to know who we are."

They all sank into silence. In the distance, they could hear the distinct *Rat-tat-tat-tat!* of guns and the *Boom!* of rockets reducing yet another village to rubble. Priscilla moved closer to Sally Beth and wrapped her arms around her. They were trapped in a quiet solitude within an outer shell of violence, the sad and desperate eye of a hurricane. None of them knew what to do. They held hands and prayed, but even as she tried to lift her heart toward God, Sally Beth felt it collapsing, folding inward and sinking back down, past her chest, past her feet even. Her prayers were useless, for God had either turned His back or had simply left altogether. She suddenly wondered why she bothered. Why pray to someone who did not care? She closed her eyes against the silence hammering her broken spirit.

John wanted to make it back to the mission before dark. If he tried to fly in at night, the Ugandans might not recognize his plane and could shoot him down. His ranch had pretty much been reduced to cinders and the cattle were gone, so all he could do was bury the dead and tell his workers to go home, or someplace safe, until he got in touch with them. He seriously doubted that he would attempt to rebuild the Kigemba station for a long time, and he wondered how to get in touch with the anonymous donor to let him know about the disaster that had befallen. But all that could wait. Now he needed to get to the mission to try to get Sally Beth and the others to safety.

He landed late in the afternoon. There would be time for perhaps two more trips to Bukoba, if he hurried. The medical crew and several others met him at the landing strip.

There was little time for conversation. They loaded what medical supplies could fit into the fuselage while Francine and Janie boarded the plane with children squirming on their laps.

"Here, I'm putting this under the backseat," said Dr. Price, shoving the cooler of whole blood they had just collected under the leather bench. "It's not much, but I'm sure it will be helpful," he added as he picked up a small child and put him on the lap of one of the older children.

After squeezing children onto laps and on top of one another, John finally hoisted himself up into the pilot's seat and looked out one last time before he started his pre-flight check.

Sally Beth put her arm around Priscilla as they watched the Skylane lift into the clouds and wing its way eastward, away from the late afternoon sun. They were silent, listening only to their hearts crying out after it.

An hour later, John landed again. His eyes were burning from the soot he had rubbed into them. He had not taken the time to even wash his face when he had left the smoldering ranch. He was sick. Sick of heart, sick of the smell of death, sick of the violence, of the evil that had descended on this peaceful place, but he pushed on, ignoring his fatigue and his nausea.

Dr. Price and Dr. Sams tried to persuade Sally Beth to get on the plane, but she shook her head. "Lilly is somewhere around here. I can't leave without her. Don't worry. Just go. Maybe she will come back tonight."

With all of her heart, she hoped that was true, that her sister would return to her and that together they would fly to safety with John, but no matter how much she listened for the Voice to tell her that Lilly would return to her unharmed, it remained silent. She did not know why God had abandoned her, only that He had. She shuddered and clung to Prissy's hand.

Priscilla would not go, either, and Dr. Sams declared he would be on the last trip out, but insisted that Dr. Price go. "You have three little children," he said. "If anything were to happen to you, I don't want to have to face them, or Jenny. Now get on the plane. You can put these two on your lap."

Dr. Price turned to embrace Sally Beth. "I'm so sorry we brought you here," he said as he held her tightly against him. "Stay right here until John comes back, and I will see you soon. I'll wait in Bukoba until I know you—all of you—are safe. God bless you, my dear." Then he squeezed himself into the front seat, a child on each knee.

When John lifted off again, Sally Beth turned to Lyla and Priscilla, and with the last ounce of her energy, smiled at them brightly. "Any more of that tea left, Lyla? I think there is a little flour still in the pantry, and I bet there's some honey, too. We might as well make some cookies." Her voice was light, but inside her heart there was only darkness.

Since she did not expect John to return that evening, she faced the approaching night feeling alone and hopeless, despite the small crowd of people who had gathered around the kitchen.

When the sound of his approaching engine drifted in with the gloaming, her suffocated heart awoke with a start and a flutter to the realization that he was here for her. It roused in her a deep yearning that rode red and warm in her blood. Brushing away a thin, frail voice from her past that whispered some nonsense about virtue, she turned her face toward the only thing that gave her hope. Amid all this horror, despite the loss of God's presence, there was a shard of glory in her love for John Smith: piercing, painful, but irrefutable, and it would not be denied.

John saw her as the lights bounced into the grass, and he saw the shift in her stance, the purposefulness of her stride as she made her way toward him. A coldness overtook him as he realized that somehow his fate had been sealed against his wishes. He loved

Sally Beth, but he was not in love with her, for there was room for only one woman in his heart, and that woman was Geneva. Yet, here Sally Beth stood, waiting for him so resolutely, standing so still, willing him to come to her. He did not know how he could disappoint her.

She did not run to him, but waited until he stopped the plane, then walked purposefully toward him. They embraced silently, but when she lifted her face, she felt his reluctance. It meant nothing to her. She had nothing but him now, and she would not accept his refusal. Her parents were dead, her best friend Holy Miracle Jones was dead, her sister had disappeared into the bloody maw of war. God had abandoned her. She might never see her home again, but if she had any control over her life at this moment, she was resolved that John would be hers, at least for a little while. She knew it for a fact; she felt it in the marrow of her soul.

Taking his hand, she led him to the courtyard by the church where they sat on the bench under the orange tree.

"You know what I want," she said at last.

He did not pretend to not know what she meant. When he saw her face, it was full of naked love, of desire. She had lost the ability to conceal the rawness of her feelings.

"Are you sure?"

"Don't patronize. This is no time for philosophy."

"I mean, you are worn out, things are out of control. How will you feel later?"

"Is there a later?"

"Of course there is. It may not be what we want, but it will come. Have you asked God about this?"

She gave a short laugh. "Oh, I know what God would say, but He isn't speaking to me right now." She was left to find her own comfort.

"I have to listen to my own heart. God doesn't know what it is like to be a child who has never seen anything but peace and the love of everyone around her, and then, overnight, to be thrown into a world of absolute evil. To be a woman who has spent her life believing that sex is a sacred pleasure between a man and a woman, a husband and wife, and then to see firsthand what men who are full of hate will do. He doesn't know what it feels like to be a virgin and see what men have done to innocent girls, to wonder if she will ever be loved by a man who will be gentle with her, to make her feel beautiful and cherished. You may not love me, but I was hoping you could pretend." She did not cry, but the sadness in her voice ripped at his heart.

"I cannot pretend, Sally Beth. It wouldn't be right. Not to you, not to me."

"But you can at least be gentle."

He let the words sink in. Sitting in the dark, holding her hand, he smelled the oranges in the tree above them and the smoke and grime on his own skin, the fear and traces of blood on hers. He could not refuse her, so open, so trusting, so hopeful that they could create something good amid this horror, but this was not the time. He was too tired. He did not want this—to see the rawness of her pain or her feeling for him, to try to pretend to love her when he knew he could only hurt her and ultimately increase her despair. If he were to make love to her, the least he could do would be to make it as beautiful for her as possible, and right now, so little of him was available, so little was possible.

"I would do you no good tonight," he said, his voice heavy with regret and fatigue. "Can we wait until tomorrow?"

She thought about it. She did not want to let go of the heat of his hand. She had held too many cold and dying hands in the past few days. She needed his wholesome blood to put some warmth into her own veins. "Will you sit with me awhile here tonight?"

"I will stay with you all night. Wait here. I'll go get blankets."

She was leaning against the trunk of the tree when he returned with blankets and even a pillow, and she helped him to spread them out on the ground, pushing aside the fallen oranges to make their bed smooth. Then they both lay down, he put his arms around her, and she laid her head on his chest, her arm holding him tightly.

"Thank you," she breathed.

He hugged her closer. Peace settled over them, and before she remembered that God had forsaken her, she prayed for the safety of her sister. In the empty stillness afterward, she thought she might have heard His voice whispering gently, *I know, my beloved. I know.*

Eighteen

October 31, 1978

John awoke to an empty space beside him and the sun in his
eyes. He sat up, rubbed the grime around on his face, and got
up, rolling up the blankets and pillow before he made his way to
the clinic. Sally Beth was there, alone. She was clean and in a fresh
dress. Her newly washed hair shimmered on her shoulders. The
look she gave him was one of pure delight.

He did not know how to respond. He had made a promise to
her last night that he was not sure she wanted him to keep. "Good
morning," he said, running his hand through his sooty hair. "You
left me."

"I was feeling nasty." She stopped, a startled look on her face.
"Literally. I needed a bath." She did not want him to think she had
felt sullied by her desire for him. She started again. This was no
time to be coy, so she faced him directly. "I still want you."

He saw how hard it was for her to speak so frankly, so he
merely nodded as he studied the floor. "I need to go see if I can get
everybody else out today. Red and Dr. Sams are the last Americans,

besides us, and there's Falla and Jenna, the pastor and Lyla, Prissy, and some others, all African. I don't want them left here once the Ugandans know the Americans are gone. What do you want to do? Are you still going to wait for Lilly?"

She nodded. "Try to talk Pastor Umbatu and Lyla into going, and Priscilla."

"If they go, it will just be you and me here tonight."

"I've thought about that. It's not right asking you to stay, so I'm releasing you from your promise. If something happens to you because you stayed with me, it would be worse than if something happens to Lilly. I'll be okay. They are leaving the mission alone, so I'll be safe here. I'm hoping Alethia's place is still standing. It's way off the main road, so maybe it is. Will you fly over it on your first trip out and let me know? If it is, I can go get some food from her pantry. There's not much left here."

He nodded again. The thought of leaving her here alone was an impossibility. "I'll stay," he said, "as long as you do," then he pushed off the doorframe, battling the thoughts that flung themselves around like live grenades inside his head. He could think of nothing but the promise he had made to her and why she had asked it of him: not the war, not his own possible death, but only of how he had seen her disintegrate before his eyes and how much she needed him to be something beyond what he could be. This war had robbed her of the God she knew, and in her loss, she needed him to step into His place and give her fragile heart something to beat for.

What was he to do? He was cursed if he did, cursed if he didn't, cursed by his own heart and by this lovely woman who trusted him not to hurt her, but was already so hurt she could be slain by a mere breath, a single word. He tried to ignore his twisting gut as he finally caved into the inevitable. He would have to go through with this, and he would do it right for Sally Beth's sake, even though he knew in his very marrow that this night could destroy at least one of them.

"I'll stay," he repeated. "And I'll love you as best I can." His heart lightened at the radiance of her face.

Alethia's house was still standing. It was tucked up under some trees on the edge of a forest, which kept it partially hidden from the air. The meadow beside it basking in the open would serve as a landing field. He wondered what would happen if his plane was seen on the ground outside the protection of the mission, then sighed with resignation. It didn't matter. He and Sally Beth both could be dead by morning, but there was nothing he could do about that.

He flew back and forth all morning, taking people to the Bukoba airport, dropping them off, returning as quickly as he could to gather more. By noon, only seventeen remained: that meant five or six more trips before the mission would be completely abandoned. Besides Sally Beth, there was Dr. Sams, who had begged her to go, then declared he would not leave until she did, Jenna and Falla, Red, Pastor Umbatu and Lyla, Priscilla, and nine other Africans who had come only this morning seeking refuge. They all pleaded with Priscilla to go on the next trip, but she stood before them defiantly, her head up, looking much older than her fourteen years.

"I will stay with Sally Beth and Lyla," she declared. "I know this land, and I can get them away from here if I need to. I am not a helpless, uninformed child. I am Ugandan, and I have known war, war much worse than this."

At this speech, Sally Beth nearly broke her resolve to wait for Lilly, but she could not give up hope that her sister was still alive, and she could not leave as long as the ember of that hope still glowed. She put her arms around Priscilla.

Pastor Umbatu was resolved to stay with his church until the last in case more refugees came seeking shelter. Lyla said, "You are all I have left in this world. I will stay by your side until death takes us." Then she turned to Sally Beth. "Sally Beth, I understand that you have the qualifications to marry two people. I love this man, and I want to be his wife. James Umbatu," she said, "I don't want to wait another six weeks. Will you become my husband now?"

He threw his head back and laughed a booming, joyful sound that sent a startle through the soft, rainy afternoon. "Will I be your husband? Lyla, you are a treasure above rubies!" He turned his beaming face to Sally Beth. "Sally Beth, will you honor us with the sacrament?"

Everyone laughed. Sally Beth knew she was not legally privileged to perform the marriage ceremony, as she knew that her heart was not deserving to perform a holy sacrament in the name of God, but at such times, what did it matter? To spread joy and love in the face of death was an honor, an exultation of the soul. She hurried to her room to find her best dress for Lyla to wear, feeling happiness warming her and filling her with strength. There would be a wedding! Sally Beth grew giddy with the thought of it.

With one voice, everyone insisted on staying to see the ceremony. "We don't all have to leave today," declared Red. Nothing will happen tonight, and John is probably worn out from all this flying and trying to keep things from falling apart at the ranch. Let's have a party this afternoon. Let's celebrate life. And love."

An hour later, Red stood in the hushed sanctuary beside Pastor Umbatu, and Falla stood beside Lyla. All the women wore flowers in their hair. Priscilla served as flower girl, walking slowly down the aisle, spreading the fragrant petals of the white lilies that grew in the meadow. Jenna played the piano, and Sally Beth's heart swelled when she pronounced the two husband and wife.

Afterwards, Pastor Umbatu bowed graciously and spoke in his beautiful, resonate voice. "My wife and I would like to invite you to a wedding luncheon, although I fear that you will have to help us prepare it. Please come and enjoy the best of what we have to offer. We even have a few bottles of sacrament wine. I'm sure the Lord will not mind if we drink it, if we do it in His honor."

Taking Lyla's arm, he led everyone to the kitchen where they ransacked the pantry for yams, flour, and canned beef. Several people went outside to gather fruit from the trees in the courtyard, and within an hour, the tables were spread with a modest feast. Lyla and Pastor Umbatu stood at the head, the smiles on their faces beaming peace and joy.

Sally Beth reveled in their happiness, even as her own heart pained. The newlyweds had each other, and everyone except her had family, someone waiting to welcome them home. Lilly, the only remainder of her immediate family, was gone, perhaps dead, and except for the hope that lay in John, she was utterly alone. Glancing at him to search for a glimmer of something, anything that he might feel for her, she saw that his face was a mask of grief, and she felt lonelier still. Would there never be a place for her in his heart? Would she die in this place, in the midst of horror and violence without knowing what it was like to be loved?

Oh Lord, why have You deserted me?

They had just finished the blessing when a horn blared at the gates. Rushing out, they saw a jeep, driven by a uniformed soldier, and Lilly and Phil in the back seat. Both were filthy and sunburned but robust and healthy. Lilly jumped out and ran to her sister.

Sally Beth felt joy surge through her. Lilly alive! Lilly running to her! She caught her sister, sobbing and hugging her until neither of them could take another breath.

"Sally Beth, you're still here. Oh, I'm so sorry! We've been trying to get back for days, but we had to stay off the main road because of the mines, and we had to hide from the Ugandans." She turned to the driver. "This is Samuel. He risked his life to bring us here, when he could have been safe up at Kakoma. But I knew you wouldn't leave here until we came back, and I begged them to bring us."

Samuel shrugged. "The Lakwena gave me leave to come. Who am I to question the mind of the Spirit?"

Sally Beth grasped his hand, speechless with gratitude. "Come and eat," she urged him, and when he demurred, she pulled his hand hard. "You must eat. We are celebrating a wedding."

They all sat down to eat. Before she took her first bite, Lilly exclaimed, "Sally Beth, this has been the most incredible week of my life! Wait until you hear what's been going on." She picked up her glass of wine and held it up. "To the newlyweds!" she declared. "And to life!" But she did not drink. She set the glass down and reached for a glass of water.

Lilly and Phil stuffed themselves as if they had not eaten for weeks. Between mouthfuls, they managed to spin out the story of their adventures for the last six days.

"You won't believe where we've been. Up in Uganda, with an army of civilians, soldiers, women, children, all mixed together, all under the leadership of Alice Auma, although they're calling her Alice Lakwena, because she is the medium for a spirit named Lakwena who guides them. She's like a modern Joan of Arc—she's only twenty-two, but all these people are following her orders and going into battle, and doing exactly what she tells them to. But they say they aren't fighting Amin's army; they say they are fighting evil; they are fighting a war against war, and they are doing it with God's guidance. Well, they say they are guided by Holy Spirits. Lakwena is one of them.

"Really," continued Lilly. "They are the most orderly, most loving, kindest people. They don't even want to kill—they just want to live in peace and in harmony with all men and with nature, too. They treat the land with reverence, they won't even cross a river without asking permission from it, and they throw coins and cowrie shells in and, in the most respectful voices, ask to 'purchase the right' to cross."

"But do they fight? How do they fight evil? Do they use guns?"

"Yeah, they do, but they don't point them at anybody. They aren't even allowed to try to kill anyone. They just wait until Lakwena tells them to shoot, and the Sprits direct the bullets to where they want them to go. If any of the enemy are killed, it's the Spirits that kill them, not the soldiers. They go into battle singing hymns, without their shirts on, or shoes, without any kind of armor, except they're anointed with Shea butter, ochre, and holy water. That's supposed to make them bullet proof."

"That's crazy," said John. "It seems like they would be mowed down."

"I know!" answered Lilly. "But the Ugandans are terrified when they even hear them coming. They run from them as if they see swarms of angels, or demons coming at them, singing and blowing horns, like when Gideon's army trounced the Midianites without any weapons. Soldiers just throw down their weapons and run! The Holy Spirits are wreaking havoc on Amin's forces."

"Have you seen this in person?" John asked.

"Yeah, once. Only the Lakwena determines who is allowed to go, and he permitted us, but we had to be purified. Just to be with them, we had to go through a long process to be declared righteous. You can't smoke or drink or fornicate—anybody caught committing adultery is whipped and banished—and you have to follow the orders of the Lakwena exactly. Do you remember when Alice came in after the whipping? Well, the Lakwena ordered that whipping, and the orders came out of *her* mouth! It's like she has nothing to do with what the spirit wants. Nobody does, and you'd better obey because once the Lakwena speaks, there's no getting around it.

"Anyway, we had to follow *all* the rules. You have to eat certain things and be kind and loving, honest—you know, what you would expect from churchy people. But there are a lot more rules, and even then, it's not easy to be chosen for battle. Alice goes into a trance every day or maybe twice a day, and the Spirits speak through her. So far, we've heard only two of their voices, but they tell us there are several besides Lakwena. They give very explicit orders about who can go to combat.

"We got lucky. Before one of the battles, Lakwena said Phil and I should go to record the miracles that happened. They wanted others to know, I guess." She took another swallow of water. "But we had to go through an extra purification ritual, take an oath of chastity, and a bunch of stuff, which ended in us spitting into a live chicken's mouth." She laughed. "I know, it sounds crazy! Poor Phil had to prove he had two testicles—no more, no less—is what the rulebook says, before he was declared worthy. But I gotta tell you, we've seen some miracles. They threw stones—regular rocks that glowed when they picked them up and exploded like grenades when the soldiers threw them, people getting shot at and not getting killed. It's the most amazing thing I've ever seen."

"Oh, Lilly! You went into a battle?" Sally Beth felt her heart break.

"Really," spoke up Phil. "We felt perfectly safe. We were off to the side, well away from any danger, standing up on a hill where we could see everything. Mostly we just saw Alice's army advancing, singing, and then when they stopped singing—you're not going to believe this—yelling 'James Bond!' at the top of their lungs, shooting randomly, and the Ugandans just broke and ran. Most of them threw down their guns, terrified the minute they saw them coming. It was incredible. Seasoned soldiers, throwing down their weapons and running over each other getting away."

"'James Bond'?" asked Red.

"Yeah. The chief technician, that's the guy who is the ritual expert, who makes sure everybody is properly purified and armed, so to speak, is named James, and he calls himself 'James Bond.' Everybody yells his name over and over at the top of their lungs as they are marching. It's the most surreal thing imaginable. You have to be there to believe it.

"By the way, we've written an article, and whoever is leaving out of here, will you send it to this address? And these rolls of film? Our professor is waiting for all this. He's going to submit the story to the AP wire and see what comes of it." Phil's eyes glittered with excitement. "This could make our careers. We could even get an award for covering this."

"Why don't you deliver it yourselves? We've all got to get out of here today or tomorrow. The Ugandans could decide to take this place out any day now." Now that Lilly was safe, Sally Beth was anxious to get away to safety.

Lilly paused, grimacing as she turned to her sister. Putting her hand on her shoulder and looking directly into her eyes, she pleaded. "Sally Beth, I'm so sorry. We're going back. This is just too big for us. Too important. We have to see this story through. Please understand!" She brushed back Sally Beth's hair with a tender gesture. "We just came back today to let you know we were safe and to ask you to deliver the film and the manuscript. We can't leave now."

Sally Beth felt the floor fall way from underneath her. She grabbed the edge of the table and jumped up. "Lilly! You can't go back into that. I have been in hell, waiting here for you, terrified about what was happening to you, and Priscilla won't go without me, and if something happens to her, it will be on my head, and I couldn't stand it if you were killed, or even *hurt*. I can't stand it not knowing where you are. Please! Don't do this; come home with me—" Her voice broke with a sob.

Lilly stood as well, taking Sally Beth into her arms. She seemed gentler, older, as she very quietly cupped her hands around Sally Beth's cheeks and looked closely at her. "Darling, I know you are afraid for me, for us. But we probably are safer than you are. I know we are safer than you are if you stay *here*." She hesitated, blinking back tears before she continued, "You have to understand that I have found my purpose in life," and Sally Beth could feel and hear the certain resolve in her voice. "I have somehow become the person I was meant to be, the person I never could be before now. You can't ask me to not be that person. Do you really want me to go back to being that silly, lazy, materialistic girl who always gave you such a hard time? Please don't ask me to do that. Let me be who I need to be. Somebody you can be proud of. Somebody *I* can be proud of." Tears shimmered in her eyes, then made their way slowly down her face.

Sally Beth flung herself into Lilly's arms, sobbing into her shoulder. She felt her whole world collapsing around her as she realized Lilly's resolve would not be shaken, no matter what she said or did. *Did God hate her? Why else would He take everything she loved away from her and then go away Himself and refuse to give her anything in return?* She sat down, put her head in her arms, and wept as if her heart would never mend.

Lilly and Phil left immediately after lunch. "Don't worry about us!" they insisted. "And leave! Get out of here before the Ugandans decide to take this place. *Please.* Go home, or at least go to Kenya with John." They moved to the jeep and waved as Samuel started it and roared out of the compound. "We'll get in touch when we leave, and it won't be long. Maybe a couple more weeks. We have to finish this."

Sally Beth stood looking after them, and although the others gathered around her, holding her, murmuring soft words, she felt entirely abandoned, especially when John cleared his throat and said softly, "We have to go now, if I'm to get any more people out today…" Sally Beth nodded, held up her head, and smiled through her tears.

"Of course." She walked slowly to the meadow with everyone to bid farewell to John and three refugees from nearby villages.

Before John climbed into the plane, he pulled her aside and murmured to her, "If you still want this, I will meet you at Alethia's house tonight."

Sally Beth looked at him, her eyes filled with anguish, and yet, somehow, hope. It pierced him with dread and sorrow and an ache that took over his whole being. Did she have any idea what she was asking of him? She needed him to be an impossible thing: a man who would prove to her that men could be good, that there were some she could trust to keep her safe, even as he lied to her with his body. And yet, she knew he would be lying. She had said it herself: he would be pretending to love her for one night only. What would become of her after that? Who would she hate more, he wondered—herself or him? He tried not to flinch at the hope in her eyes.

"I'll have time for a couple more trips after this one to get six more people out, and then I'll tell everyone that I'll stay in Bukoba tonight, and I'll come to you. If you can, try to find a way to camouflage the plane. Paint or something, anything so that it will be hard to notice if somebody flies over in a chopper."

She nodded. "Yes. Trust me." She looked deep into his eyes, and as if she were reading his mind, she smiled softly and touched his face. "I know how hard this is for you. I don't expect anything except a little comfort. I need something I can hold onto, just in case things don't go well from here on out."

He wondered if he should kiss her, but he decided not to. The others were waiting for him, expectant, and the sun would not be still.

Nineteen

"Falla, I'm going to run over to Alethia's house for a little while. It's still standing, but it probably won't last the war. I'm going to get some things that are precious to her—pictures and so forth. I don't want Priscilla to come with me; it might be dangerous. Would you stay with her? Tell her I'm sad about my sister and I want to be alone the rest of today and tonight. I'll be back in the morning. I don't want to chance coming back after dark."

Falla looked at her with concern. "Nothing is as precious to Alethia as you, Sally Beth. It is foolhardy to go."

"Maybe, but I really do want to be alone tonight. Please. I promise to be careful. Just do this for me, okay?"

Falla nodded. Sally Beth hated to tell the half-lie, but her life had turned into a lie of sorts anyway. Everything that she had learned her whole life—that life was good, that people were good, that God protects and guides—all those were lies to her. What was one more little lie now so she could find a moment of comfort and pleasure in John's arms? She packed a bag, fumbled around for the keys to Alethia's van, and left without another word.

It was hard going. There was almost nothing left of the road, and Sally Beth was glad she would not have to go over the river, for the bridge was precarious, although still standing. She made her way slowly around the holes, the abandoned, burned-out vehicles, and, to her horror, the decaying bodies of animals and humans scattered across the landscape. She knew she was looking at the aftermath of evil, at the very thing hell was made of and almost chuckled to herself as she remembered thinking that the desert outside Las Vegas was what hell was like. She would have given her hands to be in that desert with Lilly right now.

She drove on resolutely, meeting no one, listening to the sound of the rain on the roof, the windshield wipers swishing. The radio offered nothing but static. The world was on hold while evil roved the land. Only the rain offered a small piece of grace to her troubled soul.

The clouds cleared away as she drove through the red mud up to Alethia's house; it stood, untouched in a bright shaft of afternoon sunlight, a beacon of homeliness adrift in a sea of horror. Sally Beth parked the van close to the porch, mounted the stairs, and unlocked the front door, walking into the same sweet, cluttered room strewn with toys and bright clothing that she had left just a couple of weeks ago. The treadle sewing machine still sat on the dining table. A little blue and white dress lay draped over a chair, waiting to be hemmed.

There was no electricity, so she set about looking for candles and lanterns, and after she found them, she took a flashlight and went down to the basement, where she found the stash of fabric that matched the flowered curtains, slipcovers, and dresses upstairs. Alethia had not been exaggerating; there were at least a thousand yards wound onto scores of bolts. She took several of them up the stairs, found the scissors and thread, and sat down at the table.

Taking two bolts of cloth, she unwound them, then set to work sewing them together. When she had run a seam about fifty feet long, she cut the fabric, and then, starting at the top, began another seam parallel to the other. She did not stop after she had sewn up a fifty-foot square blanket, but went to work on another, smaller one. Finally, after an hour of sewing, she clipped the thread, took the smaller blanket outside and draped it over the van. From where she stood, it looked just like what it was, a big swath of colored fabric draped over a vehicle, but she hoped that in the dark, it would simply look like trees or bushes bedecked with blue, red, and yellow flowers.

Next, she went around back, slipped through the weedy garden, and retrieved tomatoes, cucumbers, and yams. Mangoes from the tree in the side yard were plentiful and ripe. Back inside, she rummaged through the pantry, whipped up a simple cake to put in the gas oven, and put beans on to cook.

Finally, she ran water in the bathtub, grateful for the gas water heater, then sank into the tub and waited until the sun began to settle in the west.

This would be something of a wedding night. She realized how pitifully adolescent the thought was. John did not love her, although she was certain she loved him. She was not naïve enough to believe that somehow he would be so smitten with her feminine wiles that he would fall madly in love with her. No, she knew that her plea for him to make love to her was the pathetic begging of a desperately lonely woman who could not see beyond the pain she had been facing for the last—how many days? It seemed like years. It seemed that the peace and love she had known as a child was only a vague, pleasant dream of the past. Now she knew that reality was brutal, and if she wanted any joy, she would have to grab it whenever she found the opportunity, even if it meant finding a man who could only pretend to care for her, and even then, reluctantly. She didn't care. Her love for John was the only light she had right now, and she needed him to show her that beauty was possible, even in the midst of horror.

She shaved her legs, washed, and dragged herself out of the tub wearily, then dressed in a clean summer dress, not bothering with underwear. She went downstairs to wait for the man who could, for a moment perhaps, make her forget about what life had become.

John arrived just before dusk, at that time of day photographers call the "magic hour," when light becomes alive, delightedly exploring secret corners, mischievously dashing away shadows that had tucked themselves away. Sally Beth put on her shoes, and out of habit, her pink princess cowboy hat, and went out to meet him, her arms full of the cheerful meadow she had stitched together earlier.

He was filled with dread as he approached the field beside Alethia's house, but when he saw her waiting for him draped in what looked like a huge colorful tent, he found himself forgetting his own fear, and instead felt a rush of delight. As usual, Sally Beth managed to look both beautiful and absurd, her arms full of fabric that not only mounded up to her head, but also dragged in a long trail behind her. Above that was her lovely face, her gleaming hair spread out over her shoulders, and topping that, the ridiculous pink hat, the rhinestone princess crown winking in the sun. He felt little bubbles of happiness float through his being, battling their way through the trepidation that had lived there all day.

"I made a present for your plane," she said, hefting the enormous bundle into his arms. "I think it's big enough to cover it, and we can weigh the edges down with rocks." He took the weight of it, and then felt a little shock going through him when he saw what she was wearing. A thin pink linen dress clung to her, and the sunlight streamed straight through it so that she seemed to be clothed in nothing but a pale pink glow. He averted his eyes, looking closely at what she had given him.

"Ah, it's a camouflage tent!" he exclaimed. "Brilliant, Sally Beth. Let's get this over her and see how she looks."

Together, they managed to drape the huge blanket over the plane, and when they stepped back, they both laughed at how silly it looked—like a giant child hiding under a blanket, pretending to be invisible. But when he squinted, he could see that from a distance, or at night, it just might work. Once the light failed, it very well could look like a flowery meadow or a forest of blooming trees. He shrugged. "Better than I could have done." Then he took her hand and walked back toward the house.

"I have a little supper," she said cautiously, then glanced down at herself and blushed violently. She had not realized how thin the dress was, or how the brightness of the sun would reduce it to merely a mist over her nakedness. As quickly as she could, she went to Alethia's closet and pulled out a drab robe. John pretended not to notice, but fumbled into the kitchen, saying, "My, this smells good. Did you bake a cake?"

"Yes. Dinner will be ready in five or ten minutes, just as soon as this cornbread is done."

"Good. I'm starved. Could I take a shower before dinner? I'm filthy."

"Of course." She blushed again and looked away.

He showered quickly, dressed himself in the clean clothes he had brought with him, and returned to find the table set with candles and a vase of flowers. "Beautiful," he said, meaning the flowers, but looking at her, and then the conversation faltered. They tried starting it up again several times over supper, but it was fraught with false starts and awkward stammerings, followed by long periods of silence while they toyed with their food.

Dusk settled gently around them, as softly as their silence, and they both fought with the apprehensions fluttering through the shadows of their souls. At last he stood. "Let's go see how the disguise looks."

Together they walked to the porch. To their surprise, the plane had seemed to disappear, melding into the shadows as completely as a mist flitting among the trees. "Sally Beth, you are a genius," he chuckled, and she laughed, too. In her laughter, he could hear the echoes of happiness. Only the echoes, but even so, the sound of it lightened his heart. He took her shoulders and turned her to him.

"Sally Beth, we don't have to do this. I can just hold you tonight like I did last night. I don't want you to do anything you might regret."

In response, she moved closer to him, put her arms around him, and kissed him with all the love she had to offer.

Her mouth tasted like honey and mangoes, and her touch sent tendrils of fire flashing throughout his whole being. He had prepared himself to be completely in control, to be the best lover he could be for her, but this kiss and his sudden desire sent him spiraling along a path he had not anticipated, a delicious, beckoning path that made him want to fling aside all his constraints and go running down it. Sliding his hands down her back and resting them at the base of her spine, he felt how small her waist was, how her flesh swelled out behind and to the sides in such firm plumpness that he wanted to rub the curves and marvel at their smoothness.

He remembered his task. This was about her. "Does Alethia have any records or music tapes or anything?" He laughed nervously. "Something other than church music, I hope."

Sally Beth broke from him, went inside, and returned with a battery-powered boom box, in which she had already placed a tape of The Righteous Brothers, and started the music. Then she fell into his arms, and together they moved to the music of "Unchained Melody."

The clouds had blown away, revealing a clear, black sky so filled with stars that it glowed sliver. A tiny sliver of a moon rose over their heads, the merest hint of light that was dwarfed by the majesty of the Milky Way. They danced in the billowing grass, and the more the music drifted into their hearts and minds, the more they both felt that this moment was right, that they should be here together, under the glowing sky, in the quiet of the music, feeling the rhythms of each other's bodies. John felt a shudder run through him. This was not supposed to happen, but he did not care. Sally Beth was in his arms, and nothing before had ever felt so perfect.

Sally Beth felt nothing but love. Her heart had melted the moment her lips had touched his, and all she wanted was more of him. She even found herself thanking God for bringing him here, although when she remembered that He would surely frown on what they did this night, she still felt grateful for the gift of love, for the gift of desire, of young bodies that could respond like this even in the face of danger and horror and death. She pushed that thought from her mind. For tonight, she would not think about it. She would only let herself feel the fireworks spiraling inside her, the warmth of John's body as he moved with her and with the music.

He had planned what he would do. He had told himself that he would keep himself aloof so that he could concentrate solely on her pleasure. He had not had high hopes about that: he had been with a virgin once before, when he was inexperienced, too, and it had ended in disaster—pain, tears and regret. Knowing Sally Beth's strong moral code, he feared the same from her tonight, when she remembered how cold his heart was.

But he forgot to be aloof; he forgot he could not love her, and he felt himself falling, as if from a great height, into a well of peace and happiness, into a pool of warm desire. As soon as the last notes of the last song faded away, Sally Beth took his hand and led him into the downstairs bedroom, where she gently pushed him onto the bed, then eased herself beside him, pressed herself against him, and kissed him with such passion that he had to keep telling himself that he must be slow and careful. He peeled off the robe, then the summery dress, and he felt his breath quicken when he saw the snowy perfection of her body.

After that, he forgot everything except that a beautiful woman— no, not just any woman—Sally Beth, a woman whose heart was as beautiful as her body, who loved him, who wanted him, was in his arms, and she was kissing him with such yearning he could not stop his own desire blooming through his heated blood. The perfume of her clean skin mixed with her own feminine smell, the freshness of her innocence mingled with her longing for him, the taste of her flesh—oranges and honey—all these things rose up in a heady mix, and he felt himself falling into an abyss of sweet yearning. He felt the hammering of her heart, and then realized that his own matched it, beat for beat, and he lost himself in the bliss of their touching.

She could not believe how beautiful this felt, this unbearable sweetness suffusing her body, the waves of feeling building and crashing over her that made her cry out with the unbearable pleasure of it. The perfection of his touch, the way he made her grow and blossom, made her want so much to *give* herself to him, to be a part of him, to connect on every level. She gasped, then breathed out with a cry, "Oh yes! Oh *please*, John!"

He nearly wept with joy, knowing not only that he had pleased her, but that she so unabashedly gave into her pleasure without inhibitions or restraint. Dizzy with desire, he almost could not think, but then, remembering that he had promised himself to ask her once again if she was certain this was what she wanted, he pushed back for a moment, hope of her assurance surging through his heated blood. He could not believe how much he wanted her, how much he needed her, how he ached for her. He drew breath to ask, looking into her eyes, large and luminous. They gazed back at him with naked adoration, then she blinked and said simply and clearly, "John, I love you."

Shock ran through him, and all manner of alarms rang in his head as he felt the sudden weight of his responsibility, heavy as a building leaning on him. He held her love, all of it, fragile, beautiful, in his hands, and he was stunned to realize that he was not worthy of it. Taking a sharp breath, he hesitated, floundering, and before he could recover, a tremendous *KABOOM!* resonated all around him, shaking the house and rattling the window panes. They both sat up, disoriented, still in the grips of their passion. Another blast broke through the haze, and they knew the war had come to them. They both jumped up, throwing on clothing with trembling hands. Sally Beth cast aside the summery dress, jumping into the jeans and shirt she had worn earlier.

John did not have a gun with him; there were two in the plane, but he knew they would not be able to make it to the plane and be aloft in time, even if he unloaded both of them into the enemy. They ran to the window as they dressed and looked out into the ravaged night.

Soldiers were just to the north of them, perhaps half a mile away, over a line of trees, sending rocket grenades toward a target they could not see. Nor could they see the soldiers, only the flaming rockets and the fires they started as they landed.

"We can't chance taking the plane. They'll see us. We'll have to try to get away in the van," he said, wondering if he should take the time to run to retrieve his guns. She was already out the door, yanking the blanket off the van, and had leapt into the driver's seat and started the engine. The firefight seemed to be growing closer and louder, and he decided not to take the chance to go for the pistols, but jumped into the passenger seat as Sally Beth gunned the engine and careened away. She drove like a demon, sobbing into the steering wheel, "Oh, Prissy!"

Twenty

There was no fighting, not even any noise of battle at the mission when Sally Beth and John came to the gates. They honked the horn until Red came running to receive them. Recognizing Alethia's van and Sally Beth's face, he did not hesitate to unlock the gate.

"There's a splinter of the army blowing things up just southeast of here," John told him as he leapt out of the van. "I think we'd better be prepared in case they decide to come here."

They all ran to Pastor Umbatu's apartment, banging on the door until he opened it. He was wearing a robe. Lyla stood behind him with a blanket wrapped around her.

"So sorry, Pastor, but I'm afraid the Ugandan army is back in this area. They've been shooting rocket launchers about five miles from here." John stopped. A distinct *Boom!* wafting in on the breeze sounded closer than that. The sky lit up with flames.

Pastor Umbatu spun around to Lyla. "Get dressed. Help them wake up everybody and meet me in the sanctuary. God help us if they decide to take the mission."

He rushed to the bedroom with Lyla while Red, Sally Beth, and

John ran to the rooms where the others were sleeping. Sally Beth found Prissy in Falla's room. She woke them both as gently as she could before she whispered urgently, "Get dressed, and hurry! We may be under attack any minute," she said as she stuffed Priscilla's sleepy arm into a blouse and held up a skirt for her to step into.

Everyone arrived at the sanctuary at about the same time. Pastor Umbatu stood just inside the doorway. "Quickly," he said. "Go to the pulpit. Lyla will show you.

Lyla motioned to them from behind the pulpit. As they made their way to the front of the sanctuary, they saw her holding open a small door at the base. A narrow set of stone steps led down into the foundations of the church. She pointed with a flashlight. "Go down. There's a shelter there."

One by one, with Red leading the way with a flashlight, they stooped under the pulpit, onto the cramped stairway, which led them into a room about the size of the clinic waiting room. Benches lined the walls. A row of lockers stood at the far end. Within minutes, they all, Red, Lyla, Sally Beth, John, Dr. Sams, Priscilla, Falla, Jenna, and Pastor Umbatu were standing, trembling under the low stone ceiling.

"I did not have the opportunity to radio for help; the signal seems to be jammed," said the pastor in a grave voice. "No doubt our friends will know of our plight soon, if we should be attacked. We must remain here, even if we hear any disruption above us. Now, all we can do is keep quiet and pray."

They spread out on the benches around the room. Sally Beth clutched at Priscilla. John sat on the other side of the child, holding Sally Beth's hand. Together, they formed a protective circle around her. Pastor Umbatu stood beside Lyla, his hand on her shoulder. They all bowed their heads and prayed silently.

Sally Beth no longer knew how to talk to God. She was not angry at Him, not now, and she no longer felt like the pitiful wretch who had lain in the bathtub hours earlier and contemplated His capriciousness and her own misery. Now, she felt calm. Prissy was in her arms and John's warmth suffused her. She wondered if she was supposed to feel guilty for disobeying God's commandment for purity, but she did not. Rather, she felt like a part of her had been restored, and it gave her courage. She simply held on to Prissy and John, open, waiting to see if God would speak to her.

He did not. Instead, there was a loud explosion directly above them, and a few of the stones above their heads gave way, landing with a crash in the middle of the room. Everyone jumped, but no one screamed. They gasped and looked at each other through the dust in the lone beam of light from Red's flashlight. Another explosion rocked them again, and more stones tumbled down. "We have to get out of here!" said Pastor Umbatu urgently. The floor above us could cave in! Women, come with me. You can hide behind the stairs to the balcony," he whispered. "Men, wait until the women are hidden before you follow." He opened the door and hurried out.

John pushed Sally Beth and Priscilla up the steps into the choking, swirling dust. Huge holes gaped darkly from the ceiling and one of the walls, a betrayal of the promise of the sanctuary. Glass from the windows lay upon smoking pews. She stopped for a second to look, but Lyla, Jenna, and Falla pushed her forward, rushing her toward a hidden alcove under the balcony stairway. Pastor Umbatu stood aside, motioning for them to hurry.

Suddenly, another missile came soaring through the wall, breaking another beautiful stained glass window. Sally Beth saw it shatter, saw the incendiary bomb come through, saw it land directly on the hidden place below the sanctuary. There was a sickening, crushing sound, and pews flared with a brilliant light before sliding sideways into the hole that appeared. Smoke and flames poured out of the hole, but when another piece of the ceiling caved in, the stones that fell smothered the fire in a cloud of dust and mortar. She stifled a scream as Pastor Umbatu shoved her into the alcove then wedged himself tightly in with the women.

"Do not make a sound," he warned, his voice low and menacing, or you will give us all away, and I do not need to remind you what Ugandan and Libyan soldiers do to women and children."

Sally Beth felt the oxygen being pressed out of her lungs. She gasped for breath in the dark, crushing stillness as she held Priscilla tightly, one hand over the child's mouth, the other one over her own. They waited, silent as dust, for many long minutes, but they heard nothing more. No more explosions, no more tinkling glass, no angry feet marching into the sanctuary, turning over pews and searching for victims to torture and murder. Her heart hammered steadily, and she could feel its rhythm matched beat for beat underneath Priscilla's thin blouse.

After a very long time, Pastor Umbatu slid open the secret door a tiny crack. There was nothing there. Carefully, he stepped forward, motioning for the women to stay still, and eased the door closed again. Again, they waited in silence, in fear, their blood thrumming in their ears as they waited for horrors they dared not think about. The scent of fear was strong in the tiny room, and Sally Beth forced herself to breathe regularly, in and out, in and out.

Pastor Umbatu returned. "All the men were safe on the steps under the pulpit. No one was hurt, but the space is too small for them all. Come out and I will give you directions."

They filed out into the sanctuary and huddled together behind the pulpit. John put his arms around Sally Beth and Priscilla, pulling them close.

"There are several hiding places. In the kitchen pantry behind the door, where the brooms hang, there is a secret door. You cannot see it, but it is unlocked, so you just push it open. Once you get inside, you can bolt it closed so that no one will notice. There is room there for a few of you. John, you take Sally Beth and Priscilla. Dr. Sams, go with them. Red, Falla, and Jenna, there is room in the stairwell under the pulpit for the three of you. It is still intact, and should be safe, barring a direct hit, and the soldiers won't be able to find the entrance unless they tear out the pulpit. If they find you, shout out that you are all Americans. Falla and Jenna, try to speak with an American accent, and let Red do all the talking. Lyla and I will stay in the alcove under the stairs. Go quickly, and God bless you all. If I do not see you again in this life, I will embrace you in the next." He touched John's shoulder. "Now go, but be careful."

John, Priscilla, Dr. Sams, and Sally Beth raced across the sanctuary, leaping across fallen pews and stone rubble. They ran to the back entrance, stood breathing as quietly as they could for a moment while John peered out into the darkness. Then he motioned for them to follow and sprinted across the courtyard to the kitchen. There were no soldiers visible, but they stayed under the shadows of the trees, opened the door to the kitchen as quietly as they could, and ran for the pantry.

The kitchen was still intact: the pantry stood solidly cheerful, bright with aprons and a few provisions on the shelves. Dr. Sams made his way to the back and reached for a jug of water sitting on the top shelf while John found the secret door behind the brooms, pushed it open, and shoved Sally Beth and Priscilla into the room behind it. But before he could step inside himself, the wall opposite exploded. Shelves fell, dumping pots, pans, kitchen appliances, and food on John and Dr. Sams.

Sally Beth leaned against the door, holding Priscilla behind her for the space of five breaths while the air stilled and a heavy silence descended, then, her heart pounding in her head, she opened the door slightly. Although the room was dark, the light filtering in through the open door of the pantry allowed her to see a huge hole in the wall. Plaster, shelves, food, and appliances lay strewn over the floor. Dr. Sams had disappeared underneath the debris in the back. All she could see of John was one foot sticking out from under the wreckage.

She wasted no time, heaving aside heavy boards and appliances. Priscilla joined her, digging through the rubble furiously, but they did not make much headway before they both sensed a shadow blocking the dim light coming into the room. Sally Beth looked up. A man wearing army fatigues, a rifle slung over his shoulder, stood very still in the doorway. She could not see him well, but his smell formed a palpable bulk of dirt, sweat, smoke, and evil. Pushing Priscilla behind her, she straightened, facing the dark menace. "Americans!" she shouted, her voice sounding shrill and inhuman as it rasped its way out of her throat. "We are Americans!"

He laughed. She could see the gleam of his teeth and the flash of his eyes. The rest of his face was invisible in the dark. She did not have time to cry out again before his fist flew forward and everything went blank.

John felt himself floating through a sea of boulders that banged his head and bludgeoned his shoulders, and then he felt nothing. He was surprised to look up and see that he was sitting at a table on a warm summer evening, the early gloaming just beginning to settle around the blue mountains all around him. Across from him sat Geneva. His heart skipped a beat as he saw the breeze lift her golden hair and goose bumps appear on her bare arms. She leaned toward him, a smile playing on her lips.

"So, what do you want now?"

He knew she was toying with him, and he wanted to make her understand how important this was.

"Reality. Living a real life and not just an advertisement of one."

She ran her fingers along the stem of the wine glass, then leaned toward him. "So what is reality for you, Mr. John Smith, god of fire and iron, visionary, beloved of Christ?"

He saw the uncertainty in her face, heard the faint disbelief in her voice, and he pushed his way past her mockery. "Reality is knowing God. It's working with your hands. It's walking the ridges as the sun comes up. It's the love of a good woman."

She startled, then smiled gently, as if she knew some deep secret. "That's just what Sally Beth said."

Her face wavered for an instant in the last rays of sunlight, and he felt his own confusion growing. "No, wait. I was wrong. What I really want is the challenge of you. I want adventure, I want the wide sky and the whole world, and I want to save you from the path you're on."

"Oh? But I have been saved already. It's Sally Beth who will give you the sky." She smiled again as the sun surrounded her, a golden halo

of sun and hair engulfed her face, and she said, "John, hear me. John. John!"

Then he felt a dull throbbing in his temples, heard his name called out again in a different voice, and he awoke to find himself on the floor, covered in flour, stones, blenders, and mixers. He groaned.

"John," came Dr. Sam's voice nearby. "Are you all right?"

"What?"

"Are you alive? Anything broken? I'm back here. There's a heavy board on top of me."

John pushed aside the rubble and sat up. Looking around, he could see only the mess on the floor. "Where are you?"

"Here, behind you. I can see you."

"Are you hurt?"

"Not much," Dr. Sams gasped in pain. "I think I've hurt my leg. But you have to go."

John pulled himself up to try move the shelves pressing down on Dr. Sams, but he spoke urgently again. "Go now. I'll get myself out." He stifled a moan.

"Go?" He looked around for Sally Beth.

"They have her. Priscilla, too. They took them out the back."

John struggled to his feet, grasped a remaining portion of the wall, and stood unsteadily.

"Lucky you," came Dr. Sam's tremulous voice.

"What?"

"You get to rescue Sally Beth. I've been trying to do that for over a year. Go *now!* You might be able to catch them. You *have* to catch them!"

John's head cleared. He struggled out the doorway, searched for the back door, and lurched toward it. Somehow, he found himself looking out the window in the door just in time to see two men dressed in army fatigues standing beside Alethia's van and throwing a limp Sally Beth into it.

He yelled as he reached for the doorknob. The door was stuck. He jerked it harder, kicking it and wrenching it away from the doorframe, then he leaped outside as the van roared away through the open gate.

The back courtyard stood as empty and forlorn as a prison yard; all of the cars and maintenance vehicles were gone, along with all the equipment that had been stored there. Remembering the bicycles by the shower building, he ran for them, leaped on the first one he saw, then tore off, pedaling as fast as he could through the silvery night. The van had already outstripped him, so he turned southward. His only chance was to get aloft.

The house was still intact, the front door standing ajar from his and Sally Beth's hasty exit. Glancing over, he could barely see the shape of his plane, which sat nearly invisible beneath the blanket of meadow. He pedaled right up to it on his bicycle, then, despite his spinning head and the pain in his shoulders, he struggled to pull at the yards of fabric Sally Beth had stitched together. He did not bother to remove it completely, but simply uncovered the nose and the windshield, then he stuck his head under the tent, wrenched open the door, and climbed aboard. He was airborne within a minute.

Making his way back to the Ugandan Road, he turned northward, crossing the shimmering river and the tattered bridge, and before long, he caught up with the colorful old van streaking its way toward the border. He tried to think of a way to stop it; he could shoot at it, but he was afraid. Sally Beth and Priscilla were in there.

Reaching into the box below his seat, he wrenched it open and pulled out one of the loaded revolvers. He banked, dropped altitude, then, holding his breath, he leaned out of the window, took careful aim at the roof just above the driver's seat, and fired. The van swerved, nearly veering off the road, then righted its course and accelerated. From the passenger side a man leaned out the window, aimed his AK-47 at him, and pulled the trigger, releasing a burst of bullets that whizzed by him. He pulled back at the sound of small *pops!* that seemed to buzz and zing all around him, and then, suddenly, he became aware of a searing pain in his thigh.

Grabbing his leg with both hands, he felt the warm blood flowing out over his fingers. Probing for both the entry and exit holes, he managed to stuff a handkerchief into one of them, then he ripped at the sleeve of his shirt until he had torn it off. That served to staunch the other bleeding bullet hole. With darkness spitting at his eyes and his hands off the yoke, he was helpless to ward off the trees that suddenly rushed up at him. He took hold of the controls again, pulling up just as his pontoons brushed through the utmost branches of a grove of wattle trees. Their pungent sent filled his nostrils, reviving him enough to right himself and look out into the horizon.

Lights loomed ahead of him. The Ugandan border, and he could see soldiers standing in a line, rifles raised toward him, the intermittent flashes of gunfire spitting into the night. He banked right, heading toward the dark glimmer of the lake in the distance. When he was well out over the water, he circled back north until he thought—hoped—he had gone far enough into safety. Fighting against the pain and the weakness, he headed back toward land and managed a semi-controlled landing in a long field at the edge of the lake.

It was deep night, and the darkness crept into his consciousness, but he took a great breath of the cold night air and revived enough to pull out his emergency first aid kit from underneath the seat. Blood still ran too freely from the wound in his thigh. Dizzy and weak, he found a roll of gauze, which he unwound and wrapped tightly around his thigh. It did not staunch the flow of blood as well as he had hoped. Within seconds, he could see the white gauze turning dark in the dim light of the slender moon.

He gritted his teeth and vowed not to die.

When John awoke again, he was relieved to find himself in some sort of hospital room. Out of the corner of his eye, he saw Geneva

drifting toward him, her face full of pity and concern, and then he saw the kind, smiling face of Holy Miracle Jones looking at him with love as he struggled to keep strength in his voice.

"Ah, boy, I see ye carry the pain of loss with ye, but be of good cheer. There's no loss, only happiness right here with ye. All ye have to do is look."

His eyes moved to Sally Beth, and John suddenly saw her, as if for the first time. Sally Beth, bringer of light and laughter, who lifts the burdens of all she meets. Who said that? Someone once said that. He looked at her again. Sally Beth, who had asked him to love her, smiled at him, then she lifted the crown off her pink cowboy hat and placed it on his head, saying, "I declare you king of my heart."

November 1, 1978, Somewhere in southern Uganda

Sally Beth had been awake for some time, but she kept her eyes shut and listened to the sounds around her. Her hands were tied tightly behind her back, and her feet were tied as well. The one brief blink she had allowed herself told her that Priscilla also was awake, lying on her side on the dirt floor, her hands similarly bound behind her back. She waited until she was sure they were alone in the tent before she looked at the child.

Sally Beth smiled at her and Priscilla smiled back. She did not seem to be afraid, but nodded and whispered, "My hands aren't tied too tight." She began to wriggle toward Sally Beth, turning her back.

Sally Beth's arms hurt. The side of her face felt like it was the size of a watermelon, and it buzzed with pain, but she rolled close to Priscilla, and with her back turned, felt for the cords binding the wrists.

Yes, they were not very tight. The ropes had been tied halfway up to the elbows and they were so thick that they had not snugged down on Priscilla's bony arms. She had somehow worked them downward toward her even skinnier wrists, and it didn't take long for Sally Beth's fingers to work open the clumsy knot.

She had just freed Priscilla and was watching her sit up to untie her feet, when they both froze. Voices came to them from the other side of the canvas wall.

Several men were walking toward them, speaking loudly, arguing, really, but she could not understand them. She looked at Priscilla, who mouthed softly, "Lugandes."

"Can you understand them?"

Priscilla grinned. "My native language." She stopped, listening intently. Another, more authoritative voice had begun to speak. He barked at the men shortly, and then there was silence.

"What did they say?" whispered Sally Beth.

Priscilla sat up, untied her feet, then moved to Sally Beth. "They want to have a good time with us and they are arguing over who gets to go first, but their commander told them they can't kill you. He's taking you to Kampala to hold you for ransom." She smiled wryly. "He says Americans bring a pretty good price." She picked the last knot loose.

"What about you?" Sally Beth sat up, rubbing her wrists, before reaching down to work at the ropes at her ankles.

Priscilla looked at the floor and shrugged, blinking hard, but she could not stop the tears rolling down her face. "I'm not worth anything except maybe a minute of fun."

Sally Beth's heart plunged. The image of the little girl who had died in her arms pushed itself up against her eyes until she could see into the hole in her cheekbone, black with blood and powder burns.

Oh, please, Lord. Let them do whatever they will with me, but don't let them hurt Prissy any more. I can't survive watching her die.

Whatever they did to her own body was of little consequence, as long as she could stay alive long enough to get Priscilla out. Precious Priscilla, who was brave enough to sacrifice everything for those she loved, who loved her enough to refuse to leave her, while she obsessed and whined to John about how frightened she was. Prissy, who had already lived through war and privation, who just wanted a safe home and people who would be kind, was facing horror and torture that would end in death. Sally Beth would rather die than let her be ravished and murdered by those beasts outside.

More shouting came from without, and there was a sudden burst of gunfire. She heard the running footfalls of several men, and then engines started up.

"What is it?" whispered Sally Beth.

"I'm not sure. I think some Libyans have come. I don't understand them, but the Ugandans are talking about a battle, and they're driving away. Maybe they'll leave and forget about us," she added hopefully.

Carefully, Sally Beth made her way to the edge of the tent, picked up a sharp stick, and poked at a tiny hole in the canvas. She worked at it patiently for a minute before putting her eye to the hole she had enlarged. They were in a camp with perhaps five more tents directly in her line of vision, but she knew there were more all around. Jeeps and various vehicles, including Alethia's van and one shiny black sports car were being moved around. Some were being parked, some were being driven off, careening onto a road that lead off into a forest.

Priscilla nudged her aside. She watched for a while before turning back to her. "I think they are all leaving. There's two men with rifles by our tent, but everybody else is loading up."

Sally Beth took her turn at the peephole. Priscilla was right. Jeeps and cars were clearing out. Two to four soldiers sat in each of the jeeps, their rifles bristling out like the legs of spiders, and two trucks filled with soldiers rolled by. She watched until they all left, until they were alone except for the two men who paced around their tent.

She moved back to the center of the space. "Sit back down. Put your feet together, and lay the rope over them. Make them think we are still tied up if they come in. She moved off to the side, draped a rope around her ankles, then snatched up another rope, holding it in her hands, which she moved behind her back. They sat quietly for a very long time, waiting, watching the entrance to the tent and listening to the men arguing and laughing outside.

Sally Beth wasn't sure what she would do, but she was certain she would not let anything happen to Priscilla if she had a breath left in her body. She repeatedly went over in her mind the moves that Edna Mae had taught her. How to use an opponent's weight against him. How to throw him and stomp on his windpipe. How to feint, then lunge, to grab a man around the neck and twist the head around.

She wondered if she could do it. Kill another human being. Take a God-given life. She had grown up believing peace was the answer. Her father and her mother had told her that there was always a peaceful resolution to things, that you did not have to resort to violence, that all people had some kindness in them.

But they had been wrong. They had not seen what she had seen for the last week—the desire to torture and murder, even delight in it, and she knew she had no choice. If she were to save Prissy, she would have to kill. And then she would see if God would forgive her, if she would forgive herself. She closed her eyes and prayed as honestly as she could.

Lord, I know I have done wrong. Things got hard and I just gave up on You. I wanted You to take care of me and those I love when others were dying and suffering. I know I was just thinking about my pitiful self, and I'm sorry. And maybe I used that as an excuse for my lust for John. I seduced him, and I didn't give him a choice. I know I did, I was just so lonesome and so scared. I'm not really sorry, though, because it was beautiful, except I know I probably hurt him, and I am sorry for that. But I hope You understand and forgive me, and I hope that I am never sorry for it, or him, either, and please, don't make me be sorry.

I know You love me, and I know You have better things planned for me than I could ever imagine, things here or in heaven. I don't care, because if it comes from You, it will be good, and whatever evil that happens, I know You will find a way to make some good come of it. But Lord, I cannot watch what they will do to Prissy. I can't. I just can't. Lord, these are Your enemies; they are my enemies. Give me the strength to vanquish them. I ask You, Lord, I beg You.

Sally Beth stopped praying. A man had entered the tent. He glared at her, then his eyes roved over to Priscilla's bare legs beneath her flimsy skirt, then up her body to her face. She sat up straight, her eyes defiant, staring at him as if she could kill him with only her thoughts. He laughed at her childish bravado, and Sally Beth could see the malevolent humor in his eyes. Prissy sat quietly, her legs together, her hands behind her back. Sally Beth began to tremble, but Prissy sat like a cold, heavy stone. There was no fear in her, only the burning defiance that blazed from her eyes.

Sally Beth took courage. The man held his rifle loosely in his hands. He pointed it at Sally Beth and spat out, "Bapbapbapbapbap," laughing as she flinched. Then he pointed it at Priscilla, sneering, and let loose a quick burst of fire just beside her. Priscilla jumped, and so did Sally Beth. The ropes slid off their legs, and the man, startled at the sight, let out a quick bark before lunging for Priscilla. She rolled to the side and jumped up. Flinging aside all doubts, Sally Beth leaped at him from behind and tried to get her arm around his neck.

She might as well have been wrestling a tree. He was as solid as wood, and her lightweight attempt to throttle him was almost laughable. Edna Mae had told her it was easy. Now she knew it would only be easy to die at the hands of this brute. He reached behind him, grabbing her hair, and flung her over his head as easily as if she had been a cat scratching at his back. Then he turned to her, and as he raised his hand, Sally Beth cowered against the canvas wall, waiting for the blow.

The thoughts that came to her were surprisingly clear and devoid of emotion. There would be no ransom for her, but that did not matter because she did not deserve to be ransomed. And yet, grace would come; indeed, it had already made its way into the tent, giving her a sense of peace, a sureness that all would be well. This man's sweating, sneering face would be the last thing she ever saw, but it did not frighten her, and it was not as ugly as she thought it should be.

Perhaps Death would take her quickly, she thought, and she fervently asked the Almighty that the same would be true for Prissy. She did not take her eyes from the face, distorted with bloodlust as she called aloud upon the name of Jesus.

The man's eyes flew open, as if he were surprised, and she marveled that the name of Jesus had had an impact on him, until he made a strange sound and fell to his knees. Prissy loomed up behind him, and as she watched, the child stepped forward, leaning around him with something red in her hand. A soft gurgling sound escaped from his lips as her own eyes felt something fly into them. Through a red, smeary, mist, she saw him open his mouth and close it, as if he were thinking of something to say, and while she stared at his moving lips, he toppled forward and landed at her feet. Blood spilled out of his neck and quivering mouth onto her legs.

She looked up. Priscilla stood before her, a bloody knife in her hand, an indefinable look on her face. She dropped the knife to pick up the would-be attacker's rifle, turned, strode to the corner by the opening of the tent, and waited, poised and still as a panther.

The man outside yelled. Priscilla raised the rifle. Sally Beth went to kneel in front of the dead man, facing the opening and blocking him from sight. A moment later, the man outside called again, and the two froze, holding their breath while the seconds ticked by in long, dusty silence.

The other man stuck his head into the opening and, somehow, Sally Beth found the courage to smile at him. As her eyes locked onto his, she forced herself to keep them steady, not to let them flicker over to Priscilla as the girl raised the rifle and fired at least five shots into the man's chest.

He fell over, blood pouring out of his chest and mouth, while his body continued to move feebly. Priscilla stepped forward, pointed the rifle at his head and held her finger on the trigger until the sound became empty and impotent.

Sally Beth stumbled out of the tent, falling to her knees, fighting against waves of light and darkness, and then, suddenly, without warning, she vomited into the dirt. She heaved and spewed, then heaved more until there was nothing left, and then she looked at the blood soaking into her jeans, and she heaved again. Priscilla watched her silently, then she gently laid her hand on her head. Stroking her hair, she murmured, "There, there, Miss Sally Beth. It's all over now. Those bad men can't hurt you now."

This rocked Sally Beth back on her heels. A fourteen-year-old girl had just disarmed a seasoned soldier, stabbed him in the back, slashed his throat, and then calmly waited for the chance to murder another. And now she was petting Sally Beth's head and telling her not to be scared. The roles had become mixed up, and it made her angry to be trumped by the courage and mercy of a child. Grabbing Priscilla, she dragged her into her lap and rocked her like a baby as she sobbed and stroked her head.

Presently, she began to laugh as well as cry, but Priscilla did not let her indulge in her hysteria for long. She jumped up, dragging Sally Beth with her. "We have to go." She picked up the rifles of both men, stripped the dead soldier at her feet of his ammunition and side arm. "Go get that other guy's stuff. See if you can find a canteen."

Sally Beth jumped up to follow the orders. It was more emotionally than physically hard to move the dead, bloody man enough to steal his ammunition, but she knew that if she was going to make it out of there with Priscilla, she'd better be ready to do just about anything. She dragged the clip, revolver, and a half-full canteen out of the tent.

"Do you suppose there's any fresh water?" she asked. The thought of drinking after that man made her stomach lurch.

Priscilla pointed to several big plastic jugs of water sitting in the shade. "If we can get one of those onto a jeep, we'll have enough water to last us. And maybe there's food, too. I'm starving," She looked at the puddle of Sally Beth's vomit on the ground and added, "And I bet you will be, too, soon enough."

There were two jeeps sitting under a sausage tree, neither of which had a key in the ignition, above the visor, in the ashtray, or under the front seat. Finally, Sally Beth said, "Prissy, if you help me push this thing over that rise there, I can get it started. Come on, it's not uphill too much, and it isn't far." She leaped into the driver's seat and disengaged the emergency brake, then put the gearshift into the neutral position.

Together, the two struggled to push the jeep up a short incline until it sat poised at the top. Sally Beth got behind the wheel. "Okay, just give her a little shove," she said, putting her foot on the ground to help push. The jeep rocked, rolled forward a few inches, and began to roll slowly downward. Sally Beth drew her foot in, shut the door, and when the vehicle picked up a little more speed, she popped the clutch. It started.

"I'm going to drive over to those jugs and we can try to get one in the back seat." She turned the jeep around, drove the thirty feet to the water station, and together, the two managed to wrestle a nearly-full container of water onto the back seat. Keeping the engine running, they looked into the other tents until they found some trail mix, candy, and a few granola bars. Priscilla stuffed some bananas into her pockets, then ducked into another tent and came out carrying several more rifles.

"You never know," she said, as she threw them into the back seat beside the water jug.

And then they were off, not knowing exactly where they were, but aware that the only safe place to be was south of the border. Sally Beth squinted at the sun and took off in a generally southward direction.

"I don't think we should stay on the main road," she said. "The army will be all over the place, and we'll be stopped at the border. Maybe we should head east, toward the lake. Maybe we can get a boat, or at least some help."

Priscilla shrugged. "Sure. I think I remember this area. When my family was killed and my village burned, I walked through here. It doesn't feel like we are too far from water."

"Your family was killed?"

"Yes. Amin's army, the most horrible men in the world. They live by killing and looting." She fell silent, watching the grassy plains roll by. Sally Beth wanted to keep Priscilla from dwelling too much on the horrors of her past. This day alone held enough horrors.

"Sufficient unto the day is the evil thereof," she said softly.

Priscilla smiled. "Plenty sufficient. But the day they raped and killed my mother and sisters and tortured my father and brothers to death was more evil. My father had put me up in the rafters to hide, and it was so bad I couldn't keep quiet. If I hadn't killed them, they would have done the same to me."

"You've killed men before?'

"Three of them. I just wish I had done it before they did what they did."

Sally Beth wanted to ask her how she had managed that, but that would have meant asking her to relive that terrible time. She wondered how much Priscilla suffered for the things she had seen and done. "Thank you," Sally Beth said softly. "I thought I would try to save you, but I was no match for those men. If it hadn't been for you, I would be dead, or worse."

Priscilla smiled at her. "I knew you would need me," she said softly. "Jesus told me." Her face was the sweet, plump-cheeked face of a child, but her eyes were old and wise. Behind the wisdom lurked a hundred years of suffering.

Twenty-One

The Jumpoff, Swallowtail Gap, West Virginia

Howard Graves gripped the phone tightly. When he spoke, he struggled to keep his voice calm. "Thank you, sir. You know where to reach me if you hear anything, anything at all. We appreciate what you are doing." He hung up the receiver, his face grim. Geneva took one look at it and fell into her husband's arms, sobbing. He tried to console her, but even he felt despair. "Don't give up hope, sweetheart. They still could have gotten away."

"How? The men you sent to find them can't go farther north. I can tell even the people at the mission have given up hope." She tried to stifle her sobs, but the thought of Sally Beth, Lilly, and John being in the hands of those murderers sent a spiral of anguish through her. "What did the State Department say?"

Howard Graves shook his head. "There's not much they can do at this point. It's a local war, even though the Ugandans have overrun the Kagera region, and we can't get involved. Anyway, the army is pretty much out of control, even if they could talk some sense into Idi Amin. I think the best we can hope for is that they are in the hands of some mercenaries who will hold them for ransom. They have to know that America doesn't like its citizens murdered." He averted his eyes. People in the throes of this war would not be concerned about the plight of Americans. Even mercenaries may not have enough of their wits about them to think about profiting from the return of hostages.

"What did they say when you told them we'd pay a million dollars to get them back?" She did not care now who knew she and Chap were wealthy. All she cared about was finding her loved ones safe.

"Well, it got their attention, but..." He trailed off, feeling helpless. He had not told her what he had heard about the brutality of the Ugandan army. Uncontrolled, undisciplined soldiers had been responsible for the horrific deaths of thousands of civilians. Many hundreds more, including the pastor of the mission church where Sally Beth had been living, had been marched to camps where they were held for ransom or sold into slavery. They had stolen all the livestock and burned and looted every building and vehicle they could find well to the south of the Kagera River. If it had not been for the timely arrival of the former special services men they had hired to look for Sally Beth, Lilly, John, and Phil, every person at the mission would have been slaughtered or kidnapped. He was at least grateful for that small mercy.

Seeing how distracted Geneva was, Howard Graves longed to put his arms around her, if only to comfort her, but he kept still while Howard Knight pulled her close, murmuring into her hair. He had long ago lost that right, and although he regretted it with all his heart, he was glad that Geneva was well loved by her husband.

"Darling," said Howard Knight. "We just have to pray now, and hope the guys we hired can track them into Uganda."

She shook her head, sobbing, "Chap, I can't stand this!"

He held still for a moment, bending his head toward hers. "How are you feeling, love?" he asked tenderly.

She looked at him, aghast. "What? Awful! They could all be

dead."

"No, I mean, how are *you* feeling? He moved his hand slowly down to her belly, cradling it for a brief moment.

"Oh. Fine, I guess."

"Then, let's go. We might as well be there, where we can get news a little quicker, and get to them quicker when they are found. Let's go to Kenya, to John's place, and wait there.

"Oh, Chap! You mean it? We can just go?"

He shrugged. "Why not?" He turned to Howard Graves. "You reckon you can get us seats on the next Concorde? We'll go to Paris, then to Kenya from there."

Howard Graves looked thoughtful. "We'll need visas," he said at last as he reached for the phone. "Guess it's time to call on our friend Senator Byrd again. And let's hope there are three seats available on the Concorde this week. Otherwise, it will be a long flight.

Geneva looked at him sharply. "You're going to go, too?" She had been grateful for Howard's Washington, DC connections and his guidance throughout this ordeal, but this was exceptionally generous.

Howard Graves smiled sadly. "Yeah, well, as pathetic as this sounds, outside of my mother, your family is the only one I have. And I guess you could say John is something of a brother. I don't want to lose any of them."

Somewhere in southern Uganda

Sally Beth tried to keep to the minor roads, veering eastward at every opportunity. Getting to the lake would most likely be their safest path, although she didn't know how they would get far enough into the lake to cross the border into Tanzania without being caught.

Lord, send a miracle.

The road was just a wide dirt path, now no more than a rocky, eroded mess. The rain and clouds had cleared, but the mud was so deep in places she tried to keep to the grassy shoulders. When the field beside them flattened out into plain savannah, Sally Beth slowed to a crawl, easing the car up the bank to leave the road altogether. Driving through grass would be easier than slogging through the mud.

She had just made the top of a rise when something glinting in the sunshine caught her eye. She slowed to stare at the object nearly hidden in the long grass about twenty yards away. Something told her to go see what it was. Turning the jeep, she made her way cautiously, bouncing and staggering across the grassland toward it.

It was John's plane, sitting lightly in the savannah grass, fresh and white in the morning sun. Leaving the jeep idling in neutral, Sally Beth leaped out, sprinted to the plane, and jerked open the door.

If he were alive, the only proof of it lay in the recesses of her certain, sealed heart, the heart that forbade him to die. He lay back in the pilot's seat, his face, flung sideways, the color of cold ashes. A dark, bloody bandage wrapped around his thigh was sticky with blood, and so much more blood was spilled over the seat and floor, she knew he had lost enough to kill a smaller man. The large bruise on his forehead spreading out toward his cheek served as a grim reminder of what had taken place the night before when the Ugandans had attacked the mission. Kneeling on the floor, her pulse buffeting her temples, she placed her fingertips at his neck, feeling for any life-rhythm there.

The pulse surged so faintly she wondered if she were imagining it, but his flesh was warm, and when she lifted his arm, it fell back limp; no sign of rigor mortis, no stench of death in the air. Just the strong, coppery smell of blood permeated the cabin of the plane.

"Is he...?" asked Priscilla, her voice strained with worry.

"He's alive," she murmured, overcome with relief, "but barely." She looked at the bandage on his thigh. "He's bled a lot." Still watching, still pressing his artery for the comfort of his sustained pulse, she said, "Prissy, will you get that canteen?"

Priscilla turned back to the jeep while Sally Beth gathered John in her arms, holding him close, stroking his hair, and begging God to intervene.

Oh, God! Please don't let him die. I'm sorry. I can't give him up. You saved Prissy, you saved me, so now please save him. Let him live. I'll leave him alone; I'll let him love whoever he wants, but please, let him live!

She knew this was her fault. If she had not begged him to stay the night with her, he would have taken a few more people to safety, and he would have stayed overnight in Bukoba. Because of her selfishness, he might die, and several people who stayed at the mission might be dead because of her as well. She held him tightly, rocking him, stunned by the pain of her loss, of the realization that she must, after all, be sorry for the sweetness of the night before. She kissed him, then held his head to her chest and simply held on, as if her own life could stretch across the thin membranes of skin between them and bring him back to her.

Priscilla returned with the water. Sally Beth tried to dribble some between John's white lips, but it trickled out the sides of his mouth, then he coughed without regaining consciousness. Sally Beth looked around frantically.

"We have to get him help." She looked at the open emergency kit on the seat next to him, but there was little in there to do any good: some bandages, syringes, tubing, ointments, sutures, and other basic necessities. Several seconds of rummaging yielded nothing, until her eyes landed on the most obvious thing there: the cooler that Dr. Sams had placed underneath the back seat. Somehow, John had missed this when he unloaded the supplies they had sent to the hospital in Bukoba.

She yanked it out, opened it, moved aside the ice packets, and breathed a prayer of gratitude. Just underneath a layer of ice was a plastic bag mostly full of her own blood. Dr. Sams had not taken a full unit, just enough to make her believe she was contributing. But still, it was something, and it was O negative, the universal donor. She heard herself insisting. *Go ahead. Somebody could really need this, and I'm as healthy as a mule.*

Thank You, God. You told me to do this. You made this happen. Now I know You plan for him to live!

"Prissy, you have to help," she said as she grabbed some tubing and a syringe from the first aid kit and took hold of John's arm. "I can't do it by myself."

She connected one end of tubing to the needle from the syringe and the other to the packet of blood while Priscilla tied a tourniquet around John's arm and slapped at it until a faint blue line appeared. Sally Beth carefully threaded the needle into the nearly invisible vein and held up the packet of blood. "I'm sorry this is cold, John, but maybe it will bring you around a little quicker."

They waited in agony as the sun crept higher in the sky and the day grew warm and humid. Priscilla fanned John while Sally Beth slowly nursed the blood into his vein. As she watched, her heart cheered when the lifeblood began to pink his lips and cheeks. At last, his eyes fluttered open.

"John, what's your blood type?"

He heard Sally Beth's voice, but he did not recognize the terrible-looking person gazing down at him. It was a woman, he thought, with wisps of Sally Beth's long, silvery hair, but the face, blue, red, swollen, and misshapen, was like no one he had ever seen before. The left eye was a mere slit in a puffy blue and red socket.

"What happened to your face?"

"What is your blood type? You've lost a lot of blood. We need to replace it."

"AB negative."

The hideous face disappeared, and in its place came the shining black face of Priscilla.

"Prissy," he said. "Are you alive?"

She smiled. "Yeah. Are you?"

"I guess. I hurt enough. I'm cold."

The blackened, swollen face with the silvery hair was back. Prissy rubbed his arms to warm him.

"Okay, I'm going to give you another unit of blood," said Sally

Beth, ripping out the tubing from the empty packet and inserting it into another one. He smiled. He had missed Sally Beth's voice. His arm grew cold again, and he winced, but within minutes, his vision began to clear, and he realized that the hideous face he had seen swimming above him belonged to Sally Beth's voice. He gasped and tried to sit up.

"Careful! Stay still."

"Sally Beth."

"Yes, John. It's me."

"What happened to your face?"

"Ugandans. Same thing as happened to yours." She placed her hand over the left side of her face and smiled, and he thought he had never seen anyone so beautiful.

After the second unit of blood, John was still weak, but able to sit up, then get out of the plane to stretch out on the grass. "I could give you another unit," said Sally Beth. "Or we can just get out of here. How do you feel?"

"I feel—" John was cut off by Prissy's urgent voice.

"They're coming!"

Sally Beth stood up. From the road came the distinct sound of motorcars. Looking out to the curve back to the north, she saw a line of army vehicles coming into view. "Oh, Lord, have mercy! Quick, get him back in the plane." She jerked open the door and hustled him in. Priscilla jumped into the back while Sally Beth hurried around to the pilot's seat. Without going through the checklist, she attempted to start the engine, but it failed to fire up.

"Pump the throttle a couple of times," advised John. "Forget the primer." She gave the throttle three good pumps, then tried again and shouted for joy when the engine caught.

The entire line of army vehicles halted in the road as Sally Beth spun the plane eastward, then several jeeps broke away, lurching across the road, coming toward them fast. She leaned into the throttle as hard as she could, and slowly, agonizingly, the plane began to widen the distance between them and the convoy of trucks and jeeps. Behind them, guns sang their dreaded songs. They heard their chortle and laughter, the ringing of lead on aluminum and steel.

Looking ahead, Sally Beth saw the glimmer of Lake Victoria not one hundred feet ahead and rushing at her fast. Instinctively she slowed, but John slapped her hand away and forced the throttle forward, then, as they rolled forward, their speed increasing, he lifted the yoke, and they sailed out over the blue waters, not more than a few feet above the surface of the lake. The plane dipped slightly before John lifted the yoke higher. They slowly gained altitude as bullets ricocheted off and into the plane.

"*Ahhh!*" moaned John. "I've been hit, again." He grabbed at his right arm just above the elbow.

Sally Beth looked back to see the jeeps bristling with guns firing at them, but by now, they were out of range, high up and over the lake. She grabbed the controls away from John. Prissy sat mute in the back, hunkered in the floorboard between the seats, her arms over her head.

"Are you okay, Prissy?" shouted Sally Beth.

Her head came up. "Yes, but there are holes all over back here. I can see daylight through the plane."

"John, how bad are you hurt?"

"Not bad. I think this is where I get to say, 'It's only a flesh wound'." He almost laughed. "How many units of the AB negative do we have on board?"

Sally Beth was not in the mood to joke. "None, John, so you can darn well quit bleeding!" She grimaced and tightened her hold on the yoke.

"And did you bring any fuel?" His voice had lost its lightness.

"What?"

He pointed to the fuel gage. It showed a near-empty tank, and the indicator was moving rapidly. "We're losing fuel. They must have hit the tank. We have to set her down. *Now!*" He wrenched the controls back away from her and lowered the nose, banking back toward the lakeshore.

"Don't go back!" shouted Sally Beth.

"Do you want to drift on the water until somebody fishes us out? We're heading south, and I'm hoping we can get to that swampy area just about ten miles above the border. They won't be able to drive in there, and there are plenty of mangrove trees, if we can get to them." Waving his head from side to side, searching intently, he said, "I'm looking for some island off the shoreline." After another tense moment, he brightened. "There's one!" he shouted, pushing the nose of the plane to within thirty feet of the water.

Suddenly, the engine began to sputter, and then died. They were a mere ten feet from the surface now; John fought to keep the nose up, but the small plane was dropping fast. Within seconds, one of the pontoons hit the water; the plane bounced up and hit it again, then plowed forward, water hitting the windshield like a tidal wave. The plane shuddered before coming to an abrupt stop. Both Sally Beth and John flew forward; hitting their heads on the windshield, they were knocked senseless. Priscilla slammed against the back of John's seat. None of them was wearing a seat belt.

Sally Beth woke to the sound of Priscilla's voice, quivering with suppressed hysteria, calling to her, shaking her, and when Sally Beth was able to open her eyes, she found herself looking into the face of a terrified child. Prissy threw her arms around her, sobbing.

"I thought you were dead!"

"No, Prissy! I'm okay. I'm okay, baby, just give me a minute." She rubbed the knot on her forehead, turning to John. "John!" she called. He did not respond. She shook him, and he felt like a heavy bag of sand under her hands. She flung herself at him, shaking him harder. "John Smith! Wake up! You can't leave us now. I didn't give you my blood for nothing. Wake up. I need you! *John!*" She stopped, sobbing, her head buried in his shoulder. He did not move or make a sound.

John was somewhere he didn't want to be, and he was in a panic. He saw Sally Beth falling from his plane, drifting slowly downward through clouds and mist. He knew that if he could only find the right combination of the right words, he could save her, but he didn't know what the words were. He knew one of them was "love," but none of the others made sense, coming to him in a meaningless jumble. He struggled to cry out, wanting to call her name, but he was mute, immobilized, helpless to form the words that swam in his head, "I will save you. Love. Love. Love."

After a few moments, Sally Beth realized that once again it was up to her, and she had a child to protect. She drew a shaky breath as she looked around her. Somehow, the plane had stayed upright, sitting out in the water about forty feet from the shoreline. Her heart sank. How was she going to get help now? Could she drag John through the water?

"Any ideas what to do, Prissy?" she asked, defeated.

"Uh, no. Unless you have a paddle."

"Not on me. Can you swim?"

Silence loomed up from the back seat, until finally, Priscilla answered softly, apologetically, "No."

Sally Beth reached over to shake John one more time. There was no response, so she did the only thing she knew to do.

Lord, please help!

But when she opened her eyes, the only thing she could think of was that the Lord had made an awful mistake. Straight ahead, standing on the bank, stood about fifty men holding spears and rifles. They all were looking at her.

Sally Beth's hand reached for the revolver that had slid up against the side of the door. She wanted to check how many bullets were left, but realized that even if the chamber was full, their situation was hopeless. She remembered a movie she had seen about a wagon train besieged by Comanches. The men had held a solemn conference, after which they had shot all the women and children to save them from the brutality they would face if they were captured.

Out of desperation, she searched her memory for Scripture to help her in this moment. The only thing that came to mind was the old standby, the 23rd Psalm:

The Lord is my shepherd; I shall not want.

He maketh me to lie down in green pastures: He leadeth me beside the still waters.

He restoreth my soul: He leadeth me in the paths of righteousness for His name's sake.

Yea, though I walk through the valley of the shadow of death, I will fear no evil: for Thou art with me...

They had read that at her mother's funeral, at her father's funeral, at the funeral of Holy Miracle Jones. Looking up to see the men on the shoreline pushing a boat out into the water, she knew what the words meant: they were going to die. It made her infinitely sad, not for herself, but for Priscilla, who had not had a chance to really live yet, and for Alethia, who would be in agony. "Priscilla, baby, I'm so sorry! This is my fault. If I had left when I should have, you'd be with your mama right now."

"It's okay, Sally Beth. I wish I hadn't left my sister when the army got hold of her. But she was dead. Lilly was still alive. You couldn't leave her."

Sally Beth closed her eyes. *Lord, I know You are with us, and I am sorry I have let You down. I have been worthless to You, but, please... Make them kill us outright. Take Prissy first so she doesn't have to see it.*

Voices came closer. She heard men shouting just outside the cabin, and, grasping the gun, she drew a shaking breath and opened her eyes to see kind, smiling faces. Her gaze roved upward, beyond the men in the boat. Standing on the bank, bending over as if recovering from a long run, stood Lilly, and beside her stood Phil and Alice Auma.

November 2, 1978, Lake Victoria, Uganda

The small, feisty woman looked at John's seeping thigh wound and declared emphatically. "This won't stop bleeding. The *gele* is helping, but I need something more potent to staunch it." She rubbed her chin, musing. "*Rhatany* might work, but I'm not sure it grows here. Or *ramie*, but I haven't seen any of that around here, either. Bur marigold grows in swampy places, so maybe somebody in this godforsaken place has it, or can find it for me."

"Thank you, Fajimi," said Sally Beth. "What can I do?

"Just keep sitting right there and talk to him while I go look for something to stop that bleeding, but for pity's sake, keep your right side to him. You don't need him to see your face from the left!" She gave Sally Beth a curt once-over. "And where did you get those clothes, girl?"

Sally Beth looked at the khaki pants and shirt Lilly had loaned her. "My sister?"

"A girl should wear dresses. You have no business dressing like a man. I'll find you something decent." Fajimi stalked out of the tent opening with one last disgusted look, adding, "Are you the one he keeps wanting to rescue? Maybe you should tell him he's done it. Then maybe he'll get some rest." She disappeared through the canvas flap.

Priscilla giggled behind her hand. "Bossy."

"Yes, but I'm glad she's here. Nobody else really seems to know what to do." She ran her fingers through her hair. "Do I look that bad, Prissy?"

The child tilted her chin upwards and gazed at Sally Beth's swollen and bruised face. "It will get better. Put some more gele on it, and drink some. Fajimi said it would help."

Fajimi returned two hours later, carrying a small canvas bag bulging with plants in one hand and a simple blue housedress in the other. As she swept into the tent, she gave Sally Beth an appraising glance and she tossed the dress to her, saying, "You will look better when you dress like a girl." Then she poured water into a bowl and proceeded to empty her bag on the table. Pale yellow flowers, golden daisies, and succulents spilled out. She sorted through them, washing them and placing them into various bowls. Sally Beth drew closer.

"Aloe vera," explained Fajimi. "There wasn't one speck of it in the whole camp. I had to walk up that mountain to find it." She slit the juicy stem down the side and placed it in a bowl before taking up a pestle and crushing it, then added a few bright yellow flowers, which Sally Beth recognized as St John's wort. After a moment's work, she dipped her fingers into the bowl and smeared it on Sally Beth's face. "Put this on your bruises. Should help." She stood back, nodding her head briefly before turning back to her work. "Go change your clothes. He'll never get better as long as you look like that," Fajimi said as she poked around in her bag, pulling out more golden flowers. "Bur marigold. Found it just where I thought I would, in the swamp." Tossing the flowers into a bowl, she attacked them with her pestle as Sally Beth slipped out of the tent.

November 6, 1978

The bleeding had stopped, but now John burned with fever. Sally Beth and Priscilla sat by him all day every day and for a good deal of the nights, holding his hand, doing their best to keep him cool while Fajimi went out to scour the island for medicinal herbs that might help him. She forced him to drink teas made from gele and other strange plants that she ground up and steeped in water. "I wish they would let me have wine," she muttered. "This no alcohol rule is bad medicine. But thank God his wounds have not festered."

"Why won't Alice let us leave?" asked Sally Beth for the tenth time. Fajimi sighed as she slathered more aloe vera and St. John's wort on her face.

"You know the Lakwena forbids it. Besides, the Ugandans are patrolling the lake. If you attempt to go now, we will be discovered. And if our hiding place is discovered, there will be no hope for you, or your sister, or for John. He will turn around soon. Go and comb your hair."

Instead, she went to Alice. "Alice, I know you said the Lakwena forbids us to leave, but please, John is worse today. Isn't there some way I can get him to the hospital?"

Alice looked tired. She had grown thinner over the last few days. But she smiled at Sally Beth with sympathy before replying, "We go to battle today. Under no circumstances are you to leave, or even venture to the edge of the camp. Sit with us while we prepare, and pray for victory. John will not die; the Lakwena has assured me that Fajimi's medicines will cure his fever in another three days, if you pray, if we all remain pure in the eyes of God."

Sally Beth sat in a chair just outside John's tent as the preparations for battle began. Prissy sat on the ground beside her, leaning against her knee, grasping her hand as they watched people filing into the clearing. Men, women, and children silently poured out of tents and out of the forest, walking softly, as if not to disturb the cool morning air.

They watched uneasily as the commanders and technicians brought out pots of Shea butter and ocher, laying them on the ground under the yellow fever trees for the hundred men chosen for battle. They took off their shirts and smeared the concoction over their faces and bodies, then sat in ten rows of ten men each to listen to the technician in command read out the safety precautions. He walked among them, sprinkling water from a small vessel on each of their heads, then stood before them, holding a book high, speaking soberly and so softly Sally Beth had to strain to hear.

"Thou shall not have any kind of charms or remains of small sticks in your pockets, including the small piece used as a toothbrush. Thou shalt not smoke cigarettes. Thou shalt not drink alcohol. Thou shalt not commit adultery or fornication. Thou shalt not quarrel or fight with anybody. Thou shalt not steal."

Phil moved gingerly around the perimeter of the troops, snapping pictures. Lilly crouched with her camera before Alice, who sat still and rigid, seemingly in a trance.

"Thou shalt not have envy or jealousy. Thou shalt not kill."

This sent a chill through Sally Beth. *How could soldiers going to battle be commanded not to kill?*

"You will execute the orders and only the orders of the Lakwena. Thou shalt not take cover on the ground, in the grass, behind trees, ant hills, or any other obstacle there found."

Not take cover! Do not kill and do not take cover. How had they won every battle they had engaged in over the past weeks? Sally Beth wondered if perhaps God was helping them, if Alice were indeed being led by the Holy Spirit.

"Thou shalt not pick from the battlefield any article not recommended by the Lakwena. Thou shalt not kill prisoners of war. Thou shalt follow the right words of command and never argue with the commander. Thou shalt love one another as you love yourselves. Thou shalt not kill snakes of any kind. Thou shalt not eat food with anybody who has not been sworn in by the Holy Spirit. Thou shalt not branch off to any home or shake hands with anybody while on route to the battlefield.

"Thou shalt not eat pork or mutton or oil of the same. Thou shalt have two testicles, neither more nor less. If any of you have not adhered to the safety precautions or fear that you cannot follow them, stand now and leave this place. The Lakwena will protect us only if all are found worthy."

There was a long silence while each soldier turned inward, examining his heart. Sally Beth clutched at Priscilla's hand, and from time to time, glanced back into the tent at John. He lay pale and still as a statue underneath the cool shade of the tent.

At last, a tremulous breath passed through the ranks, then three men rose and walked away. As soon as they stood, three men from the crowd began making their way forward. They took off their shirts and dipped their hands into the ochre and Shea butter pots, anointing themselves, then took the places vacated by their fellow soldiers.

"You have nine bullets and four magic stones each today," said the technician. "Remember, you are not to point your weapons at anyone. You are not to kill. Only shoot into the air over the enemy's head. The Spirits will guide the bullets to their mark as They deem." He stepped back, gesturing toward the ammunition tent, where rifles and clips were laid out beside a large pile of rocks.

"Sing continually as you move forward until I command you to stop. When you are in sight of the enemy, the first rank shall hurl the magic stones forward as far as you are able, but do not shoot until my command. When you in the first rank have thrown all your stones, the second rank shall move forward with their stones. If your heart is full of love, enemy bullets will not be allowed to move past the stones. In this way, we are assured victory. The Lakwena has declared it."

No one moved as Alice suddenly stood and made her way to the front of the rows of warriors. She stood calmly, facing the eastern sun, with her hands raised high above her head.

"We are the soldiers of the Holy Spirits, purified in the faith. With Lakwena as our guide, protecting us, shielding us, going before us, we will be victorious. Go forth!" She began singing,

> *Encamped along the hills of light,*
> *Ye Christian soldiers, rise,*
> *And press the battle ere the night*
> *Shall veil the glowing skies.*
> *Against the foe in vales below,*
> *Let all our strength be hurled;*
> *Faith is the victory, we know,*
> *That overcomes the world.*

The soldiers picked up the refrain, lifting their hands, singing, and then, as if they had seen an invisible signal, they stood as one, stamping their feet and holding their hands high. Their voices swelled in triumph as the crowd behind them joined in,

> *Faith is the victory!*
> *Faith is the victory!*
> *Oh, glorious victory,*
> *That overcomes the world.*
> *His banner over us is love,*
> *Our sword the Word of God;*
> *We tread the road the saints above*
> *With shouts of triumph trod.*

Still singing, they began to march. As they passed single file by the tent, each man picked up four stones, a rifle and a clip, slid the clip into the rifle, then continued on northward where boats waited. As they disappeared into the forest, she heard the music shift into another hymn. For some time she could hear the powerful voices floating through the forest,

> *Onward, Christian Soldiers, marching as to war*
> *With the cross of Jesus going on before*
> *Christ the royal Master, leads against the foe!*
> *Forward into battle, see his banners go!*

Sally Beth was chilled by the sight of soldiers marching off, defenseless save for nine bullets and four stones each, their faith and the supposed "armor" of holy water, Shea butter, and ochre. She closed her eyes.

Lord, protect them. And John.

The soldiers began returning sometime before nightfall, straggling in, few in numbers, wounded, beaten, heartbroken.

Lilly gasped as she saw the first ragged, bleeding soldiers stagger into the camp. "This is the first time I have seen them defeated," she said, her voice heavy with foreboding. "I don't know what this means, but we'd better think about getting out of here as soon as we can." Sally Beth felt fear building in her chest as she took John's limp hand. Her soul pressed against the wall that had grown up between herself and God, but it could not move it, and she did not know how to tear it down.

"We'll be all right," she said, smiling at Prissy as brightly as she could, but no one, including herself, believed it.

November 10, 1978, Nairobi, Kenya

Gordon Blair rushed in from the barn to answer the ringing telephone. Even with the new man he had hired, it was hard running the place without John, and he was worn out with trying to pick up the pieces of what had been left of the Kagera station at Kigemba Lake. He picked up the receiver, hoping it wasn't more bad news.

"Center for Drought Resistance Sustainability," he said into the mouthpiece.

"Good afternoon," came the voice at the other end. "Is this Mr. Blair?"

"Yes. May I help you?"

"This is Franklin Ross, with Nairobi First Bank. I spoke to your partner, John Smith, the last time I called, regarding a donation made to your organization a few months ago?"

"Yes, of course." Gordon hoped that Mr. Ross was not going to be asking for an accounting of the money spent on the station at Kigemba Lake. He dreaded having to explain that a good deal of it had literally gone up in smoke or had been carried or driven across the Ugandan border.

"Permit me to express my condolences for your misfortune and for the disappearance of Mr. Smith. I trust everything possible is being done to find him and the young woman with him? And I understand there are others who have disappeared as well."

Gordon was surprised to hear this. *How did Mr. Ross know about Sally Beth, Lilly, and Phil?* "Thank you, Mr. Ross. Unfortunately, it is very difficult to track down the whereabouts of my partner and the others. All we know is that they are likely somewhere in Uganda, and it's impossible to get any news from there."

"Of course. That's why I'm calling. My client wants to help and has asked me to let you know that if you need anything at all, please call me with your request. He feels partly responsible for your troubles because he insisted on your establishing a station in Kagera."

"Thank you. I can't think of anything at the moment, except perhaps, if your client is so inclined, there might be something he could do for the employees who were helping John. Three have been displaced because of the war, and four have died. They have families."

"Yes, I am aware of that, as I am aware that there are several refugees from the mission where Mr. Smith often stayed when he was in Kagera. My client has instructed me to let you know that we have arranged for accommodations for anyone associated with Mr. Smith—his employees at Kigemba, people from the mission, anyone connected with him who has been affected by the war. He wishes you to bring them to Nairobi to stay until they have recovered from any injuries and have found living accommodations. Mr. Smith also may have some relatives or friends who might be coming to Africa to help search for him or offer support. They all will need to be housed during their visit."

Gordon wondered if he was supposed to round up all those people as Mr. Ross continued, "I have engaged the Victoria Inn for the next month, which I believe will provide the most suitable lodging for a large group. Of course, if it is necessary, I will extend the rental until it is no longer needed."

"The Victoria Inn?" Gordon was taken aback. "How many rooms?" The Victoria Inn was the most luxurious hotel in all of Nairobi, a colonial palace that had hosted every British monarch from Queen Victoria to George VI. Even after the end of the occupation, it continued to set the standard for luxury, becoming the most sought-after place for dignitaries and personalities who came to Nairobi. It was outrageously expensive. For someone to reserve rooms for a month was unthinkable.

There was a chuckle at the other end of the line. "Well, not the whole Inn." But we did manage to reserve a block of fifteen rooms. If more rooms are needed, we will try to find another hotel as close as can be arranged." Mr. Ross paused. "By the way, it might make sense for you to stay there as well, to be the host, so to speak, or at least take some time to help ease the adjustment of some of the refugees. No doubt, some will be feeling vulnerable and frightened, and will need a kind friend nearby. I know it may be difficult for you to run the ranch and entertain a diverse group of visitors, but my client would be most appreciative if you can. He encourages you to hire help, at his expense, of course. We chose the Victoria Inn because it is so close to your ranch. I hope you will be able to assist us."

"Of course," stammered Gordon. It would, in fact, be quite difficult for him to keep up his responsibilities at the ranch and play nursemaid to twenty or thirty frightened refugees, but who was he to refuse the generous benefactor who had just given them half a million dollars? He reckoned he would be able to survive the ordeal, especially given the fact that the Inn boasted some of the best chefs in Kenya. He hung up the phone mystified, terrified, and excited.

Lake Victoria

John had shown no signs of improvement. Sally Beth watched in anguish as he grew thinner and paler. Four days ago, Alice had promised her that John would begin to heal in three days. But then, she had also assured her soldiers of victory in battle. She wondered if something was amiss, if the fever would defeat John just as Alice and her men had been overrun. She had prayed incessantly by his bedside, but the coldness of her spirit seemed to extinguish every flame that rose up as she cried out to God, turning it into a curling puff of smoke before it even left her heart. Restless and desperate, she sought for something different.

"Lilly," she said to her sister, "I need to get away from here, to go someplace quiet where I can be alone with God. I just need to get out of this murky air, someplace I can breathe. I see that big hill over there. Do you know how to get to the top? Would you go with me?"

Lilly eyed her with sympathy. "I've been there. It's pretty, and it would be a good place for you to pray, but Sally Beth, it's a lot higher than it looks, and it's terrifying to climb. We went there for the purification ritual before I went to battle with the troops, and it was all I could do to make it to the top and back down again. I can't even think about going back there without panicking." She looked at Sally Beth regretfully. "I'll ask Alice to send someone with you, okay?" she said softly.

"Lilly! You flew from Bukoba to the mission in a creaky little old plane—with *me* flying, and I had never even taken off before. You weren't the least afraid then. How can you still be afraid of high places?"

"It's funny. Planes are fine. I can look down through the clouds and not feel a thing; I can even enjoy it. But when my feet are on the ground and I look down and imagine it falling away, I get this crazy feeling that I'm going to jump, and that scares me to death. I get that same feeling in tall buildings. I know it's weird."

Sally Beth put her arm around her. She could feel Lilly's distress. "It's okay, sweetheart. I remember how hard it was for you at the Grand Canyon, how hard it's always been on mountaintops. Never mind. I'll ask Alice."

"Ask me what?" came a voice from behind her. She turned to see Alice leaning against a mangrove root.

"Alice, I'm glad you are here." Lilly put her arm around Sally Beth and pushed her forward an inch. "Sally Beth wants to go to Memmee Hill to pray, and I know it is forbidden for a woman to walk through the forest alone. Would you find someone who knows the way to go with her?"

Alice regarded her coolly for a long moment before she replied, "Perhaps I could go with you, Sally Beth." Pushing away from the tree, she added, "I, too, wish to go to a high place to pray. The

Spirit must be speaking the same thing to both of us today." She took Sally Beth's hand. "Natiko's dress is becoming to you. I hope it lifted the spirits of our friend John. Is he improving today?"

"No, Alice. He has not improved at all. He is still fevered and talking out of his head a good bit of the time. That's why I want to go pray. I need a quiet place where I can be alone."

"I see," said Alice slowly. "He did not make a turn for the better after three days as the Lakwena promised?"

"No, if anything, he might be worse. Fajimi's herbs seem to be keeping his wounds clear, but she doesn't know why he has fever." She fought back tears. "Will you go with me?"

Looking at Sally Beth with narrowed eyes, Alice mused, "There is something you urgently need to speak to God about? The Lakwena is unable to discern the light of the truth when there is a darkness in a man's or a woman's heart." She took a few steps forward. "Come. I will take you to Memmee, and you can unburden your spirit."

Alice was quiet as they made their way up to higher ground. After they had crossed through the deep shade of the forest, they found themselves suddenly facing a cliff more than a hundred feet high rising up before them like a wall of stone. Sally Beth looked up along a precipitous path that had been scratched into the face of the cliff and found herself wondering how Lilly had ever made her way up the side of this mountain. A year ago, such a climb would have been impossible for Lilly, and Sally Beth felt a small surge of pride for her sister's strength and determination. Following Alice, she grabbed hold of the rock and pulled herself up onto a narrow ledge.

"When you get to the next ledge, be sure you begin the climb with your left foot, Sally Beth," came Alice's voice from above her. When you get near the top, you will need to reach out with your right foot, and you won't be able to shift your feet at that point. Do you understand?"

"Yes." Sally Beth concentrated on balancing on the balls of her feet as she reached upward, feeling for a place to grab onto the rock above her. This was far more precipitous than she had imagined it would be.

After nearly ten minutes of climbing the sheer face of rock, they reached a wide ledge, and from there the path grew easier. It was still very steep, but she was able to walk nearly upright, using her hands only to steady herself against the cliff side. Then, before many more minutes had passed, she found herself at the top, where she turned to face out over the vast, shimmering waters of Lake Victoria. The breeze coming up from the water below lifted her hair from the back of her neck, cooling her and bringing the fragrance of the monkey-tree blossoms below. Long, silky grass at her feet rifled in the wind, and the sun beamed its soft, generous rays. The lake spread out in three directions, and as she looked out, she knew this would be a good place to pray. She had not felt such peace since before the war had begun.

Alice stood beside her, looking down to the water. "I will leave you here," she said quietly. "I wish I could tell you to take your time, but we should go back within an hour. My troops need my presence among them." She nodded briefly before making her way over the gentle terrain toward a grove of trees a few hundred feet away. Sally Beth sat on a rock and faced the water, lifting her face into the tender wind.

She took a breath. Never had she found it this hard to pray. "Lord," she began, speaking aloud in case God could hear her voice when He could not hear the cries of her soul. After the first few words of invocation, she faltered as her thoughts turned toward John and his silent suffering. Disquiet seeped into her spirit like a dark, oily smoke stealing through every fissure in her fragile armor. She was barely on speaking terms with God; her prayers still felt heavy and flightless, like a bumblebee with stunted wings. She took a breath and began again.

"Lord, I don't know how to pray. I feel tired, dead inside. I feel like I've been fighting so hard and for so long that I don't know how to just let go and let my thoughts fly up to You. And I feel as if You and I are not friends any more. Have You given up on me?"

Her mind wandered into the horrors of the past weeks; she saw the suffering children, the anguished eyes of women, the bloody, broken people who looked at her with hope while she knew there was no hope. She saw the child with the hole in her face, the piles of rotting bodies along the roadside. She saw John, bleeding and white, fevered, thin, and then she saw his face looking at her, his eyes soft and full of wonder. She saw herself look into those eyes, wanting to lose herself in them, to make him lose himself inside her. The only good thing she had known in the weeks of terror and pain was John. John holding her, whispering promises of safety and warmth, John's hand on hers, and she whimpered, "Lord, why won't you heal him? Is it because I sinned?"

And then something fell into place, and she recognized the truth of what she had been hoping she could ignore. She had sinned against God, against His holy ordinances. Not because of her desire for John, but because she had lost faith in what God could and would do. She had shut her eyes against the God she had known since her youth and had turned instead to find her hope and salvation in a mere man. It broke her heart to admit it. *But shouldn't she be allowed to love a man? Shouldn't a woman be allowed to want a man to protect her? What did God want from her, after all? Was she not to know what it was like to know the joy of human love? It didn't seem fair.*

Sally Beth knew she had to really look at herself and her spirit and be honest about what she had done. At last, she sighed and gave into the judgment. Drawing a deep, steadying breath, she spoke aloud.

"I know, I've been resisting this confession. I wanted him, Lord, I wanted him so bad I was willing to exchange You for him, at least for a little while. I know I didn't give him a choice, but did all I could to seduce him, knowing it was wrong, not just because You told me it was wrong but because I made demands on him that he couldn't fill. He couldn't love me, but I wanted to make him love me. I know, I confess that sin. And now he is sick, and I'm afraid You will take him from me forever, and all this is my fault. But Lord, please, I am willing to give him up if that's what You demand. I don't want to, but if I have to, I at least ask You to make me want to, because more than anything, I want You to be my Lord again. And I want You to heal John, and if it takes giving him up, I will do it."

Tears ran down her face as she struggled to say the words she had so long fought against saying. She didn't want to regret her hours with him, she didn't want to regret the sweet, overpowering pleasure, the feeling of safety and promise in his arms, but if that's what it took to give him life, she would do it.

"There is a sin in you that you had not confessed?" The voice beside her was hard.

Sally Beth jumped and turned to see Alice standing behind her. "You are burdened with sin? And it's been unconfessed since you have come here? Sally Beth! You have put us all in danger." Alice's eyes flashed with anger as she advanced upon Sally Beth. "We went into battle when one among us was lying in the luxury of her fornication! The Lakwena cannot see through the darkness you brought, and now you have brought disaster upon us all."

Sally Beth blinked through her astonishment. "No, I did not!" She stopped, then started again, "I mean, I am not guilty of what you say. I just..." She felt the blush rise to her face. "I wanted to, but I did not." She tried to explain away her guilt, but at last merely dropped her head, weeping. "I'm sorry," she said at last.

Alice did not answer. She turned, quickly making her way back down the path. Sally Beth followed her silently, feeling the misery of the burdens that had been placed upon her, the burdens that kept growing heavier as she groped for handholds in the face of the cliff. She was moving too slowly. Alice was nearly at the bottom of the cliff, and Sally Beth knew that she would not be able to find her way back to the camp if she let her out of her sight. She quickened her pace, despite the heaviness in her limbs and in her heart.

She managed to keep Alice in sight until they had both made it back to camp. Alice disappeared into her tent without speaking or even turning to look at Sally Beth. Confused and miserable, Sally

Beth made her way to the infirmary tent, but before she arrived, Priscilla and Lilly met her. "Sally Beth!" Prissy cried. "I've been looking for you. John is awake, and his fever is gone. Oh, Praise God for His glorious healing!'

Sally Beth looked at Lilly, who was beaming. "It's true," she confirmed. "He's been asking for you in between sips of water. I don't know what you prayed for up on that mountain, or what you promised God, but it must have worked. He's going to be fine."

Twenty-Two

November 23, 1978, Victoria Inn, Nairobi, Kenya

Half of the long table sat in a pool of sunshine, the other half under the dappled shade of strangle fig trees. The rain had held off for most of the day, allowing for a cool, almost dry breeze.

John sat at the head of the table. This was the first day he had been able to walk without the use of a cane, although he still limped and could not stand for long. As he looked at the crowd, he saw the faces of friends and strangers he had never imagined would be assembled together in Nairobi, certainly not at Thanksgiving, and he took a moment to bask in thankfulness for all they had survived.

Nearly everyone he cared about was there, including the one person he had been longing to see for the past four months. Geneva sat halfway down the table beside her husband, looking radiant and beautiful. He studied her discretely, waiting for his heart to tell him what he needed to know, if it would ever be free of her. As she lifted her eyes to meet his, she somehow did not look like the Geneva he had so desperately loved last summer in that time of windswept delirium. That Geneva had been so full of sunlight that she had seemed almost transparent, nothing but glittering edges, sharp and diamond-like, and the image had blinded him, had made him dizzy with the desire of possibility. In that splendid transparency he had felt that he could layer in all of his dreams.

This Geneva was more substantial, softer, and obviously happier. He had wanted to fill in the transparencies, to make her whole. Now she was whole, and that meant she was now both more and less than sunlight. He could see something he had not seen there before: a woman's beating heart, flesh and bone, and he suddenly realized he had been chasing a dream, a fiction. He had wanted her not for who she was, but for what she was not: he had wanted her restlessness, her incompleteness so that he could rewrite her to fulfill his fantasies. He had wanted someone to save, someone with whom he could script a heroic ending. And he had been a fool.

He almost chuckled as he realized that he had wanted to be her champion, but she had done the rescuing. She and her family had flown here just to help find them; they had hired mercenaries who had come to the mission and saved everyone there from certain death. He could not pretend to play the hero any longer.

Next to Geneva sat Sally Beth, bouncing Geneva's baby on her lap, laughing at something Lilly, to her right, had said. Although his heart felt leaden with guilt at how he had hurt her, he could not help but smile—laughter danced in his heart every time he caught sight of her. Sally Beth was fun and funny, and she was able to make him delight in the most ordinary of things. If only he could love her in the way she had wanted him to, his life would be simple and serene, uncomplicated. He had tried, but Sally Beth's safe, steadfast, faithful love was not what he needed. She was the opposite of the adventure and challenge that he craved in a woman. He lowered his eyes in sadness, hoping she would someday forgive him for what he had not been able to do or be.

Beside Lilly sat Howard Graves, of all people. Why he had come was beyond him; it seemed that he had somehow been involved with the mercenaries and had been instrumental in getting everyone here.

John's life had changed in ways that he never would have asked for, but he was grateful for most of the changes. His heart full, he slowly struggled to his feet. "My dear friends," he said, looking at the crowd of people and knowing they were truly his friends. "This is the most thankful Thanksgiving I have ever had. If it weren't for the absence of Pastor Umbatu, it would be perfect. To have you all here, to be surrounded by so much love and support... well, I can't thank you enough." Feeling his throat close, he took a deep breath before lowering his head. "Father, we are truly thankful for all the blessings you have showered down on us, for friends, for love, for hope, for healing, for salvation. Now we ask that you keep Pastor Umbatu safe and that you return him to us soon."

Then he lifted a glass. "To friends," he said, "and family, and to the Lord God who looks after us, who saves us from our enemies."

Everyone raised their glasses, echoing his words. Alethia's girls giggled. They thought John was the handsomest man they had ever seen, even though he was white. He wasn't fish-belly white, though, like most of the Americans at the table, but golden, like the sun on the dry grass of August. What made them love him most was the fact that he had saved them all from the Ugandans who had destroyed their home, had brought them to Kenya, and was building a new home for them high in the mountains, far away from Idi Amin.

Sally Beth thought he was the handsomest man she had ever seen, too, but, unlike the six little girls, she tried not to look at the green-eyed, sun-bronzed Adonis who stood at the head of the table. He would never return the love she bore for him, so rather than let herself gaze at him with longing, she turned to Lyla sitting across from her at the table.

"Don't you worry," she soothed. "They'll find him." Sally Beth was certain of it. More than three weeks had passed since Pastor Umbatu's kidnapping, but still, she believed he was alive, and that he would be back one day soon.

"Yes," spoke up Red. "I know it, too." He raised his glass. "To

Pastor Umbatu, a real hero. May he come home soon. If it hadn't been for him, some of us wouldn't be here today. I'll never forget. We were all cowering in our hiding places while soldiers were tearing apart the sanctuary. He stepped out, and just as coolly and kindly as could be, said, 'Gentlemen, may I help you in the sweet name of Jesus?' He was so gracious the soldiers didn't know what to do. He had to be the one to suggest they take him and hold him for ransom. They quit looking after that, or they would have found us." He paused while everyone lifted their glasses, thinking of Pastor Umbatu and murmuring his name.

Lyla smiled as she said, "My husband, the hero. He has always been a hero to me."

Red had not finished. Smiling at Geneva and her husband, he lifted his glass again. "And to Howard and Geneva Knight, and Howard Graves, too, you good folks from America who worked so tirelessly to help us. The men you sent to look for us came just a few minutes after the soldiers left. I don't know what would have happened, how we would have gotten out of there if it hadn't been for them. Thank you."

"Thank you," came the voices from around the table.

Alethia stood. "And here's to John, who risked his life to bring my children to safety, and to Lyla, who sheltered them, and to Sally Beth, who mothered them when I was not there."

John wanted to toast Sally Beth, too, and when he tried to formulate in his mind the words he would say to let her know how grateful he was to her, the long list gave him pause. She had saved his life more than once, she had been courageous in the face of danger and death; she had nursed him during his long delirium on the island; she had given him her own blood; she had loved him when he didn't deserve to be loved. It made him grieve to think that this exquisite woman had wasted her love on him, that he had turned his back on something so beautiful and sweet as the heart of Sally Beth. But what could he do? He could not make himself love. All he could do was try to find a moment to raise a glass to her in thankfulness and in acknowledgement for all she was. He sat, mute and miserable, feeling the sting of his ingratitude.

He hesitated too long. Sally Beth had jumped up. "Here's to Alethia, the best mother I know."

Immediately Geneva jumped to her feet. "Here's to Howard Graves, who is a true friend. He has been the one who managed all this, arranging for the rescue team, for getting us over here."

John started to speak again, but Lilly's laughter rang out before he drew breath. "Okay, okay, let's face it, we're all wonderful, so let's just acknowledge that fact and get on with it—I'm starving. Here's to wonderful us!"

"To wonderful us!" they all echoed with laughter, although more than a few were also wiping tears from their cheeks.

"Wait just a minute," spoke up Phil. "You all can go ahead and start passing around the food, but I have something to announce that I've been sitting on for two days now so I could make it a part of this celebration, and I can't wait another second or I'll explode." He grinned at Lilly, who grinned back. Reaching under the table to bring out a copy of *The New York Times*, he opened it to the front page of the world news section and held it up for all to see. Lilly let out a squeal, and the others realized what it was.

A picture of Alice Auma, dressed in army fatigues, and looking very young and vulnerable, standing in a jeep on a jungle road, a shaft of sunlight bathing her fresh, innocent face was splayed across the front page. Underneath the photo was the headline: "Modern Joan of Arc Hears Spirit Voices, Leads Army Against Amin."

"Look here, six inches on the first page of this section and more on page five. Story by Phillip Bayman and photographs by Lilly Lenoir!"

Lilly squealed again and so did Sally Beth. The others all cheered and applauded.

"Read it, Phil!" shouted Howard Graves.

"No, it's too long," he said modestly. "I'll pass it around so you all can read it. There is another picture on page five. Lilly's amazing."

"Yes, she is," said Howard Graves. Lilly blushed as Sally Beth caught her eye. Geneva grinned at her and started to say something, but Sally Beth knew that whatever she said would embarrass her sister, so she piped up.

"Have some of these sweet potatoes, Lyla. It's my mother's recipe, and I bet you've never had anything like them."

Lyla made a wry face. "I love you, Sally Beth, but your sweet potatoes are too sweet for me." She smiled a little. "But I do not complain at how sweet you are."

Lilly broke in. "You ought to try living with her, Lyla. You might change your mind after you've been around all that sweetness for long. It's enough to give a body diabetes." She put her arm affectionately around Sally Beth's shoulders and gave a squeeze. As Sally Beth hugged her back, she saw John looking at her, and she felt her own heart being squeezed.

After dinner, Geneva made her way to where John sat. "You look tired," she said. "I hope today hasn't been too hard on you."

He shook his head, smiling, but his face was lined and sad. "Thank you for coming. It was kind of you. Generous." He didn't know what else to say; he suddenly felt overwhelmed and lost, unable to think of what he should do next. She sat beside him and gazed at him, her chin resting on her fist.

"What's going on between you and Sally Beth?" Geneva asked him without preamble.

"What do you mean?"

"You're avoiding each other, and both of you keep looking at the other one when you think nobody's noticing. Something has happened. I keep thinking about that day Holy Miracle—the day he died—told us that she was the one for you, and I'm wondering if you've realized it. He called her 'your happiness'."

John looked up, surprised, realizing that she had heard it, too.

"So what transpired between you?"

He made a futile gesture. "We almost made love. Would have, but the Ugandans started shooting at us. She wanted to. I didn't."

He glanced at her sheepishly. "I wasn't over you. I let her know that she was playing second fiddle."

Geneva winced. "You idiot."

"I know."

"Looks like you've made a career out of turning down Lenoir women." It was his turn to wince. "And I thank you," she laughed. "At least for turning me down. I had a few lessons to learn. Thank God I learned them in time. Anyway, what are you going to do now?"

He shrugged; his shoulders sagged. "I don't think Holy Miracle got it right."

"Well, now I know why I needed to be here. To keep you from continuing to be an idiot."

He smiled at her sadly. "I'm not ready to love anybody just yet, Geneva. I need more time to heal, I think," and with that, he rose unsteadily and limped back into the hotel, leaving Geneva feeling confused and saddened, wondering how hurt Sally Beth had been over all this. Hoisting Blue higher on her hip, she went in search of her cousin.

Geneva found her sitting at the window in her room, wrapped in the ragged cloak of her sorrow. Her face was white with grief. Not bothering to knock, Geneva went right in and put her arms around her sweet, uncomplicated Sally Beth.

"Something wrong between you and John?" she asked.

"There was nothing ever right between us."

"I don't think so. I think he's just been through a lot, and deep down, I think he loves you. He just needs some time."

Sally Beth shook her head. "I am not fit to be loved by anybody."

Geneva sat up. "What on earth are you talking about? Sally Beth, you are the fittest person in the world! You are—you are the *best*. Ever!"

"Oh, no." She shook her head. "I've been selfish and manipulative and I've been mad at God, and now we aren't even really on speaking terms, and I don't know how to make it right unless I just forget about John." She sniffled.

"You and God aren't on speaking terms? You mean you've quit talking to Him?"

Sally Beth didn't quite know how to respond. "Well, not exactly, but He doesn't hear me anymore."

"And what makes you think this?"

"Because I'm arguing."

"Is it a sin to argue with God?"

She paused. "Well, no. I guess it's more like I've resisted what He wants me to do."

Geneva smiled as she put her arms around Sally Beth again. "Oh, honey, you are talking to the queen of manipulators, of selfish, of resisting what God wants. And a year ago, I was thinking pretty much the same thing you are right now, and you know what?"

Sally Beth looked at her tentatively. "What?"

"My favorite cousin in the whole world who is infinitely wiser and kinder and more godly than I am told me something that I'm going to throw right back at you now. We *all* are a mess. We screw up; we do awful things and expect God to give up on us, but that just makes Him pursue us harder. I remember plain as day you saying, 'If God didn't love anybody who wasn't broken,'—and that means manipulative and selfish and resistant to His will—'then He wouldn't love *anybody*.' Do you remember that, Sally Beth?"

Sally Beth paused. "Well, yes, but this is different."

"Different how?"

"I knew better."

Geneva tried not to snort. "Do you know of *anybody* who gave in to some sort of temptation who *didn't* know better?"

Sally Beth stopped to think as Geneva pressed on. "Eve? King David? Abraham? How about Jonah? Peter? Sally Beth, I could go on all day if I knew my Bible better, but if you think about it, there isn't anybody who passes that test!"

Sally Beth nearly smiled. "Well, there's the Virgin Mary."

Geneva couldn't stop herself from hooting this time. "Oh, I see. You're bucking for sainthood, is that it? You expect yourself to be *that* good!" She shook her finger in Sally Beth's face. "Silly girl. *There's* your sin. You think you are capable of being perfect. And it's killing you because you aren't. Close, but believe me, I couldn't stand you if you were." Geneva laughed and hugged her again.

Sally Beth hugged her back, letting loose the torrent of tears she had been holding back for weeks. She wept and laughed, nodding her head, sensing the rightness of what Geneva had said, but still wondering if it could be as easy as that. To just wait for God and quit trying so hard. She wasn't sure. The faithlessness of her recent past still haunted her, and she felt she had some making up to do.

Suddenly, Lilly burst into the room, followed closely by Lyla. "Pastor Umbatu has been found!" she shrieked. "We just got a message from a church up in Bugala Island. He escaped from prison in Kampala and met up with the Holy Spirits army. He's with them at their camp!" She gave a little hop. "Hot dog! Sally Beth, you've got to to get him, and I'm going with you. And Phil, too. What a story."

"Me, too!" exclaimed Lyla. "You're not going without me!"

"If I take all of you, there won't be room for Pastor Umbatu to come back," protested Sally Beth."

Lilly waved that off. "That's okay. Phil and I can stay a few days. You can come back and get us." She turned toward the door. "Come on! I'll grab a bag and meet you at the plane."

Geneva watched as Sally Beth hesitated, glanced at her hopefully, then squared her shoulders and ran out of the room after Lilly.

The news had reached the others by the time Sally Beth made it out to the lawn. John was nowhere in sight, but she did not take the time to look for him. Lyla was already racing for the plane, and Lilly was flying out the door with her bag and cameras over her shoulder.

"Wait a minute!" shouted Phil. "Are you going *now*?"

"You betcha," answered Lilly. "Come on." As she turned to sprint down the hill, she bumped into Howard Graves, who had stepped up behind her.

"Hey!" he said, raking his fingers through his hair in exasperation and exclaimed, "Crazy woman! Am I going to have to follow you to the ends of the earth just to get to know you?"

Lilly's smile turned incandescent. She paused for a dramatic moment, flickered her eyes at him, and said in mock demure tones, "Maaaaybe," then took off. Howard did not hesitate before he ran after her.

John appeared. "What's going on?"

Gordon answered, "Pastor Umbatu is with the Holy Spirits and Sally Beth is going to get him. Lyla, Lilly, and Phil are going, too." He watched the group racing toward the planes. "It looks like Howard wants to go, too. Should I take him?"

"No," spoke up Geneva. "John will." She looked at John meaningfully.

"He really shouldn't..." began Gordon.

"Yes, he should." She wasn't sure why it felt so urgent to her, but she knew without doubt that John must be there for Sally Beth. She put her fist on her hip, glaring at John, willing courage and strength into him. "Sally Beth is going to need you."

"I don't have a plane. It was shot up and is still being repaired."

"Oh. Well, what is Sally Beth flying?"

"The old Super Cub. She's been flying it since we got back. I haven't been strong enough," he admitted, realizing that he probably still wasn't strong enough. "She's been helping Gordon while I've been recuperating."

Geneva looked at him intently. He looked tired and thin, and he probably was too sick to make the trip, but she couldn't stand the thought of Sally Beth flying off into Uganda without him. Pushing aside her doubts, she turned to Gordon. "Give him the keys to your plane," she demanded. "No," she added, shaking her head as he started to protest. "John needs to be the one to go."

John knew Geneva was right. Sally Beth had never flown by herself with more than one passenger, and if she had to land in the water, she might need him to help. The thought of her alone and vulnerable and responsible for so many people made him anxious, too. He shrugged as he held out his hand, feeling the weight of his responsibility to Sally Beth. Never mind that he was still weak and feeling all of his injuries. He had to man up. "I need your plane, buddy."

Gordon reluctantly reached into his pocket. "Try not to bring her back full of bullet holes," he pleaded as he placed the key in John's open palm.

Sally Beth, Lyla, Lilly, and Phil had already climbed aboard the Super Cub. Howard Graves stood outside, holding the back door open, arguing with Lilly.

"I'll be back when I'm back!" Lilly shouted at him. "Pastor Umbatu will need my seat, so I'll have to stay until somebody can pick us up. Besides, you never know what may be going on up there, and I can't miss this story."

She slammed the door as Sally Beth fired up the engine, leaving Howard standing forlornly in the grass. After a second's hesitation, Lilly leaned out the window. "Don't worry," she said softly. "I'll come back." Then she leaned out farther, grabbed him by the back of the neck and pulled him toward her, kissing him long and hard. "Or you can come find me."

Sally Beth and the Piper Cub were out of sight by the time John had hobbled to Gordon's Skylane. As he pulled himself into the cockpit, Howard Graves materialized by him. "Can I come along?" he asked.

"There's a war on. It won't be a luxury trip."

"Seems like those Lenoir women aren't into luxury." He grinned. "I've discovered I like that."

"You don't know the half of it, buddy. Come aboard," John said as he began the preflight checklist.

The Skylane was a faster plane than the Super Cub, so John caught up with Sally Beth quickly. He had half a mind to pull alongside of her, but he was afraid that would rattle her, and she had enough responsibility already. He put on his headset and spoke softly into the radio. "Skylane 235 niner Juliet to Super Cub

18472. You copy?"

The radio crackled, and then Sally Beth's sweet, soft voice came floating into his head. "Copy Skylane. No need for you to be here. Over."

He chuckled. No one ever said, "Over," but Sally Beth loved saying it. She had said it made her feel like an official pilot.

"Roger that. But I'd like to be around when you land that thing. You're carrying more weight than you're used to, and the engine isn't as powerful. Keep the nose up. You roger that?"

"You forgot to say 'Over.'"

"Roger. One more thing. Stay off the radio when we get close. Someone may be listening. Over."

"Roger that. Over and out."

Over and out. Sally Beth hoped that would shut him up. It was hard enough to concentrate, without the sound of his voice in her head, and she was carrying three precious lives. It was scarier than she thought it would be.

The Holy Spirits army had moved. Sally Beth peered down into the mangrove swamps, looking for any sign of the camp. She buzzed low once over the island, but then decided she should climb and look from higher up. If the Ugandans saw her obviously searching, she would give away the position of Alice and her company. Climbing higher, she saw that John had hung back, circling low over the lake, barely visible on the horizon. He was thinking the same thing and was waiting for her to find the Holy Spirits before he ventured in.

"Okay, everybody keep your eyes peeled. They're probably expecting us, and they'll have somebody in the open to signal us. Or look for campfires, for tents, anything."

"There!" shouted Lilly. "Over there—on the east side—just where that peninsula starts to narrow." She focused on the island and began snapping photographs.

Sally Beth saw it. Ten men stood at the narrow strip of land between the water and the forest. She realized she would have to make a water landing, something she had never done before. In her memory, there was only that terrifying moment when John had wrenched the controls away from her, diving down, and the sudden splash as the pontoons sliced the water and they all were flung into the windshield. "Is everybody buckled up?" She held her breath and ran though the procedure in her head.

John watched from a distance as Sally Beth pushed up into the clouds almost out of sight, and he waited until he was sure she had sighted the army. As soon as she began to descend, he circled back toward the island. If they had trouble, he wanted to make sure he was there. Sally Beth was a natural, and a quick learner, but she had landed a plane only a few times—the Super Cub only three times—and never in the water. He took a breath, watching the fragile vessel winging downward, and concentrated on what she should be doing, willing her to set the nose at the right angle, imagining how the water would rush up to meet her, how confusing the shimmer of the lake surface would be. He pushed his mind toward her, hoping to help her settle down smoothly, like a dragonfly on a flat, untroubled surface.

She gritted her teeth, drew a breath, and hearing her heart pounding above the roar of the engine, she muttered, "Lord, if you were ever with me, be with me now," then narrowed her focus on the silvery surface of the lake. Beside her, Lyla murmured her own prayer, and from the back seat, Lilly yelled out, "Sweet Lord Jesus, keep this thing upright!"

"What was I thinking?" asked Phil, as the plane bobbed on the lake water and they all were taking a moment to still their pounding hearts. "When you all took off running, it never occurred to me that somebody other than you could fly. How many times have you landed this thing, anyway?" It had been obvious that Sally Beth was not an experienced pilot.

"This plane? A few times. But never in the water."

"Oh, get over it, Phil," scoffed Lilly. Any landing you can walk away from is a good landing. And look—there they are." Some of their old friends in army fatigues, carrying guns, shields, and spears arrived at the shore just as John skimmed smoothly to a stop beside them. One of them called to them.

"Don't leave the planes here. You can be seen. Move them around to that inlet where you can hide." He waved toward the southern end of the island. Dutifully, Sally Beth and John fired up the engines again and steered the planes into a small cove tucked into a stand of mangroves.

Alice's men met them with boats, which took them through shallow water for some distance, and when mangrove roots became so thick the boats could no longer move, they got out to fight their way through papyrus reeds growing in the marshy wetlands. Finally, soaked and caked with mud, they put their feet on solid earth, where they found Alice and Pastor Umbatu waiting. If they had resented their ragged, soggy journey, they forgot about it when they saw Lyla flying like a sprite over the last of the muddy banks to throw herself into the arms of her husband.

Twenty-Three

The camp was in disarray. Bundles and crates had been piled onto carts. People milled about, cooking on small fires or packing up the last of their belongings. Alice stood in front of one of the few tents still standing, surrounded by several men who bore rifles and spears, their kind, but watchful faces glowing darkly. She held her hand up when the group appeared at the edge of the camp.

"All of you wait here. The Lakwena wishes to speak to Sally Beth," she said, giving Sally Beth a meaningful look, then she turned and strode into the tent. Sally Beth followed her inside to find her settling into a chair that dwarfed her small frame. Alice gazed forward, unspeaking, before she sat up, stretching her neck, giving Sally Beth a long, appraising look.

"My friend, the Lakwena sees something in you that he cannot decipher, something bigger and stronger than even he is," she said in her light, girlish voice. "Although I had feared your sin had caused us to suffer loss in battle, he tells me otherwise."

Alice stopped suddenly and her eyes went blank, as if dead: the pupils shrank to mere pinpricks. Her young face hardened. "Prayer

Warrior, who has the ear of Almighty God, you are timely come," came the low, guttural voice of the Lakwena. "I call upon you to preserve the life of my servant Alice and her army, for I can protect them no longer. The enemy has learned the secret of this place, and they are at the door. You must pray for my servants, for they will suffer great defeat in the days to come."

Alice took a breath, the life came back into her eyes, and she said simply in her soft, Alice voice, "Did the Lakwena tell you I must be on my way?"

"Yes, and I am to pray for you," replied Sally Beth, biting her lip and wondering how helpful her prayers could be. *How could she preserve the life of Alice and a whole army?*

"Good. The Lakwena has told me that your soul is pungent with the Spirit; your prayers are like incense." Alice rose, going out of the tent as she called to her soldiers. Sally Beth did not have the heart to tell her that the Lakwena was mistaken, but she felt a small flutter of life in her spirit, and she took hope.

Lilly broke into her thoughts as they strolled through the camp, saying goodbye to the friends they had made during the days they had lived among them. "It's tough, seeing them go, knowing things are probably over for them, for Alice. The day I went with them, I somehow felt like we were invincible. I guess those days are done now. They've lost the last three battles. Once Amin's army figures out they aren't bullet proof, the whole charade falls apart." She looked up to see Howard Graves standing nearby, his eyes locked on her.

"You'd better go rescue Howard," Sally Beth teased. "He looks as pitiful as Lamentations when Jimmy Lee's been out of sight too long. And he sure doesn't look like he belongs in this place. If he tries to go through the swamp without you, he's likely to be eaten by something." Lilly laughed and squeezed her hand as she slapped at a mosquito.

"He'll at least be eaten by these mosquitoes. Shoot, we all

will be if we don't get out of here." She looked at Howard with wistfulness before she added, "You'd think I'd develop a taste for the rugged type. They're much handier at getting you through the jungle, but I can't stop myself from looking at those pretty city boys." She walked toward him, stepping lightly, and as Sally Beth watched Howard's face, she felt a sweet hope for her baby sister pierce her heart.

Already, the army had completely broken camp. They had hauled boats to the edge of the island opposite the swamp and had loaded them, waiting for darkness before they attempted their escape. A sad aura of defeat hung about the place. Sally Beth watched them quietly moving about, until John appeared beside her. "We need to leave now," he said gently. "The guide is waiting." He nodded toward a soldier standing with Phil, Howard, Lilly, Lyla, and Pastor Umbatu.

"I know," she said, reluctant to leave. "I'm sad for these people. They had such good intentions, and now, I see defeat in their faces. You didn't see them the day they marched to battle, before their first loss. You've never seen anything like it. Such confidence and joy." They turned toward the forest, leaving the camp and the defeated people behind them, walking side by side for a few paces before John finally cleared his throat and spoke.

"I owe you an apology, Sally Beth. For all the stupid things I've done."

She was surprised. "You didn't do anything stupid."

"Oh, I think so."

"You mean risking your life to go after me? Taking a couple of bullets? Keeping me from crashing into the lake? I wouldn't call that stupid. I thought it was kind of sweet."

"Sally Beth! Did you just make a joke about the danger I was in? I never thought I would see you be snide."

She laughed. "John, I'm the one who owes you an apology. And I'm not even sure I've realized all the things I've done to wrong you. I need some time to think before I come clean. I've already made a big enough fool of myself."

"And pray tell, exactly how did you make a fool of yourself?"

"You know." She blushed, then stopped and turned to him. "John," she said earnestly, "I love you, you know that, and I don't regret what happened between us. But I took advantage of your generosity. I know I put you in an impossible situation, and I'm sorry. I was a little crazy, I guess, but I'm not making any excuses, and I'm sorry I did that to you. I was wrong, and I knew it was wrong, but I did it anyway, and while I appreciate your trying to make me feel better about it, you can't. You just have to leave me alone for a while and let me get over it."

John felt a great weight settle around his heart at the thought of her uncomplicated love—too generous, too freely given to him. He knew what he had done to her twenty-four days ago. She had lavished all of her love on him, and, in her most vulnerable moment, he had let her know he could not return it. And yet, she did not fault him for his cruelty. "You love me still? After all that?"

"Well, why ever not? You think I can get over you just like that?" She snapped her fingers.

"I thought you were—I thought I had hurt you, and you couldn't forgive me."

She looked at him as if she thought he was crazy. "Hurt me? You've never been anything but kind to me."

"When I, when you—" He didn't want to say it, to admit that he had fallen apart at the depth of her feeling for him. He shut his eyes against the vision of himself as she had looked deep into his soul and uttered the words, *John, I love you.* He knew he had flinched, had hesitated, had shown her his callous heart. He paused, took a breath, and launched in.

"Sally Beth, in case you are wondering, when I look at Geneva now, all I see is a friend and I realize I never loved her like I thought I did. I was just in love with the idea of being lovestruck. To tell you the truth, I've been running from the real thing, and I was using her—my supposed heartbreak—as a shield, a shield against anyone who might want to love me. I have to admit, I don't think I know how to really love anybody. I look at you, and I see beauty and grace and love and goodness and strength. I just wish I could love you the way you love me. And I am sorry I hurt you."

She pressed her hands against his chest. "You don't understand. This is not about you and me. Whatever hurt I've suffered, I brought on myself. This is between me and God, and it's complicated."

"Complicated how?"

She sighed. "I let God down, and now things aren't right between us. I need time to sort through some things, to beg His forgiveness, to learn how I'm supposed to love Him again before I can even think of anything else."

"Things aren't right between you? Lilly told me you went to the mountain to pray for me, and while you were there, my fever broke, and I started getting better. How could things not be right between you?"

She shook her head. "I don't think my prayers even reached Him," she said miserably. "Either He chose to heal you without my intervention, or the medicines finally started working. I was just up there arguing with Him."

"Well—how did you let God down?"

"I quit listening. I wanted what I wanted without even caring what He wanted. I got mad at Him. I ignored His will. I did my dead level best to seduce you." She intoned the list like a somber clanging of bells. He didn't know what to say, but he wanted to reassure her.

"Sally Beth," he said hesitantly, "We—we didn't do anything." He groped for the words. "You're still a virgin, if that's what's bothering you."

She made a dismissive gesture. "This isn't about my body parts, what's been altered. In my mind, in my heart, my spirit, I *did* do something. I tried to run from God." She hated to admit the next part. "I—I put you in His place. I wanted you—your love more than I wanted His. That's worse."

John listened quietly, his head down as she continued. "And I wronged you, too. I asked you—demanded that you do something you knew was wrong, and I didn't give you a choice, not even a little out. I made you feel like you would be a horrible person if you didn't make love to me, and, John, I'm sorry! I knew at the time what I was doing." She bit her lip and fought back the tears. "I'm so sorry! I was really, really weak, and I was feeling desperate and lonely, and I was so in love with you, and you loved Geneva. Oh, John, I'm so sorry. Please forgive me. I understand why you can't love me back."

John was taken aback, and instinctively, he reached for her, wanting to comfort her, wanting her to know she was worthy of love from the right man, but just as he touched her shoulder, a sudden explosion rocked both of them from their feet. They fell to the ground as mud rose up, splattering them. The hill behind them erupted with people running and shouting. Raking the mud out of his eyes, John searched the area, only to see wild confusion. People streaked through the forest, running for safety, and behind them streamed an army of Ugandans, yelling and indiscriminately shooting automatic rifles. People were falling: men, women, and children screamed and collapsed, the blood flowing from their bodies, mingling with the mud, turning the place into a red quagmire where Death danced.

"Run!" he yelled, pulling Sally Beth to her feet. Dragging her into a grove thick with mangrove trees, he pushed her underneath a root. Half submerged in thick water, they held onto each other and watched while dozens of men in Ugandan uniforms attacked the fleeing people.

They waited, shivering in the quagmire of a sluggish stream until the last man passed, not daring to move until the noise had moved away from them, and then they bolted, rising to their feet, running downstream, falling through the swampy morass, until at last they came to the boats they had left tied to mangrove roots. Alice's guide had already hustled Pastor Umbatu, Phil, Lilly, and Lyla into one of them. He sat with a white-faced Howard in the other one, grim, waiting. As Sally Beth and John emerged onto the wider swamp, the guide pulled her into the boat while John jumped aboard. They were just about to push off when they saw movement in the forest above them.

"Get down!" hissed the guide, as he maneuvered the boat among the sedge. The other boat followed closely behind. Waiting in the thick air, heavy with the suffocating stench of rotting vegetation, the group felt fear rising and hovering above them, nearly as palpable as the cloud of mosquitoes attacking them. They did not have to wait long before they saw two men stumbling down the hill, carrying a limp Alice Auma.

The guide sitting in the boat stood cautiously. "We are here!" he said softly, waving his hand. The men changed course, picking their way through the trees. Sally Beth recognized Francis and another man known as Tabor, although their faces were altered by fear and smeared with blood. A dark patch of blood stained the shoulder of Tabor's shirt, and Alice was covered in blood from her shoulder to her hip.

"Alice has been shot," gasped Tabor, just as he sank to his knees.

"Quick!" said Francis. "You must take her with you. She is alive, but you must get her to a hospital as quickly as you can." He dragged his young commander down the hill toward the boat as the guide and Pastor Umbatu jumped out to run toward them, followed by all the others. Together, they laid Alice on the bank.

She had been shot in the gut. A great, gaping wound slowly pulsed and sucked, seeming to inhale and exhale, breathing blood. Sally Beth bent to examine the injury. "Somebody give me your shirt or something we can stop this blood with," she said. Several items of clothing were handed to her, which she stuffed into the gory, throbbing hole.

"You must save her!" said Francis. "We still have time to get away; they are waiting for us on the other side of the island, but only you can get her to a hospital in time. Please take her in your plane."

Alice stirred. "No," she moaned. "I have not been granted permission. We have not purchased the right..." she groaned loudly. Francis and Tabor looked at each other.

Francis leaped to his feet, pulling coins and cowrie shells out of his pockets. "Give me what you have of value," he said urgently." I will take responsibility for this." He flung the items from his pockets into the air. "Great Spirits, give us leave for Alice to enter the air!" Snatching coins from outstretched hands, he threw them high out over the water, watching them arc above the papyrus and sedge, then he turned to Alice and gently laid his hand on her cheek.

"Alice," he said softly. "We have purchased the right. The air will allow you transport, with the blessings of the Spirits."

She did not hear him. Her face had become still and gray, and the bloodstain continued to spread out over the compresses that could not stem the flow.

Sally Beth stood to look around. Fajimi had used bur marigold on John's wounds to staunch the bleeding, and she knew it grew in swampy places on this island. She jumped up to the firmer bank, walking quickly, searching, until her eyes landed on a patch of yellow daisy-like flowers growing in a sunny spot. Running to it, she grabbed a handful.

John felt a sudden unease as he watched her walking away. When he drew breath to call her, a glimmer and a flash caught his eye, and to his horror, a Ugandan soldier stepped into the sunshine, wrapped an arm around Sally Beth's waist, and pushed a knife against her throat.

She gasped, but silenced herself when the knife pressed closer. Out of the corner of her eye, she saw John standing in deep shade, looking at her. The blood was slowly draining from his face.

John crouched, halting into a stuttering half-step in which he pivoted his left leg forward, the right hip turned slightly back, obscuring his holstered revolver. He had learned from his past mistake not to venture out into a war zone unarmed, but still, he was woefully unprepared for battle. Out in the open like this, even hidden by shade, he knew that if the soldier saw him, he would not be able to reach for the revolver and flip off the safety before the man drove his flashing knife into Sally Beth's throat. He eased sideways, creeping higher up the bank to the shelter of the trees above him. In the eternity that passed second by second, he sensed the tension of the others behind him. Glancing back, he saw that they were partially hidden, crouched behind the sedge, but the boats still lay in the water, highly visible in a shaft of sunlight. If the soldier glanced in their direction, he would surely see them.

Alice's guide was armed, but John did not know if he would be willing to kill in order to save Sally Beth; the Holy Spirits soldiers were trained never to shoot directly at the enemy. He did not know if the man who held Sally Beth was alone or if companions were nearby. There were sounds of distant gunfire and grenades, but all around the immediate vicinity lay deadly quiet. If he were to fire his revolver, anyone nearby would hear it.

Sally Beth concentrated on breathing and on keeping the eyes of the man who held her from straying to John. He was not easily visible, for they were standing in bright sunlight and John was in deep shade, but she could sense that he was slowly moving upward toward the trees. *Oh, Lord, please keep John safe. And Lilly. I don't care what happens to me, but let them get away. Tell me what to do to help them.*

The man hoisted Sally Beth in one arm, the knife pressed in the soft, white place underneath her chin. She did not struggle, but risked one backward glance to John. He saw the terror in her clear blue eyes, and felt a jolt hit him full in the chest as he realized that her fear was not for herself, but for him. Those eyes begged him to run away, to leave her behind and find safety for himself. And beyond that, he could see the authentic soul of Sally Beth, and he remembered the way those eyes had looked into his when her words had come, without guile, without pretensions, *John, I love you.*

The heavy air suddenly lightened, turned clear and transparent, and in a flash, he recalled the sound of Holy Miracle's voice floating to him, *Your happiness is standing right in front of you.* All of a sudden, he knew it was true, and that he had been blind and obtuse. Even as he had denied it, Sally Beth was everything he had ever said he wanted: here was his adventure, his challenge, his chance to be a hero. But all that meant little, for what he had said he wanted was simply a fiction he had created—what he thought he wanted, what had seemed to be a holy grail of his manhood. But as he looked into her eyes, limpid with love and fear *for him*, he knew that he had lied to himself for years. What he really wanted was the Sally Beth he saw standing before him, looking at him with such love pouring from her clear, honest soul, full of longing and hope and fear *for him*. She was more than beautiful, so much more than the script he had written, and he realized he could not live without her.

His heart beat against its cage. What had he done? Twenty-four days ago, she had told him she loved him. Twenty-four days ago, she had been willing to give herself to him. Twenty-four days ago, she had looked into his eyes, he had seen the golden heart of Sally Beth, laid bare and open to him, and he had flinched, had closed his heart. She had seen it, had seen his cowardice, his shallowness, and still she loved him.

He would have given his own life if only he could go back to that moment and take with him the love he felt for her now, if he could have, in that moment, made her know that her heart was safe with him, that he would cherish it as it deserved to be cherished. He forgot his weakness, his pain. He would die before he lost her, but more important than that, he knew he was capable of killing, more than capable. He would find a deep satisfaction in killing this man who was threatening Sally Beth.

Already, the man had begun to slowly back up, dragging Sally Beth with him. Within seconds, they would vanish into the forest. John steadied himself and locked eyes with Sally Beth.

She saw him shift his focus to look at her and saw his face soften, saw the raw, naked feeling for her, saw the anguish etched there, and she knew he was willing to die or kill for her. It made her sad, to think about the missteps they had taken, the love that they had juggled between them like a hot stone, tossing it from hand to hand, and up into the air, but never able to hold it together, never quite able to find a way to let it warm both of them at once. She wanted to shout out to him that whatever happened, she needed him to know that she loved him, loved him with her heart's blood, with her spirit, with her soul. If she died in this moment, she wanted to send him the message that he had awakened something in her that was worth cherishing.

As the man began to drag her away, she fought to keep her eyes on John's and saw his gaze harden, then he subtly moved his head to the right and let his eyes flicker in the same direction. She nodded, steadied herself, drew a sharp breath, and jerked her head upward, away from the knife. She tried to spin out of the man's grip, but it seemed that he was a mountain of strength while she had the weight and power of a butterfly. All she managed to do was make him more aware of her. He tightened his arm around her head and laughed as it began to crush her.

During the struggle, John had managed to pull his revolver and snap off the safety. But before he could take aim, the attacker suddenly noticed him and swung Sally Beth around so that she was between them. Frustrated, John took a step forward, but the Ugandan reached behind him to flip his AK 47 around from his back, and he was forced to stop again.

Sally Beth saw the situation in slow motion. It was going to be up to her. If she did not disarm the Ugandan now, he would kill John, and most likely, everyone there. Taking the moment that the knife was absent from her neck, she spun around, lifted her knee sharply, and jerked it hard into the man's groin while she simultaneously pressed her fingers against his carotid artery. She knew she did not have the strength to throw him, but if she pressed hard and long enough, she might be able to incapacitate him. His eyes bore directly into hers, and there were demons in them.

Not taking his eyes from hers, he grinned, then swept his arm upward, knocking her backward. She staggered and fell, skimming down into the water, just as a shot rang out. The soldier spun backward, clutching at his shoulder as another shot sang through the air. He cried out as he fell, blood blooming at his groin, his hands clutching at air, and John rushed forward, gun in hand, shooting again and again until the revolver clicked impotently, spent. That did not stop him. He raised his gun above his head, then pummeled the man's head with a rage that filled him as he felt the satisfying crunch of metal on bone. Seconds passed before he felt Sally Beth tugging at his arm.

"John, stop! We have to go. Stop! There may be others."

His vision cleared, and he saw the bloody revolver in his hand, the limp form of the man at his feet, the now-feeble pulsing of blood staining his uniform and the ground below him. John took Sally Beth's hand, and they ran.

One of the boats was in the water, with Phil, Pastor Umbatu, and Lyla already paddling away. Alice lay in the bottom of the boat, her gray, chalky face resting in Lyla's lap. The second boat remained at the bank, half in the water with the guide sitting in the forward section, but both Lilly and Howard Graves were crouched beside it. Lilly had her eye pressed to the viewfinder, intently focusing and shooting. Howard was next to her, a rifle in his hands, and he, too, had his eye to the scope.

Francis and Tabor suddenly rose from the reeds at the shoreline to hustle Howard and Lilly into the boat. They held it steady as John and Sally Beth reached the bank, splashing through the water with agonizingly slow steps. He picked her up, dumped her into the boat, and then grabbed the hands reaching for him to haul him out of the water.

"Get away!" whispered Francis urgently as he shoved them off. "Our country depends on her." Then they slipped back into the shadows of the forest as John and Howard picked up their paddles and began the frenzied task of steering away from the bank.

When they had gone about a hundred feet, the first bullet whizzed by. Another hit the water beside them, and several others embedded themselves into the wood. Yet another splintered the oar that Howard held. He threw it away and picked up the rifle beside him. Throwing himself down, he leveled the rifle toward the shore just as another burst of fire spat into the water nearby. Two men stood at the edge of the forest, rifles pointed toward the small boats hurrying through the swamp.

Lilly lay beside Howard in three inches of water, and more water slowly poured into the craft riddled with holes. Her camera rested on the edge of the boat, her face, calm, concentrated, was plastered to the viewfinder. She was snapping and advancing film nearly as fast as the AK-47 fired bullets at them. Sally Beth dove on top of her, grabbed her by her blonde hair, and yanked her head toward the soup at the bottom of the boat.

"There are only two of them," said Howard as he raised himself to one knee and took careful aim. He fired once, then again, and silence suddenly fell upon the reedy water. After a long moment, Sally Beth raised her head enough to look over the edge of the boat. There was nothing but marsh grass and mangrove trees visible in the tranquil, dappled, empty forest.

"Howard!" cried Lilly. "When did you learn to shoot like that?"

Howard sat in the bottom of the boat, stunned, the rifle lying beside him in the water. "This summer. After what happened last year when that boar attacked Geneva, I figured I ought to learn. How to ride, too." He looked up, pale and shaking, and tears rimmed his lashes. "I didn't know I would ever actually kill somebody."

"I know what you mean, buddy," came John's choked voice from the other end of the boat. He sat still, his paddle hovering above the water for a moment before he flung himself at Sally Beth and gathered her into his arms.

November 24, 1978,
Lawn of the Victorian Hotel Inn, Nairobi, Kenya

John woke, shivering, with lights bouncing off his eyes. The sound of the Super Cub's engine rattled his ears and his head, and he jumped up from the lounge chair in which he lay, only to feel such pain piercing his thigh that he fell flat on his face. As he was trying to pull himself up, he felt gentle arms around him and the sweet, warm smell of Sally Beth.

"Why aren't you in bed? You're shivering. And you're wet. Did you sit out here in the rain all night?"

"Didn't notice. It was bad enough I didn't go to Bukoba with you. The least I could do is wait for you. Gordon is sitting by the radio. I could have gone to you if you needed me."

"John, there was no need. We made it fine, and you needed to get the others back. Howard, help me get him up to his room. He's freezing and plumb done in." Howard Graves appeared at his other side, putting his arm around him. "Okay, man. You've played the hero enough today. No need to die of exposure just because we had to take a side trip. None of us are full of bullet holes, you know."

"How's Alice?"

"She'll make it. We waited until she was out of surgery, but if we had known you were going to stay out here all night waiting for us, we would have come back sooner."

Together Howard, Lilly, and Sally Beth helped the limping, shivering John up the hill to the hotel. "Don't go to bed yet," he said to Sally Beth when they had brought him to his room. "I'm going to take a hot shower, and I'll be quick. Could you get me a cup of coffee?"

"Don't you want to sleep a little? The sun won't be up for another hour."

"No, if you can stay up a little longer. I just need some coffee. Please. I need to talk to you, and I need coffee."

Everyone fell quiet, assessing John's condition. He looked better. At least he wasn't shivering, and his eyes looked tired but more alert. At last, Sally Beth said, "You two go on. I'll run down and get him some. The kitchen will be open by now." Howard and Lilly looked at John and Sally Beth, then at each other. Something flashed between them, and Sally Beth thought about giving some cautionary advice, but then she reconsidered. Lilly was her sister, not her child. "Go on," she said, as she slipped out the door. "I'll be right back, John."

When she returned ten minutes later, bearing coffee for each of them, he was dressed and sitting at the table waiting for her. "Thank you," he said as she handed the coffee to him. "I'm sorry to make you go get it for me, but I got stiff out there, and walking is—"

She cut him off. "Don't be silly. You have already done too much. You shouldn't even have gone with us, but I'm so glad you did. How are you feeling now?"

"Fine, I guess. Except I've realized that I'm the world's biggest idiot." He paused, then his words came out in a rush. "Sally Beth, I'm so sorry. I don't even know where to begin. How to begin. I've been blind; I've been arrogant; I don't know why I've resisted loving you. But when I saw you with that knife at your throat, I knew that I can't live without you." He stopped. His hands were shaking, and he was dangerously close to bursting into tears.

"Hush," she said. "You just got scared, and you feel responsible for me. You know, when you save somebody's life, you think you're accountable to them forever, or something like that. I think you just need to get some sleep. You'll feel better."

"I can't feel better until I've told you. Until you know I love you. Until I have done right." He put his hand to his forehead, blinking back tears, then looked at her again, imploring her to understand.

She chose her words carefully. "John, you're overtired." She did not say that she was overtired, too, and right now this was more than she wanted to deal with. When John had looked into her eyes there on the banks of the swamp, when the knife was pressed to her throat, she thought she had seen his feelings for her, but in reality, she knew that was just wishful thinking. John did not love her, but he really wanted to, he wanted to do the right thing, and he was willing to believe he was in love with her to make her happy. She sipped at her coffee, inwardly writhing at how painful this moment was. "Why don't we talk about this after we've both rested a bit?"

He saw the doubt in her face, her misgivings. Drawing a shaky breath, he began again, "Yes, we can do that. But Sally Beth," he said as gently and as non-threateningly as he could, "would you do something for me? Return a favor?"

"Of course, John."

"Stay with me a while. Curl up with me on the bed and sleep with me. I need to hold you, and I can't sleep unless you are here with me. I need to feel you, alive, in my arms."

She remembered the night he had offered her the comfort of sleep in his arms, and how beautiful that night had been, under the stars, under the orange tree, an oasis in the midst of terror. Blinking back tears, she nodded. "Yes, I will," and she stood and held out her hand.

He awoke hours later, feeling calm and warm. Sally Beth's head was on his shoulder, her hand on his chest, and his arm was wrapped tightly around her. As he allowed consciousness to lighten his being, he felt the rightness of having her beside him, the sweetness of her regular, soft breath, and he felt an overpowering urge to hold her there forever. He studied her face for a long time, newly astonished at her beauty. *The face of an angel.*

At one time, he had said he wanted a woman who had read *War and Peace* and who could discuss it with him. Sally Beth, barely literate, would never read *War and Peace*, or anything like it, but she had lived through war and peace, and she had emerged from the darkest moments stronger and more beautiful than any woman he could imagine. *What kind of fool had he been?* The chuckle rose unbidden in his throat as he considered his own arrogance, his pretentiousness at trying to construct the "perfect" woman, and how Sally Beth was so much more than that.

She stirred, opening her eyes, but she did not move. "Good morning, my love," he said. "You don't have to wake up just yet. Sleep all day if you want to."

She smiled as she sat up. "I'm hungry. And really, really dirty." Lifting her arm, she gazed at the mud caked on it. He had not even noticed the mud until now. She was covered with it, and streaks of blood fouled the blouse she was wearing. He remembered anew the blood foaming from Alice's stomach, the blood spewing out of the man's shoulder and groin. Only her face and hands were clean; she must have washed them at the hospital while they were waiting through Alice's surgery.

"Oh, gosh, I really need a shower, and clean clothes," she said, looking forlornly at the filthy pink skirt and white peasant blouse. It had been her favorite outfit, the one Lilly had bought her for her birthday, and she had donned it for the Thanksgiving lunch as a private tribute to her sister. Now she would never be able to wear it again, for the memory of yesterday lay over it like a violation.

"I don't want you to leave." He was afraid she would never come back.

"I just want to get cleaned up. We can go to breakfast. Or lunch, whatever time it is." She smiled at him, and hope fluttered in his heart.

"Go shower and change and meet me at the landing strip in thirty minutes. I'll bring something to eat."

He was glad she had not walked with him. Shards of glass seemed to find their way into his thigh and work their way up to his hip with every step he took, and he felt nearly helpless trying to manage the picnic basket as he hobbled the hundred yards to the plane through a shimmering drizzle. By the time she arrived, he was already in the cockpit waiting for her, and although he would have liked to help her get in, the best he could manage was having the door open for her. He did not want her to see him so helpless.

By the time they were aloft, a soft silence had inserted itself between them. She was feeling fretful and lost, reliving the horror of the death and suffering she had seen the day before; he was facing the urgent need to make amends for how he had failed her. They flew southward until the majesty of Kilimanjaro rose out of the mist before them, and John settled the plane down in an open savannah. The rain had settled into a whisper of drizzle, falling onto grass that had turned impossibly green from the rains. Rivers thundered through grottos and rocky draws nearby, and lakes had appeared in the grassy valleys. Everywhere lush flowers bloomed, perfuming the air with their sweetness mingled with the scent of rainwater, while Kilimanjaro glimmered white and silver in the distance. As Sally Beth climbed out of the plane, she gasped at the wonder around her, from the shimmering, emerald grass at her feet to the towering clouds above her, and the glorious, nearly infinite, sparkling mountain beyond. Sally Beth inhaled the purity of the air around her, feeling her spirit being cleansed from the horrors of the day before.

John limped out to an acacia tree with wide, spreading branches, the white blooms drooping like wisteria, exuding a scent as sweet as mimosa. There he spread a blanket over the lower branches to keep out the rain and another on the grass, and together they laid out the small feast he had procured from the hotel kitchen. They both fell onto the food as if they had not eaten for weeks.

After the first flush of their appetite had been satisfied, John sat up, looking at Sally Beth with watchful, sad eyes. He began hesitantly. "Sorry about last night. This morning, I mean. I was insane with worry."

"I know. It's okay. Are you feeling better now?"

"Yes. I've told you how I feel, and that hasn't changed. Will never change. Now will you tell me?"

The question took her aback. She was not quite sure how she felt. She loved him, that she knew, but she was not convinced of his love for her, and her soul was greatly troubled. People had died and they had been responsible, things were not resolved between her and God, and His silence was oppressive. How could she begin anything new unless she knew for certain His blessing lay over it? "I... feel... confused. And sad at all that has happened. All this death, the defeat of Alice's army. I feel like you and I need to sort of fall back and regroup. Do some thinking, I guess."

He felt his heart plummet. "Whatever you need. I'm here. I love you. I'll wait; I'll follow you; I'll be here. But I won't be apart from you. I can't let you get away from me. I'd rather die than lose you."

"It's hard to think about love right now, with all that happened yesterday. You killed a man, John. Doesn't that… hang over you, *oppress* you? Make you feel lost?"

"No. I only feel glad that I killed him because it means that you are alive. I would be oppressed and lost if you were not here. Does it bother you? You've seen plenty of death these last few weeks."

"I know. And I have been at least partly responsible for three deaths. This man yesterday, and two more when the Ugandans took Priscilla and me. She killed one of them with just a knife, and I helped her. John, it haunts me. I was raised to believe you never take the life of another, and I've been putting my own life and the lives of people I love—basically what *I* want, what I think *I* need— above that. It's hard to live with."

He edged closer. "Pray with me, Sally Beth," he said, taking her hand. She hesitated before moving closer to him, and they both bowed their heads.

"Lord," he said, "we have been caught in a war, and we have taken lives, and we don't know if You will forgive us for it. Ease our hearts, Lord, not just about what has happened, but about loving. Let Sally Beth know how much I love her, how much I am willing to do for her. Let me love her, Lord, and let her love me."

Sally Beth glanced up, and she couldn't help but smile at John's heartfelt, but selfish prayer. *Not me, me, me,* she thought. *What can I do for You?* She lifted her eyes to the silver mountain before her just as the sun broke through the clouds, and an unbearably bright shaft of light shone down on it, glancing into her eyes and making her squint.

Beloved, it is that easy, came the Voice as clear as the air and the raindrops shimmering in the sun. *It always has been. My Grace is as great as My Might.*

She startled. "What?" she asked.

John repeated himself, "I'm asking for you to love me."

His words were rich and sweet, like honey, falling into her ears as softly as her own thoughts. Subtly, quietly, she felt a shifting in her spirit, a lightening of weight as she lifted her eyes to the bright snowcapped mountain, as she thought of her own green hills and of Holy Miracle Jones. A flock of blue swallows winged their way across her line of vision. From somewhere nearby came a birdsong, and behind the song was a memory: *Sally Beth, the man God has planned for you will run from you before he runs to you, and when he catches you, you will know what it means to be loved.*

"How long do you think it will be before you can run, John?" she said. She liked the idea of him running to her. She was tired of chasing after him.

"I can hobble pretty fast now. If you run slow, I think I could catch you. Why don't we take a little break from all this and run away together?"

"Where to?"

"I've heard that West Virginia is a beautiful place. A good place to raise a family. I know of a little farm where I could run a clinic, right next door to the most charming family. He's a physician; they have four little girls who would play with our children."

She shook her head. "That sounds lovely. But I just realized how much we have to do here first. I don't think it's time to rest, yet."

He sighed, and then he laughed. "I don't know why I ever thought loving you would make me lazy. But I have an inkling of what I'm in for. Marry me. Marry me right now. Then we can get busy."

Get busy echoed the Voice. *I have plans for you two.*

Sally Beth laughed as the joy welled up, sudden as a cloudburst, spreading from her belly to her chest to her head, and in celebration, she lifted her face into the sun and the stunning clouds of light and let herself be enfolded in the sky's embrace.

Epilogue

December 30, 1996, Nairobi, Kenya

*D*ear Mom and Dad,
    I'm here! Tired as all get-out because we stayed up most of the night talking, and the jet lag is starting to catch me. The place looks amazing—the new school and workshop look even better than we imagined it, and John has added about 300 head of cattle to the program, so the new barns are full already. I can't wait to get started, which is a good thing because John says he can't take a break for a minute now that calving season is going full tilt. He says I got here just in time.

Sally Beth loves the books on tapes you sent. She had finished with all the Dickens you sent for Christmas and was hoping for more. War and Peace *will be first—she said she's always wanted to read it. She is as pretty and sweet as ever, and still wearing the craziest hats! They've gotten a lot glitzier now that the fashion design operation is going. There are about thirty women working full time, and they pretty much consider themselves rich. It's amazing to see how much she has changed the lives of the poorest people here. One girl about my age has only been here for about six months, and she has real talent. Sally Beth says she's going to take her to New York in the spring to talk to some retailers about her designs.*

All the girls are a big help at the workshop so that Sally Beth can spend most of her time on the anti-FGM campaign. Annilee is a good manager, even though she's only fourteen. She looks so much like Sally Beth it's kind of hard to tell them apart. And both James and Carl look more like John every day. They're both going to help with the calving this year. It's nice to see them so grown up, but they're still so much fun.

Since Sally Beth has cranked up the anti-FGM thing, Prissy has quit her job at the hospital to come help her. They had a run-in with some village elders who tried to get them to keep out of it, and John said it was like World War III starting. Prissy told them that every time she operates on a girl who's been cut, she wants to take her scalpel to every village elder who encourages it and do a number on them. Whew! I think those guys had better stay away from her. She is tough when she gets mad. So is Sally Beth, although she hides it better.

Alethia and some of her other "girls" came for Christmas, and their husbands, too. Alethia's husband is a lot like her—very energetic and kind. They left to go back home today, so it was good to visit with them last night. By the way, did you know that Becky has been offered a professorship at Cornell? All of these ladies are amazing. They make me feel like a lazy bum for wanting to take a year off. But if I'm going to be a vet, I might as well take the opportunity to learn from the best.

I miss you guys already, and I can't wait until March when you get here—nearly three months. John and Sally Beth are planning a safari down in Tanzania when you get here, and I can fly you down.

Lilly called last night. She's covering the genocide in Rwanda—she says it's really bad and she can't wait to get away, so she's going to go meet Howard in Paris while he's there next week working on some big international deal. She's hoping they'll go to Tanzania after that to go trekking on Kilimanjaro, and if his schedule works out, they'll drop in here for a few days to see me. It will be great. It's been two years since I last saw them.

And speaking of Rwanda, Sally Beth and John probably are getting another child from the orphanage there. This will make a total of nine. Sally Beth is all excited, of course. He's three, and she says three-year-olds are the best, except when she's saying babies are the best, or ten-year—olds are the best, or... ha ha! John just says he's glad it's a boy this time because he needs some help in the fields. He made the mistake of saying it out loud so the girls all jumped on him and tried to tickle him to death. They all are so cute, and John is such a good dad. It goes without saying that Sally Beth is a good mom. They're almost as good as you two.

Anyway, that's a lot of news considering I've been here less than twenty-four hours. You won't be hearing from me much for a while since I'll be out riding the range with 400 head of cattle. Yippie! My love to all of you, and of course to Jimmy Lee, Edna Mae, Aunt Rachel and Uncle Wayne and the cousins and give big kisses to my baby sisters (only don't tell them I called them babies), and tell them I miss them and can't wait until Spring Break so they will be here for the big safari. I love you. Write!

Your son,
Blue

Author's Note

The historical events described in this story are true. In October of 1978, Idi Amin, the brutal despot who called himself the President of Uganda invaded Tanzania, leaving in his wake a wasted countryside and thousands of raped, tortured, and murdered civilians. Those who were not killed were captured and sold as slaves. If you go to Google Earth, you will see the ruins of a church standing by the Kagera River in Tanzania, only twenty miles from the Ugandan border, destroyed by Idi Amin's army the night of October 31 to November 1, 1978. This place caught in this war became the inspiration for my story about how Sally Beth's uncomplicated faith and love are tested.

Alice Auma and her army are historical. Although I did not make them up, I did take some literary license by placing them slightly out of their time. Alice was Ugandan and she did lead a band of soldiers called the Army of the Holy Spirits, but she actually did not come on the scene until 1986. Born in 1956, she would have been only twenty-two-years-old at the time of the Ugandan-Tanzanian war: young, but not too young to listen to spirits and lead an army after the fashion of Joan of Arc.

Alice channeled several spirits, especially one dead army officer called Lakwena. Because the Acholi believed Lakwena was a manifestation of the Holy Spirit, Alice became the head of the Holy Spirit Movement. According to her biographer, anthropologist Heike Behrend, the movement appeared to be a blend of Orthodox Christianity, African witchcraft, and nature worship. I did not try to dress up Alice's beliefs or actions to make her more "Christian," nor did I point out flaws in her theology. I just let her stand as she stood in Uganda when she led the Army of the Holy Spirits across the war-torn landscape.

All of the information about Alice and her army mentioned in *A Saint in Graceland* are factual, including the most farfetched bits, such as the parts about "James Bond," requiring new recruits to spit into a live chicken's mouth, and the necessity of exactly two testicles, among other things. With such a character hovering in the wings, I couldn't pass up telling her story. I like to think the few weeks of victory Alice enjoyed when she was twenty-two in this novel was just a prelude to the larger campaigns she led eight years later.

The character of Alethia Bagatui (and Sally Beth's passion for helping children) was inspired by a living person. Katie Davis, a white, upper-middle class homecoming queen and class president, went to Uganda on a mission trip right after her high school graduation in 2006, and she is still there. She gave up her comfortable life, a college education, and the boy she had planned to marry to live in Uganda and formally adopt fourteen (at last count) little girls. She also founded and runs the Masese Feeding Outreach, a program that provides meals, medical care, and education to 1,600 children who might otherwise be forced to beg in the streets. In addition to all this, she began a vocational program to help adult women earn income to support their families by making jewelry that her foundation markets in the United States.

I decided to make Alethia of African descent with personal ties to the people of the region because the story of Katie's journey from pampered prom queen to the mother and benefactor of Ugandan children is too extraordinary to be easily believed, especially in the historical context of this novel. Like Alice's story, Katie's is more fantastic than any fiction I could write. If you want to know more about her and the work she is doing, read her blog at katiedavis. amazima.org. Prepare your heart. This woman makes you realize what it really means to love and serve God.

It was emotionally difficult to research and write about the practice of female genital mutilation (FGM), or female circumcision, as, I expect, it was difficult for you to read about it. But I knew early on that if I was going to describe the horrors that led to Sally Beth's spiritual collapse, I could not leave out this important cultural practice.

FGM is still common in all African nations. Westerners have been vocal about the brutality of the tradition for a very long time, and Africans have found their objections condescending and insulting. The story about the Finnish woman who spoke out against it being circumcised and murdered in her own home is true.

There has been some progress, although it is heartbreakingly slow. In May, 2015, Nigeria became the 26th African nation to criminalize or discourage the practice, but such laws have been largely ignored, superseded by generations of ingrained tradition, and FGM is still common in many African nations. Unfortunately, even while attitudes are gradually changing in Africa as native women begin to lead in the battle against mutilation (see desertflower.org), FGM is gaining in popularity among immigrant populations worldwide, including Europe and the US. (see Newsweek, 2/6/15. "Female Genital Mutilation on the Rise in the U.S," by Lucy Westcott). At present, there are an estimated 130 to 150 million victims of FGM around the globe. Activists like Sally Beth and Priscilla have their work cut out for them, but thankfully, there are thousands of men and women who are working tirelessly to end this horrific practice.